DARK STORM

KEL RICHARDS

RiverOak®

Good News in Fiction

COOK COMMUNICATIONS MINISTRIES
Colorado Springs, Colorado • Paris, Ontario
KINGSWAY COMMUNICATIONS LTD
Eastbourne, England

RiverOak® is an imprint of
Cook Communications Ministries, Colorado Springs, CO 80918
Cook Communications, Paris, Ontario
Kingsway Communications, Eastbourne, England

DARK STORM
© 2004 by Kel Richards

First Printing, 2004
Printed in the United States of America
1 2 3 4 5 6 7 8 9 10 Printing/Year 08 07 06 05 04

Cover Design: Koechel Peterson & Associates

Unless otherwise noted, Scripture is taken from the HOLY BIBLE, NEW INTERNATIONAL VERSION®. Copyright © 1973, 1978, 1984 International Bible Society. Used by permission of Zondervan. All rights reserved. Scripture marked KJV is taken from the *King James Version*. Public Domain.

Library of Congress Cataloging-in-Publication Data

Richards, Kel, 1946-
  Dark storm / by Kel Richards.
      p. cm.
  ISBN 1-58919-018-1 (pbk.)
  1. Archaeologists--Fiction. 2. Hurricanes--Fiction. 3. Australia--Fiction. 4. Islands--Fiction. I. Title.
  PR9619.3.R485D37 2004
  823'.914--dc22

                                          2004008140

Contents

Acknowledgments

I wish to acknowledge the influence, first, of E. F. Benson (1867–1940), whose ingenious short horror stories succeeded in conveying the reality of evil (I have drawn on two of his ideas in the following tale).

Second, I acknowledge the influence of Charles Williams (1886–1945), who demonstrated in his novels that gripping storytelling is able to convey deep and serious ideas.

But above all I wish to acknowledge the influence and inspiration of C. S. Lewis (1898–1963)—Oxford don, Cambridge professor, Christian apologist, and master storyteller.

It was from Lewis that I first learned this world is a battle zone, divided between the forces of light and the forces of darkness, and that the one option not open to human beings is neutrality.

Throughout this book I have drawn upon Lewis and his writings, which I hope will bring pleasure and delight to my fellow Lewisians everywhere.

EXPEDITION

"The sun will be turned to darkness and the moon to blood before the coming of the great and dreadful day of the LORD."
—Joel 2:31

1

*F*eatures?"

"That's right, Nick, features," said Frank Gordon, leaning back in his leather chair until it creaked in protest.

"I'm an ambulance chaser, Frank," protested Nick Hamilton. "You know me, I'm an old hack. I'll live and die on police rounds."

"Wrong on both counts. You're not old, and you're not a hack. You're a good writer, Nick, a fact that has not gone unnoticed. On top of which, George's wife is pregnant. I don't want to give him a big project that'll just be dropped the minute the baby's born. Features, Nick—it's a great opportunity."

Nick turned to stare out the glass wall of the editor's office. Beyond the glass stretched the newsroom—a vast, open, untidy

space, cluttered with desks, journalists, telephones, computer termi-
nals, piles of old newspapers, and plastic cups half filled with cold
coffee. Noticing some of his colleagues had hastily looked away,
Nick realized they were wondering what this meeting was all
about.

"Most journalists would leap at the chance to write features,"
continued the editor.

"I know you mean well, Frank," Nick replied, "but stop trying
to plan my career for me. You sound like my mother."

"This paper is my baby, and I intend to put you where it will
be best for the paper. Give up, Nick, you're not going to win this
one."

"Can I go back to police rounds if this doesn't work out?"

"Of course."

"All right," Nick relented. "Where do I start?"

"I have your first assignment right here," Frank said with a smile
as he slid open a desk drawer and pulled out a manila folder. "Have
you ever heard of Cavendish Island?"

"Cavendish Island? No, I can't say I have."

"Not many people have. It's an isolated outcrop of rock, soil,
and sand, covered in low scrub and pounded by the waves of the
Pacific Ocean."

"Whereabouts exactly?"

"Almost 800 kilometers northeast of Sydney. Some 150 kilometers north from Lord Howe Island. Although it's uninhabited,
legally it's still a dependency of New South Wales."

"Still? What does that mean?" asked Nick as he continued to
pace up and down his editor's carpet.

"Sit down, Nick. I can't talk to you when you're pacing around
like that."

Nick sank into a leather chair facing the editor's desk.

"Where was I? Ah, yes—Cavendish Island is still legally part of
New South Wales. It was mapped and named by Lieutenant Henry
Ball, commander of HMS *Supply*, on his way to Norfolk Island from

Port Jackson in 1788. In 1821, a penal settlement was established on the island. It consisted of convicts from Botany Bay who had been convicted of committing further crimes while in Australia. For some reason it failed and was closed two years later. Then in 1825, Norfolk Island took its place as the extremely harsh penal settlement for paroled convicts who committed additional crimes."

"So this is a historical piece you want me to write?" Nick complained disbelievingly.

"Just listen, Nick. There's more to the story."

"I'm listening."

"Apparently during its short life, Cavendish Island was an absolute hellhole. The troops who were sent there as guards called it *Cadaver Island*. The convicts weren't so kind—they nicknamed it *Rotgut*. According to this file," Frank continued, "the commander of the place, a man named Colonel ...," he flipped over a few pages to find the name, "... Colonel Godfrey Black, was a real sadist."

"Anyway, the place closed down in ... what? 1823?"

"Yes, 1823."

"So, why is it a story?"

"A group of archaeologists are about to go back there to dig in the ruins and write up the story of the island. And I want you to go with them, Nick."

"With them? So I'll be away from the office for how long?"

"A few weeks."

"A few weeks? Missing all the good stories. Who gets police rounds while I'm away?"

"I've decided to give Terry a go."

"He doesn't have the contacts," Nick snapped.

"Then you can help him out," said Frank, picking up the empty pipe he used to smoke, and turning it around in his fingers. "Take him down to police headquarters. Introduce him to some people."

Nick silently fumed. He knew he was stuck with this job. But handing over his carefully built-up contacts to somebody else would not be easy.

"Why not send Terry out to this ... whatever it is ... Cavendish Island? He'd do a good job. Leave me on police rounds. Come on, Frank," he pleaded. "You know that what I do best is what I love most. How about it?"

"Give it up, Nick. I've made up my mind. What you won't admit, but everybody else on the paper can see, is that you write well. You're a good color man. There have been times when we have front-paged your stories simply because of the way you wrote them. Terrific, vivid stuff. I mean it, Nick."

"Yeah, and I like you too, Frank," the reporter replied sarcastically, "but buying me a beer and talking like a used-car salesman won't make me feel any differently."

"Then just accept the fact that you're going on this trip, and that it's a better story than you think it is."

"Not from what I've heard so far."

"Then shut up, stop whining, and listen." Frank took a deep breath, turned over some pages in the folder in front of him, and continued. "There are ruins on the island, left by the convict settlement— some wooden barracks, a quarry, and a stone building. Apparently this Colonel Black decided that his convicts should be doing hard labor, so he had them digging and moving blocks of stone."

"What sort of a building is it?"

"Well, it's a ruin now, but from the looks of it, the plan was for it to be a church."

"A church?"

"Don't look so surprised. Black wouldn't be the first churchman who was also a real, certified sadist."

"So that's what this expedition is going to study—a quarry, crumbling wooden barracks, and a ruined church?"

"Yeah, that's pretty much it."

"I still can't see the story in it."

"Hang on, Nick, there's more."

Nick sighed impatiently and waited until Frank had gathered his thoughts. "As I said, the place has been uninhabited since 1823.

But there has been the occasional visitor, usually unintended," Frank said. "Back in the 1950s, a yacht called the *Dolphin*, owned by a rich American named Paul Korbis, sailed into the one safe harbor the island offers to shelter from a severe storm. While Korbis's party was there, they explored the place and took some photographs. Then, six years ago, a New Zealand family, the Wiltshires, in their yacht the *Promise,* were caught in the edge of a cyclone and blown off course. They limped into the harbor at Cavendish Island to repair their mast and recover from the battering. They also took some photographs."

"This is leading somewhere, is it, Frank?"

"Keep your shirt on, Nick. Here are some of the pictures they took."

Frank pushed half a dozen eight-by-ten black-and-white photos across the desk. Nick picked them up and leafed through them slowly.

"So?" he asked. "What am I supposed to see?"

"You tell me," said his editor, leaning back in his chair and folding his arms. "You tell me what you see."

"Well, they're mostly photographs of the stone ruins. The first thing is that it's an odd-looking church. There must have been stonemasons or sculptors, in that penal settlement, because this church is not just square lumps of stone—there are gargoyles and strange-looking statues and ... things I can't describe ... in the ruins."

"Quite right," said Frank smugly. "Now, what else?"

"Nothing else really. Except that the building has deteriorated quite a lot between the two visits. In these earlier pictures the building is not in bad shape. It's a ruin, I grant you, but you can still see the faces of the gargoyles and ... things. In these later ones they've crumbled away. Or eroded away."

"The difference is striking, isn't it?"

"Yeah, quite noticeable."

"Except that you're looking at the pictures the wrong way around."

Nick looked up with a puzzled expression. "I don't under-stand," he said slowly.

"The ones that show the most damage were taken back in the 1950s. The photos that show the stonework to be in better repair—the faces on those stone creatures clear and unweathered—they were taken recently."

"Impossible."

"The evidence is quite clear. Now, that's a story, isn't it?"

2

Sydney lay basking in sun and brown haze. The air was still, and the yellow-brown smudge sat without moving over the tall office buildings and the sparkling blue water of the harbor. To locals it was familiar. To a visitor like Cathy Samson, it was surprising—that the residents could allow such a beautiful city to be spoiled by pollution.

The unmoving hazy blur looked as if a medieval wizard, risen from his grave, had cast a curse upon the city, a curse which lay like an evil haze, creeping into the mouths and lungs of the inhabitants.

Cathy stepped off the polluted street and into the quiet air-conditioned hum of her plush, central city hotel, where she took an elevator to the fifth floor. She was short, what fashion designers call "petite," with dark hair and large brown eyes. Those eyes blinked intelligently behind gold-rimmed spectacles that gave her the appearance of an owl caught in daylight—a rather pretty owl. Men often called her cute, and the label irritated her.

As the elevator doors opened, Cathy went to step out, but she was pushed aside by a young woman in a hurry. *How rude,* thought Cathy as the doors closed. She believed it was polite to let people out of an elevator first, before barging in.

She was still fuming as she walked down the carpeted corridor of the hotel trying to juggle her shopping parcels and her room key at the same time. Eventually, after dropping one of her parcels and picking it up again, she managed to get her door open, stagger into the room, and drop all her bags onto the bed.

Before they became crushed, Cathy put the clothes she had bought on hangers, and then hung them in the wardrobe—or, at least, the small area in the hotel room that took the place of a wardrobe. She had purchased checked flannel shirts, corded jeans, and a cotton-lined canvas jacket. They were attractive but still functional for the expedition.

The sound of running water came loudly through the wall of her room. *Someone in the next room,* she thought, *is taking a bath,* which she decided was a good idea. She had just arrived in Sydney that morning and had spent most of the time since her arrival strolling around the shops. Shopping had left her hot and dusty, the pores of her skin clogged by the grit that drifted through the city air.

A few minutes later she had stripped off her clothes and was standing under a hot shower, feeling the tension drain out of her muscles. For a long time she stood under the soothing stream of steaming hot water, feeling it massage her body and ease her tension.

Eventually Cathy stepped out of the bathroom wrapped in a terry-cloth robe and vigorously rubbed her hair with the thick bath towel. After a minute she stopped rubbing, stood still, and listened. The bath water was still running in the room next door. *Perhaps one of the occupants has had a bath, and now another person is running a fresh bath,* she thought. Still, something about it struck her as odd.

Cathy blew her hair dry, then she brushed it into shape and turned her attention to making a cup of coffee. As she filled the little electric pot and turned it on, she noticed that she could still hear the sound of running water from the next room.

This time she started to worry. What if someone had slipped and fallen in the bathroom next door? What if he or she was lying there in pain, or unconscious, and in need of help? She picked up the phone and dialed.

"Hello? Front desk? My name is Cathy Samson; I'm in room 509. In the room next door to mine, 511 I think it is, there's the sound of running water, like someone's running a bath. The thing is, it's been running like that for … well … nearly an hour now, I guess. I'm concerned that something might be wrong. Would you look into it? Thank you very much."

Hanging up the phone, Cathy went back to making her coffee. Twice she opened her door and looked around. Both times there was no one. She sipped her coffee and paced up and down. Then she looked again. This time there was a young man in a dark suit knocking at the door of the next room.

"I'm the person who called," she said. "Cathy Samson. Can you hear the water?"

"Yes," replied the young man, turning toward her and revealing a lapel badge that read *Lindsay Van Arnt, Asst. Manager.*

"No one has replied to my knocking. Have you heard any other sounds from the room, Miss Samson?"

"No, just the running water. Do you think someone went out and left the bath water running?"

"You go back to your room, Miss Samson. I'll check it out."

As Cathy stepped back inside her room, she could see that he was opening the door with his passkey. Soon afterward, the sound of running water stopped.

Cathy gave the incident no further thought as she dressed and then phoned her family in Melbourne. As she hung up the phone, the sounds of footsteps and voices in the corridor reached her through the thick walls. Curious, she opened her door and looked out.

There was a small cluster of people gathered around the open door of the next room—among them uniformed police officers.

"That's her," said a voice from the group. It was Van Arnt. "That's the young lady who reported the running water."

A middle-aged man in a rumpled gray suit detached himself from the group and walked toward her.

"Detective Potter," he said, flashing an I.D. card at her. "May I have a word?"

Confused but curious, Cathy nodded and stepped back into her room.

"When did you notice the noise from next door, Miss ...?"

"Cathy Samson. I got back from my shopping around four o'clock, I guess. Maybe a little past four. I wasn't keeping a close watch on the time."

"And you heard the noise as soon as you stepped into your room?"

"Yes, I did."

"Did you hear anything else?"

"Not a thing. Just the running water. It sounded as though someone was running a bath. What's happened?"

"Did you see anyone leave or enter the room?" Potter ignored her question.

"No, no one. Not this afternoon, that is. There was a dark-haired woman in her late thirties coming out of that room this morning."

"No one else?"

"I'm afraid not. Look, what's happened? What's going on?"

"We're just inquiring into an incident at the moment, Miss Samson."

"What sort of incident? What's happened?"

"If we need you again, how can we contact you?" persisted the detective.

"Well," said Cathy, "I'll be here until Saturday, and then I'm leaving."

"Leaving for where?"

"I'm an archaeologist, part of a team. We're leaving for Cavendish Island on Saturday."

"And you'll be gone for ... how long?"

"Four weeks. At least, that's the plan."

"It's most unlikely that we'll need you," said Potter, smiling and trying to look gracious, "but just in case we do, can you be reached there?"

"There's a radio phone on the boat, I believe, but I don't have the number at the moment."

"Here's my card, Miss Samson. Could you make inquiries, and as soon as you have that number, give me a call and pass it on? Just in case, you understand."

"Certainly. If you wish." Cathy accepted the card.

Potter shuffled toward the door, then he turned. "What about your home address and phone number? Where can we contact you when you get back?"

Cathy gave him her parents's address and phone number in Melbourne.

"Can't you tell me anything about what's happening?" she asked again.

"Thank you for your assistance, Miss Samson," said the policeman, pulling the door closed behind him.

Cathy was not satisfied, and for the next few hours she listened carefully, opening her door every ten minutes or so to see what was happening. She stopped a passing maid and asked, "What's going on next door?" The woman just shrugged her shoulders and kept walking.

People kept coming and going in the next room late into the evening. From what she had seen on television, Cathy thought it looked like a full police investigation team.

Shortly after nine o'clock, several loud bumps caused Cathy to look into the corridor again. This time she saw a gurney being wheeled out of the next doorway. She couldn't see who was on the gurney, because the sheet was pulled up over the face. However, it was obvious that what was being removed was a dead body.

3

From the journal of Lieutenant Edmund McDermott, officer of the New South Wales Corps.

July 7th, 1821

*T*his day I was summoned by His Excellency, Governor Macquarie, and informed that it was the governor's pleasure that I should accompany Commander Black on his expedition to establish a new penal colony at Cavendish Island. I was somewhat taken aback by this appointment, since I find myself well settled here at Port Jackson and not in the least desirous of removing to another place. However, His Excellency's secretary explained to me, when, as I was departing, I did venture to mention some small degree of dissatisfaction, that I had been chosen in large measure because I am a single man. Since all the convicts to be transferred to the new establishment will be male, it was thought inappropriate to transfer married officers and their families to such a remote and desolate island as their guardians.

Although I understand such thinking, it hardly appeases my concerns, or makes me any the more pleased with the disjunction this unforeseen assignment will cause in my affairs. I will now have to appoint a manager to look after my grant of land at Rose Hill. And then, given the nature of the inhabitants of this place, I shall have to request one of my brother officers to supervise my appointed supervisor. It is a most vexatious business.

Upon learning of my appointment, I proceeded at once to the dwelling of Commander Black to consult with him about his plans and about the preparations he desired me to undertake on his behalf. Upon my word, I found him to be very strange man indeed. He seemed little interested in the contributions that I might be able to make to the planning and preparations for this new colony. Indeed, he told me that all was already well in hand and the only tasks that he entrusted to me were the merest trifles that an enlisted man could have undertaken.

Although it was well before noon when I visited the commander, I suspect that he was either slightly in his cups or else under some sort of strange excitement. His eyes seemed to glow in a preternatural manner, and his speech was hurried and disconnected. However, he did give me a list of the convicts he had selected to take with us on this voyage of establishment. They were all, he informed me, men who had proved themselves to be villains of the deepest and darkest dye, offending repeatedly since their arrival in the colony. These were men, said the commander lustily, that the lash could not cure, but that complete isolation and hard labour might.

At the commander's suggestion, I took the list of names to the court-house to have their transfer to the penal colony of Cavendish Island recorded. This list was not a long one, since the establishment party is to consist of only fifty convicts, twenty troopers, a sergeant, the commander, a surgeon, and myself. Given the brevity of the list, I decided to wait in the office of the court-house whilst the clerk made his official copy. Whilst thus employed, I occupied my time consulting the records of some of these convicts selected to accompany us to our God-forsaken island.

Some of the men whose records I consulted did indeed prove to be criminals of the most wicked and habitual sort. By way of example, I found on our list the name of William Cauldron, known to the convicts as Black Billy. He is a giant of a fellow, standing over six feet tall, and being solidly built. Unfortunately, this evil man uses his size and strength for no better purpose than to terrorise and intimidate his fellow convicts.

He had originally been convicted and sent to the colony as a particularly brutal and ferocious footpad. Since his arrival he has been flogged on numerous occasions for his insolent and villainous attacks upon certain of his gaolers. As for his reputation amongst his fellow criminals, I can only record that several who had reason to disagree or dispute with him over some matter are known to have disappeared. It is widely rumoured that he has murdered them. But, since their bodies have never been found, it has been officially presumed that they are amongst those who have sought some fugitive freedom in the bush, and William Cauldron has thus managed to escape the hangman's noose; which, I have no doubt, he richly deserves.

There were other names on the list almost as bad as Cauldron's. For instance, I found both Jack Fletcher and Richard Edgar amongst those who will journey with us—men of such evil repute that it requires no further comment from me in this place.

However, other names on the commander's list rather puzzled me, and I could not comprehend why they should be regarded as deserving of further punishment or isolation. One such was a youngish man named Edward Cavell known to me, in my occasional capacity as a building supervisor, to be an excellent stone mason. He has worked in a gang under my command during the construction of the colony's hospital, and I could find no fault with either his work or his manner. Why was such a man, I asked myself, being sent to some fearful island, remote from even those limited comforts of our primitive civilisation in this colony?

Another whose name struck me as being out of place on the commander's list was a man no longer young, known as Arthur Jellicoe. This man, who had once been a forger, has turned his undoubted talents in a happier and more innocent direction since his arrival at Port Jackson more than a decade ago. There is more than one public house in this colony that sports a sign-board painted by Jellicoe, whilst in Government House there is a fine bust of His Excellency carved from the local sandstone by this same Jellicoe. I knew of no occasion of his giving fresh offence to the law, and, therefore, could not understand his presence on this voyage to Cavendish Island.

The clerk of the court having once completed his task of copying the list, I returned to Commander Black's dwelling to raise with him my concerns. I must record here that the commander's response to the matters I raised fell a great deal short of satisfactory. Far from being prepared to proffer an explanation for the strange mixture of convicts selected for re-assignment, the commander spoke to me in a most ungentlemanly and offensive manner, suggesting that I had no concern in looking into the composition of the list and that I had exceeded my authority by so doing. I reminded him that I had been appointed as his second in command. Commander Black's only response was to roar abuse and order me from his house.

He is a strange man, and I shall find serving under him a difficult task indeed.

4

The next morning Cathy picked up the newspaper lying outside her hotel room door and then searched through it feverishly for some news of the tragedy that had occurred in the next room.

She found the story at the top of page three: "Murder in City Hotel."

The headline alone was enough to make Cathy put down the paper and draw her breath. She had never been this close to a murder before. Reading on, she discovered that the victim, a woman, had been found naked in the bathtub. She had been stabbed seven times. According to the paper, police had identified the victim but weren't releasing her name until her next of kin had been notified. The body, said the article, had been discovered by the hotel staff.

"Hmmff," Cathy snorted. "I didn't even get a mention." Then she felt guilty—a violent death had occurred, and she was thinking only of herself. But, somehow, perhaps because it had happened to a stranger in the anonymity of a hotel, the whole affair felt remote and impersonal.

She read and reread the short report several times. When had the murder happened? Presumably, while she was out shopping. For a while she toyed with the idea of calling her parents and telling them about her brush with melodrama, but then she decided that her mother would only worry.

Having finished the rest of the paper, Cathy dressed, brushed her hair, slipped her key into her purse, and left the room. The next door down the corridor now had a police seal pasted across it. And standing in front of the sealed door was a young man dressed in jeans and a leather jacket.

"Ah, the neighbor," he said, as Cathy pulled her door closed with a loud click. He turned toward her and smiled. Cathy guessed him to be two or three years older than she was and quite good looking, in an untidy sort of way.

"You weren't here last night by any chance, were you?" he continued.

"I'm sorry, do I know you?" replied Cathy, in her haughtiest voice.

"Humble apologies. I should have introduced myself. I'm Nick Hamilton, from the *Mirror*."

"A journalist?"

"Guilty as charged, Your Honor."

Cathy must have continued to stare at him for several seconds, as though he was an insect, because he quickly added, "Well, we can't all have honest jobs, you know."

That made her laugh. "I'm sorry if I was rude," she said.

"It's impossible to be rude to a journalist—well-known fact. Have you eaten yet? Can I buy you breakfast? Or at least a cup of coffee?"

"You want to ask me about what happened last night?"

"Something like that," he admitted.

"I have to warn you that I don't know anything interesting."

"I'll take a chance on that. So which will it be? Coffee? Breakfast?"

"Since you want to talk to me, you may as well pay for the privilege, Mr. Hamilton. I was just on my way to breakfast."

"Lead on then, and I will follow," he said. When they stopped at the elevator, he added, "By the way, I don't know your name yet."

"Cathy Samson."

"Samson, Samson," he muttered to himself as they stepped into the quietly humming elevator. "I know that name from somewhere … I've got it. You're on my list."

"What list?"

"The list of the members of the expedition to Cavendish Island."

"Yes, I'm a member of Professor Royston's team," Cathy said with some surprise, "but how did you know?"

"I'm coming too."

"You are?"

"The *Mirror* was offered a place on the expedition boat, and I have been ordered to fill it."

"You don't sound exactly thrilled by the prospect," she remarked as they walked across the grand lobby of the hotel.

"I'm happy where I am—on police rounds," muttered Nick through gritted teeth, "but I wasn't given a choice."

"We'll have to try to make the archaeology not too boring then," shouted Cathy over the sound of the traffic as they stepped out onto George Street.

She led the way to a small coffee shop on York Street she had noticed the day before.

Cathy ordered croissants and a small cup of black coffee. Nick ordered a flat white, then pulled out his notebook.

"I wonder if it's a coincidence that you and the victim were staying in the same hotel," he muttered, half to himself.

"The victim?" asked Cathy. "You mean you know who she was?"

"Of course."

"But it wasn't in the paper."

"We don't print everything, especially those things the police ask us not to. Anyway, I have contacts. Whether it's for publication or not, I usually know."

"Well then? Who was she? Why might it be a coincidence?"

"Because she was also connected with the Cavendish Island expedition. Her name was Jenny Marshall. She was married to—"

"Dr. Paul Marshall," volunteered Cathy.

"Yeah, that's the guy. An American historian apparently, whose area of special interest is Australian colonial history."

"Dr. Marshall's work is quite famous. The poor man. I presume he won't be joining the expedition after all."

"I guess so," agreed the journalist. "Depending on whether he still wants to come and on whether the police let him."

"Why would they want to stop him?"

"Wife dies, husband is always the first suspect. That's the way it is."

For a while they drank their coffee in thoughtful silence.

"By the way," asked Nick slowly, "why were you in the same hotel as the Marshalls?"

"Professor Royston made the reservations. Or his office did. I assume they booked everyone from out of Sydney into the same hotel."

"And you didn't know the Marshalls were next door to you?"

"I had only just arrived. Mind you, even if I had seen him, I wouldn't have recognized him. I've read one of his books, but I've never even seen a photograph of the man."

"So tell me what you saw and heard last night."

"I had to read the paper to find out what had happened."

"Yeah, but even so, I might be able to do a color piece out of what you tell me."

Cathy obliged the journalist with a detailed account of the previous afternoon and evening. Nick filled several pages of his notebook.

"You still do shorthand?" she remarked in surprise. "I thought all journalists used those little tape recorder things these days."

"My father insisted I learn," Nick said with a grimace. "He was a newspaperman of the old school. So I learned shorthand to keep him happy. It's not hard, and it can be useful."

"Anyway, now you know everything. I told you it wouldn't be of any use to you."

"I know that you alerted the hotel authorities, and that's a new fact that no one's told me before. And I know that Potter's involved in the investigation. He owes me a favor; maybe I can squeeze a bit of information out of him."

"I wonder …" said Cathy slowly.

"Wonder what?"

"Whether Mrs. Marshall's death could have anything to do with the expedition. Do the police have any leads?"

"None that I know of. And I think if they had a good lead, I'd know. Your thought is an interesting one. Is there someone who doesn't want the Cavendish Island expedition to go ahead? And will he murder to stop it?"

The early morning sun was glinting off the waters of Rose Bay under a cloudless sky. Moored at the end of the Rose Bay wharf and standing by to receive supplies was a twenty-meter oceangoing cruiser—the MV *Covenant*—gleaming white in the early sunlight.

Standing on the wharf looking down onto the deck was a weather-beaten man in his mid-fifties. His arms were folded, and a look of grim anger occupied his face. He watched as a small, red-headed man mopped the deck.

"Any idea how it happened, Toby?"

"I haven't a single idea, Captain," replied the deckhand.

"When did you tie up?"

"Just after ten o'clock last night. Just like you told me to."

"And then you were back this morning … when?"

"Not long after six."

"And there was gasoline all over the deck then?"

"Aye, you could smell the stink, Captain, halfway up the wharf. As bad as an oil refinery, it was."

The captain turned away looking puzzled and worried. He rubbed his hand thoughtfully on his chin.

Striding toward him up the wharf was a woman about his own age with short, gray hair and a businesslike manner.

"I'm looking for Captain Nagle," she announced as she drew closer.

"You've found him. What can I do for you?"

"Uh, Captain. I'm Dr. Ingrid Sommerville. Due to depart with the Cavendish Island expedition on Saturday. I'm here to check the medical supplies."

"Let Toby finish mopping the deck before you go aboard," said Nagle, making a sweeping gesture as he spoke. "It shouldn't take much longer."

The doctor put her black bag down on the timber of the jetty. "Is there a problem?"

"Not so much a problem as an oddity, as you might say," replied Nagle. "When Toby here arrived this morning, he found the decks awash with gasoline."

"A curious accident." The doctor glanced over her shoulder to the point, about halfway up the wharf, where two pumps stood side by side—one gasoline, one diesel.

"Yes, it might have come from there," said the captain, following her glance, "but how that could have happened, well, I've no idea. Mind you, if I catch the idiot who did this, I'll blast the barnacles out of him."

Ingrid raised her eyebrows, and the captain smiled. "I like to talk like an old sea dog occasionally—it amuses the customers."

The doctor was about to make a comment when a huge shadow stepped between her and the sun. She turned around and found herself facing a giant of a man—a tall, solidly built Polynesian, a Tongan, with a huge grin on his face.

"Morning, Sam," said Nagle. "Meet Dr. Sommerville, one of our passengers to Cavendish."

Ingrid found her hand being swallowed up in the Tongan's huge fist as she shook hands.

"Doctor, this is Sam Fangatofa, one of our deckhands. The Irishman behind the mop over there is the other, Toby O'Brien."

At the sound of his name Toby looked up and raised his cap in respect.

"What happened, Cap'n?" asked the Tongan.

"There was gasoline all over the deck when Toby arrived this morning."

"That's bad. Very bad. How did that happen?"

"We don't know, Sam. Accident maybe."

"Maybe," said the deckhand doubtfully.

"I think I've just about finished here, Captain," Toby called out from the deck.

"You can go aboard now, Doctor," said Nagle, "just mind your step." He took her hand and helped her down from the wharf to the deck.

Nagle had no sooner seen Ingrid below when he was summoned by a voice from the shore—a young, female voice.

"Yoo hoo! Could someone give me a hand with my cases please?" she called plaintively.

"Come along, Sam," muttered Nagle, "let's see what the young lady wants."

They walked briskly down the length of the wharf to where the young woman was standing.

"I'm Captain Nagle, and this is Sam Fangatofa, one of my deckhands. Now, how may we be of service to you, ma'am?"

"I'm Holly North," she said, "pleased to meet you."

As she spoke she extended her right hand, while using her left to hold her floppy straw hat in place as a gust of wind whipped across the water. "I'm the expedition photographer. My gear is in the trunk of that taxi," she added, nodding toward the road.

"We'd better go and get it then," said the captain.

The captain and his deckhand retrieved several black cases and a wooden chest from the taxi and carried them the length of the wharf.

"Thank you for doing this," gushed Holly. "It's awfully kind of you."

"What's in the chest?" asked Nagle.

"It's a portable darkroom," explained the photographer. "Well, just about. All the chemicals and paper I need and a small enlarger."

"Sam," said the captain, "carry this stuff on board and help Miss North find someplace to stow her gear."

"It mustn't get too hot, Captain," Holly cautioned.

"Away from the engine room then, Sam."

"Aye, sir," said the big Tongan. He hefted the wooden chest onto one shoulder and tucked two of the larger black cases under one arm. "Follow me, miss," he said, "I show you the way."

Once they were out of sight, Captain Nagle began prowling around the aft deck, still troubled by the spilled gasoline. He got down on his hands and knees, searching under the seat that ran around three sides of the deck.

"Lost something, Captain?" asked Toby as he reappeared on deck.

"Still puzzled, Toby, that's all," was the reply. A moment later the captain made a grunt of discovery and pulled from its hiding place deep under the seat an empty gasoline can—with its cap missing.

"What do you make of this, Toby?" asked Nagle holding his find aloft. "This doesn't look like an accident to me."

"But, sir, why would someone pour gasoline all over the deck in the middle of the night, and then not ..."

"Not set fire to the boat?"

"That's sort of what I was thinking, Captain."

"Perhaps they were disturbed ... or perhaps they never intended to strike a match. Perhaps it was just meant as a warning."

"A warning of what, Captain?"

"A warning that someone doesn't want this expedition to go ahead."

5

_____

The room was small and windowless. There was one door, one table, and three chairs. The walls, floor, and furniture were all a nondescript gray. On the table was a tape recorder.

Paul Marshall sat on one side of the table. Facing him were two police officers. The older of the two reached forward and pressed the machine's record button.

"Interview with Dr. Paul Marshall. Thursday, nine o'clock. Those present, D. S. Potter and D. C. Ingrams. You understand, don't you, Dr. Marshall, that you are here voluntarily to help us with our inquiries and that you are free to leave at any time?"

Paul nodded.

"For the tape please," instructed Potter.

"I understand."

"And you also understand that you may have a lawyer present if you wish and that you are not required to say anything, but that anything you do say will be part of the official record and may be used in evidence?"

"Yes, yes, I understand."

"How long have you been in Australia, Dr. Marshall?"

"Six … no, seven days."

"What is the purpose of your visit?"

"I've been invited by Professor Earl Royston to join his expedition to Cavendish Island."

"Cavendish Island? Where is that exactly?"

"In the Pacific Ocean, between Lord Howe and Norfolk

islands. It was a penal colony for a couple of years in the early nineteenth century. A rather brutal and harsh settlement, according to all reports. Although, to be honest, very little is known about it. Hence this expedition."

"I met another member of your party yesterday, a Miss Cathy Samson. Do you know the name?"

"I've never met her, but her name was on the list sent to me by Professor Royston. I believe she's an archaeologist, a Ph.D. student."

"Her room was next door to yours at the hotel. It was Miss Samson who raised the alarm."

"Maybe I should be grateful, but … it was too late anyway."

"Is it some sort of coincidence that Miss Samson's room is next to yours?"

"Royston's secretary made the room reservations for those of us from out of town, so it's hardly surprising."

"And you'd never met Miss Samson before?"

"She's a very junior team member. I probably won't meet her until Saturday, when the boat departs for Cavendish."

"You'll still go on the expedition then? Despite the death of your wife?"

"Unless you stop me. There's nothing I can do for Jenny now, and these expeditions take a lot of time and money to set up. It's too late to pull out now."

Potter consulted his notes for a moment. "What makes an American academic interested in Australian colonial history?"

"In my field, you've got to specialize these days. Every square inch of American history has been staked out already, so I was looking for something different. Look, is this getting us any closer to finding my wife's killer?"

"Just be patient, Dr. Marshall. I need to understand the background."

"Well, you've got enough background. Now get out and find out who killed my wife!" Paul rose to his feet; his eyes narrowed to slits. His face was flushed with anger, and a muscle in his cheek twitched nervously.

"Sit down please, Dr. Marshall," Potter said, quietly but firmly. "We know our job. There are officers out now, making inquiries. But we need your help. So if you can just be a little patient with us ..."

"Sorry," muttered Paul, running his fingers through his short dark hair. "I guess I'm a little rattled."

"Naturally you're upset. Now, can we proceed?"

"Yes, yes, of course."

"The preliminary forensic report put the time of your wife's death at between three and four yesterday afternoon. Where were you at that time, Dr. Marshall?"

"With Professor Royston. I've been with him all day, every day for the past ... three ... no, four days."

"Doing what?"

"Planning this expedition. He's archaeology, I'm history—the two disciplines have to work together on this one."

"Why were you chosen as team historian? Why not an Australian?"

"Because my university is providing part of the funding. A lot of the funding, in fact."

"So you were with Professor Royston yesterday afternoon?"

"Yes. All afternoon. Ask him if you don't believe me."

"We will, Dr. Marshall, we will." For a long minute Potter stared at the American in silence, trying to penetrate the steely cold glare of those eyes. "And where was your wife during this meeting?"

"Jenny said she was going shopping."

"When was the last time your saw her?"

"I've answered all these questions before."

"I'm sorry, but we have to go over it again."

Paul shrugged his shoulders in resignation and said, "She came with me to the university in the morning. She had lunch with us there. Then she called a cab and left for the city. She said she was going shopping."

"Did your wife have any friends or acquaintances in Sydney?"

"No. This was her first visit."

"But not yours?"

"I've been here often."

"Why didn't you bring your wife on your many previous visits?"

"Jenny is my second wife. We've been married just under two years. This is my first visit since the marriage."

"I see. Can you think of anyone who would have a reason to kill your wife, Dr. Marshall?"

"No one. No one. Look, her death doesn't make any sense. It must have been a burglar—broke into the room, thought it was empty, panicked when he found Jenny in the bathroom, and killed her."

"That may well be exactly what happened, Dr. Marshall. It's certainly one of the possibilities we're investigating. But, of course, there's one small difficulty: How did the thief get into your room?"

"That's what burglars are good at, isn't it?"

"There were no signs of forced entry," said Potter quietly, leaning forward across the table.

"Then maybe he stole a key. How should I know?"

"Where was your room key, Dr. Marshall?"

"Well, to tell the truth, it was in my coat pocket. With me, at the university."

"You didn't hand it in to the front desk when you went out for the day?"

"I know I was supposed to, but I kept forgetting to do that."

"And as a result, your wife had to get the assistant manager to let her into your room."

"I guess she must have."

"And your copy of that room key, did it stay in your coat pocket the whole afternoon? Where was your coat, Dr. Marshall?"

"Hanging up outside Royston's office."

"And can you swear, from your own knowledge, that the key never left that coat pocket all afternoon?"

"No. No, I can't swear that. I don't know it for sure."

"Could your key have been used, without your knowledge, to gain entry to the hotel room for the purpose of murdering your wife?"

"I ... I guess so ... but who would want to do such a thing?" For the first time Paul looked worried. He licked his lips nervously and ran his fingers through his closecropped hair.

"Ah, that's the big question, isn't it, Dr. Marshall? The really big question."

6

From the journal of Lieutenant Edmund McDermott, officer of the New South Wales Corps.

July 8th, 1821

*S*lept badly this night, being deeply disturbed by the occurrences of yesterday, and, in particular, my unpleasant encounters with Commander Black, who is to be the commandant of the Cavendish Island Penal Settlement, and my new commanding officer. Having breakfasted, I went to seek out my brother officer, Mr. Wardle, to ask if he knew anything of this Commander Black's reputation, so that I might, at least, be forewarned as to what I might expect once we reach the island.

I found Wardle in Bridge Street, supervising a gang that was repairing the small wooden bridge that crosses the Tank Stream at that point. Wardle left the convicts under the supervision of his sergeant, and we repaired to a quiet spot where we could see the men but not be overheard by them. I then presented him with the name of Commander Black and asked him if he had heard anything of the man.

The news that my friend Wardle was able to pass on to me was deeply disturbing indeed. It appears that Black had been the officer in charge of an iron-gang employed as lime burners on the banks of the Hawkesbury River. There, so Wardle was able to inform me, Black had a reputation for brutality and insensate cruelty that went beyond the bounds of discipline and into the realms of hellish wickedness.

It was, so Wardle informed me, a well-known fact that Black took pleasure in rousing up the poor half-starved skeletons of fellows at midnight to load lime, when the boats happened to come in with the night's tide. They used to have to carry the baskets of unslaked lime a great way into the water in loading the boats; by which means many of their backs were raw and eaten into holes. He went on to say that he had heard from several different sources that Black was well known to have killed a man with a handspike, and was never tried for it.

"I have got a man under me now," said Wardle, "who received 2,600 lashes with the cat-o'-nine-tails in about five years when under the supervision of Commander Black, and the poor fellow's worst crime was insolence to his overseer. The fact is, this man is a red-hot Tipperary man; and when his blood gets up, you could not make him hold his tongue if you were to threaten to hang him. Since I have had him he has never had a lash, just because I take no notice of what he says. The consequence is, there is nothing in the world that man would not do for me if he could. Several years ago, in Black's lime-burning gang, a man actually died under the cat: Of course it was all quietly hushed up."

On another occasion, so Wardle was able to inform me, when Black was commandant of a road-making gang, whenever he intended to send a man to the lock-up for the night, he made the lock-up keeper start three or four buckets of water over the floor, under pretence of keeping it free from vermin, but really for the purpose of tormenting the culprit by compelling him to walk about all night: there being no where dry to sleep. And then he would have the poor wretch tied up to the triangle first thing in the morning, before breakfast. This Wardle swore to be true, having got it from the lock-up keeper himself.

I took my leave from Wardle deeply disturbed by his report of Black's disgusting brutality, which exceeded anything I had yet heard of as practised under the sanction of British law.

Concerned as to what future course of action I should take, I sought an audience with my friend Mr. MacCallum, a respected magistrate in the colony and a Christian gentleman. I laid before him my experiences of the day before and the information that Wardle had been able to share with me. MacCallum gave the matters I laid before him serious thought and did not rush to answer too quickly. When at last he spoke, it was to advise me to exercise some caution in rushing to judgment on Commander Black's character. The colony, he reminded me, is a breeding ground for gossip, rumour, and innuendo. This being so, he regarded discretion as the better part of wisdom when stories were being handed around for the apparent purpose of damaging an officer's character.

MacCallum encouraged me to withhold judgment until I had some firm evidence of a more direct nature. I pointed out that by the time such evidence is to hand, it may be too late to repair the damage. By then we may well be settled on Cavendish Island, and Commander Black may have established a reign of terror based upon brutality and an ill temper. If that should prove to be so, said MacCallum, then I should take it as my God-given duty, as second-in-command, to ameliorate the situation, so far as it is in my power to do so. Indeed, he added, such a task—namely the task of restraining Commander Black's malevolence—may well be the reason why Divine Providence has placed me in the position of being a senior officer of this new penal colony.

Encouraged by MacCallum's advice, I determined to call upon Commander Black after luncheon, to once again offer my services in the business of preparing for our departure for this new penal settlement. Consequent upon this decision, I called upon the commander's residence at about the middle of the afternoon. To my undisguised relief, I found him in a more settled and amenable frame of mind than I had on the preceding day. We discussed many practical matters in considerable detail and in a most frank and friendly fashion.

As the afternoon wore on, the commander brought out a bottle of port, and we relaxed and talked together of our various experiences as officers of the New South Wales Corps. Or, rather, I should say that I talked, for I found Commander Black somewhat reluctant to reminisce about his own biographical details. As night began to draw on, he pressed me to stay and share his evening meal with him, which I agreed to do.

It turned out that his domestic establishment was managed for him by his daughter, his wife having died some three years previously. The meal of roast pork and potatoes was excellent, but I was somewhat surprised that the daughter, by the name of Jessica, did not join us. Black explained that she preferred to eat with the servants in the kitchen. This was yet another oddity of which I made a mental note. As the meal wore on, Black drank more and more of the port, and, as a consequence, his behaviour became increasingly belligerent. Indeed, I observed that Miss Black, whenever she entered the room to supervise the laying or clearing of the table, eyed her father warily and seemed to be in great fear of him.

Several times in the course of the evening I endeavoured to depart. However, these endeavours provoked aggressive protests on Commander Black's part, as he insisted that I not withdraw my company until he gave me permission to do so. At length, the amount that he drank took its toll on his consciousness, and he fell asleep at the head of the table, snoring loudly.

This I took as my opportunity to depart. Miss Jessica Black saw me out at the front door, and as she did so, I asked her whether she would accompany us to Cavendish Island as a member of her father's household. To which innocent enquiry she gave the following astonishing reply: "Not if there is any mercy in this world, dear sir, not if there is the slightest amount of mercy."

7

The room was lined with dark, polished wood and floor-to-ceiling bookshelves. A faded Turkish carpet covered the floor. In one corner was a large desk, piled high with papers and unsteady stacks of books. There were four people seated in the over-stuffed armchairs that furnished the room—a man and a woman who looked to be in their early sixties and two women in their twenties.

A long, heavy silence hung over the room, broken only by the loud, slow ticking of a carriage clock on the mantelpiece.

"Well, Vicky." The man's voice broke the silence. "Do the police intend holding Paul, or will they release him to join the expedition?"

"I've asked them, Professor, but so far I haven't been able to get a reply out of them." The young blonde who spoke had cool blue eyes, a stenographer's notebook on her lap, and a pencil in her right hand.

"I see," muttered Professor Royston, rubbing his chin with his hand thoughtfully. His face had the soft, puffy appearance of one who had lived too well and indulged himself too often.

"Apply some pressure to them, darling," said the older woman. "Get our lawyers on the phone. Tell them to get a writ of *habeas corpus*, or get him out on bail, or something."

"I don't think that will be necessary, Stella," replied her husband. "What do you think, Vicky?"

"Well, Dr. Marshall seemed quite confident that the police

would not want to detain him for long. After all, he was here with you and Miss Myles at the time when they say his poor wife died."

"True, true," agreed Royston. "Lois, have the police contacted you?"

"I haven't spoken to them yet, Professor," replied the tall, plain young woman seated in the shadows in the far corner of the room. "But I checked my desk on the way to this meeting, and there was a message asking me to call a Detective Ingram."

"I see. Once you and I have provided an adequate alibi for Paul, I assume the police will have no reason for holding him. So you see, Stella, it will not be necessary to call in the lawyers."

"You'd better be right, Earl my dear. Nothing must go wrong with the expedition."

"Nothing will go wrong with it. Everything that is planned will happen. And it will happen on schedule."

"It had better. If not, there will be consequences," murmured his wife with quiet intensity. Her voice carried a ring of command about it, as if she expected obedience and was rarely disappointed.

"Will Dr. Marshall still want to come?" asked Lois Myles. "Won't he be too upset to come with us to Cavendish Island?"

"I know him better than you do, Lois," replied Royston. "The last time he was in Australia was, let me see, almost three years ago. You would still have been an undergraduate then. Dr. Marshall is dedicated to his work—obsessed, one could almost say. Hence, unless the police restrain him from doing so, I have no doubt that he will sail with us on Saturday."

"There is one thing, Professor," said Vicky, tapping her short-hand pencil on her notepad.

"Yes?"

"Mrs. Marshall was also due to sail to Cavendish Island. Following her death, there is an empty berth on the boat."

"Yes, that is correct."

"Well, I was wondering, seeing as how I worked as Dr. Marshall's secretary during his last visit, whether it would be at all useful if I came along. I don't want to push myself forward. It's just that—"

"Lois, what do you think?" interrupted Royston.

"Hmm. There's always a lot of paperwork on a dig like this. Someone who can type and do shorthand might be very useful. Just so long," she added, turning toward Vicky, "as you are prepared to help with the dirty work as well?"

"Anything," replied Vicky. "I'll help with anything at all."

"You're very keen to come, aren't you, my child?" Stella asked suspiciously.

"Yes, Mrs. Royston, very keen," Vicky admitted.

"Would we be better off filling the extra berth with a trained person?" asked Lois.

"Well, Jenny Marshall had no training," Royston said.

"None of Marshall's women ever had any training," sneered Stella. "They were all empty-headed bimbos."

"Jenny would have worked on record keeping," Royston continued, ignoring his wife's interruption, "and cleaning objects and fragments that we found. I'm sure Vicky would be able to do everything Jenny Marshall would have done."

"I have no objection then," concluded Lois.

"Let me think about it overnight," said Royston, "and I'll let you know in the morning. How would that be, Vicky?"

"That would be fine, Professor. Thank you very much."

"Well, Vicky and Lois, I needn't detain you any longer. Thank you for sparing me some time this morning."

Taking this statement as a clear note of dismissal, the two young women left the room. As soon as the door closed behind them, Stella remarked, "You know what's really going on, don't you, Earl?" The normally regal and arrogant expression on her full, round face was replaced by a look of cunning as she waited for her husband's reply.

"What do you mean, my dear?"

"That young woman's in love with Paul. I'm sure they had some sort of affair while he was out here three years ago. This is just a ploy on her part to resume it."

"Quite possibly. But if her presence will help the expedition, either because she can do some of the donkey work or because she keeps Paul happy, I don't care. Just so long as nothing rocks the boat."

"Just remember, Earl my love," said Stella with more threat than affection in her voice, "if anything goes wrong—consequences, dire consequences."

With that, she swept up her handbag and left the room.

Professor Royston returned to his desk, where he sat in thoughtful silence for some moments before picking up the telephone and dialing.

"Dr. Max Taunton please. Max? It's Royston here. That young stenographer who works for your department, Vicky something. Yes, Vicky Shaw, that's the one. She's just offered to take the empty berth on the *Covenant* when she sails on Saturday. What do you think? Yes, I see what you mean. But I don't think there's any hidden agenda. Or, at least, none that won't work to our advantage. Stella thinks Vicky's in love with Paul, wants to resume an old relationship. Exactly, it would keep Paul preoccupied and allow us to get on with the real agenda. If you're agreed then? Fine. I'll let her know she can come."

The two young women were walking down the stone corridor that linked the archaeology and history departments of the university. When they reached a wide bay window, they stopped and stepped over toward the tall mullioned windows, away from the pedestrian traffic in the corridor.

"How do you think the meeting went?" asked Vicky, looking like a pretty but very artificial doll beside her tall, plain companion.

"Just fine," replied Lois. "Very well, in fact."

"I'm not so sure. Do you think I'll get that extra berth on the boat?"

"You will," said Lois. "Don't worry about it."

"I am worried about it. Our orders are to get me on that boat. And you know, they don't take it well when orders are not carried out."

"Just relax. You're in. I'm certain you are."

"You could have supported me more strongly, you know," accused Vicky, a touch of bitterness in her voice.

"I didn't need to. And I decided it was better for me not to come on too strongly, waving flags and arguing for your inclusion. You know how suspicious the Roystons can get. Especially her."

"If I'm left out—"

"You won't be. So stop worrying. The plan worked. Stella is convinced you're in love with Paul. She thinks that's the only agenda you have. So she, and the prof, will think it's perfectly safe to let you join the expedition."

Vicky thought this response over in silence for a few moments. "If Royston says no, is there time to try another tack?"

"If he says no—and he won't—offer to go for free. Say you'll take your vacation time, so the expedition doesn't need to fund your salary."

"Won't that make him suspicious?" Vicky asked nervously, biting the bright pink lipstick off her bottom lip.

"Turn on the full 'woman in love' performance. He won't be able to resist that."

"Perhaps." Vicky sounded doubtful.

"It won't come to that," Lois assured her. "They bought the story today. You're in. Stop worrying."

"I guess you're right."

"I know I'm right."

"So, how many of us will there be on the island?"

"Just the three of us—you, me, and Paul," replied Lois. "But that's enough."

"I thought there were plans to send more."

"There may have been at one stage, but, if so, they've been dropped."

"Is three enough? Can we pull it off?"

"Of course we can. Three is more than enough. Especially considering that we don't have to do anything concrete, just stop the others from going ahead with their plans."

"Yes, you're right, of course. Who will be in charge?"

"Paul has been given leadership. You just follow his orders."

"And what about you?"

"I will coordinate my actions with yours and Paul's. But they've given me a special role to play."

"Which is what, exactly?"

"You don't need to know."

"So Paul and I work together, and you run your own show?"

"Something like that."

"And they think that will be enough to stop these people?"

"I'm sure they're not counting on us three alone. They will have other plans in operation as well. But what those plans are, we don't need to know. We just need to keep our heads down and do our part. Now, we'd better move on. We don't want to be seen talking together. The less the Roystons know about our connection, the better."

"What have you got for me?" asked Frank as Nick walked into his office.

"I've filed an update on the Marshall murder," said Nick, "and I've got a call in to Potter at police headquarters to see if I can find out any more."

"Good. Do they suspect the husband?"

"My sources suggest he's in the clear."

"I always suspect the husband when a wife is murdered. Most of the murders I covered when I was on the road were done by spouses."

"Frank," Nick said with a sigh, as he lowered his lanky frame into a comfortable chair, "you haven't been an on-the-road reporter for twenty years. Times have changed."

"I'll bet most murders are still domestics."

"There's more organized crime these days, Frank."

"Yeah, I guess so. You ready for Saturday? Keen to go?"

"I've got a bag packed. And I guess I'm looking forward to it now."

"This is an interesting change," the editor said with a grin. "What brought this about?"

"I met a member of the expedition today. An archaeologist named Cathy Samson."

"And she's pretty, is she?"

"I guess I'd say that she's … all right."

Frank laughed out loud. "That means she's pretty. And that's why you're now quite happy to go."

"Lay off, Frank."

"All right already. By the way, did you see the piece we ran in last Saturday's paper about the Royston expedition to Cavendish Island?"

"Yeah, I saw it."

"Well, it's provoked some religious fruitcake to write to Royston asking him to cancel the expedition. A copy of the letter was also sent to us."

"Why? Why cancel the expedition, that is?"

"It's all to do with mysterious dark forces. Here, read it for yourself," said the editor, digging through several untidy piles on his desk, and finally, with a grunt of satisfaction, handing over a photocopy of a neatly typed letter.

Nick glanced over the note, which was typed on plain paper—no letterhead—and signed "W. H. Muir," with no indication of whether this was a man or a woman's name.

"Read it," urged Frank. "Go ahead and read it out loud."

"Dear Professor Royston," Nick read. "I was alarmed to read in today's edition of *The Sydney Morning Mirror* of your intention to lead an expedition of archaeologists and historians to Cavendish Island, there to unearth the evil remains of that unholy settlement. I write for the single and sole purpose of persuading you to abandon your aims. It is unfashionable in this scientific age to speak of non-material spiritual forces; nevertheless, I must do so.

"Even among those who accept the existence of such forces, there is nowadays a terrible mistake that is commonly made— namely, assuming that all spiritual forces are benign and helpful. Would that this were so. The tragic truth is that there are non-material spiritual forces every bit as evil as Adolf Hitler or Joseph Stalin—forces that desire to hurt, kill, maim, and inflict suffering and pain. Furthermore, such forces are always deceptive. They present themselves as 'angels of light' while being, in reality, agents of horrifying darkness.

"You are probably unaware of a booklet published in 1893 entitled 'The Dark History of the Secret Coven.' However, I have come across a copy of this booklet, and the story that it tells is an appalling one. There were deeds done on that island during its brief period as a penal colony that are wicked beyond description. They have left a cloud of evil clinging to Cavendish Island that it would be most unwise to disturb. I beg of you: Abandon your foolish plans to unearth this awful past. You will only be exposing yourself and the members of your party to powerful evil forces.

"Yours sincerely, W. H. Muir."

"So, there you are, Nick," said Frank with a cheerful grin. "Don't say you haven't been warned."

8

Saturday morning dawned bright and clear. As Nick Hamilton stepped out of his taxi at Rose Bay, he slipped his hand into his inside top pocket to make sure that he had not forgotten his copy of "The Dark History of the Secret Coven." He had found three columns of Muirs in the Sydney telephone directory, but only one W. H.—it had been the right one.

The voice that had answered the telephone was elderly and suspicious but warmed immediately to Nick's promise to read the booklet and take the warning seriously. Nick had then arranged for a courier from the *Mirror* to pick up Mr. Muir's copy of the booklet. So far he hadn't had a chance to read it, but the voyage to the island would give him plenty of time for reading.

"Good morning, Nick," said a bright voice from several meters away. Nick looked up and saw Cathy Samson, who was also in the act of paying her cab driver.

"Good morning, Cathy," he responded, thinking again how pretty she looked—she seemed to shine in the bright morning sunlight—"allow me to give you a hand with your bags."

"I do seem to have a lot, don't I?"

"For a small cabin on a motor cruiser, you certainly do."

"I see that you travel light," Cathy remarked.

"Journalists learn to do that. This one canvas bag holds all I need."

Nick slung his bag over his shoulder and picked up one of Cathy's bags in each hand.

"Can you manage?" she asked, her brow furrowed.

"Of course I can," said Nick. "You lead the way."

Cathy picked up her remaining suitcase, the smallest of the three, and Nick's briefcase and led the way down the timber decking of the wharf.

A giant Tongan was standing on the aft deck of the MV *Covenant* awaiting new arrivals.

"Here, I take those," he said with a grin. Nick handed the luggage down as he introduced himself and Cathy.

"Hi, I'm Sam," replied the deckhand. "Welcome aboard."

"Thanks. Are the others already here?"

"Everyone except Professor Royston and his wife."

Nick held Cathy's hand as she crossed the gangplank and jumped onto the highly polished wooden planks of the deck.

"Morning," said the journalist to the small redheaded Irishman coiling a rope toward the aft of the deck.

"Top of the mornin' to ya," he replied. "I'm Toby. And I heard that you two are Nick and Cathy. Welcome aboard."

The names sound good together, Cathy thought. Immediately another part of her mind scolded her for being foolish.

A short, steep companionway led down into what Toby had called the main lounge. It occupied the width of the entire boat, had a long, continuous settee built into the walls around most of its circumference and was lined with large windows down both sides.

Half a dozen people were standing around talking.

"Ah, newcomers." A man with a weather-beaten face and grizzled hair stepped forward. "I'm Captain Nagle; welcome aboard the cruiser *Covenant.*"

Once again Nick and Cathy introduced themselves.

"Meet your fellow passengers," continued the captain. "This is our ship's doctor—at least for this voyage—Dr. Sommerville."

"Oh, do call me Ingrid."

"And this young lady is your expedition photographer."

"Holly North."

Nick shook hands with the slender young woman with the sun-tanned face and the wind-blown brown hair.

"I'll have to talk to you about the possibility of you taking some pictures for the paper," he said.

"That would be great," Holly replied.

The captain continued the introductions. "Now this is Lois Myles, Professor Royston's assistant."

"We'll be working together," said Cathy warmly.

"So I gather," responded Lois, a rather plain-looking, hard-faced young woman with a noticeable lack of enthusiasm.

"And this is Dr. Max Taunton," continued the captain, ignoring any note of coldness in the social undercurrents.

The man he introduced was a sandy-haired, middle-aged man in a crumpled tweed jacket and an open-necked shirt that had not been properly ironed.

"And what's your part in the expedition, Dr. Taunton?" asked Nick.

"Oh, call me Max, please. I'm a historian."

"I thought Dr. Marshall was filling that role."

"Well, we can't allow all the history to be done by an American, now can we?" Max replied with an embarrassed smile. He then added, "There'll be more than enough work for both of us."

"Nick, Cathy," resumed Nagle, "there's tea and coffee there at the forward bulkhead, just help yourselves. Unless you'd like to go down to your cabins first and settle in?"

"Yes, please," said Cathy, "I'd like to unpack first."

As Cathy followed the captain out through a companionway at the far end of the main lounge, Nick poured himself a cup of strong, black coffee and let his eyes slowly travel around the room.

"What makes the *Mirror* so interested in this expedition?"

Nick turned around to discover Ingrid at his elbow.

"Surely this is history, not news," she added.

"Perhaps it would be, except for the photographs," explained Nick.

"What photographs?"

"You don't know about them?"

"I know the ruins have been photographed twice since the Second World War, but I don't know that there's anything remarkable about the photos."

"In the later photographs," explained Nick, "the ruins appear to be in better repair than they were in the first photos."

"Oh, I see. 'Extraordinary phenomenon, the island where time runs backwards.' Something of that sort."

"Something like that," replied the journalist, adding defensively, "but history alone makes the trip worthwhile."

"Let me tell you, young man, the remarkable history of Cavendish Island is a far better story than some tabloid nonsense about The Unexplained," the doctor said mockingly.

Just then, the swinging door that led to the companionway stairs flew open, and two people emerged. The man was in his forties, with thick black hair, deep-set black eyes, and the most extraordinary bushy eyebrows that met above the bridge of his nose. He was followed by a young woman in her twenties, small and quite pretty, Nick thought, with honey-blonde hair.

They were introduced as Dr. Paul Marshall and his temporary secretary, Vicky Shaw. *So, that's the recently bereaved Dr. Marshall,* Nick thought. *What an unfortunate appearance he has—his face seems to be fixed in a permanent scowl.*

After the introductions were over, Paul cleared his throat loudly and held up his hand asking for everyone's attention.

As silence fell over the main lounge, he said, "While everyone is gathered here, and right at the beginning of our time together, I'd like to make an announcement." His scowling gaze swept the room for a moment, and then he said, "I did not kill my wife. I want everyone to be perfectly clear about that—I did not kill my wife."

9

From the journal of Lieutenant Edmund McDermott, officer of the New South Wales Corps.

July 22nd, 1821

*T*his morning I stood facing the waters of Port Jackson, with my back towards Sydney town, knowing that by nightfall this town would be my home no longer, Commander Black having decided to sail upon the night tide. Having attended Morning Prayer at Holy Trinity Church in Argyle Place, as was my usual habit, I walked through Argyle Cut until, upon reaching the harbour, I found myself facing the King's Wharf, tied up at which was HMS *Covenant, the three-masted barque that was to take us to Cavendish Island.*

A gang of men in irons was passing barrels from hand to hand. The chain began at a heavily loaded wagon and ended at the foot of the gangplank leading to the deck of the *Covenant.* Going aboard I made myself known to Captain Pyne, who has the charge of carrying us safely to our destination. Having been assured that the loading of the ship with provisions was well under control, I left the captain and wandered towards the prow of the ship, and there I stood for many minutes, taking a long, fond look at the harbour I was leaving behind.

Here and there points of land—bare, grey, and boulder heaped—jutted out into the water; in other places the waters retreated from view into deep bays, whose shores were clad with a dense tangle of evergreens. The wind was fresh, and waves were breaking on Garden and Pinchgut Islands, both of which fell within my purview. Away to my left, the waters began to gradually narrow until they formed the stream that becomes the Parramatta and, in a minor branch, the Lane Cove Rivers.

This place, which had seemed so strange and alien upon my first arrival on these shores, now felt to me like home. So stricken at heart was I at the prospect of leaving all this for I knew not how many years, that I almost turned and hurried to Government House to make one last plea to be released from this duty. Common sense quickly told me that such a plea would be useless and that I must turn my face into the wind and make the best of my circumstance as I was able.

Turning around and looking back over the aft of the ship, I could see George Street, the main thoroughfare of Sydney town, full of pedestrians and vehicles, lively with bustle and activity. It stretched all the way from the King's Wharf to the houses at the foot of the Brickfield Hill, a distance of some mile and three-quarters.

I made enquiries of the second mate as to whether anything had been seen of Commander Black on the Covenant that morning. He replied that the commander had briefly visited the vessel and then departed again saying that he had an appointment to keep at the Market House—this being a well-known public house in the vicinity of the marketplace. Upon learning this, I set out at once for the Market House, intending to discover what specific orders my commanding officer might have for me on this, the day of our departure.

Upon entering the Market House, I found the large taproom to be very crowded, despite the early hour, with settlers who had brought their produce to the market in their carts and drays. These were, in the main, those poor people usually called Dungaree settlers, so called because of their frequent attire—that blue Indian manufactured cotton known as Dungaree. Casting my eyes about, I could see nowhere in all that crowd any sight of Commander Black. Almost everybody was drinking rum in drams, or very slightly qualified with water; nor were they niggardly of it, for I had several invitations from those around me to drink with them.

Many of the men were either quite intoxicated or much elevated by liquor. Their chief conversation consisted of vaunts of the goodness of their bullocks, the productiveness of their farms, or the quantity of work they could perform. The whole company was divided into minor groups of twos, threes, and fours, and the "dudeen" (a pipe with its stem reduced to three, two, one, or half an inch) was in everybody's mouth. But, peering however hard I did though the thick, smoky atmosphere of that place, I could not spy my commanding officer anywhere.

With many apologies and excuses I pushed my way through the throng, glancing over heads, and around packed groups of bodies. At length, at a table in the far corner, I spied a bent back and the back of a head that I thought might belong to Commander Black. I began at once to make my way in this direction. What with stepping over sprawling legs and colliding with drunken farmers, I made slow progress.

It seemed to me that Commander Black was deep in conversation with another man, an individual of the most unprepossessing appearance, for he had a deep scar down one cheek and the golden earrings of the sailor in both ear lobes. The taproom was a noisy place; hence it was impossible to hear a single word that passed between the two men. However, from their gestures and movements I took it that they were arguing about something. Whatever the argument was, they finally settled it, at which point the commander produced his purse and counted out upon the table a prodigious number of golden sovereigns. The amount of money that was changing hands in that transaction fair took my breath away.

The swarthy and unattractive individual drinking with the commander counted the money a second time, and then, in exchange, he produced some small object wrapped in a piece of oilcloth. Now consumed with curiosity, I pushed forward to see what could possibly be so valuable. The commander, the side of *whose face I could now see quite clearly, eagerly unwrapped the cloth to examine its contents. Imagine my surprise, when it was revealed to be—a book!*

Now, what book, I asked myself, could be worth so much money to my commanding officer? The book was about the size of a small Bible, and was bound in leather. Craning my neck forward to gain a better view, I could see that it was not, in fact, a Bible—unless it were like no Bible I had ever seen before. For marked upon its leather cover were bizarre runic inscriptions that looked to my eyes to belong more to some ancient pagan world than to anything that might be called Christian civilisation.

10

Y ou're in cabin nine, Mr. Hamilton," said Captain Nagle.

The door swung open to reveal a small room: a single bunk, a porthole, a desk and chair, a small chest of drawers, and hanging space for clothes.

"The head is next to the stairs from the main lounge," said Nagle.

"The head?"

"The toilet, the lavatory, the john, the loo—whatever you call it. And next to it is the shower."

"Only one for all of us?"

"The Roystons have a small, private bathroom next to their cabin, which is the big cabin, and so do I. The rest of you share."

Nick threw his canvas bag onto the bunk and dropped his briefcase on the desk.

"What did you make of Dr. Marshall's strange outburst?" he asked as he unzipped the canvas bag.

"He's been under a lot of pressure over the past few days," said Nagle. "I'm sure of that. First, he lost his wife, and in addition, so I gather, the police have questioned him at length. No doubt his nerves are rubbed raw."

With that observation, the captain turned to go, remarking over his shoulder as he left, "A few days at sea will settle his nerves."

Nick hung up a couple of pairs of jeans and stuffed T-shirts, sweaters, underwear, and socks into drawers. Then he knelt on the bunk, opened the porthole, and looked out. The sun was glinting off the waves that skipped across Rose Bay, and a salty breeze was blowing across the harbor. Closing the porthole again, he left the cabin, pulling the door closed behind him.

He was standing in a narrow corridor that ran almost the entire length of the boat, with doors opening off it on both sides. The deck beneath his feet was vibrating with the silent throb of a powerful diesel engine. Nick could see a steep, narrow stairway not far from his cabin leading down to the engine room, with a large red and white sign reading *Crew Only.*

Returning to the main lounge, Nick found it empty. Presumably the passengers had drifted out onto the aft deck to enjoy the sea breeze and, perhaps, a last glimpse of Sydney. He decided to join them.

As he emerged from the main cabin, a voice called out, "Could someone give me a hand with the professor's bags and cases?"

Looking up, Nick saw Sam standing on the end of the wharf. Nick glanced around, saw that none of the crew were on the deck, and replied, "I'll help."

He climbed up the gangplank and then followed the big Tongan down the wharf and on to New South Head Road, where they found a small mountain of suitcases, bags, and boxes on the footpath, and a gray-haired man, with a pointed goatee beard and a flushed face, arguing fiercely with a taxi driver.

"Oh, for goodness sake, Earl," snapped a middle-aged woman wearing a scarf around her head and large dark glasses, "forget about it. Just pay the man."

With a snarl of reluctance Professor Royston pulled several notes out of his wallet and thrust them into the driver's hand. The driver immediately walked toward the door of his cab.

"What about my change?" yelled the professor.

"You mean I don't get a tip?" asked the driver with an impudent grin.

In response, the professor swore at him and held out his hand for the change. This he received, and the cab sped off.

Nick and Sam walked around the small mountain of luggage, trying to figure out where to start. Nick was standing beside Professor Royston when he heard the sound of a car engine being gunned. He looked up and saw a blue BMW roaring toward them. Nick grabbed the older man, flung him toward the footpath, and leaped after him.

The big car thundered past within inches of Nick's feet.

"That was mighty close," exclaimed Sam.

As he helped the professor up, Nick said, "I could have sworn that guy was driving straight at us."

"Oh, he was," gasped the professor. "I'm quite sure he was. That was a deliberate attempt on my life."

The room was paneled with dark wood and was dimly lit. There were thirteen men in dark suits seated around a long, board-room table. A decanter of whiskey was being passed slowly from right to left around the table. Several of the men were smoking cigars.

"Is everything in place?" asked the shadowy figure seated at the far end.

"We've increased the number of agents who will be on the island from three to four," replied a big, beefy man, speaking between clenched teeth that held a cigar.

"What about Dr. Marshall?"

"He still believes that he is in charge of our operation."

"And he doesn't suspect …?"

"He has no idea that we found it necessary to dispose of … or, perhaps I should say 'replace' … his wife."

"It was foolish of him," said a quiet voice from the center of the table, a voice that was little more than a whisper, "to marry an outsider in the first place. If he wanted another woman, we could have arranged it."

"As, indeed, we have now," remarked the chairman from his place in the shadows at the head of the table. "And he understands what his instructions are?"

"I have stressed to him time and again," said an American voice at the chairman's left, "that this operation is purely negative. His task is to stop the others from carrying out their intentions. Once that objective has been accomplished, I told him, the council will decide what use to make of the power source."

"And he accepted this explanation?"

"Of course he did, Mr. Chairman. He has been part of the organization since his youth. He knows there is only one penalty for disobedience."

"That's right," grunted the beefy man. "Disobedience means ... death."

VOYAGE

What fellowship can light have with darkness?
—2 Corinthians 6:14

11

Nick Hamilton was rather proud of Sydney Harbour, with its beautiful expanse of glittering green water, the pretty white and pink houses that tumbled down the foreshores, the green fringes of trees and shrubs, the scattered islands, and the surprising twists and turns of bays on either side. The Roystons and their luggage were on deck, the ropes were slipped, and the MV *Covenant* began moving out of Rose Bay and down the harbor.

"Lovely," sighed Cathy, as if reading Nick's mind. "What's that lighthouse-looking thing over there on the left?"

"It's not on the left," Nick said.

"Yes it is, there on our left."

"On our port side, you mean. We're at sea now."

"Don't be smart," Cathy said. "Now, what is it?"

"It marks the Sow and Pigs—a large submerged rock and several smaller rocks. Best avoided."

They were standing at the bow of the boat, leaning against the railing, the wind whipping into their faces. Nick watched the green waves dashing toward them.

"Professor Royston was looking rather grim when he came on board." Cathy raised her voice slightly as the vessel gained speed. "I wanted to introduce myself, but it didn't seem to be the right moment."

"Good guess on your part," Nick agreed, turning toward her. "So, you haven't met him before?"

"He employed me by telephone and correspondence from Melbourne. I thought I'd told you. Anyway, what was he so upset about?"

"Just after he got out of his taxi, he was almost run down by a car."

"I guess that shook his nerves."

"I'm sure it did," agreed Nick, "but more than that, he claimed it was deliberate."

"Deliberate?"

"An attempt to kill him, no less."

"Did you see it?"

"Oh, yes, I was there. I saw it all right."

"So, what do you think? Was it deliberate?"

"Of that, I'm not so sure. But the professor seemed pretty certain."

"Odd."

"Yes, *odd* seems to cover it."

"Especially coming on top of everything else," mused Cathy.

"What else?" asked the journalist, his curiosity aroused.

"While you were up getting the Roystons' luggage, I was talking to Toby O'Brien, the deckhand, and he told me about the gasoline."

"What gasoline?"

"It seems that one night last week, while the *Covenant* was docked at Rose Bay, someone poured gasoline all over the decks."

"Poured? Or spilled?"

"Toby said the crew was certain it couldn't have been an accident."

"As you say, odd. And before that was the murder of Dr. Marshall's wife. Are they connected," speculated Nick "or separate incidents?"

"That's the question, isn't it?" asked Cathy, shivering a little more than the fresh ocean breeze justified and pulling her jacket more snugly around her shoulders.

Captain Nagle dispatched Vic Neal, the ship's engineer—a thin, wiry man who seemed to live in grease-spotted T-shirts and old jeans—to the engine room, while he stood on the bridge, one hand on the wheel, the other operating the radio that kept him in touch with harbor traffic control. The rest of the ship's company was gathered in the main lounge. Some of them were drinking, but most were gathered in twos and threes at the big windows that lined the lounge, watching the foreshores of the harbor slip by.

"Max, be a darling, and fetch me another sherry," purred Stella Royston. She was seated on the plush settee that ran around the perimeter of the main lounge. The scarf was gone, but she was still wearing the dark glasses. In response to her command, Max hurried across to the bar at the forward bulkhead and poured a generous glass of dry sherry.

"Earl, come here," she commanded, once she had the sherry in her hand. "Take a seat by my side. I wish to speak to you."

Professor Royston excused himself from Ingrid and Holly and hurried to his wife's side.

"Max, another sherry for my husband," Stella ordered. She sipped her drink in silence until the professor had been served, and the faithful Max had tottered away.

"You behaved very foolishly on the road a short while ago, didn't you, my dear?" She spoke in a threatening hush that was only a little above a whisper.

"I was angry," replied her husband, fingering the collar of his shirt nervously.

"Discipline. Control. Those must be our watchwords," hissed his wife.

"Do you think I don't know that? I'm sure there was no serious damage done, but just to make sure, I'll have a quiet talk with the journalist at the first opportunity."

"You'd better."

"I just said I will, and I will. Hamilton is no threat. He's just a journalist with a room-temperature IQ. I can handle him."

"Well, here's your chance." Stella gestured with her glass. "He's just come in off the deck, with that new assistant of yours, that Samson woman. Go and talk to them."

"I was just about to. There's no need to point out the obvious," snapped her husband as he rose from his seat.

"You two look a bit wind-blown," Royston said cheerfully as he approached Nick and Cathy, his gray goatee bristling incongruously out of his round, fleshy face.

"We've been out on the forward deck," said Nick.

"But we're approaching the heads now, and we had to come in as the swell was getting up. If we'd stayed any longer, we'd have been drenched by the spray. By the way, I'm Cathy Samson, your new assistant."

"I'm delighted to make your acquaintance, Miss Samson—in the flesh, as it were, rather than on the phone."

There was a peculiar inflection in Royston's voice as he pronounced the word *flesh* and Cathy felt a distinct shiver run down her spine.

"Your credentials look excellent on paper," the professor was saying, "and the reference from your master's degree supervisor was glowingly fulsome in its praise. I think we can find some most unusual colonial masonry for you to work on, Miss Samson, most unusual."

Again there was that strange tone in his voice and Cathy found herself taking an involuntary step closer to Nick.

"Now, Hamilton," resumed Royston briskly, "I made an unfortunate remark earlier. After the near-accident, you know."

"I know," Nick said, "and it had nothing to do with the notion of an accident as I recall."

"Ill temper. That's all it was. My nerves have been on edge, you'll understand. Preparing for an expedition like this one is a great responsibility."

"I'm sure it is," the journalist concurred, "not made any easier by the murder of Dr. Marshall's wife."

At this reference to the murder Professor Royston became noticeably uncomfortable. "Yes indeed, most regrettable. With all of these concerns, you'll understand why my nerves were on edge, and why I might have made a … uh, a foolish, and uh … an unguarded statement."

"Think no more of it, Professor."

"You would not think of including it in any of your reports for the *Mirror,* would you?"

"A little incident like that? Of course not."

"Good. Good. Excellent. Now, Miss Samson, let me brief you a little on what we may expect on the island." He took Cathy by the arm and led her away.

Odd, thought Nick. *In fact, odder and odder.* All of his journalistic instincts told him that anything someone wanted suppressed was important. Royston's remarks had ensured that Nick would be careful to remember the incident on the road and keep puzzling about its significance.

12

From the journal of Lieutenant Edmund McDermott, officer of the
New South Wales Corps.

July 22nd, 1821

McDermott, what are you doing here?" spluttered
Commander Black, hastily stuffing the small book into his pocket,
apparently hoping I hadn't seen it.

"I've come for my orders, sir," I replied. "They told me on the
Covenant I'd find you here."

"I'm glad you've come, my boy," said Black in an unnaturally hearty manner, rising from the table and throwing an arm
around my shoulders as he spoke. At the same time, although
he thought I couldn't see the gesture, he was waving at his
strange, scar-faced companion to go away.

"Your main responsibility today, my boy," continued Black,
steering me towards the middle of the taproom, "is to get the convicts on board the Covenant. Those fifty men and boys who are
our first consignment are being held in the stockade at the
Brickfield Hill end of the George Street barracks. Take Sergeant
Davis and a company of troopers and escort them to the ship."

"Yes, sir."

"And, I want them battened down in the hold of the ship by
lunch time."

"But sir, we don't sail until the night tide."

"Do you think I don't know that, McDermott?" snapped
Black, his natural ill temper surfacing once more. "My first task is

to break the spirit of these villainous re-offenders. And being locked in the hold during the heat of the day is a good first step towards that noble goal."

"But, sir—"

"Just do as you are told, man! And don't question my orders."

With that he whirled on his heel, disappeared into the crowd, and was gone. I walked back into George Street with my head full of questions. Pondering all I had seen and heard, I made my way through the warmth of a sunny mid-winter's day in the Colony of New South Wales.

Those who have never left England's shores will not understand that in this wretched climate, winter quite often behaves in a most unseasonable way, with clear skies and strong sunshine through the middle parts of the day. And so it was today, as I entered the main gates of the barracks in search of Sergeant Davis.

Davis was a man I knew by sight but had not served with previously. His appearance did not recommend him, always looking, at least to my eyes, to be somewhat slovenly and unkempt. Not withstanding this slight failing, he had a reputation for strict discipline and for being able to extract the maximum amount of work from a gang of convicts.

I located Davis in the sergeants' mess, playing cards with three of his comrades. Having introduced myself and explained that we were charged by Commander Black with the removal of the convicts from the stockade to the ship, and that by lunchtime, I added my comment that this would be unnecessarily harsh on the prisoners and suggested that we consider delaying the action until later in the day.

"Oh, no, sir," said Davis quickly. "I couldn't be a party to that, sir. You see, sir, I have served with Commander Black in the past, and I know that he is uncommon particular about his orders being carried out just as he gives them. Right down to the dots on the 's,' sir. Most particular indeed. So I would propose that I rouse the

company immediate like, sir, and get the business under way.
Unless you have some objection to that, sir."

Put in that way I could not, of course, object. Sergeant Davis
then showed commendable energy and alacrity in assembling the
company, and within the half-hour I inspected the troops as they
stood in their ranks on the parade ground. The sergeant having
declared them to be all present and correct, I gave him the order to
march them to the stockade and begin the removal of the assigned
convicts.

They were a sullen and unhappy lot, the fifty men and boys,
dressed in uniform gray and wearing iron shackles on their legs,
that we escorted the length of George Street to the King's Wharf.
Their prison for the duration of the voyage was to be the main
cargo hold of the Covenant, between decks. Upon our reaching
the ship, the main cargo hatch was thrown open, and a rope ladder let down into the hold. A blacksmith on the wharf then
removed the shackles from the convicts, and, one by one, they
climbed up the gangplank, and down the rope ladder.

When the last of them reached the foot of the ladder, it was
withdrawn, the hatch covers thrown closed, and barred.

"There you are, sir," said Sergeant Davis smugly. "All snuggled
down and tucked up as neat as you could want, sir. And all done
by the noon hour."

"You may take the troops back to their barracks for their lunch,
sergeant, then have them pack their kits and be back on the wharf
by sunset."

"Yes, sir," he responded with a careless salute.

As the sergeant and his men departed, I was approached on
the poop deck of the Covenant where I was standing by a red-
faced, middle-aged individual who introduced himself as Dr. Curtis
Fraser, ship's surgeon.

"What is the meaning of this, sir?" he demanded.

"The meaning of what?"

"Of placing these wretched fellows in the hold so early in the day? Are they to be fed? Or are they to sit there, hungry and thirsty in the darkness until the morrow?"

"This was not my decision, sir, nor was it my desire," I explained, and went on to tell him of the explicit orders of Commander Black. At the mention of Black's name he instantly became subdued and disinclined to question or criticise. However, he did have sufficient humanity to arrange for a barrel of hard-tack, a barrel of dried beef, and a barrel of water, to be lowered into the hold, for the supply of the convicts.

After taking luncheon at a public house near the wharf, I supervised the loading of my sea chest and my kit bag aboard the Covenant.

As dusk was drawing on, I spied a pony trap rattle down George Street and onto the boards of the King's Wharf. Driving the trap was Commander Black. Seated beside him looking uncommonly miserable, was his daughter Miss Jessica Black.

I immediately walked around to where she was seated and offered my hand to help her down.

"Leave her alone, McDermott," shouted Black. "She is as fit as a bullock. She can take care of herself."

I looked at the commander somewhat stunned. However, he did not stay to see if I obeyed his instruction, but leapt down from the trap and walked briskly up the gangplank. As soon as he was gone, I again held out my hand, which Miss McDermott grate-fully accepted, and thus I helped her out of the vehicle.

As she stepped down, a gust of wind off the harbour blew her bonnet back from her face, and there I saw, right down one side of her face from the hairline to the chin, a large, ugly, purple bruise. She seemed embarrassed by my discovery and hastily pulled the bonnet back into place.

The next hour was occupied with last-minute preparations for departure. During all this time, Miss Black sat on a packing case on the wharf with her head lowered. At some moments she appeared to be sobbing.

At last Captain Pyne, commander of the HMS Covenant, was ready to give the order to raise the gangplank and slip the ropes. It was at this moment that my commanding officer realised that his daughter had still not stepped on board.

"Jessica!" he bawled loudly, leaning over the ship's rail. "Come aboard at once! Step lively!"

Miss Black, for her part, stood up, but instead of boarding the ship, she gathered up her skirts and ran off the wharf and up the George Street hill. Somewhat stunned and confused, I turned to Commander Black and asked, "Should I follow her? Or send one of the men after her?"

In response he swore viciously, and then muttered, "Let her go. She has no resources and no friends. She will die in a ditch. Which is no better than she deserves. Let the wretch go.

Turning he shouted, "Captain, weigh anchor. I have no desire to miss the night tide."

13

Cathy slept late on Sunday morning, lulled by the sound of waves lapping the side of the boat; the gentle, distant throb of the engines; and the constant sighing of the sea breeze.

Even after she woke, she found it easier to lie in her bunk, feeling the gentle rise and fall of the ocean swell, than to leap out of bed full of energy. Then she felt guilty about staying in bed so late and rose quickly and dressed in jeans and a sweater.

When she opened her cabin door, she noticed that the door of the cabin opposite was standing open. Iinside, sprawled fully clothed on his bunk was Nick. He was engrossed in a book, and for a long minute Cathy stood silently and looked at him—the blunted nose, the dark hair that was never quite tidy enough, the lopsided eyebrows over twinkling blue eyes, the good-humored mouth and wickedly cleft chin … just then he looked up and caught her staring.

"Ah, Sleeping Beauty has risen at last," he said with a smile. He laid aside the paperback book in his hand—its lurid cover declared it to be *That Hideous Strength* by C. S. Lewis.

"Would you care to join me for breakfast?" he asked, thrusting his lanky form up off the bed.

"Since I think I can smell bacon cooking, that is an invitation impossible to resist," she answered.

They climbed the companionway to find the main lounge transformed into a dining room. Sam Fangatofa emerged from the small galley at one end carrying a covered tray. Apparently he was cook as well as deckhand.

"There's something about the smell of the ocean that whips up an appetite," said Nick as he loaded a plate with bacon, scrambled eggs, fried mushrooms, and toast.

"This, I take it," commented Cathy, "is not your usual breakfast?"

"At home I'm strictly a muesli man."

"Your wife doesn't cook you a hot breakfast?"

"I'm not married," Nick said after a pause, "if that's what you wanted to know."

"I'm sorry," mumbled Cathy. "I'm prying. None of my business."

"No, no. Don't be like that. I don't mind you asking at all. What about you? Did you leave a husband and seven children behind?"

Cathy laughed. "Like you," she said. "Similarly single."

"Inviting the journalist was not a good idea, Earl," Stella Royston said firmly.

"The world must learn of our news," her husband disagreed, "and we are better off having a representative of the media with us, to be the eyes and ears of the world, as it were. When we have control of the power source, we will use this journalist as our channel, to convey our demands to the world."

They were sitting on the aft deck, well away from casual eaves-droppers. Stella was once again wrapped up in her scarf and ever-present dark glasses. The professor resembled an American tourist in a brightly colored open-necked shirt and brown slacks.

"You had just better keep him under control, that's all."

"I will, Stella. I will. And anyway, it's only until we have achieved our goal. After that nothing, and no one, on earth will be able to resist us. Hamilton will do exactly as he is told. When we reach that point, you will see how useful it is having him with us."

"Just remember," said his wife, in a voice so quiet that he had to strain to hear the words, "that I am the channel. It flows through me."

"I can never forget that," said Royston bitterly. "Never."

He rose from his seat as the subject of their conversation emerged from the main lounge with Cathy and walked over to greet them.

"Beautiful morning, is it not?" the professor said, in the forced manner of one to whom pleasant conversation comes unnaturally. "May I have a word with you, Nick?" Royston took the journalist's arm and led him to one side. "Just excuse us for a moment, won't you, Miss Samson?"

"Yes. Yes, of course," replied Cathy, puzzled.

"Now, Mr. Hamilton," said the professor, once they had reached the far corner of the deck.

"Nick, please."

"Certainly, Nick. I take it your editor briefed you on this expedition?"

"Yes, of course."

"Of course he did. He would. And what did his briefing focus on?"

"Well, the history, of course."

"Yes. And what else?"

"The mystery of those photographs. The building that appears to be repairing itself."

"It is, Mr. Hamilton. I'm sorry, *Nick*. That's exactly what's happening: The building is repairing itself."

"How? Why? What's going on?"

"The fact is, Nick, that Cavendish Island is the source of an extraordinary power. It is a place where the ley lines converge, if that means anything to you. It is like a massive electrical generator."

"What sort of power?"

"Ancient power," whispered the professor, his face crinkling in a peculiar expression of greed that was almost lust. "Extraordinary ancient power. The power that has driven this world for more thousands of years than you and I could guess."

"Tell me more."

"Not now. Later. The important thing is that you do exactly

what I tell you, when I tell you. Do that, and you will see and hear things no one has seen or heard for thousands of years. You will be the sole reporter covering the biggest story of the century. Perhaps of any century. Trust me, Nick. Do what I say, and you will become the most famous journalist in the world."

With that Royston patted Nick on the arm in a paternalistic way, and walked off.

The last thing I'll ever do is trust you, thought Nick, irritated by the professor's patronizing attitude.

Just then a large swell slapped against the side of the boat, and everyone lurched to one side, then struggled to regain their balance. Stella fell heavily against the railing near her seat, knocking her dark glasses onto the deck.

Nick hurried to her side and helped her back to her deck chair.

"My glasses! My glasses!" she shrieked. Nick bent down, scooped up the dark glasses and handed them back to her. Covering her face with her hand, she slipped the glasses back into place.

"Thank you, dear boy," she managed to say once her glasses were secure and she was comfortable again.

"Think nothing of it," Nick said, then slowly made his way back to Cathy's side.

"Most extraordinary thing," he said, when he reached her.

"Mrs. Royston's fall?" asked Cathy.

"No, her eyes."

"Her eyes?"

"She held up her hand to cover her face, but I caught a brief glimpse of her eyes. The pupils are ... well ... pink, is how I think you'd describe them. I've never seen eyes like them."

"Perhaps she's an albino. Don't they have pink eyes?"

"Yes, they do. But she's not an albino. Look at her skin, and hair—both dark. And I've met people who were albino. Her eyes are not like that. They're totally different. They're not like any eyes I've ever seen. At least, not in a human being."

14

___

 *H*is pink scalp was covered by wispy, white hair. He was dressed in an old-fashioned, dark blue business suit with a white shirt and red bow tie. On his feet were brown suede shoes. He was sitting in the straight-backed chair outside the editor's office, his hands clasped on the silver handle of his walking stick. Every so often he glanced at the editor's secretary. She, for her part, looked away, embarrassed.

For the fifth time, she left her desk and went into the editor's office. Once she had closed the door securely behind her, she said, "He's still there, Mr. Gordon."

"Who's still there?" asked Frank Gordon without looking up from his work.

"The old man."

"Hmm?" Frank raised his head, blinking. "You mean Mr. ... what's his name?"

"Muir. Mr. W. H. Muir. That's his card on your desk. He's been waiting for three hours now."

"I told you to tell him that I'm busy."

"I told him, sir, but he insists on waiting. He won't go away. What should I do? Should I send for security?"

"No. We can't do that," muttered the editor with a deep sigh. "That man is a fruitcake—a religious fruitcake, Rhonda. It will be a waste of my time to talk to him. Just ask him to leave, that's a good girl."

"Would you please come out and ask him to leave, Mr. Gordon?"

"Me?"

"Please, sir."

"But that's your job, Rhonda."

"I don't think I can do it, sir. He's such a nice old man."

"Hmm. All right. All right. I give in. Tell him I'll give him five minutes. That's all, Rhonda. Five minutes. Not one minute more."

"Oh, thank you, sir."

A moment later Frank was standing at his desk and shaking hands with his visitor.

"Have a seat please, Mr. … uh …"

"Muir. Wallace Humphrey Muir. At your service, sir."

"Please have a seat, Mr. Muir."

The old man lowered himself with some care into the leather chair facing the editor.

"Now, you have five minutes of my time, Mr. Muir. What can I do for you?"

"It's about the Royston expedition to Cavendish Island. I know you received my letter, because I had a phone call from your Mr. Hamilton."

"Yeah, Nick told me he was going to call you."

"Well, he did as he had indicated he would. He seemed like a very nice young man on the telephone."

"He is. He's a great guy."

"And for that reason I am worried about him. In the first instance, about him. But, ultimately, of course, about us all."

"Now you've lost me."

"Allow me to explain, Mr. Gordon." Muir settled himself more comfortably in his chair. "In my letter I mention a booklet entitled 'The Dark History of the Secret Coven.' When your Mr. Hamilton called, I sent him my copy. Part of the story in that pamphlet concerns Cavendish Island, and the things that happened there during its brief, unhappy occupation."

"What sort of things?"

"The sort of things that would put a Nazi concentration camp to shame, Mr. Gordon."

"Really?" the editor asked, brightening visibly. "And Nick has this booklet? Well, that'll make a great angle in the story."

"Oh, dear me," muttered the old man. "How can I get this through to you? It is more than just a *good angle* that we are talking about here—it is the power of darkness."

"What power?" asked Frank, skeptically.

"First, let me ask you, if I may, Mr. Gordon, what do you believe in?"

"Believe in? Anything I can see or hear or touch or taste or smell, I guess."

"That little? Oh, dear me."

"What do you mean, 'that little'? I believe in the physical universe around me, and that's a heck of a lot."

"But you don't believe in anything you can't see?"

"No," the editor doubtfully replied. "I don't think I do."

"Then you don't believe in love?"

"Love?"

"Or hope? Or faith? What about electricity? You can't see that. Do you believe in electricity, Mr. Gordon?"

"Ah, I've got you there, old timer. I can't see electricity, it's true, but I can see the things electricity does. I can see its power in action."

"And in just the same way, I can see the power of God in action. I have seen him heal alcoholics and drug addicts and change lives in most remarkable ways."

"Is this getting us anywhere?"

"Whether you see it or not, Mr. Gordon, whether you believe it or not, there is another realm. Let's call it the realm of the spirit. It is what gives a nation courage in wartime; it is what heals the deepest emotional scars; and it is what gives ordinary believers purpose and meaning and direction in their lives."

"I make my own purpose and my own direction, Mr. Muir," said Frank confidently and leaned back in his chair.

"But unless you function in accordance with the spiritual laws of the universe—God's laws, Mr. Gordon—you will come unglued in the end."

"Your five minutes is almost up, Mr. Muir," snapped Frank, irritably.

"You have made it abundantly clear that you are not a Christian, Mr. Gordon."

"You've got the message, old timer."

"And I take it the same is true of your Mr. Nicholas Hamilton."

"Ah ha. That's where you're wrong. I happen to know that Nick is a churchgoer. Takes it all terribly seriously. Keeps a Bible in his desk drawer. Goes to a lunchtime Bible study with some other journalists here in the city somewhere."

"Indeed? That changes the whole situation. In that case, perhaps Mr. Hamilton is not in danger after all."

"Then you can go home and stop worrying." Frank began rising from his seat.

"But the rest of us still are in danger," continued the old man. "There is a dark power that may be unleashed."

"Time is up, I'm afraid, Mr. Muir. Thank you for coming by. My secretary will show you the way out."

Despite the editor's words, the old man remained in his seat, staring into the distance, apparently lost in thought.

"Mr. Muir?"

"I'm sorry. I was just thinking about something. Tell me this: Would it be possible for me to contact your Mr. Hamilton?"

"There is a radio phone on the boat."

"May I have the number please?"

"Well, if you called the charter company, they'd give it to you anyway, so I guess it won't hurt." Frank sat down at his desk, flipped open his teledex, and copied a number onto a scrap of paper.

"But if I give you this, Mr. Muir," said the editor, holding out the slip of paper, "I want you to promise me something."

"Yes, sir?" asked the old man, his bushy white eyebrows rising in a question.

"I want you to promise that you won't pester Nick—that you won't do anything that will slow him down or make it harder for him to do his job."

"The very opposite, Mr. Gordon. I promise you that I will do all I can to facilitate his job. His task has suddenly become immensely important."

15

The night air was so warm that after the evening meal most of the passengers took their drinks out onto the aft deck. There they gathered in little groups, linked by low, murmured conversations. In the northern sky a yellow edge of new moon could be seen; to the south the stars were blacked out by low banks of gathering clouds. The vessel pitched in a gentle, rhythmic pattern, and the powerful diesel engine provided a soft background hum.

"When should we sight the island, Captain?" Nick asked.

"Sometime tomorrow, if the weather continues to hold as fair as this," replied Nagle, "and it will."

"How can you be so sure?" asked Max.

"Everything comes from satellites these days, Mr. Taunton," Nagle answered. "We plot a precise position by means of navigational satellites, and we are kept in touch with the weather by meteorological satellites. Even our radio phone link is bounced off a satellite."

"What time tomorrow?" asked Paul.

"If I don't make a firm promise, then I won't disappoint you. And you'll go on thinking I'm a canny old sea dog," said Nagle with a guttural laugh.

"So, what is your special area of historical interest, Dr. Marshall?" Nick asked.

"Paul's major work is a book called *Crime and Punishment in 19th Century Australia*," Vicky volunteered before the American could answer.

"Thank you, Vicky," growled Paul. "I'm quite capable of answering for myself, thank you very much."

"I'm sorry, Paul," she responded, her eyes downcast.

"That being so," Cathy said quickly, smoothing over Paul's ruffled feathers, "Cavendish Island may be a gold mine of information for you."

"A fresh, untapped gold mine, that's the big thing," he explained. "Having made a close study of both Port Arthur and Norfolk Island, I have a couple of good yardsticks to measure Cavendish by."

"Do you teach a course on Australian colonial history back at your home university?" inquired Nick.

"At UCLA? Yes, I do. And, I might add, it's very popular. My students are typical young Californians, always looking for novelty. The Australian colonial story gives them that." He swallowed the last of his drink in one gulp. "This warm ocean breeze is making me sleepy. If you folks'll excuse me, I think I'll hit the sack. Come along, Vicky."

"I'm coming, Paul," said the little blonde, and she followed in his footsteps.

"Why does he need Vicky to help him hit the sack?" asked Nick. "Is that a secretary's job?"

"It depends on exactly what their relationship is, doesn't it?" Cathy said knowingly.

"Oh, I see," said Nick, with a nod. "It's like that, is it?"

"It has been ever since we came on board," she remarked, a hint of disgust in her voice. "Haven't you noticed? Men! Honestly, you're so unobservant sometimes."

She stood up abruptly and walked over to the ship's railing. Nick followed. For a while they stood in silence, looking at the starlight silvering the waves.

Eventually Nick spoke, "Now that you point out what's going on—and assuming you're right—I agree with you, it's pretty disgusting."

"Well," Cathy responded, "Paul may be a slimy worm, but he's right about one thing—ocean travel makes you sleepy. I'm off to bed. 'Night, Nick."

"'Night, Cathy."

As Nick turned to watch her leave the aft deck, he was surprised to discover that he was alone, the others also having retired for the night. Nick slumped down in a deck chair and stared at the stars. There were so many stars, he thought, far more than he could see through the polluted air of Sydney. Each one an unimaginable distance away. The sheer scale of the universe was something that Nick could never get used to.

He thought about what Cathy had been saying. She had, he thought, as many wonderful features as there were stars in the Pacific sky. Rarely did Nick ever wish for the gift of poetry. In fact, he normally had little time for poetry. His reverie startled him, and he lowered his eyes from the stars to the boat.

The lights in the main lounge had been turned out. Apparently he was the only passenger who had not yet turned in for the evening. But it was such a warm night, and he was feeling so relaxed, that he felt no urge to leave the deck.

Looking out across the water, he noticed that some of the stars were disappearing. *Clouds blowing up?* he wondered. A few minutes later he found the answer as the first few wisps of fog drifted across the boat. The fog seemed to come out of nowhere, and soon the air around him was thick and the ocean invisible. The drifting vapor stung him with its cold, sour smell. The white fog enveloped the *Covenant,* and the world was blotted out.

Nick stood up and walked to the starboard railing. He could see no more than a few meters. The boat's navigational lights where caught by the fog and shone dimly back again. The surge of the sea and the sound of the wind seemed to die away. There was a strange quietness that came with the fog, an eerie stillness in which every creak and groan of the boat could be heard.

But some of the creaking and groaning of timbers seemed to be coming not from the boat, but from the fog. *It's an illusion,* thought Nick at first. *My ears are playing tricks on me.* But then it came again—louder and clearer this time. Off to starboard was the definite sound of creaking timbers, and something else. What was it? *The rattle of ropes, that's it,* he thought.

Peering into that thick fog, Nick thought he could make out a shape. A large, looming, unformed shape. Then there was a point of light, somewhere in the midst of the dark shape. Not a steady point like the *Covenant's* own electrical navigation lights, but a light that flickered unsteadily, like an oil lamp.

The fog began to lift slightly astern, and Nick was certain that something was coming up on them on the starboard quarter. He stood back from the railing, uncertain as to whether he should immediately rouse the crew or not.

Then it appeared out of the fog. It was a ship. A sailing ship! A great three-masted vessel, with a cloud of canvas aloft. *It must be one of those naval training ships,* thought Nick. And still he didn't rouse the crew. There was clearly no risk of collision—the other vessel seemed to be making better speed than the *Covenant* and was going to pass it on the starboard side.

She was coming up fast, that old timer, but Nick couldn't understand where the wind was that was driving it, for there was not enough breeze on his cheek to blow out a candle. The fog lifted a little more, and it became clear that the old vessel would pass the boat with twenty meters or more to spare. Nick stood watching, rooted to the spot by the spectacle.

It was a great, high-sided vessel, riding quite high in the water, as if carrying little cargo. As it drew closer, he could see masses of rigging and great, wide yardarms necessary, no doubt, for all that bunch of canvas. As the prow of the ship passed by, Nick peered through the remaining fog, trying to read the vessel's name. Then he remembered there was a flashlight in a locker under the aft deck seating. He got down on all fours and felt around for the locker. He found it, pulled it open, and groped around for the flashlight. In a minute his searching fingers found what he was looking for.

Hurrying back to the railing, Nick flicked it on and pointed it at the prow of the passing ship. Painted in dark, old paint on the high bow of the sailing ship was a name. Nick's eyes were excellent, but the distance was a challenge. He began to spell it out, letter by letter. Then, with a gasp of astonishment, he realized that the sailing vessel beside them was called the *Covenant*.

Puzzled and confused, Nick ran the beam of the flashlight down the length of the ship. Her decks appeared to be deserted. Except on the high afterdeck. There, at the great wooden wheel, stood one man. Nick could see him quite clearly. He was young, perhaps in his late twenties, with a pale face and a shock of red hair. He was staring at Nick even as Nick was staring at him. He was wearing some sort of military uniform. An old-fashioned military uniform. He stared at Nick with a look of sheer terror—a look of total, undisguised horror. And his lips were moving. He was saying something, not to Nick, but to himself. In the dead quiet of that fog-bound sea the words drifted faintly across the waves—and Nick recognized the words.

"The Lord is my shepherd; I shall not want. He maketh me to lie down in green pastures: he leadeth me beside the still waters. He restoreth my soul: he leadeth me in the paths of righteousness for his name's sake. Yea, though I walk through the valley of the shadow of death, I will fear no evil: for thou art with me; thy rod and thy staff they comfort me."

The man was reciting the words of the twenty-third Psalm, Nick realized. Terrified out of his wits, the strange young man was saying the words out loud as a source of comfort. In the stillness it was uncanny: the quiet slap of small waves, the creak of timber, the rattle of ropes in the rigging, and the young man's voice.

"Thou preparest a table before me in the presence of mine enemies: thou anointest my head with oil; my cup runneth over. Surely goodness and mercy shall follow me all the days of my life: and I will dwell in the house of the Lord forever."

Then the high stern of the great wooden ship had passed, and the whole vessel disappeared into a bank of fog. After some minutes Nick realized that he was staring stupidly at blank fog and ocean, and his flashlight beam was still turned on. He flicked it off. Then, moving like a man in a dream, he returned the flashlight to its place in the under-seat locker.

Walking back to the side of the boat, the journalist grabbed the railing firmly, as if he was trying to hang on to a sense of reality, or perhaps to his own sanity. The fog was lifting now, and the stars were reappearing. Within a few minutes, the last drifting traces of fog were gone. Nick stared across the starlit waves. There was no sign of the great three-masted sailing vessel. In fact, there was no sign of any ship at all.

"Did I dream it all?" Nick asked himself. "Did I imagine it? What on earth is going on here? Or is it something that is not *on earth* at all?"

16

From the journal of Lieutenant Edmund McDermott, officer of the New South Wales Corps.
July 31st, 1821

I write these words by the dim light of a stub of candle in the officers' mess shortly before midnight, at the end of the strangest day of my life. It began as a breathlessly still tropical morning, the air hot and heavy, the sky brazen and cloudless, and the shadow of the Covenant lying solitary upon the glittering sea.

I woke early this morning and, feeling stifled by the close air in the officers' cabin, made my way up to the deck. The sun was low in the eastern sky, a large, blazing white ball just above the horizon. The air was still, and the sails above my head flapped listlessly. Save for the man at the wheel and the guard at the quarter railing, I was alone on the deck. Looking across the low, oily waves of the silent ocean, nothing could be seen except the hideous fin of a silent shark.

The seams of the deck were sticky with melted pitch, the sails flapped and the ropes rattled against their masts, and the bowsprit rose and fell with a slow, sickening regularity. I walked across to the battened hatches that covered the main cargo hold. If I stood very still, I could hear the faint moaning of the poor creatures locked up between decks. There were now forty-eight convicts, two of them having died from heat stroke. Commander Black had appeared quite indifferent.

When it came to the matter of the commandant's treatment

of the prisoners, I did my best to plead for some humanity, and I had an ally in Captain Pyne, the commander of the Covenant who seemed to have an unusually sensitive conscience for a naval man. But our words were of no avail, as Commander Black seemed to hold the whole ship in the grip of some awful terror. Even the most hardened sailors watched him warily, seeming nervous that he might at any moment explode in another abusive display of ill temper. The only one who appears to not be afraid of the commandant is Sergeant Davis, and he, although it pains me to say it, appears to take pleasure in every act of cruelty of that excessively cruel man.

As soon as the unseasonal heat began, I suggested the convicts should be allowed a greater access to fresh air and an increased supply of water. With a cruel smile playing on his lips Commander Black rejected both of these proposals. "Mr. McDermott," he said in that quiet, guttural way of his, "two hours' exercise is graciously permitted each afternoon by His Majesty King George the Fourth to prisoners of the Crown, and two hours' exercise is what our convicts shall have."

The two hours' "exercise" to which he referred was the two-hour period each afternoon when the hatch covers were thrown open, and fresh air and sunlight allowed to penetrate the cargo hold. Our ship not being designed as a convict carrier, there were no facilities to allow the poor wretches onto the deck for anything like real exercise. This being so, I could see no harm in the hatch covers being opened for a far greater period, preferably during the coolest parts of the day, the morning and evening. Commander Black took pleasure in refusing and often strolled near the hatch covers during the hottest parts of the day, a smile on his lips as he heard the convicts groaning loudly.

Furthermore, since our voyage was a relatively short one and the ship was well stocked with fresh water, I proposed that an additional barrel of water be lowered into the cargo hold every second day, to ensure that none of the poor wretches should die of thirst.

"They have their official ration of water, Mr. McDermott," snarled Black, "and their official ration is what they shall have."

By the end of the second day of severe heat, two of the troopers and one of Captain Pyne's sailors had taken to their bunks with heat stroke. On the morning of the third day, shouts from the hold informed us that two of the convicts had died from the heat and thirst. The commandant raised their bodies from the hold on ropes, and then made the entire company stand on deck, in the hottest part of the day, whilst he held a burial at sea for them.

Captain Pyne read the service, constantly interrupted by Commander Black, who protested that he was reading too quickly and should slow down. The more the troopers looked uncomfortable in their dress uniforms in that heat, the more Black appeared to want the burial service dragged out.

Finally, today, I could take it no more, and as firmly as a junior officer dare with his senior officer, I took the commandant to task for his treatment of the convicts and his lack of interest in the well being of his own men. In the most abusive language imaginable, he accused me of insolence and insubordination, and informed me that if ever I should speak that way to him again, he would have me flogged. Indeed, I believe that he is capable of ordering a fellow officer to suffer under the cat, and I begin to feel in my bones a deep fear and hatred of this man.

"As it is," he continued, "so many are now suffering from heat stroke, that the ship is shorthanded, hence your punishment shall be that you will take the wheel and stand the night watch tonight and every night until we reach the island."

Thus it was, that I was alone on the deck, at the ship's wheel, when a fresh breeze finally sprang up, and the dreaded heat was at last defeated. As the sails filled, I could feel the wheel kick beneath my hands, and I had to take care to keep a close watch on the compass, in its solid brass case near my right hand, and to keep the ship on the course that Captain Pyne had set.

When the breeze first sprang up, about two hours after sunset, some of the officers and men came out onto the decks to enjoy the cooling change. However, as the night drew on they retired to their bunks, and I was once again alone on deck.

With the hour drawing on towards midnight, I saw something strange upon the water dead ahead of us. It was a bank of fog, perhaps the product of the sudden change from hot to cool conditions. Under a moonless sky filled with stars I could clearly see the rolling, drifting bank of fog, as white as any snow, as it drew closer.

Then, in a moment, or so it seemed, it was all around us, damp, sour, and dense, blocking all view of the starlit ocean. Indeed, in that fog it was impossible to see one end of the ship from the other. The lamps on the port and starboard beams that were our riding lights had become mere dim, yellow smudges in that fog.

Then my senses began to play tricks upon me, or so it seemed, for I thought I could hear sounds drifting over the water, from within the densest part of the fog bank. The sound was of a low, almost inaudible, throbbing, as of some large beast that growled constantly. The noise was off the port beam and somewhat ahead of us. As I leaned forward over the wheel, straining my eyes, I thought I saw something. And then, to my utter amazement, it emerged to view as the fog lifted slightly.

It appeared to be a vessel of some sort, but like no vessel I had ever seen before. It was painted white from stem to stern, and seemed to have some sort of cabin, or low building, that occupied most of its deck space, and, strangest of all—it had no sails! The low, threatening, throaty growl was definitely coming from this strange, nightmarish vessel.

As we passed within twenty yards of this beastly apparition, I thought I saw a figure moving on the aft deck. Peering through the fog, I looked again for some sign of movement, and this time I was quite certain that there was someone, or something, moving about on the aft deck of the ghost ship, for I was now convinced that was what it was. Suddenly, and without warning, the ghostly pilot of the phantom ship lit a lamp, but a lamp such as I have never seen, that cast a narrow beam as white as sunlight across the intervening waves.

In an access of terror I turned to prayer, and asked my gracious Heavenly Father to protect me from the demon ship and from all dangers and terrors of the deep. Having prayed, I sought to reassure myself of my Heavenly Father's love and care by saying aloud the words of the twenty-third Psalm.

Slowly we drifted past the ghost ship. And then, just as it was about to pass from view, the strangest thing of all happened: I caught a glimpse of the name of the white ship, painted in large black letters on its bow. And the name was—Covenant. What could this mean? I thought. Is this some dreadful phantom of ourselves?

Then, as suddenly as it had arisen, the fog dissipated. As the last, lingering, white wisps of fog lifted, I hurried to the aft rail and looked over our wake for a final glimpse of the white ship. But it was not there. The ocean was empty. We were the only vessel within the whole, wide horizon.

As soon as I was relieved on watch, I came down to the officers' mess to record in my journal the strange glimpse of the supernatural world which I had been privileged to see. However, as to what this vision might mean, that is entirely beyond my capacity to guess.

17

The colonel was not in uniform. He was wearing a dark gray business suit, a blue shirt, and a dark blue tie. He was sitting very straight and erect on one of the polished wooden chairs in the minister's reception room.

His face was weather-beaten and absolutely expressionless. The only indication of his impatience was his habit of occasionally running his hand through his close-cropped, steel-gray hair.

Secretaries and minor public servants hurried back and forth, carrying bundles of files and looking important. The reception room, or hallway, was wide with a high ceiling and deep carpets. It had an almost cathedral-like hush about it. People talked little, and when they did, it was barely above a whisper.

Eventually a young, fair-haired woman with a haughty expression walked up to the colonel. "The minister is available now. If you would come this way please."

The colonel followed her through high double wooden doors into the minister's inner sanctum. There she left him, closing the doors behind her as she did so.

The office was huge and carpeted with deep pile. Along one wall was a bookshelf filled with bound law volumes, and along another a window that rose all the way from the floor to the ceiling. The colonel walked over to the window and looked out over the city. Then he turned back toward the room as a door behind the desk opened, and the minister bustled in.

"My dear Colonel, I'm terribly sorry to keep you waiting for so long. But, you know how it is, the pressure of official business," he said, smoothing down the long wisps of brown hair across his balding scalp as he spoke.

"I quite understand, sir."

"Have a seat, please have a seat. Did my secretary offer you any refreshment? Can I offer you coffee? Would you like a cup now?" The minister buzzed for his secretary. This slowed down the conversation as they had to talk of trivial matters until the coffee had been served. The colonel swallowed his irritation, reminding himself that the role of the military was to serve the civil administration.

"Very well, Colonel," said the minister, once they were alone again, "your report please."

"They have almost reached the island, Minister."

"Indeed? I had imagined it would have taken them longer."

"The *Covenant* is quite a powerful boat, sir."

"And how are you keeping track of them?"

"At the moment, mainly by tracking their satellite contacts. The Defense Signals Intelligence Unit is running a twenty-four-hour monitoring service. Every time they log into a navigational satellite or a meteorological satellite, we know about it."

"What about their communications?"

"Also by satellite, and we are monitoring and recording all their radio telephone calls."

"What have you picked up so far?"

"Only routine matters. The captain speaks to his shipping office once each day, the journalist called his editor once, and one of the party—a Dr. Max Taunton—called his mother. There have been no other calls."

"So far."

"Indeed. As you say, Minister, so far."

"But you will keep monitoring, of course."

"Of course, sir."

"And what about visual observation. Are you doing anything about that?"

"Again, only by satellite. At least at this stage. We have one of our 'weather' satellites in a position where it can photograph the island regularly. The pictures, once they are electronically enhanced, show remarkable detail."

"Will that be sufficient, do you believe, Colonel?"

"I'm afraid not, sir."

"So, what do you want me to authorize?"

"Putting a man on the ground with them, sir."

"Do you think it will really be necessary to put in one of our field officers?"

"I'm afraid so, sir."

"I see. And how will you accomplish this task?"

"We have constructed several scenarios. Depending on the situation, on how circumstances develop, and on how quickly we need to act, we will choose the appropriate scenario."

"But you will have no difficulty placing an agent in position without arousing anyone's suspicions?"

"We can do that, sir."

"I have every confidence that you can, Colonel. Do you want me to sign an authorization for that action?"

"Yes, sir. I have brought the necessary document with me. I assumed that you would not want it to pass through the usual channels."

"You assumed correctly, Colonel."

While the minister sipped his coffee, the colonel retrieved a one-page document from his briefcase and laid it on the desk pad before the minister. The canny old politician carefully read every word, then signed his name with a flourish at the bottom. He handed it back to the colonel, who returned it to his briefcase.

"And what about the worst case scenario, Colonel?" asked the minister. "What happens then?"

"You mean, if they uncover ...?"

"Precisely. If they stumble into the wrong places and uncover the wrong things. What do you do then?"

"The senior planning group came to the conclusion that gas would be the cleanest way to handle it. Cyanide gas."

"In other words you would …?"

"Act on the authority you gave us at the beginning of this operation, sir. We would terminate with extreme prejudice."

"I'm afraid I don't speak your language, Colonel."

"We would kill them all, sir."

Sam Fangatofa was on the forward deck, hanging over the bow, looking for submerged rocks as the *Covenant* entered the harbor of Cavendish Island. Toby was beside him, also keeping a lookout; Captain Nagle was on the bridge, having taken the conn personally as they approached the island; Vic Neal was in the engine room, running the engines as slowly as possible as the boat crept forward cautiously into the bay.

For the passengers, crowded onto the aft deck, there was no sense of the dangers posed by a poorly charted bay, only the excitement of reaching their destination.

Before them were great cliffs of black rock, encircling a calm harbor of crystal-blue water. The rocks seemed to rise vertically straight out of the water and tower above them like dark, jagged thunderclouds. Along the top edge of the cliffs was a low tangle of green shrubs. As the boat moved forward, the cliffs seemed to reach around and embrace them like the powerful, muscled arms of a wrestler seizing an opponent.

Holly was talking as she was taking photographs. "Look at those peaks on both sides of the bay. Pretty steep, I'd say. You'd have to be a rock climber to get up them."

"And the cliffs," added Ingrid, as sunlight broke through the clouds and caught the black rocks, reflecting off the hard, shiny surface. "With cliffs all the way around, how do we get to the interior of the island?"

"There's supposed to be a trail," Max explained. "According to the historical records, there is a trail that leads up from that small beach to the top of that cliff. That one over there." He was pointing directly ahead as he spoke. Nick squinted and could just make out indentations in the rock face that were too regular to be a natural feature. "It was cut by the first party of convicts," Max continued. "Until then, they'd camped under canvas on the beach."

"It's a pretty small beach to camp on," Ingrid commented.

"Well, perhaps some of them stayed on their ship," responded Max. "At any rate, they cut a trail at the southern end of the beach that winds up to the cliff top. It was big enough for them to carry all their supplies and materials up, so it should be sufficient for us."

"If it's not overgrown," said Holly, still snapping with her SLR.

"They cut it out of the rock," said the historian, "so it's unlikely to be overgrown. Well, not too much, anyway."

Paul leaned against the railing, watching the arms of the bay slowly wrap themselves around the boat as the *Covenant* made its cautious progress. He stared at the island with a hard, but strangely hungry, look. Close by his side huddled Vicky.

"Oh, look, Paul. I think I can see it."

"See what?"

"The ruins. There, on top of the cliff. You can just catch a glimpse of a stone wall, or something, through the bushes."

"Yes," murmured the American quietly, "yes, so you can. If this is what it is meant to be, well ..." He left the thought unfinished, staring at the fragment of wall that could just be seen between low, windblown trees.

Lois Myles was standing beside the Roystons, her face blank, her eyes squinting in the bright sunlight.

"Well, what do you think, Lois?" asked Professor Royston cheerfully. "There it is, that black shape you can just make out through the foliage. That's where we'll be doing most of our work. Are you looking forward to it?"

"I'm looking forward to gathering useful material for my Ph.D. thesis," she replied, "and, of course, to working with you, Professor."

"Don't be so serious about it, Lois. The point about field work is to enjoy it."

"Oh, I'll enjoy it all right. Never you fear, Professor. I'll enjoy every moment of it." With those words she drifted away to the opposite railing.

"Strange woman," muttered Royston.

"Why did you bring her?" challenged his wife.

"Because I did not want an experienced archaeologist on this trip. You know that, Stella dear. We agreed, students only. That was the safest thing. We decided."

"But surely you could find a more suitable student."

"Lois will be fine!" snapped Royston irritably, and for some moments the two of them stood in silence watching the small beach and the towering cliffs draw closer. It was Mrs. Royston who broke the silence.

"I can feel it, Earl," she whispered. "I can feel the power. It is very strong. And very dark. It is going to be magnificent."

Professor Royston glanced at his wife and, for a fleeting moment, a look of fear passed over his face.

Nick saw the professor's expression and wondered what it meant. He and Cathy were standing slightly apart from the others near the aft railing.

"It's rather forbidding, isn't it?" Cathy asked.

"In what sense?"

"Well, cliffs towering around us on three sides. And the rock is so dark," she explained.

"That's basalt, I think."

"Quite right. Well done, Nick. It's a volcanic rock formed by lava. At some time in the primeval past, Cavendish Island was a volcano."

"It's certainly a dark, oppressive-looking place. There's none of the warm, sunny sandstone you see around Sydney."

"Feeling homesick?"

"I'm not one of the world's great travelers," he admitted. "I don't need to be. Not when I live in one of the most interesting cities on earth."

"As a girl from Melbourne, I have to take issue with that," said Cathy with a laugh, as she turned to watch Sam and Toby checking the water's depth.

Sam was swinging a leadline over the bow of the *Covenant,* and Toby was calling the numbers up to Captain Nagle who had slid open the windows on the bridge. As soon as he gauged the boat to be far enough inside the arms of the bay to be sheltered from storms, he signaled an all-stop to Vic in the engine room.

After the engines had stopped, the captain allowed the vessel to keep drifting slowly toward the beach for a while. When he was satisfied that he was close enough, he called out, "Drop anchor, Mr. O'Brien."

"Aye, sir."

Nagle locked off the equipment on the bridge, climbed down onto the deck, and made his way to his passengers.

"Well, folks," he said, taking off his cap and mopping his forehead, "we've arrived. Welcome to Cavendish Island."

ISLAND

The way of the wicked is like deep darkness;
they do not know what makes them stumble.
—Proverbs 4:19

———◆———

18

*I*t was the sounds that Nick noticed first—the occasional cry of a distant sea bird, the whistling wind, the crash of waves on the rocks far below. He stood on the cliff top and looked toward the ruler-straight line of the distant horizon. Then he looked down toward the narrow strip of sand where they had first landed. There was, he thought, a strange quietness about the island—a sense of desolation.

One by one the members of the expedition joined him at the top of the cliff. They had needed Sam to cut away the overgrown and overhanging bushes before the old winding path to the cliff top was usable. But that had been done, and now they were gathered and ready to start.

"Lois and Cathy, you come with me to the ruins," Royston commanded. "Holly too. I'd like you to start photographing the building. And, of course, my wife will accompany us." He turned to the American. "Dr. Marshall?"

"We'll take Sam to help us cut away the undergrowth," stated Paul, "and try to uncover the sites of the barracks and stockade. Max will come with me, and Vicky, of course."

"I'd like to go with the historians," volunteered Ingrid.

"Very good. And I suggest you do the same, Mr. Hamilton … uh, Nick," Professor Royston said with a smile.

"Why not," responded Nick pleasantly. "I'll catch up with the ruins later."

"Excellent. Excellent. Well, I suggest we plan to all meet on the beach at five o'clock."

When Royston said this, everyone glanced instinctively at their watches. Then there was a general bustle of movement as they shouldered their backpacks and set off.

Cathy followed Royston's lead around the cliff top toward the ruined church. The only undergrowth was long grass and low bushes stunted by constant exposure to sea breezes. It wasn't long before Cathy could hear Royston exclaim, "Wonderful!" from somewhere just ahead. She followed Holly around a clump of shrubs, and there, facing her, was the building.

It looked at first glance like a small country church, except that it was made entirely from the island's black basalt rock, which made the structure look dark and forbidding. The more Cathy stood and stared, the more oddities she saw. There were gargoyles, statues, and other carvings. She had known to expect these, but confronting them, in this strange and desolate spot, was oddly disconcerting.

"Look at all the fancy stone work," said Holly. "I pity the poor guys who had to work on that." She raised her camera and started snapping away.

Cathy walked a little closer and looked at some of the details of the building. The windows were simply empty openings. She didn't know if there had ever been windows fitted, or if the building had ever been properly finished. Above the arched, open doorway was some lettering carved in the stone.

"Look at that," said Cathy to Lois. "There. Above the doorway."

"Ah, yes. Can you read it?"

"It's pretty weathered. Someone may have to climb up and clean the mold and lichen off it before we can read it clearly. But the first words seem to say 'The Cathedral Church of ...' I can't make out any more."

"That's ridiculous," Lois snapped, "calling something as small as this a cathedral."

"Come on, inside everyone," urged Royston. His wife had already stepped into the interior of the building.

The first thing Cathy noticed was that the roof was intact, which surprised her. Then she noticed the smell. It was putrid and revolting. She quickly pulled out a handkerchief to cover her mouth and nose. She looked at the others to make a comment and was startled to see that neither of the Roystons seemed aware of the odor. They were certainly not showing any response to it. Lois also appeared to be unaware of it.

Just then Cathy was joined by Holly, who said, "This place really stinks, doesn't it?"

"It's almost unbearable," agreed Cathy.

Tentatively she sniffed at the odor. It was, she decided, the smell of meat that had gone bad. Yes, that's what it was: the smell of rotting, maggot-riddled flesh.

Nick found himself in the lead, walking between Sam, with his machete dangling from his belt, and Max, who carried a map and a compass.

"A little farther in this direction," said Max, consulting first the map and then the compass.

"What exactly are we looking for?" asked Nick.

"Well, according to the records, there were two barracks buildings, a larger one for the convicts, and a smaller one for the troops. Then there was a separate house for the commandant, and a high fence that surrounded both the commandant's house and the troops' barracks. The area inside that fence was called the stockade."

"It sounds as though they were afraid of the convicts," Sam remarked.

"Well," said Max thoughtfully, "either afraid of the convicts, or of something else."

He didn't explain his remark, but pushed on through the long grass and low scrubby bushes.

Some fifty meters farther on he stopped again, and this time the rest of the group caught up.

"I suggest we spread out," said Paul. "The buildings were made of wood, and they will have rotted to pieces and fallen apart by now. What we are looking for will be foundations that will give us the building alignments and any remnants of the buildings or their contents that might be lying among the grass and bushes."

"Then we should be looking down around our feet," said Sam.

"Right," Paul said. "Max, you can be the center position for our line. Ingrid, you, Sam, and Nick spread out to the right of Max. Vicky and I will move over to the left. We'll cover more territory that way."

The group took up their positions, and then moved slowly forward, looking carefully at the ground over which they were walking for telltale signs of habitation.

They had not gone far when a cry from Ingrid brought the rest of the group to her side.

"What have you found?" asked Max breathlessly.

"A piece of stone work," replied the doctor, nudging a lump

with her foot. Nick knelt down and brushed away the dirt and grass.

"I think it's a tombstone," he said.

"Hey, that's great," said Paul enthusiastically. "Is there an inscription?"

Nick ran his fingers over the surface of the stone, and then said, "Yes, I think there is. But it's caked with mud and dirt."

"I have a brush in my kit," volunteered Vicky. As she spoke she dug into her backpack, a moment later producing a stiff-bristled brush which she handed to Nick. Sam prized the heavy slab off the ground and propped it up against a low stump. For several minutes Nick worked in silence, brushing away more than a century of accumulated dirt, mud, and bird droppings out of the grooves of the lettered inscription.

"There, I think that's got it," he said at last.

"What does it say?" asked Paul.

Slowly, deciphering the faded letters one at a time, Nick read: "Here lies Alfred Trelawney Davis. Sergeant, New South Wales Corps. Born, September 7, 1790. Died, December 15, 1822. A true and loyal servant of His Satanic Majesty."

Unable to stand the smell any longer, Cathy turned and fled the building. She ran unseeing toward the cliff top, only stopping when she realized how close to the edge she had come. She stood there for some minutes, the strong sea breeze blowing directly into her face, gulping down lungfuls of fresh air.

"Don't tell me you've given up work for the day already," said a voice behind her.

Cathy turned around to find Lois staring at her with a cynical smile on her face.

"I just couldn't stand the smell."

"Smell? What smell?"

"The dreadful, putrid odor inside that building."

"There is no smell. You're imagining things." Lois's square, plain face was hard and unsympathetic.

"But it wasn't just me," said Cathy. "Holly could smell it too."

"Then you're both imagining things. Come back with me. You'll see that I'm right. Come on."

Cathy followed Lois back to the site of the ruined building. The bay over which the church had been built lay on the western side of the island. The church had been erected on an east-west axis, with the main door facing the cliff top, and the altar at the eastern end.

Pausing at the open doorway to steel her nerves for the stench that lay within, Cathy looked at one of the carvings that decorated the lintel: a curious, leering face, with its forked tongue out. She ran her finger over the face, and found it smooth to the touch.

"Lois," she said, "this face here, on the lintel of the door. There's not a mark upon it. No sign of weathering at all."

Lois stepped closer and ran her fingers gently over the old carving. "Yes, you're quite right," she said. "There's no mark of aging at all. That is odd."

Instead of stepping into the building, Cathy took a step backward, to look again at the church as a whole.

Then, nervously, and tentatively, she followed Lois back into the dark chamber that was the ruined church. To her utter astonishment there was no smell—no stench, no odor of any kind. She was puzzled. What had happened? Had she imagined it? Had she dreamed it? No, that couldn't be the case, for Holly had seemed to smell it too. Cathy decided that she must talk to Holly about it as soon as possible.

"See there," said Lois, triumphantly. "No smell. Just as I promised you."

"What's all this?" asked Stella as she approached.

"Cathy ran away," said Lois, very much like a tattling schoolgirl, "because she imagined that she could smell some sort of awful stench."

"I didn't imagine it," insisted Cathy. "There really was something."

"Don't be stupid, girl." Stella's voice cut like a knife. "Now take out your notebook and go and help my husband at the stone altar. There are inscriptions to be recorded."

With the only light coming from the doorway and from narrow windows, it was dark inside the church. A light like tarnished silver came in through the western door, but little of it found its way as far as the altar. As for the windows, the small light they gave was tinted green by the foliage that overgrew them.

"It's gloomy in here, isn't it?" said Cathy as she walked up to Professor Royston.

"Ah, there you are, at last," he snapped. "This is not a holiday, Miss Samson, and I don't want you imagining that it is."

"No, Professor," returned Cathy, "I know I'm here to work. Please don't misunderstand me."

"Well then, stop chattering and get out your notebook. I want you to make a detailed and accurate copy of the decorations and inscriptions on this altar. I will return in half an hour to see how you've done." With that, he turned on his heels and left.

Puzzled by the professor's hostility, Cathy examined the five panels across the front of the stone altar, each carved directly into the stone in bas-relief. The first four panels showed the four horsemen of the apocalypse: conquest, war, judgment, and death. Each panel had a reference to a text in the biblical book of Revelation at the bottom of the vivid, violent illustrations.

The first showed the rider on the white horse, with his bow of conquest and around him slain and bleeding bodies. The next showed the rider on the red horse, with the sword of war and around him violently clashing armies. In the third was a black horse, whose rider held a pair of scales, and in the margins were terrified people hiding in caves and behind rocks from the awful judgment. The fourth showed the pale horse whose rider is called Death and Hades, and around him were hordes of hungry, ravenous demons.

All of this Cathy could understand because of her knowledge of the Bible, but the fifth panel she found puzzling. It appeared to show the front door of this very church itself. In the doorway stood the figure of a robed monk holding up a cross. He faced a terrible creature like a gigantic slug that reared itself up in front of him. Below ran the legend *Negotium perambulans in tenebris*, and a reference to one of the songs, or psalms, in the Bible—Psalm ninety-one.

"How are you doing?" said a voice over her shoulder, which interrupted her speculations.

"Oh, Professor. This text here, *Negotium perambulans in tenebris*— 'the pestilence that stalks in the darkness'—what does that refer to?"

"It is not something I have ever personally encountered. At least not yet. And it's not something I would ever wish to encounter. Unless, of course, I could be sure that I was protected from its power."

19

Nick walked slowly through the long grass, scuffing it up with his boots as he walked. By searching through the bushes he and his group had found five more gravestones—all of them recording the deaths of various troops, but none bearing the strange inscription found on the Davis tombstone. Then Paul had located what he thought were the foundations of the commandant's house.

Nick was now concentrating on finding objects or evidence of the commandant who had once lived there, but he was finding it hard to focus on the task.

He had told no one, not even Cathy, about the "ghost ship" he had seen. He was certain he wouldn't be believed, even if he was listened to sympathetically. And he could hardly blame people if they put it down as a dream or a nightmare experienced during a confused half-waking state, rather than reality. Indeed, he was starting to think that was what it must have been. Consequently, he did not feel the least bit inclined to tell anyone.

Slowly the group began to turn up small objects. Vicky was the first, then Ingrid, and then everyone was finding artifacts. There were old, rusty nails; pieces of broken crockery; a small green glass bottle, still unbroken; a brass button, green with verdigris; and numerous other small items. Vicky placed each into a plastic bag, then Max labeled the bag with a key number.

"These finds are hardly world-shattering," remarked Nick, as his patrol of the search area took him close to Paul.

"Yeah, it's too bad, isn't it? This is not our work. The archaeologists should be doing this. Historians only really come into the picture once there are documents to look at."

"Which means this whole expedition is mainly archaeological?"

"I guess you could say that. But I have brought with me copies of the historical accounts of the Cavendish Island penal settlement, and one of my goals is to fit those accounts into the landscape of the place."

"In other words, to make a better reading of the documents?"

"Yeah, something like that. Mind you, that graveyard is a real find. By the time Vicky has recorded all those inscriptions, I'll have some real material to work on."

The journalist and the American professor drifted apart again, continuing their search in silence. Five minutes later, Sam called out excitedly, "Hey, boss. Over here. I think I found something."

The whole group hurried to Sam's side.

"What is it, Sam?" asked Ingrid.

Instead of replying, he pointed to the stone slab, lying flat at his feet.

"I think it's hollow underneath," he said. "I tap on it with my knife, and it sure sounds hollow under there."

"Can you move it, Sam?" asked Max.

"I tried once. It's heavy. Maybe if we all try."

The men knelt down in the grass, got a grip on the slab, and tried pushing in unison.

"It's not working," puffed Paul after the third attempt. "Is there any way of lifting it first, and then pushing it to one side?"

"Maybe I could lever it up with my machete."

"Let's try."

Sam pushed the blade of his machete as far into the crack around the stone slab as he could, then he applied his weight and strength, using the tempered steel of the heavy blade like a crowbar.

"It's starting to lift," shouted Max. "Now, everyone push together."

They did, and the slab moved. A second time it moved even farther. Several attempts later it came free and slid away, revealing a small, stone-lined, underground cavity.

"What is it?" asked Nick.

"A secret compartment," said Paul with confidence. "This was the commandant's own private little hidey-hole."

The small cavity was half filled with green, slimy water, but Paul didn't hesitate. He rolled up his sleeves and plunged both arms into the water. A moment later he retrieved a book, or the remnants of a book, falling apart and soaking wet. Then he plunged in again, and this time withdrew a bundle wrapped in oilcloth. Further searching produced nothing.

The group gathered around the two treasures on the grass.

"What do you make of them?" Ingrid asked.

"Well, my guess is that this cavity has been dry for most of the last century and a half; otherwise, the book would have disintegrated entirely. I'd say the water in that compartment comes from a fairly recent storm. We've just been unlucky, not getting here before the water did."

"But part of the book is still readable, isn't it, Paul?" asked Vicky plaintively.

"Oh, I'm sure we'll recover something from it."

"What about this other bundle?" said Nick. "It looks more interesting."

"Yes," agreed Paul. "Let's unwrap that and see what we've got."

Slowly he removed the oilcloth that was tightly wound around the parcel, eventually revealing another book. It was a small, leather-bound volume with bizarre, ancient-looking runic symbols on the cover.

20

From the journal of Lieutenant Edmund McDermott, officer of
the New South Wales Corps.
October 30th, 1822

*T*his day I took to my bed with a fever. My room is simply
one end of the troopers' barracks, and through the thin, timber
petition I hear the men moving about from time to time during
the day, although none of them come to visit me in my sickness.
The reason for this I know full well: They are terrified of the
commandant. A soldier who resists his will is treated as badly as
any convict; although, I must add, that sadly there are those who
wear our uniform who seem to take pleasure in Commander
Black's evil schemes, and chief amongst these is Sergeant Davis,
who should be my good right hand and my chiefest supporter.

How I contracted this fever I do not know, since I eat and
drink only what my men do, and they are not similarly afflicted.
Likewise, I cannot blame my condition upon the weather, because
although the season is devilishly hot, this island does not have
what I would call an unhealthy climate. Perhaps I have been bitten by some strange tropical insect, I do not know. All I know is
that I alternately sweat and shiver, that all of my joints ache, and
that I am as weak as a newborn kitten.

This morning I found myself unable to rise from my bed, the
condition having come upon me with great suddenness, since last
night there was no hint of the fever. If my moans and weak calls
for help were heard by anyone, they were ignored. At last

Sergeant Davis came to my room, when I had still not emerged well after the hour for morning muster. Discovering my condition, he said he would inform the commandant and instruct one of the men to bring me a supply of water, as I complained of a thirst that fain would kill me.

I know not what caused the delay, whether Davis neglected to tell a trooper or whether the man he told was neglectful of following his instructions promptly, but whatever the cause I lay upon my bed of sickness, in a tangle of blankets, in great discomfort, for several hours more before a man arrived bearing a cup and pitcher of water. These he placed on my bedside table and left again with scarcely a word.

This is something I have noticed since arriving on Cavendish Island: how little people speak to one another. It is almost as though a blanket of sullen and terrified silence keeps each man in a solitary world of his own interests. The usual camaraderie of crime has not united the convicts; instead they have been uncommonly inclined towards aggressive disputes among themselves, in between long periods of sullen and angry silence brought on by sheer exhaustion.

The soldiers have spent so much of their time being either tired or terrified that the usual laughter and joking has been absent from the barracks. As for myself, my only brother officer is the odious Black, who early repulsed my attempts at polite conversation and who chose instead to alternate bouts of excessive, not to say obsessive, work with bouts of late-night drinking with Sergeant Davis, who appears to be a boon companion of the commandant's from of old.

As I lay upon my sick bed, I drifted in and out of consciousness, occupied by visions that were half nightmares, half waking dreams. I saw upon my inward eye those early dreadful months after our arrival, and after HMS Covenant had departed. We camped, in cramped conditions, under canvas on the small beach in the island's one and only bay while the prisoners were set to the task of digging a pathway out of the solid rock at the most accessible end of the beach. When this was completed, the camp was transferred to an area of level land at the top of the cliff, and conditions became slightly less cramped.

The commandant then ordered the clear felling of all the trees on the island. At the same time a saw pit was dug, and the timber thus obtained was sawn into planks for building purposes. As odious a man as Commander Black is, I must grant that he is a determined and hard-driving man who succeeded in having erected barracks for convicts and soldiers and a house for himself in a shorter time than I would have thought possible.

In fitful dreams, as though seen through a purple haze, I saw again the pleasure the commandant took in putting the convicts to hard, stone-breaking work in that part of the island that he designated "the quarry." As blocks of stone began to emerge, Sergeant Davis supervised a gang of builders whose task it was to erect a stone building on the cliff top overlooking the beach.

When I first saw this work beginning, I ventured to ask Commander Black what type of building was under construction, this information not having been previously vouchsafed to me. He replied, with a snarl of preternatural ugliness on his face, "It is a church, Mr. McDermott, a church. That should satisfy your pious little soul."

To say the very least, I was astonished by this announcement, for I had never in my entire life encountered a man more irreligious than the commandant. These reminiscences filled my mind as I tossed and turned, huddled under blankets, alternately shivering and then shaking with heat. Sweat streamed from my body, and soon the bedclothes were soaked. Still I was left alone in my misery, without a soul to nurse me or supply my needs.

In my desperation I prayed often, and, although my bodily aches continued, I found great peace of heart and mind in my prayers. Reaching out to my bedside table I found my Bible, and during my waking periods read from its pages, finding further comfort in the Holy Word of our great God and Heavenly Father. I found particular assurance in the words of Psalm ninety-one:

"He that dwelleth in the secret place of the most High shall abide under the shadow of the Almighty. I will say of the LORD, He is my refuge and my fortress: my God; in him will I trust. Surely he shall deliver thee from the snare of the fowler, and from the noisome pestilence. He shall cover thee with his feathers, and under his wings shalt thou trust: his truth shall be thy shield and buckler. Thou shalt not be afraid for the terror by night; nor for the arrow that flieth by day; Nor the pestilence that walketh in darkness; nor for the destruction that wasteth at noonday."

21

Show me your notebook," demanded Professor Royston.

Cathy handed over her notebook containing the sketches of the altar decorations.

"Hmm. Not too bad. Now start making measurements of this altar and record them in your notebook. I will return shortly."

Cathy looked at his retreating back, her blood boiling. She was not some high-school kid in a work-study program. Telling herself that such anger was unchristian, she took a deep breath and set to work.

After a while she took a break and dug into her backpack for the small bottle of fresh water she had packed before leaving the boat. She drank about half the contents, refastened the lid, and sat the bottle on top of the stone altar. Then she resumed her work.

As she measured all the smaller dimensions of the altar, Cathy noticed that Lois was just a few meters away, doing the same thing with a stone pulpit. And while they were working, the Roystons were at the other end of the church, admiring the stonework and speaking to each other in hushed tones.

Having done all the measuring she could do alone, Cathy called out, "Lois, could you give me a hand here? I need someone to hold the other end of the tape measure."

With ill grace Lois strolled across, took the other end of the tape, and assisted Cathy with the remaining measurements. Then she returned to making sketches of the stone pulpit.

Cathy picked up the still half-full bottle of water that had been sitting on top of the stone altar, unfastened the lid, and put the bottle to her lips. At moment later she spat out the mouthful of water she had been about to swallow.

"What's wrong?" asked Lois, looking up.

"It tastes foul," said Cathy, screwing up her face in horror. "It tastes bitter and ... slimy ... and ... just horrible."

"Where did you get the water from?"

"I filled it up on board, before we left the boat."

"Well, when we get back, you'd better warn Captain Nagle that one of his water tanks has gone bad."

"No. That can't be the problem."

"What do you mean?"

"I drank half the contents of the bottle a little while ago, and it was fine. Then I sat the bottle on top of the altar, and when I drank some more ... well ... I told you what it was like."

"That's ridiculous," sneered Lois. "It makes no sense."

"Here, taste for yourself."

Lois accepted the offered bottle, raised it tentatively to her lips, and took a small sip. Immediately she wrinkled her nose and screwed up her face.

"Yuk," she said. "That's what I call really bad."

"This time I'm not imagining things, am I?" insisted Cathy.

"Not this time," admitted Lois. "Although how it went bad, I can't explain. Unless it has something to do with ..."

"To do with what?"

"Oh, nothing. Never mind. It's just that there may be some power, or some influence, that has changed the water."

"But I can't imagine any earthly power that could do that."

"Perhaps," said Lois, speaking more to herself than Cathy, "it wasn't entirely earthly."

"What do you mean?" Cathy asked. But her question went unanswered, as Lois, looking puzzled and preoccupied, returned to her own work.

Paul began to slowly turn over the pages of the small book that had been found inside the oilcloth.

Leaning over his shoulder, Nick could see that the text was in Latin, and that it was illustrated frequently with what looked like medieval woodcuts. These showed strange monsters out of ancient mythologies. There were gargoyles, griffins, basilisks, ogres, giants, elves, fauns, and leviathans swimming in great oceans, mixed in with other grotesque creatures it would have been hard to name.

"What's it all about?" asked Sam.

"I won't try to translate it here," replied Paul abruptly. "I'll study it back on the boat tonight."

"May I?" Nick extended his hand for the book.

"Very well," said Paul reluctantly after a long pause. "Handle it very carefully, and you can look at it for a moment or two."

He passed it to the journalist, although his reluctance to let it out of his hands was obvious. Slowly Nick turned the pages. Some seemed to contain chemical or mathematical formulas, others contained diagrams of buildings with the measurements all carefully marked. And everywhere were the woodcuts of strange beasts— things with armor, claws, and wings. On one page was a beast like a giant bat, but it had the head and vicious, tearing beak of a vulture. On another was a horrible slug-like creature, under which were the words *Negotium perambulans in tenebris.*

"I just wish I could read Latin," Nick remarked.

"If you've finished with that now," said a nervous Paul, holding out his hand. Nick returned the book. "It's getting late," continued the American. "Let's start heading back to the beach."

"If it's all right with you, Paul," said Max, "I'd like to lead us back by a different route, so we can have a quick look at the quarry."

"Okay. Lead on, Max."

Max and Sam took the lead, followed by Paul and his faithful shadow, Vicky. Nick and Ingrid brought up the rear.

Constantly checking his map, and his compass, Max led them directly north. After tramping in silence for some time, he signaled for a halt.

"The old quarry should be somewhere around here. Just ahead of us, I think," he said.

"I'll take a look," volunteered Sam. Using his machete, he cut his way through some especially thick undergrowth, moving ahead in a straight line.

"Here," he called from the undergrowth a few minutes later. "Follow my path."

The others followed in single file, and soon found themselves standing on the edge of a small lake.

"This it?" asked Sam.

"It must be," said Max.

"Obviously the quarry has filled with rainwater over the years," commented Paul.

Nick wandered a few meters away from the others, and stood looking down into the thick, algae-green water that filled the one-time quarry. As he looked, he thought he saw a movement—some large, dark shadow, gliding through the green, slimy water. In a moment it was gone, and he was not sure whether he had imagined it.

Then he saw it again. There was nothing distinct, just a sense of a twisting, sinuous movement. Nick glanced across the weed-covered surface of the water and saw it heave up and then settle again, as if being rippled by something underneath. *There is something alive in that water,* thought Nick. *Something big. Something very big.*

Eventually Cathy finished her work on the altar. As she packed up her things, she glanced around to where the others were. Through the arched doorway, silhouetted against the evening sky, she could see Holly was still taking photographs, Lois was just finishing her work on the pulpit over to one side, and the Roystons were standing near one of the narrow, slit-like windows, engaged in what looked like a whispered argument.

Just then a movement caught the corner of Cathy's eye. She turned and looked in the direction of the movement, but, as far she could make out, there was nothing—and no one—there.

Still, it had been a very clear and distinct impression. She stared hard into the dark corner, and saw, or thought she saw, a deeper shadow within the darkness—a shadow that seemed to radiate darkness just as a lamp radiates light.

Then she shook herself. She was being foolish, Cathy told herself, allowing her imagination to run away with her.

"What are you worried about?" said a voice at her elbow. Cathy jumped.

"Sorry. I didn't mean to startle you," said Holly. "It's just that you looked as though you were trying to solve the problems of the universe."

"It's all right. My mind was wandering, that's all. I was, what my little brother would call, off with the pixies."

"Just so long as they were friendly pixies," Holly said with a laugh and then crouched down and began taking flash pictures of the altar. As the brilliant, blue-white flashes fired, Cathy again looked around the building, looking to see what those flashes might expose, crouching in some distant corner. But, although she looked hard, she saw nothing.

Cathy made her way to the front door, where she was joined by the Roystons.

"It's almost five," said the professor. "Time we were heading for the beach to meet the others."

"We will spend a full day here tomorrow," said his wife, "and uncover some of the ancient secrets of this cathedral."

Cathy found it odd that Stella should refer to the building as a cathedral, but she was not sure why it struck her as odd. She walked out onto the steps and glanced up again at the inscription over the door. There she could clearly read the words: "The Cathedral Church of All Hallows."

With a hollow feeling in the pit of her stomach, Cathy remembered that just a few hours before part of that lettering had been so heavily encrusted with moss and lichen as to be unreadable. Now it was quite clear. And no one had cleaned it, of that she was certain. It would have taken a ladder to reach the top of that arched door, and they did not have a ladder with them.

Suddenly she was very afraid of that old building and wanted nothing more than to be away from it—the farther away from it the better.

"Come on, everyone, we're leaving now," Professor Royston was shouting. "Lois, Holly, come along. It's time to meet the others on the beach."

In response to his call, Lois walked out of the gloom of the church and stood on the grass near the steps, between Cathy and Stella.

"Holly, come on," yelled the professor, a note of irritation creeping into his voice. "You're holding everyone up."

Silence was the only response.

"Where is that woman?" demanded Stella angrily. Then she shouted loudly, adding her voice to that of her husband, "Miss North! Come here at once, and stop being so inconsiderate!"

Her words echoed around the stone building and came back again, but there was no other response.

"I think we should go and look for her," said Cathy anxiously.

"Nonsense," snorted Stella. "If she doesn't come when she's called, she should be left behind."

"But something might have happened to her. She might have tripped or fallen or something," Cathy insisted.

"Very well then. Go and look for her, if you wish. But I'm staying here."

Cathy, Lois, and the professor went back into the church.

From his pocket the professor produced a small, pen-sized

flashlight. He turned it on and shined it around the empty stone vaults.

"Holly? Holly? Where are you?" called Lois.

Cathy went over to the stone altar. It was hard to see anything in those dark shadows and against that black stone, but it was clear that Holly North was not there. Cathy walked slowly around the altar. On the eastern side her foot bumped against something. She bent down to look at it, then called out, "Professor. Lois. Come here. It's her camera." Cathy held up the large SLR camera that Holly had worn around her neck all afternoon.

"Where was it?" asked Lois.

"Right here on the floor."

Professor Royston scanned the whole area with his flashlight. There was nothing but bare stone and no sign of the photographer.

"All right. This time we'll spread out and search the whole building. I'll get my wife to help."

The professor called his wife into the building, showed her the camera, and explained the situation. Then the four of them spread out in a search pattern and moved slowly from one end of the building to the other, with Professor Royston searching every dark corner and every shadow with his flashlight.

By the time they had regrouped at the front door of the ancient church, one thing had become clear: Holly had vanished.

22

There's something alive in there," said Nick. "In the water."

"I can't see anything," Paul declared impatiently. The group was standing, strung out in a line, along one edge of the artificial lake that had once been a quarry.

"Let's head back."

"Wait a moment," urged Nick.

"I think I see it," said Sam. "There. Look."

Everyone looked in the direction he was pointing.

"You're imagining things," complained Paul. "Nick planted the idea in your head. That's the trouble with journalists, too much imagination."

"No. I saw it. A large, dark shape," Sam insisted.

Just then Vicky gave a squeal. "Paul! Paul!" she said, "I think I saw something moving. Down deep in the water."

"Shut up Vicky. You're just easily led, that's all. You can't see anything deep in that water. It's black down there."

"But Paul …"

"I said shut up."

Just then there was a ripple of movement as a broad patch of weeds moved, as though lifted from underneath.

"What was that, Dr. Marshall?" asked Ingrid. "A figment of someone's imagination?"

Sam bent down, picked up a large stone, and then waited expectantly. The watchers on the edge of the water stood silently for a long minute. Then another patch of thick weeds moved, as though the whole pond was breathing. Sam threw his stone, very straight and very hard. The response was another sharp movement in the weeds, and then they saw it. Just for a fleeting moment they saw a broad, smooth back. And then it was gone again.

"Something there all right," said Sam, and added with a broad grin, "Should I go and get my fishing line?"

"It might be dangerous," said Max nervously. "It might be something like a crocodile."

"There couldn't possibly be a crocodile on the island," responded Paul with weary impatience.

"You know what I mean," persisted Max, "an amphibious reptile of some sort. Something that could come out of the water and … and … attack us."

"It's certainly very big," said Nick quietly. "I'd be happier standing here if I had a gun."

"Then I propose we get a move on," said Ingrid in her brisk, nononsense way, "and return tomorrow, properly armed."

"Yes. Yes. Very sensible," urged Max as he turned and led the way back toward the cliff tops and the path that would take them back to the beach.

Because they were returning by a different route, well away from the trail they had to cut on their way to the old convict site, they had to wade through grass that was hip deep in places. Several times Nick stopped and cocked his head to one side, listening hard. He thought he heard a sound, a slithering sound of movement, somewhere behind them. In his imagination he saw some primeval monster that had climbed out of that foul swamp and was now tracking them. But when he stopped and listened, all was silent, and he blamed his own fears for imagining things.

His thoughts were interrupted by Ingrid who was walking beside him.

"Just take a look at that, Nick," she said enthusiastically.

"What? Where?"

"That flowering bush over there. Isn't that spectacular? Wait for me while I go and pick a few flowers."

"Don't be long," urged Nick.

"It will just take a moment."

Ingrid stepped off the rough trail cut by Sam's machete and began wading through the long grass toward a small, flowering bush.

"Hold on, up ahead there!" shouted Nick. "We're getting left behind."

"Catch up then," shouted Paul. "Get a move on."

"Wait a moment," Nick yelled. "Dr. Sommerville has stopped to pick some flowers."

"Flowers," Paul said in disgust. Nevertheless, he stopped. Farther ahead Nick could see that Max and Sam had also come to a halt.

Just then an ear-splitting scream tore the air, and Nick spun around in time to see Ingrid disappearing from sight. She seemed to be sinking into the earth. Nick imagined, for a split second, that she might be in the jaws of some gargantuan swamp creature.

He ran as hard as he could to the spot where she'd been standing. "Dr. Sommerville!" he yelled. Her screaming had stopped. There was neither sight nor sound of her.

"What happened?" asked Sam, who stood puffing beside him. Within a few seconds everyone was there.

"What's happened to Ingrid?" asked Vicky, a note of panic rising in her voice.

"I'm not exactly sure," said Nick, inching carefully forward through the thick grass.

Then he felt his foot slipping and stepped back quickly. Looking down, he saw it: a hole, almost a meter across, hidden by the long wild grass.

"She's fallen down here," Nick said to the others. "It must lead to a cave or … something."

"It's pitch black down there." Sam leaned forward cautiously.

"Dr. Sommerville, can you hear me?" Paul called out, leaning toward the opening.

There was no response.

"The fall must have knocked her unconscious," said Max.

"Or killed her," added Paul.

"I'm going down there," Nick volunteered.

"I'll go, Nick," said Sam.

"I'm thinner than you, and this opening might get narrower farther down. You stay here; I might need your strength on the surface to help pull us out."

Nick sat on the edge of the opening, feeling his feet dangling in space, then lowered himself cautiously over the edge, groping with his feet for some sort of hold. He could find none.

"Take my hands, Sam," he said, "and lower me down."

Nick felt large hands grip his, then his weight was taken by the giant Tongan's arms. He was lowered farther into the vertical shaft. Still he could feel nothing with his feet.

"I must be near the bottom," Nick called. "Let go, Sam. I'll drop the rest of the way."

"I don't know, Nick," Sam replied. "Don't sound smart to me."

"Do it!" shouted Nick. "Let go!"

Nick felt the hands release their grip, then the world disappeared as he fell into total blackness.

23

It was an ordinary suburban brick-veneer house. Each time the front door bell chimed, it was opened by Mr. Wallace Humphrey Muir, who welcomed the newcomers and led them into the living room.

The group was a varied one. There were young couples in their twenties, some who were approaching middle age, and one couple almost as old as Mr. Muir himself.

"Everyone, Margaret and Angus are here, and young Sebastian arrived just as I was letting them in. Now, who would like tea, and who wants coffee? There are chocolate cookies, and Melissa brought some of her wonderful homemade cake."

When everyone had been served, Mr. Muir settled himself in a large, overstuffed armchair. He fished a pair of gold-rimmed glasses from his pocket and perched them on the end of his nose. He ran his pink blotched hand over his thin, wispy, white hair and picked up a large Bible from the coffee table at his knee.

"Tonight I'd like for us to spend some time in prayer," he began, "before we do our Bible study."

The others looked at him expectantly. He flipped open his Bible and began to read, "Ephesians, chapter six, verse twelve, says this: 'For our struggle is not against flesh and blood, but against the rulers, against the authorities, against the powers of this dark world and against the spiritual forces of evil in the heavenly realms.' My dear friends, there is just such a struggle going on right now."

"Mr. Muir?"

"Yes, Sebastian?"

"Who are these rulers and authorities and powers?"

"A very good question, Sebastian. Some have argued that these words refer to national governments—evil governments, such as Nazi Germany or Stalin's Russia. Nevertheless, the words mean exactly what they appear to mean. In the spiritual realm there is a battle going on between good and evil just as there is in this world."

"That's rather frightening," said Melissa.

"Well, it is, and it isn't. Dark cosmic forces can certainly manipulate and deceive and hurt human beings. But we do not live in what is called a dualistic universe, in which the forces of good and evil are equally matched. No, that is not so. Jesus has already won the decisive battle, and the final defeat of the evil forces is just a matter of time. But in the meantime, they are still dangerous, just as a well-armed sniper can still be dangerous, even after his army has been defeated."

"Why is this important just now?" Margaret asked.

"Because of an expedition currently underway to Cavendish Island. In case you haven't heard of it, Cavendish briefly was a penal settlement—a very harsh one, like Norfolk Island or Port Arthur."

"What's the problem with this expedition?"

"Some people believe there is a history of Satan worship on that island, and as a result they believe that by going there they can reactivate, and release into their own control, those dark powers."

"And can they?"

"Our world is always in danger on an outbreak of moral evil. I think there is great spiritual danger in what they are doing."

"So, what should we be praying for, in particular?" Andrew asked.

"In the first place, for a man named Nick Hamilton, a journalist accompanying the expedition. He is, so I understand, a Christian. Where he is, right now, is a very dangerous place for him to be."

"Isn't there a risk of taking all this too seriously," suggested

Margaret, "and becoming obsessed with cosmic forces and battles and all the rest?"

"There is certainly a danger of becoming obsessed with anything, of dwelling more than we should on things that stir our imagination. On the other hand, surely it is just as dangerous to ignore these things altogether."

"I suppose so."

"Well, then, let's begin."

Nick found himself lying in total darkness, stiff and sore. He raised himself up on one elbow. Nothing seemed to be broken. Struggling to his feet, he found that he had been lying on a steeply sloping bed of lose shale that slid dangerously under his feet when he tried to move.

"Nick! Nick, can you hear me?" It was Sam's voice.

"Yes. I can hear you, Sam."

"Are you all right?"

"A bit bruised, that's all."

"What do you need down there?"

"A flashlight. Urgently, please. It's pitch black. If I'd had my wits about me, I'd have stuffed a flashlight in my pocket before I jumped."

"Can you see the light of the opening above you?" called Paul.

"Not at the moment. Hang on, I'm going to move in the direction of your voice."

Slowly Nick clambered up the slope of lose shale until he could see a circle of darkening sky above.

"I'm right underneath you now," he shouted.

"Good," yelled Paul. "I'm dropping my flashlight down to you now. It's just a small one, so it won't be too heavy. Here it comes."

A moment later Nick saw a small object hurtling straight down toward him. He managed to catch it before it hit the rocks. "Got it," he called out to the watchers above. He tried the switch. "And it still works. I'm going to search for Dr. Sommerville now."

"Nick, we've sent Vicky back to the boat to fetch some rope."

"Great. As soon as I've found the doctor, I'll come back and let you know."

Nick allowed himself to slide down the steep slope of gravel and shale until he reached a flat, rock surface. Then he switched on the flashlight and stood up. Almost at once he found Ingrid. She was lying unconscious on her side at the foot of the slope.

He felt for a pulse and was relieved to find it strong and regular. One side of her face and one arm were badly grazed. Nick tried feeling the major bones of her arms and legs, and, as far as he could tell, none were broken, but one foot was twisted at an odd angle.

"Dr. Sommerville, can you hear me? Come on, wake up, Doctor," said Nick, but there was no response, not even a groan.

He straightened up. Until she regained consciousness, he feared there was nothing he could do. He turned his attention to the cavern he was in, shining the flashlight beam over the rocky walls and ceiling. It appeared to be quite large, and at the far end there was an opening that he presumed would lead to another cave or tunnel.

Looking down at the still-unconscious figure, Nick decided to find out.

Keeping the beam focused on the uneven rocky floor, the journalist made his way to the far side of the cavern and the almost circular black hole that opened into an even deeper blackness beyond.

"It must be vast," he muttered to himself, feeling a gentle breeze blowing out of the darkness onto his face, "but this is not the time to explore."

He returned to the doctor. As he reached her side, she began to moan.

"Dr. Sommerville. Dr. Sommerville, can you hear me?"

She moaned again. Louder this time.

"Ingrid, it's me, Nick. Come on, speak to me, Ingrid."

"Nick?"

"How are you feeling?"

"Sore. Very ... very sore. What happened?"

"You've had a fall. Don't you remember?"

"A fall? Ah ... yes ... I remember now ... oh, it hurts."

"Where does it hurt?"

"Everywhere. Every inch of my body is aching."

"We need to get you back to the boat. We have this really good doctor on our team; she'll take care of you."

"Very funny, Nick. Now put your arm around my shoulders and help me sit up."

"How's that?"

"Ooof. Tomorrow my body will be one massive purple bruise."

"Is anything broken?"

"That's what I'm trying to figure out. I seem to be able to move my arms and legs. Ah! Oh no. I think my left ankle is broken."

"We're getting some rope. We can get you back up to the surface in a rope sling. I'm going back to the entrance to see what's going on. You just wait here for a moment, okay?"

"I'm not going anywhere, Nick. I promise."

Nick climbed back up the steep gravel slope until he stood under the pale circle of sky that represented the way out.

"Hello, up there," he yelled.

"Nick?"

"Who's that?"

"It's Sam. Have you found the doctor? Is she alive?"

"Yes on both counts. But she's got a broken ankle."

"Is she there with you now?"

"No, there's a steep slope of gravel and shale here. She's down at the foot of it."

"Can you bring her up so that she's under this opening? If you can do that, we can haul her up. Toby and Vic have arrived with a rope."

"Okay. I'll go and tell her the good news."

It took Nick the better part of twenty minutes to half lift, half carry the doctor up the slippery slope of gravel. She helped as much as she could, but she found the effort too painful and exhausting to be of much assistance. If was a great relief to Nick to see her being lifted upward in the rope sling.

Before leaving the cavern himself, Nick decided to go back and take one last look at the bigger cave system beyond. On the far side, at the entrance to the large cavern system, he flashed his light around, but the battery was starting to die, the beam was dimmer and yellow, and he could see very little. As he turned to go, he stepped on something that crunched under his foot.

Looking down, he saw a skeleton—old, brittle, and white. It was about the size of a large dog, but unlike any dog Nick had ever seen. Its jaw was elongated and filled with sharp, curved teeth. Its feet ended in sharpened claws like talons.

"I wouldn't like to meet one of those in the flesh," he muttered to himself. A sudden chill ran down his spine as he wondered how many of these creatures might be living in the cave system. He had no intention of waiting to find out.

When he arrived back under the hole, a rope was dangling down, and Sam was calling his name.

"I'm here, Sam," he yelled back.

"Thank heavens. I was getting worried, Nick. Grab the rope, and I'll haul you up."

24

*L*ate that night on board the *Covenant,* the expedition team ate a quick-fix meal in depressed silence.

Ingrid had been taken to her cabin where Captain Nagle, who turned out to be well-trained in first aid, cleaned and bandaged her wounds and splinted and bound her ankle. She administered a painkiller to herself and shortly afterward fell asleep.

Cathy was in tears over the disappearance of Holly North. Nick hugged her and comforted her. She was so upset, she was unable to eat. Nick sat with her in her cabin, talked to her for a long while to settle her down, and left her when she started to get sleepy.

Having taken care of Cathy, Nick went to the boat's communications desk on the bridge and placed a radio phone call to Frank Gordon's home.

"Frank? It's Nick. How late is it there?"

"Just after eight o'clock. I just walked in. How's it going?"

"Disastrously."

"Sounds like it's a good story," said the editor. "What's happened?"

"Our expedition doctor is out of action. She fell through a hidden opening into a cave and broke her ankle. Incidentally, there appears to be a whole system of linked caves and tunnels and huge caverns under the island. I intend to explore them as soon as I get a chance."

"Take care of yourself, Nick. I don't want you breaking an ankle too."

"I'll be careful."

"But a broken ankle doesn't rate as a disaster. What else has happened, Nick?"

"The expedition photographer, Holly North, has vanished."

"Vanished? Like, disappeared?"

"Precisely."

"How could she vanish? Has she fallen off a cliff or something?"

"I don't think so. A search party from the boat combed the island for an hour, and it's not a big island. We'll resume the search in the morning."

"Where did she disappear from?"

"The old stone church," said Nick.

"Ah. The building that mysteriously repairs itself. Clearly a case of The Unexplained," responded the editor.

"I don't think it's a clear case of anything, Frank."

"By the way, I got a fax today about your expedition from some group in California."

"That's odd. How did they know about it? Who are they?"

"Hang on, I'll go get it out of my briefcase."

Nick waited on the phone until, with a loud thump on the end of the line, his editor returned.

"They call themselves The Order of the Crimson Circle. As far as I can make out, they're some sort of New Age group. I had Rhonda look them up in the *Mirror* library. They're into channeling and crystals and tarot cards and what they call white magic. All that sort of thing."

"Technically they are neo-pagans then. What did they want?"

"For us not to report the expedition. According to them, it's very important that the world not hear of Cavendish Island, at least not yet. 'The world is not ready for this truth'—that sort of thing."

"At least it kept you amused, Frank."

"True. I faxed them back one of my famous heavily ironic,

tongue-in-cheek memos. Of course, they won't understand any of my jokes. They take themselves so seriously, these people."

"Anything else?"

"Oh, yes. Old Mr. Muir came to see me. He seemed like a nice old guy, so I listened to what he had to say, gave him a cup of tea, and sent him away. At least I think I gave him a cup of tea. I can't remember now. Too much Scotch."

"Listen, Frank. As soon as we find Holly—or her body—I'll file a story. But you'd better clear it with the police first; her relatives will have to be informed."

"We'll take care of all that, Nick. You just take care of yourself."

Back in the main lounge, Nick found that Sam and Toby had set up a buffet-style salad bar for the passengers to serve themselves.

Paul and Vicky were seated on the long lounge, both eating, and Lois was in a corner, reading a magazine. The others, Nick assumed, had eaten while he was on the radio. The place was deathly quiet: There was the almost inaudible throb of the marine engine that provided their electrical power, the slap of waves, the eerie whistling of the wind, and the occasional cry of a night bird.

Just as Nick had finished his salad and was pouring himself a cup of coffee, Professor Royston burst out of the companionway, his face bright red with anger.

"Paul, you have something of mine," he puffed. If he hadn't been so out of breath, it would have been a shout.

"I'm sorry. What was that?" asked the American.

"You heard me. And you know exactly what I mean."

"I'm afraid I don't. You've lost me completely, Earl. You're clearly upset about something, but I can't imagine what."

"Don't pretend," hissed the professor venomously. "Max has told me what you found today."

"What we found?"

"He means the book, Paul," Vicky offered. Paul gave her a black scowl. "Oh? The book? Is that what you want, Earl?" He tried to sound casual.

"I want the book—*the* book. It is the key to the island. I came here for it. You know that. Now hand it over."

"Well, I'm not so sure about that."

"Just what do you mean?" growled Royston.

"I mean that documentary materials should be handled by the historians on the team, not the archaeologists. Just as soon as I've translated it from the Latin, I'll let you have a look at it. Or, maybe, just give you a copy of the translation."

"You're playing a dangerous game, Paul. A very dangerous game. I just hope you realize that."

"A game? A game, Earl? This is a scientific expedition. We're just here to work together uncovering an interesting corner of your convict past."

"Please, Paul," murmured Vicky, placing her hand on the American's arm. "Don't make him angry."

"I know what I'm doing," said Paul irritably, shaking off her hand.

Lois had put down her magazine and was watching the proceedings with great interest. Nick looked around, trying to interpret the undercurrents. There were unspoken assumptions in the conversation that he couldn't follow.

"You'd be well advised to take Miss Shaw's advice, Paul," said Royston with quiet intensity. "For the last time, will you hand over the book?"

"For the last time, Earl, no, I will not."

Nick watched the professor storm out of the main cabin, and then walked out onto the aft deck, his coffee cup in hand. Vic Neal, the boat's engineer, was leaning over the railing, smoking a cigarette. Nick walked up beside him.

"Beautiful night," said Vic. "The air's as warm as milk, and the sea's as soft as a silk sheet. It least, it would be a beautiful night if the expedition hadn't got off to such a bad start."

"Very true. Were you in the search party?"

"I was. And what I can't figure out is just how the lady got out of the church."

"What do you mean?"

"There is only one doorway, the windows are just narrow slits, and there were four people between Miss North and that doorway. How could she slip by four people unseen?"

"Today I discovered there is an extensive network of caves under the island," suggested Nick. "I wonder if there is a link. Perhaps a passageway that leads underground from the church?"

"Like a secret passage? What would a convict prison want with secret doors and panels and passages?"

"It does seem unlikely. But what other explanation can there be?"

For a long time they stood there in silence, each lost in his own thoughts.

The quiet was broken only by the slap of waves and the occasional cry of a night bird. Even the wind had died. In the starlight, for the moon was behind clouds, Nick could see a large black bird picking over the carcass of a fish on the beach. When the bird threw back its head and released its harsh, throaty cry, the sound came across the waves as if the predator was right beside them.

Vic was squinting, and his head was tilted to one side, as if he was listening hard.

"Can you hear that, chief?" he said.

"Hear what?" asked Nick.

"Just listen," said the engineer.

Nick closed his eyes and concentrated on listening intently. Then he heard it. There was a deep, almost inaudible rumbling, and with it a grinding of stone on stone, as if the grindstone of a mill was turning very, very slowly.

"Yes," he whispered, "I can hear something."

"It's coming from up there, isn't it?" Vic nodded at the cliff where the ruined building lay invisible in the darkness.

"I'm not sure."

Both men returned to their concentrated listening. There it was again: heavy stone moving ever so slowly over heavy stone.

"I'm not a superstitious man, chief, but if I were, well, I would swear that building's *alive*."

Nick said nothing, but he shivered as if the night had suddenly turned cold. He concentrated his eyes and ears on the building. The moon came out from behind a cloud, and on the cliff top a fragment of the church became dimly visible—rimmed in pale, blue light.

Nick peered at the moonlit shape. He could see part of the wall and one of the narrow windows. For a moment he thought he saw a flicker of light—as if one of the stars was gleaming from *inside* the building, instead of in the night sky. But it was there so fleetingly that Nick distrusted his own senses.

But then there was something else—at the top of the church wall, rising up above the height of its roofline. For a moment that darker blackness against the points of stars moved, and in that movement it looked like a giant wing, as of a bird or a bat. But it was there for just an instant, and then it was gone. *Did I really see it at all?* Nick thought.

"Well, I'll be ..." began Vic. "No. I must be imagining things."

He flicked his cigarette stub into the sea and turned to go. Just then a loud crash, an explosion, thundered out behind them, and both men spun around toward the main lounge.

They ran across the deck and into the lounge. The air was full of acrid, drifting blue smoke. Professor Royston was holding a revolver in his hand. There was a bullet hole punched through the toughened glass of the lounge window, just behind Paul's head.

"You could have killed me!" screamed Paul, recovering his wits.

"Yes, I could have, couldn't I?" replied Royston with a sinister smile. "Now, you will give me the book."

"Never."

"You seem to forget, Paul. I am the head of this expedition. In that capacity, I hereby dismiss you from the expedition team. You now have no official standing. Max Taunton will take over the history work from you. Any expedition property you currently have in your possession you must hand over immediately; otherwise, you will be guilty of theft."

"I don't believe this. You're not serious."

"Oh, I'm deadly serious. I find myself confronting a self-confessed thief who is refusing to part with official expedition property to which he has no legal claim. And I am forced to use this weapon to defend expedition property from this known thief. That is the situation we are in, Dr. Marshall. Now, will you fetch the book for me please?"

There was a very long silence, during which the two men stared pure hatred at each other. It was a battle of wills. Captain Nagle came up the companionway from below decks. He opened his mouth as if to speak, but Vic, who could see the intensity on Royston's face, signaled his captain to hold his peace.

Somewhere in the distance a seagull shrieked. The breeze had sprung up again. It blew through the bullet hole behind Paul's head and ruffled his hair. Vicky, seated beside him, was white with terror, and silent tears were trickling down her cheeks. The standoff made the air electric with tension.

"All right," said Paul, finally. "No book, no historical artifact, is worth this tension, this ... this ... performance."

Saying these words, he dug into the pocket of the sports coat he was wearing and pulled out the small book still wrapped in its protective oilcloth.

"Very sensible, Dr. Marshall," said Royston smugly. "Now, you will kindly leave the boat."

"What?" yelled Paul in protest.

"You heard me. I want you off the boat tonight."

"Now, Professor," interrupted Nagle.

"You stay out of this, Captain," snapped the professor. "This boat has been charted for my expedition, and the only persons permitted on board are your crew and the members of my team. Dr. Marshall belongs to neither category, and he must leave." The revolver quivered in his hand.

"But there's nowhere for me to go," yelled Paul.

"You can sleep on the island. I should think the beach would be quite a comfortable place. One of the deckhands can run you ashore in the inflatable runabout."

"But ... but ..." Paul spluttered.

"I am not an inhumane man, so I will allow you to take a tent and sleeping bags from the expedition stores, if you wish."

"If I'm sleeping on the beach, then I certainly wish!"

"Fine. That's settled then."

25

From the journal of Lieutenant Edmund McDermott, officer of the New South Wales Corps.

October 31st, 1822

I slept badly last night, and the fever appears to be getting worse. The settlement's surgeon, Dr. Curtis Fraser, finally came to see me. He claimed he had been himself unwell yesterday, and for that reason was unable to attend me. I made no comment, although I knew full well that he had once again been the worse for liquor.

Surgeon Fraser has been provided with accommodation in one room of Commander Black's house, and the commandant, for reasons that quite escape me, seems to encourage the doctor's indulgence in alcohol. After conducting a cursory examination, Fraser recommended bed rest and regular medicinal doses of brandy. He said, "The fever must be allowed to run its course," and then departed.

He left me with a bottle of brandy from his own supply. I drank a little of it, and then fell back on the bed and tried to sleep.

As I fell into a fitful doze, still burning with fever and dripping with sweat, strange pictures came into my head, pictures of things that have happened since we arrived on this benighted island. There was the day I found the body of a young convict, one Edward Cavell, at the bottom of the ever-deepening hole that is the rock quarry. Every bone in his body appeared to be broken. Two of the convicts who saw his death told me he had been flung from the top of the quarry by Black Billy Cauldron, a huge and powerful man. However, they were not prepared to give evidence against Cauldron for fear of their own safety. Cauldron himself swore that Cavell had fallen. The commandant accepted Cauldron's account, and once again that evil man escaped the punishment for murder that he so richly deserves.

I seemed to sleep for a while. Half-waking, I remembered that it was only a few months after that incident that Commander Black took Black Billy under his wing as his own personal servant. For his part, Cauldron seemed to become devoted to the commandant and would do anything to serve his master. This did nothing but increase the reign of terror by which the commandant already held the island community in thrall.

At about midday, Trooper Kelly, a thoughtful young man, arrived at my room with a meal. I was able to sit at my desk to eat this, and while I ate, Kelly brought fresh blankets and changed the sopping bed linen. When I fell back into bed after lunch, I drank a good deal more of Fraser's "medicinal brandy" and then slept dreamlessly for several hours.

When I awoke, there were two men in my room speaking in low tones. Keeping my eyes closed but listening carefully, I identified the voices as belonging to Commander Black and Sergeant Davis.

"It must be tonight, Davis," the commandant was saying. "As you know full well, the date is correct. And we will please those forces we seek to master if we use this date for their beneficence."

"I'm sure you're quite right, sir."

"You are to bring McDermott to the cathedral shortly before midnight. All four of us will be needed for the ceremony. Make sure the others are ready and fully prepared. I will arrange for Cauldron to stand guard while we do what has to be done."

"Yes, sir," replied Davis, and then I heard his footsteps departing. What was it these men had planned? And I had heard my name mentioned: what part was I to play in their arrangements?

Keeping my eyes closed, I heard Black moving around my room. He appeared to be picking things up and shifting things about. Shortly he was joined by another man. When he spoke, I discovered it was the surgeon.

"Fraser, all of McDermott's things should be moved out of this room by daylight," said Commander Black.

Moved out? I was being moved somewhere, then. But where? And why?

"Trooper Forbes can take care of that, Mr. Black."

"And I'm telling you to do it, Dr Fraser. Do you dare to question my orders?"

"No. No, commander. Not at all. Never that."

"Very well then. After the ceremony is over, and before the dawn, I want McDermott's things removed and burnt."

Burnt? Were these foul fiends then planning nothing short of my death? In an access of fear and panic I tried to move my arms, to open my eyes, and to my inexpressible horror found that I was unable to move a muscle.

"Will he wake again before midnight?" the commandant asked.

"Almost certainly," replied the surgeon. "The mixture of brandy and laudanum I gave him will have to be repeated during the evening."

"See to it yourself. Even if you have to pin him down and force it down his throat. He must be alive but under our control when we consecrate our 'black church' tonight and summon to our command the goat-headed one himself."

Unable to move, I faced the prospect of my own death as calmly as I could. I know that I belong to the family of our Heavenly Father by the grace of his one and only Son, our Lord Jesus Christ. Therefore, for me, death does not hold the fears it

may for some. As St. Paul said, to be absent from the body is to
be present with the Lord.

However, while I can contemplate my death quite calmly,
the business of dying fills me with terrors, for I do not think
those men intend my departure from this world to be an easy or
a pleasant one. All I can do is pray to God for strength, surren-
dering my soul to him, knowing that at all times I am in his
powerful and loving hands.

As the darkness faded, I felt the power of Fraser's drug
wearing off, or, at the very least, beginning to weaken. No doubt
he shall soon appear and, by force if necessary, compel me to
drink some more of the draft. Hence, I take this opportunity of
the regaining of a little of my strength for the writing of this, in
all likelihood the last entry in my journal.

When I have completed it, I intend to hide it under a loose
floorboard near my bed. Perhaps from that hiding place it will
one day be found. And possibly then someone, in some place, at
some time, will know the truth about this island of death and
about my fate.

26

___

*F*rank Gordon poured a finger of Jack Daniels into a whiskey glass just as David Letterman was saying goodnight. He hit the off button on his remote control and opened the manila folder lying on the coffee table near his left elbow. Scrawled on the front of the folder were the words: The Order of the Crimson Circle—b/g material.

As he sipped his drink, he slowly turned the pages. It was mostly a computer printout from the AAP files, supplemented with a photocopy of a *Mirror* story on the Australian branch of the Circle and an interview with the founder taken from an American magazine.

"Typical Californian screwballs," muttered Frank to himself. Crimson Circle founder Eliaphas Crowley, a middle-aged former physics professor and former devotee of Zen Buddhism, had renamed himself Apollonius. The magazine article quoted him as saying: "The occult has found many devotees throughout Europe and North America over the past 200 years. There was, in fact, an upsurge in spiritualism in the 1800s, especially after the publication of Darwin's *The Origin of Species* in 1859. During the 1970s there was an occult explosion. Witchcraft, astrology, spiritualism, channeling—they are all growing in popularity."

"Only because charlatans like you are ready to exploit the gullible," he snorted.

In the article, "Apollonius" went on to say: "We in the Crimson Circle hold a monistic world view that has much in common with

Hinduism. We see the entire universe as a living, unified whole. The Power permeates the entire universe, and in a sense every person is a part of The Power. The Power and humanity are therefore one."

"The Power," scoffed Frank into his whiskey glass. "Why don't you just call it The Force and then you can pretend you're Obi-Wan Kenobi."

Many of the printouts concerned the predictions, uttered from time to time by Crimson Circle spokesmen, that a day was coming of "Global Awakening and Cosmic Consciousness." No specific date was ever mentioned, but the prophetic announcements had an increasingly urgent tone.

"Hysteria," snarled Frank, tossing the file to one side, finishing his whiskey, and stumbling off toward his bedroom.

Some minutes later he lay there in the dark, aware as always of the empty half of the double bed. He missed his wife, and occasionally he allowed himself to feel a pang of regret for the affair that had destroyed his marriage of twenty years. The affair was over, the marriage was over, and Frank was alone. Relaxed by the whiskey, he drifted into sleep.

Frank found himself standing in a street he didn't recognize. It might have been one of those northern English industrial cities he had visited as a journalist many years earlier. The street was lined by grim, narrow-terraced houses on one side, while on the other were several grimy, dirty-looking shops sandwiched between the brick walls of factories. The street was deserted. It was nighttime, and it was raining.

Frank had a feeling that he had been wandering for hours in similar mean streets, always in the rain, and always in the darkness of night. None of the shop windows were lit, and no lights showed from any of the houses. He began to walk. But no matter how far he walked, he never seemed to come to the better parts of town.

With his hands in his pockets and his coat collar turned up against the chill wind, he walked past dingy lodging houses, small tobacconists, billboards from which posters hung in rags, windowless warehouses, echoing railway stations that had not seen a train in years, and small bookshops whose dusty stock seemed to be limited to textbooks on accounting or psychiatric nursing.

After what felt like hours of endless trudging, he decided to knock on a door, inquire about his whereabouts, and ask for directions to a bus stop. The problem was, which door? Most of the houses looked to be deserted, lifeless.

Just then he heard the sound of voices. It was a man and a woman engaged in a bitter argument. He hurried up the front steps and knocked on their door. As soon as he did so, the arguing ceased. But no one came to the door. He knocked again. And again. His knocks echoed inside the house. But there was no other sound: no voice, no movement.

At last he gave up and moved on. He hadn't gone ten paces down the street when he heard the bitter, savage argument resume behind him. He shrugged his shoulders and kept going. "Where am I?" he kept asking himself. "Where am I? And how did I get here?"

Frank felt a deep, aching loneliness within, one that was quickly replaced by a fierce pride that refused to admit that he was lonely or that he could ever feel lonely.

Then, in the distance, he spotted a light and quickened his step. He had to walk for a long time before the light appeared to be even a little closer. The streets were unchanging in their dullness and dark emptiness. Some were wide, with tram tracks down the middle and sparse, inadequate street lamps on the corners. Others were little more than narrow lanes that ran past the back fences of houses and factories, and Frank had to be careful not to stumble over the garbage that spilled out onto the street.

After what felt like an eternity, he turned a corner, and there was the house with its front window shining brightly. He hurried up its front steps, and before knocking, he looked in through the uncurtained window. Inside was a man—a short, fat man in an old-fashioned double-breasted suit—walking up and down. Without pausing or changing his pace, the man walked steadily back and forth across the room.

With a shock of recognition, Frank realized that he knew the man. It was Sir Alfred Stocker—the first proprietor Frank had ever worked for as a young cadet journalist. But that could not be. Stocker had been dead for years. Whatever the explanation, here was someone who could help him. Frank knocked on the door loudly and clearly. There was no response. He waited a few minutes and knocked again. Still no response. He went back to the window and looked in again.

Stocker was still there, still pacing up and down. As he paced, he was muttering to himself. Frank listened very carefully to what he could hear Stocker saying: "I own *The News* and *The Advocate* and *The Standard*. I own three houses. I own the sheep station and the yacht. I own *Sporting Weekly* and *Woman's Journal* and four radio stations. I own *The News* and *The Advocate* and *The Standard*. I own ..."

That's all it was, over and over again—a recital of all the things he owned. Sometimes the list changed as he remembered some long-forgotten possession. But the recital never stopped. It was as though he was afraid that if he forgot the list he would no longer own all those things.

Frank went back to the front door and pounded heavily. A few minutes later he pounded again, even more loudly. There was no response and with a shrug of his shoulders Frank gave up and stepped back into the rain.

Once again he was walking down cold, dark asphalt streets that gleamed with rainwater. "What have I just seen?" Frank asked himself, "and what does it mean?"

Suddenly there was a sensation in his chest like a sharp pain as he realized: *If Stocker is here, and Stocker is dead, then I must be dead too! I have died—and gone to hell!*

Frank woke up abruptly, bathed in sweat. He switched on his

bedside light and looked at the time. It was 3:00 AM. "I've been dreaming," he muttered. "What a hell of a dream."

He found it impossible to fall asleep again. He tossed and turned in the dark for some time, then turned his bedside light back on. He picked up a book to read, but, for some reason, his thoughts kept going back to Nick.

For no very logical reason he was beginning to feel that his journalist was in very great danger.

He read a page and a half of a biography of Richard Nixon, and then, unbidden, the picture of Nick returned to his inward eye.

"What could happen to him on that island?" Frank asked aloud. "Surely there can't be anything safer than archaeology."

But these answers were strangely unsatisfying. And Frank couldn't deny, even to himself, that the expedition had got off to a bad start.

"Almost as though there's a curse on it," he muttered. But what could he do to help Nick? Then he thought of W. H. Muir. "That weird old man expected the expedition to be dangerous. Perhaps I should talk to him again. Privately. Outside the office. Maybe if I just frankly tell him I'm concerned, he might suggest something. Might even be able to do something."

Feeling restless, Frank got out of bed, went to his wardrobe, and hunted through the pockets of his tweed jacket. There he found the scrap of paper with Muir's phone number.

"I'll call him," Frank decided. "Not now. Not at this hour. In the morning. At a more reasonable time."

At that moment Frank's phone began to ring.

Oh no, thought the editor as he picked it up, *a crisis at the paper.*

"Hello," he said, "Gordon speaking."

"Mr. Gordon," said the quavering, elderly voice, "I apologize for calling at this hour. I was awake praying—I don't sleep very much any more—and I had a very strong feeling that I should call you. It's Wallace Muir."

27

Nick was among the first of the party to go to the beach in the morning. Cathy, still shaken by the events of the previous day, stayed close by his side. When they climbed down from the *Covenant* to the inflatable runabout, Sam Fangatofa was already sitting in the bow of the small craft with a shotgun nestled across his knees.

"What's that for?" asked Cathy.

"After yesterday," explained Sam, "I want to be ready for anything."

Lois and Professor Royston were also passengers, while Toby sat at the aft tiller. After they had splashed ashore, Toby went back to pick up another group. Paul, unshaved, red-eyed, and looking somewhat hung over, emerged from his tent on the beach, closely followed by Vicky, who had chosen to share his exile

Nick watched Professor Royston with interest, to see whether he would look at all embarrassed or ashamed by his actions of the previous night. But there was no sign of it. Instead, the expedition leader looked very pleased with himself, and full of life.

"Today," he exclaimed, standing on the beach, with his hands on his hips, "we will unlock the secret of the old church."

"After we've found Holly North," Cathy reminded him.

"Oh yes, of course, my dear. I was not forgetting the tragic case of Miss North. But after that, the old building will be forced to give up its secrets to us."

Paul stood watching this performance from farther down the beach. Royston, however, never once looked in Paul's direction.

The inflatable runabout arrived back at the beach, this time carrying Mrs. Royston, Max, and Captain Nagle, as well as Toby who pulled the inflatable up above the high-water mark.

The captain explained, "I've left Vic Neal on duty on the *Covenant*. The rest of us can form the search party for Holly."

"I would be happy to help," said Paul, coming over.

"Don't bother us, Paul," snarled Royston, his face growing blacker. "This search is for expedition members only."

"I'll take charge of the search, if you don't mind, Professor," intervened Captain Nagle, "and in my view we need all the help we can get. You're welcome, Dr. Marshall, and Miss Shaw as well. Everyone assemble in front of the church in five minutes."

Cathy, Nick, and Sam were the first to hike up the steep trail to the top of the cliff.

"This way, Nick," called Cathy, leading the way. "Come and have a closer look at this weird building."

The three made their way along the narrow path that wound around the cliff, at times perilously close to the edge, until, at last, they rounded a clump of bushes, and there it was.

"It's strangely impressive, isn't it?" said Cathy, with a proprietorial air.

The journalist didn't respond, but began to slowly walk about the perimeter of the church. Along each side, and against the buttresses at each corner, were griffins, basilisks, gargoyles, and strange, indescribable creatures—ugly, prehistoric reptiles in the main.

"I've seen all these before," said Nick at last. "At least, I've seen the designs for them."

"Where?"

"In that little book that Paul found yesterday. The one our two esteemed leaders were fighting over."

"Designs for all of these creatures were in that book?" asked Cathy skeptically.

"It's true," insisted Nick. "Whatever that book contains the plans for ... well, this was built to those plans. Come on, show me the interior."

Cathy felt a strange reluctance to reenter the dark, damp building and stood back to let Nick and Sam go first.

As Nick stepped in through the arched doorway, he felt his skin brushed by something cold and clammy; something that resembled a cold, wet, clinging spider web or, perhaps, the edge of a leathery wing. Nick looked around. There was no spider web, but instinctively he brushed his hands over his clothes and hair.

Their footsteps rang upon the stone floor as they advanced slowly forward.

"You know something," said Sam softly. "What amazes me is how it can be so dark in here when it is such a bright sunny day outside."

"And how it can be so cold in here," added Cathy, "when it's so warm outside."

"That too, Miss," nodded Sam.

There were pillars at regular intervals down the length of the building, and, at the far end, a stone altar and a stone pulpit. Nick stopped in front of the altar and stared at the carvings.

"These were in the book too," he remarked.

"Hold on," interrupted Sam. "I think I hear something. Listen."

They all listened. From the farthest, darkest corner came a sound like a shivering breath, followed by a quiet whimper.

"Nick, have you got your flashlight?" asked Cathy.

"I didn't forget it today," replied the journalist.

He unhooked it from his belt, flicked it on, and pointed it into the corner. There was a small, huddled person there, looking like a bundle of rags.

"Holly!" cried Cathy. "It's Holly!"

All three ran to the corner and knelt down beside the pathetic figure. It was indeed Holly. She was curled up tightly into a fetal position. Her clothes, face, and hands were filthy, smeared with a mixture of ash and clay. Her fists were tightly clenched. Her eyes were open and staring blankly into space.

"Holly. Holly. Are you all right? What happened to you?" asked Cathy anxiously.

There was no response.

"Holly, can you hear me?" Nick asked gently. "Are you hurt?"

Holly didn't move and did nothing to acknowledge their presence.

"She's in shock," said Nick, standing up. "Poor kid. She's probably been here all night."

"Impossible," Cathy said. "This building was searched three times last night. I was part of two of those searches. Every corner, every nook and cranny was searched. She couldn't have been here."

"Then where has she been all night?" asked Sam, puzzled.

"Let's worry about that later," suggested Nick. "In the meantime, we'd better get her back to the boat, where she can get help."

He bent forward to pick her up, but the moment he touched her, she screamed.

"Cathy, see if you can settle her down."

"There, there, Holly," Cathy said soothingly, as she gently stroked the young woman's arm. "We won't hurt you. We're here to help you. We have to take you back to the boat. You'll be safe there."

"Keep it up, Cathy," said Nick. "You keep her calm. Sam, you pick up Holly and carry her down to the beach. I'll run and tell the others."

28

The inflatable runabout—carrying the shivering wreck of Holly North, along with Captain Nagle, Sam, Nick, and Cathy—approached the stern of the *Covenant*. The occupants of the runabout were surprised and pleased to see Ingrid on the aft deck of the large boat. She was leaning heavily on an improvised walking stick ship's engineer Vic Neal had made for her from pieces of strong plastic piping.

Sam was the first to climb the ladder up the side of the boat, carrying Holly in one of his gigantic arms.

"Good grief. What on earth has happened to her? Where has she been all night?" cried Ingrid in alarm as she caught sight of the huddled figure. "Holly, Holly," she continued. "Have you been hurt? What has happened to you?"

Holly turned her head slightly in the direction of the speaker but showed no indication of recognition or comprehension.

"Take her down to her cabin," said the doctor. "Cathy and I will clean her up and see what can be done for her."

As Sam disappeared below with Holly in his arms, closely followed by Cathy and the doctor, Nagle turned to Nick. "What's your opinion? What do you think happened to Miss North?"

"I don't understand it, Captain. It's a mystery, as far as I'm concerned."

"Whatever it was," muttered Nagle, "it was clearly a most horrible experience. I have half a mind to tell Royston the expedition's canceled. If it turns out that she needs urgent medical attention, I will definitely do that."

"Royston won't thank you for it."

"After last night," said Nagle with disgust, "I couldn't give a toss what Royston thinks. He offered to pay for the repair of the glass—and I'll make sure he does—but that's hardly the point, is it?"

"It can't be allowed to go on," agreed Nick. "This adolescent feuding between Royston and Paul has got to stop."

"I agree, Nick, I absolutely agree," said the captain. "There is something rotten at the heart of this whole expedition. Something absolutely rotten."

At one end of the beach Lois and Vicky stood close together, engaged in whispered conversation.

"Paul is losing it, Lois," said Vicky, whose simpering sycophant look was replaced with a hard, cold expression. "He's falling apart."

"That's pretty obvious from the way he handled that debacle last night. He should have realized that Royston would demand the book. He should have come up with some way of delaying handing it over, rather than simply refusing. That was pretty stupid."

"What can be done about him?"

Lois thought for a while and then said, "We're going to have to forget about him. Just carry on as if he weren't here. Which, quite frankly, he might as well not be."

"And what will that mean?"

"You'll come under my command. For the time being, stay with Paul, keep on eye on him, make sure he doesn't cause any more trouble. When it's time to move, I'll give you your new strategy."

"Right. Uh oh, here's trouble now."

"Where?"

"Paul. He's climbing the path up to the cliff top. If he follows the Roystons to the old church, there'll be another row."

"You'd better follow him," commanded Lois. Vicky obeyed immediately and set off at a trot to catch up with Paul.

Dr. Sommerville walked into the main lounge, where the captain, Nick, and Sam waited for news.

"Well, how is she?" asked Nick.

"I've given her a sedative, and she's sleeping soundly. Cathy is sitting with her," replied the doctor, leaning heavily on her walking stick as she moved across to a sofa and sank down into it.

"What injuries does she have?"

"Well, that's the hard part to explain. She appears to have no serious physical injuries of any kind. A few minor cuts, scratches, and bruises—that's all. She got off more lightly than I did. At least, physically that's true."

"But mentally?" prompted the captain.

"Ah, mentally she's in a state of deep shock. It's a deeper shock than I've ever seen before. She's retreated inside herself, gone back to an infantile, or pre-infantile, state. At the moment, she's literally uncontactable. All we can do is keep her physically comfortable, make sure she gets plenty of sleep, and see whether nature can heal the soul. But something else is troubling her."

"What do you mean?" asked Nick.

"Well, as I said, she hasn't been physically *injured*—but she *has* been changed."

"In what way?"

"She has aged. Overnight she has aged dramatically. I'm not sure exactly how many years, but at least twenty, I would say. You couldn't see it through the filth until we cleaned her hair, but most of her hair has gone gray. And it's grown. So have her fingernails and toenails. Then there's the lines in her face. She has deeply etched lines today that weren't there yesterday."

"I don't understand it," said Nagle.

"Neither do I, Captain," said Ingrid, "but there it is."

"Is it a threat to her health?"

"Not as far as I can tell. Not an immediate threat, anyway. She's just older, that's all. Well, older in the body, younger—much younger—in the mind. Poor Holly."

Vicky caught up with Paul at the top of the steep trail up from the beach.

"Where are you going, Paul?" she puffed breathlessly.

"I think it's high time," replied the American, "that you and I, Vicky, took a good look at this old stone church. How can we research the island's history without studying its major artifact? So that's what I'm going to do."

"But, is this the best time, Paul?"

"What do you mean, Vicky?"

"It's just that Professor and Mrs. Royston are there right now. There might be a scene. Why don't we come back later."

"Royston doesn't own the island, and he can't stop me from looking through the church—which is exactly what I intend to do."

With that he set off, striding rapidly along the path. Vicky had to run to keep up with him. When he rounded the last group of bushes and was face to face with the building, he froze in his tracks. Vicky looked at him anxiously. His face had lost all its color—he suddenly looked pale and ill.

"Paul," she said, "are you all right?"

He didn't reply, but stared fixedly at the building.

"Paul? Paul?"

He began to walk slowly forward, like a man in a dream or a hypnotic trance. When he was less than a meter from the wall, he reached out one hand and touched the face of an ugly gargoyle. Suddenly he withdrew his hand with a cry of pain.

"Paul! Paul!" cried Vicky. "What's happened?"

As he wrapped a handkerchief around his bleeding fingers, the American historian grunted, "It bit me. It bit me."

29

Stella Royston looked slowly and lovingly around the building, before saying, "It's coming back to life, you realize that, don't you, Earl? It is coming back to life, and it is demanding blood."

She knelt down before the hideous altar and ran her fingers over the ugly carvings. "It's all real," she crooned to herself, "all real. And all filled with power. Soon, very soon, that power will fill me, and the rest will kneel before me in terror."

The professor didn't hear these words; he was halfway down the body of the church tapping the paving stones with a crowbar he had brought with him from the *Covenant*.

"A crypt," he said aloud, as he slowly walked and tapped. "There must be a crypt."

"What's that, Earl?" barked his wife, irritated at being interrupted in her reverie.

"I said there must be a crypt somewhere."

"Why must there be a crypt?"

"Because some of the ceremonies of Commander Black and his inner circle would have been too secret to hold in the church. I am certain that Black would have included a crypt in his design."

"Quite possibly. But if so, why haven't we located the entrance?"

"Obviously because it's concealed. Ah, what's this?"

"What have you found?"

"This slab here, the one that extends under the pulpit—it rings hollow when I tap it. Listen."

Tilting her head to one side, Stella listened carefully as her husband made the crowbar ring with firm blows on the stone slab at his feet.

"Now, I'll tap one of the other slabs so you can hear the difference."

This time the crowbar awoke only a dull thud from the stone.

"Yes, I can hear the difference. We'll have to pry up that slab there and see what's underneath it."

"And to do that, we'll have to move the pulpit. Come and give me a hand. If we both get behind it and push in that direction—toward the center of the building—we should be able to slide it far enough to lift the slab."

The Roystons both put their shoulders to the stone pulpit and pushed. It refused to move. After a few minutes both were red in the face with the strain.

"Stop. Stop," gasped Stella. "Let me catch my breath."

"We can't do it on our own," panted the professor. "I'll have to get help."

He began to walk toward the entrance, mopping his sweating forehead as he walked with a large, dark red handkerchief. As he paused to pocket the handkerchief and replace his spectacles, he looked up and saw two people standing in the doorway—Paul and Vicky.

"Ah, it's you two," he hissed.

"You don't own this building, you know, Royston," said Paul primly. He was calmly applying an adhesive bandage to a cut finger as he spoke. By his side, Vicky looked nervous, like a child who is expecting a loud explosion at any moment.

There was a long and heavy silence. Then a slow smile spread over Royston's face.

"Of course I don't own it, my dear chap. I would never pretend that I did. Come in, come in, by all means. Take a look around."

Paul hesitated, a puzzled expression on his face.

"I fully intend to," he said at last, and then added, reluctantly, "Thank you."

Royston stood to one side as the American and his young sec-retary entered. He followed them with his eyes as they walked slowly around the dark building, taking in its strange and eccentric features. Stella Royston stood by the altar watching the proceedings with close interest but saying nothing.

"Remarkable," said Paul quietly. "Most remarkable. And all this was built by convict labor?"

"It was indeed," replied Royston, with the smug pleasure of a proprietor. "In a little under two years."

"I've seen a lot of excellent convict stone work in my time, but this is … so … so different, I guess."

Royston chuckled. "What a simple way of expressing it," he said. Then he stood in silence, as Paul, with Vicky close behind his heels, resumed his tour of the building.

"We need photographs. And drawings of these carvings," he said at last.

"All organized," responded Royston smugly. "Mind you, it is my view that the most interesting elements of this building are yet to be uncovered."

"What do you mean?" asked the American.

"Why, the crypt, of course," said the professor.

"There is a crypt?"

"There is sure to be."

"Where is the entrance?"

"As it happens, Stella and I uncovered what we believe may be the entrance just a moment ago. Over here. Let me show you."

Having said this, Professor Royston repeated his demonstration with the crowbar.

"Well, let's get on with it," said Paul impatiently. "Move the pul-pit, pull up the slab, and let's see what's there."

"My thoughts exactly. Unfortunately, the pulpit is too heavy for Stella and me to move on our own. We had just given up trying at the moment you arrived."

"Well, let's all four of us try," said Paul. "Come on. All four shoulders should be able to move it."

"Excellent idea," cried the professor. "Come along, Stella my love. And you too, Vicky. Here beside Dr. Marshall and me. Let's all heave together."

While the others put their shoulders to the stone and took the weight, Stella quietly stepped back a pace. This was not work, she decided, for someone like her. The other three grunted and strained, and, as they did so, the stone pulpit began to move.

"It's coming," grunted Paul. "Push harder."

All three were red in the face, and their muscles were taut, but slowly the heavy pulpit was sliding across the floor, with the sound of stone grinding on stone.

"There," puffed Royston at last. "That's far enough. We should be able to get at the slab underneath now."

"Yes, it's clear, my love," said Stella, in a quiet, calm voice. "Get your crowbar now, and lift the slab."

"Give me a minute to catch my breath, my dear," complained Royston. But he was so excited that he already had the crowbar in his hand.

"Here, I'll do that," said Paul. "I'm younger and fitter than you."

A red-faced Royston, still trying to catch his breath, didn't argue but handed the crowbar to the American.

Nick and Sam walked side by side, pushing their way through the long grasses and low, scrubby bushes of Cavendish Island.

"Are we going in the right direction?" asked Nick. "I'm not the world's best navigator, and I don't have a great sense of direction."

"I do," said Sam with a huge grin. "This way, two hundred meters."

"If you say so."

They pushed on, Sam leading the way. Nick was carrying Sam's shotgun under his arm, both barrels pointed safely at the ground.

Two hundred meters later they broke through a low barrier of tough, thorny bushes and found themselves standing on the edge of the swamp, or lake, that had once been the island's stone quarry.

"I'll never doubt you again, Sam." Nick smiled as he handed Sam the shotgun and took the machete in exchange.

The surface of the water in front of them, dense with its covering of weeds, was silent and unmoving. For some time they stood in the still, mid-morning heat, watching the water, looking for some sign of the presence that lurked beneath its surface. Sam rested his gun in the crook of his arm, ready to raise it to his shoulder at the first sign of movement.

"Let's walk around the edge," suggested Nick. "We might see more from the other side."

"Good idea," agreed Sam.

In silence they made their way slowly around the edge of the swamp. Several times they had to pause while Nick hacked away at obstructing bushes. About halfway around, the journalist stopped and pointed ahead with the machete.

"Look," he said.

"Where?"

"Right there. Just ahead of us. Look at that trail in the grass."

Sam stepped closer and looked over Nick's shoulder. Two meters away was a flattened area of grass, as if some large animal had moved through it recently.

"Look at this," cried Stella. "Here, where the pulpit was standing, a corner of the slab is chipped away. You should be able to get your crowbar into that corner and lever it up."

"I'll try," said Paul. "Stand back."

Paul's face was bright red, and beads of sweat were standing out on his forehead. Finally, after much effort he let go of the crowbar and stood back.

"That slab," he puffed, "is either very heavy, or else it's jammed into place somehow." Vicky hurried up to his side and offered him a tissue. He accepted it without a word of thanks and wiped the sweat off his face.

Slowly the American walked around the slab, examining it from all sides.

"I don't understand it," he said at length. "It should move. It doesn't look to be that thick. Maybe if we both put our weight onto the crowbar, Royston?"

"Certainly, my dear fellow," said Royston agreeably. "Let's try together."

The two men settled into place over the crowbar, then both pushed as hard as they could. There was not the slightest sign of movement from the stone slab.

"Perhaps you need a longer crowbar," suggested Vicky. "You know, more leverage."

"What we need," said Stella, "is that big Tongan man—that Fangatofa, or whatever his name is—a man with some real muscles."

The grass was simply flattened, as if a great weight had been pulled over it, making a trail almost a meter wide that led from the water's edge toward the center of the island.

Nick knelt down and ran his hand over the flattened grass. Despite the heat of the day, it was still damp. But not just damp with water from the swamp; it was covered in some kind of thick slime.

He stood up and looked at his hand in disgust, then washed it in the swamp water and wiped it on a thick clump of dry grass.

"My guess is that it's been here fairly recently," he said.

"Whatever it is," added Sam.

"Have you ever seen a trail like this before?"

Sam was silent and thoughtful for a long time. Finally he said,

"I once saw trail made by a python. Flat grass it was, about ten centimeters across. But this, no python made this."

"So, something that moves like a snake but is about a meter across," said Nick thoughtfully. "There is *nothing* like that."

"That's what worries me."

"Well, are you game?"

"I'm game. I have the shotgun, Nick. I'll lead the way."

The sun was beating down relentlessly, but it was not just heat that caused the big drops of sweat to trickle down their foreheads as they followed the trail of slimy, flattened grass.

Both men were tense, moving forward in a half-crouching position. Sam nursed the shotgun—both hammers cocked, and his finger resting lightly inside the trigger guard. Nick held the handle of the machete firmly in his right hand with the blade slightly raised, ready to use.

The trail didn't follow a straight path, but weaved sinuously around, confusingly changing directions every ten meters or so.

"Which way are we heading now?" asked Nick. He spoke in a whisper, although why he was whispering he couldn't be sure.

"Toward the church," replied Sam also in a whisper.

The trail stayed always among the long grasses, weaving and twisting to avoid the short, thorny bushes that studded the island landscape. By keeping an eye on the sun, Nick calculated that the trail was turning around again, and heading in another direction.

"Which way now?" he asked.

"Back to the swamp," whispered Sam.

Nick could feel his shirt sticking to his back, soaked with sweat. And ahead of him he could see the same kind of dampness staining Sam's shirt.

As the trail curved back toward the creature's lair, back toward the swamp, Nick and Sam walked more slowly, more cautiously, and in complete silence. After ten minutes Sam stopped and cocked his head to one side as if listening. Then he turned back to Nick and tapped his ear, as if to say, "Can you hear it?"

Nick listened carefully. At first he could hear nothing. Then he heard it too: a faint, distant sliding or slithering noise of a heavy weight being dragged through the grass. Nick looked down and realized that the slime that covered the flattened grass beneath their feet was fresher and wetter.

Sam turned back toward their quarry and resumed his cautious forward progress. Nick made a few practice swings with the machete as he followed in Sam's footsteps.

The curves in the trail were sharper now, and the grass was almost two meters high. Nick and Sam felt as though they were walking down a twisting, turning, treacherous green tunnel.

Suddenly, from not far ahead of them, came the sound of a loud splash, and Sam broke into a run.

A moment later the two men were standing on the edge of the swamp, its surface a mass of ripples, causing small waves to break at their feet.

"We've missed it," said Sam.

Nick walked a couple of meters around the edge of the water, peering down into its dark, impenetrable depths.

"It's back in its lair," he agreed.

At that moment the floating weed began to lift and move. Both men waited, muscles tense. Then, just for a moment, there was a glimpse of a broad, rounded, shining back—and Sam pulled the trigger. Both barrels fired in a loud, sharp explosion. The back reared. Then it sank. Huge bubbles broke the surface of the swamp.

"Have you killed it?"

In reply Sam shrugged his shoulders, but at the same time he reloaded both barrels of the shotgun.

For a long time the two of them stood there watching the now calm, flat surface of the swamp. At last they decided there was nothing more to be done for the moment and turned to go. As they did so, from behind them came the sound of a loud splash and a cry that sounded like a creature in pain.

Nick whirled around and caught a glimpse of something, he

wasn't sure what, plunging back under the water. The cry, the scream of pain, echoed in his ears.

"Did you see it?" he asked Sam.

"No, boss," said the deckhand. "Afraid not."

"At least we know you hit it."

"But I didn't kill it. And some animals are more dangerous when wounded."

30

The colonel's office was in a basement. The concrete walls were painted light battleship gray, and all the furniture was standard military issue—in dark battleship gray. Dressed in uniform, the colonel was seated behind his desk with a cigar clamped between his teeth when the buzzer on his desk sounded.

He looked up at the monitor to see who was waiting in the corridor. He recognized the face and pressed the release button that opened his office door. A young, dark-haired man clad in military garb stepped inside, closing the door as he did so.

"Have a seat, Captain," said the colonel. "Would you like a cigar?"

"No thank you, sir."

"Have you been following the progress of the Cavendish Island affair?"

"As you instructed, sir, I have been reading the intercepted signals."

"And what have you noticed?"

"The journalist is the problem, sir. Unfortunately, he has stumbled onto the caves, and he apparently intends to explore them."

"Exactly. You understand that this must not happen. Or, if it does, the journalist must die."

"Yes, sir."

"There's another problem that you aren't aware of yet."

"Sir?"

"There's another radio on the island. Apart from the ship's radio, that is. And someone is using it to send coded signals."

"Who? Why?"

"We have no idea."

"The signals haven't been decoded yet?"

"No. And they probably won't be. They are electronically coded, and without a copy of the master chip used in the transmitter, it would take weeks, perhaps months, to crack the code."

"Do we know what organization is behind this second signal source?"

"No, we don't, Captain. That's one of the things you'll have to find out."

"I'm going in then?"

"I think we have no option now but to place you on the field. We need a rapid insertion, so we'll employ Plan Alpha. You are familiar with the region, I believe?"

"Yes, sir. I was part of the Operation Rainbow Warrior field team."

"Ah, yes. Of course."

"What about backup?"

"One small, fast patrol boat will also be dispatched to the general region. It will be available for you to call in if, and when, you need it."

"When do I start?"

"Immediately."

As the inflatable runabout touched the side of the *Covenant,* Captain Nagle grabbed the ladder and hung on. Toby cut the motor and tied up, and then he and the captain climbed up to the deck.

Nagle made his way to the wheelhouse, where he found Vic leaning back in the navigator's chair, reading a book.

"How's everything, Vic?"

"Fine, Captain. No problems."

"Good. What's the weather doing?"

"A low-pressure system is building up north of Noumea. We'll need to keep an eye on it to make sure it doesn't turn into a tropical cyclone and then decide to head in our direction."

"Make that your responsibility, Vic."

"Aye, Captain."

Nagle left the wheelhouse and made his way below decks.

He tapped gently on the door of Holly North's cabin and entered. Ingrid was sitting in a chair beside the bed, wiping her patient's forehead with a damp cloth.

"How is she?" asked the captain.

"No improvement," replied the doctor.

"What can be done for her?"

"Nothing. At least there's nothing I can do, apart from keeping her settled and resting. Perhaps at one of the big city hospitals they could do something. But even then ..." She shrugged.

"You see, Doctor," said Nagle, sitting down on the end of the bed, "the decision I am facing is this: should we stay here at the island, or should I take responsibility for canceling the whole expedition?"

Paul Marshall and Professor Royston's futile attempts to remove the slab were interrupted by Vicky, "Oh, that's horrible. It's disgusting."

"What is?" asked Stella sharply.

"That smell."

"I can't smell anything."

"Come over here, Mrs. Royston. The smell is coming from underneath this slab we were trying to remove. See, there's a piece missing where the corner is chipped."

"Of course there's a piece missing," snapped Stella impatiently. "That's where the men have been trying to insert the crowbar to lever it up."

"Well, that's where the smell is coming from. Come closer, and you'll be able to smell it for yourself."

Reluctantly Stella walked over to Vicky's side and bowed her head to smell whatever aroma might be rising from floor level. She sniffed delicately, and then her face contorted.

"The child is right. Come over here, Earl."

Her husband obeyed her command, and he too stepped back in disgust. Paul repeated the experiment with the same results.

"Well," drawled the American, "I don't think much of your crypt, Royston. You have my permission to explore it on your own. I certainly won't be going down there. Come along, Vicky. We are leaving these two to enjoy the sort of odor that suits them so well."

With that, he stalked out of the building with Vicky hurrying behind him.

"What an odious man," snarled Royston. "I think we should leave him stranded on the island when the *Covenant* departs."

"That won't be necessary, my dear," purred his wife.

"What do you mean?"

"Once I have the power, he will be completely under my command. He will be able to do nothing except whimper for mercy and feel the lash of terror I can inflict."

Royston looked at his wife cautiously, a flicker of fear in his eyes. Eventually he spoke. "Well, Stella my dear, for that to happen we must first complete the reactivation of this building. Or, perhaps I should say, this power source. And then, in order for the transfer to occur, we must conduct the ceremony, fully and properly, with a satisfactory sacrifice."

The scraping of sandals on the stone floor alerted the Roystons to the arrival of a newcomer in the building. They abruptly broke off their conversation and looked up. Lois was standing in the doorway.

"At last," snapped the professor, a note of genuine anger in his voice. "Where have you been all morning? There's work to be done."

"I'm sorry, Professor. When Holly was found—"

"Never mind about Holly North. Forget about her. You have work to do, and you should have been here."

"Yes, Professor."

"And where is Miss Samson? Why have neither of my assistants been here this morning?"

"Cathy is back on the boat. I believe she is helping Dr. Sommerville take care of Holly."

"How dare she. She was not hired as a nursemaid to look after foolish young women. She works for me. She should be here."

This tirade was interrupted by Stella's voice.

"Earl. Come here. My dress is caught."

Unlike the younger women, who wore jeans, Stella was wearing a long peasant frock that swept the floor. She was standing over the slab they had been trying to move, and the edge of her dress appeared to be caught in the jagged hole in the corner of the slab.

"I've been trying to pull it free," she said in exasperation, tugging again at the dress as she spoke, "but it seems to be caught fast."

"I'm coming, dear," said her husband as he hurried to her side. "Here, leave it to me. I'll work it free."

Professor Royston knelt down on the stone, grasped the fabric firmly in his right hand, and worked it back and forth.

"It's caught on something underneath the slab," he grunted.

For another minute or two he wrestled with it and then said, "It's being held fast."

"This situation calls for a woman's touch," volunteered Lois. "Here. Let me."

"Just get on with it, you two," snapped Stella, "instead of twittering at each other. Do you think I enjoy standing here, stuck fast?"

Lois got down on her hands and knees and began tugging and twisting the fabric, trying hard at the same time not to tear it.

"Get a move on," said Stella imperiously.

"I'm doing my best, Mrs. Royston," replied Lois, through gritted teeth. "But it's just no use. It won't come free. It's held fast."

"I'm going to have to tear it loose, my love. There is no alternative," said the professor.

"All right then, do it," sighed his wife. "Get on with it."

Professor Royston knelt down once again, got a firm grip on

the fabric, and with a savage tug, tore it free. The sound of ripping fabric echoed around the building.

"Just look at that torn edge," said Lois, incredulously.

Royston looked where his young assistant was pointing: The torn edge of the fabric was covered with black, evil-smelling slime.

"Now look what you've done," snapped Stella. "This thing is ruined. I don't know what that disgusting stuff is, but I'm not wearing this dress any longer."

"I'm sorry, my dear. But it really wasn't my fault."

"I'm not interested in pathetic excuses. I'm going back to the boat to change."

The surface of the swamp was absolutely still beneath the baking heat of the tropical sun as Nick and Sam stood up to leave.

"I guess there's no point in hanging around," said Nick. "Let's get back to the others. At least we can warn them there is something in here."

The big Tongan nodded his head, moving off down the trail, once again taking the lead.

"Hold on, Sam," said Nick. "I'd like to go back by the old convict buildings. It's no farther that way, and I'd like to have another look. After all, I am supposed to be writing feature articles about this place."

"If you say so, boss," said Sam, as he turned around and changed direction slightly.

For the next few minutes they hacked their way through the low undergrowth until they found the path they and the others had cut the day before. From there on, the going was easier. It was now late in the morning, the sun was high in the sky, and the heat and humidity were sweltering.

Eventually they came to the site where the convict buildings had once stood. Here the undergrowth was less dense. Partly because of the extensive clearing the convicts had done in their time, but mainly because the jumbled mess of stone foundations and rotting floorboards prevented thick growth.

"Now, over there is where the commandant's house stood," mused Nick, mopping his face with a handkerchief. "And that's what we looked at yesterday. So that must mean that this is where the barracks stood. Let's prowl around here, Sam, and see what we can turn up."

"Shouldn't the professor be doing this?"

"If we find anything, we'll pass it on to him," replied Nick with a shrug of his shoulders. "Come on, help me look."

Cathy sat beside Holly as she slept. Every so often she reached over and wiped the beads of perspiration from the photographer's troubled face. The temperature in the tiny cabin was stifling, but the huddled figure on the bed was shivering, as if she was terribly cold. From time to time she moaned aloud in her sleep.

Cathy stroked the young woman's forehead gently and said, "There, there. It's all right now, Holly. You're back on the boat. You're quite safe. Nothing can happen to you here."

The photographer pulled back from Cathy's touch and began to whimper and gasp for breath. Suddenly she sat bolt upright in bed, her eyes still tightly closed, but her face titled upward, as though staring at something only she could see. She raised her hands as though trying to push away something horrible that was approaching her. Then with a loud cry she fell back onto the bed.

Cathy picked up the damp washcloth and began wiping Holly's fevered brow again. The photographer's lips were moving, and, very faintly, she was starting to speak.

Ingrid entered the cabin and rushed to Holly's side.

"I heard Holly cry out," she said. "How is she?"

"She seems to be having nightmares of some sort," replied Cathy. "And look at her lips moving. I think she's trying to speak."

"That would be excellent," said the doctor. Cathy moved back from the bed to let the doctor come closer. "If only she would start to speak again, that might be a sign that she is beginning to recover."

Holly's lips were definitely moving in a regular pattern, but whatever she was saying was quieter than a whisper, and neither Cathy nor the doctor could make out a single word.

"Is she just talking in her sleep?" asked Cathy.

"Even that is better than losing the capacity for speech entirely," said Ingrid.

Suddenly all the breath and life seemed to drain out of Holly's body. As she sank back into her pillow, she began to whisper clearly: "… keeper of the keys … bringer of fire … night roamer … tail-swallower …" And then her whispers faded away to nothing.

"How is she?" asked Cathy anxiously.

Ingrid didn't reply immediately, but listened to Holly's heartbeat and then checked her blood pressure.

"She seems to have fallen into a deep sleep now," said the doctor at last.

"What were those words she was saying?" asked Cathy.

"Who can tell?" Ingrid mused. "Perhaps the memory of a childhood nightmare."

Nick and Sam walked slowly over the site of the troops' barracks, kicking over objects with the toes of their boots and occasionally picking up some small thing to examine.

At one point Nick stepped on some rotten, ancient floorboards, which gave away underneath him. He fell ten centimeters to the ground beneath. As he recovered his balance, he began to pull away at some of the rotted boards with his hands.

"You okay, Nick?" asked Sam.

"Fine."

"You find anything?"

"So far only a couple of empty rum bottles."

"Then I say we go back. It's nearly lunch time, and I'm hungry."

"Hang on, there's something here."

"Where?" asked Sam.

"Behind these rotten floorboards, separate from the rest. As though someone once had a secret place, a hiding place, under the floor of the barracks."

Nick stood up and kicked at the boards with the toe of his boots. The aged wood split under the blow and broke apart to reveal a small compartment, lined on all sides by pieces of wood.

"Anything in it?" asked Sam.

"I'm just checking," replied Nick as he got down on his hands and knees and reached in among the pieces of crumbling wood. "I just hope there are no spiders in there, waiting to nip my fingers."

"I hate spiders," said Sam with a shudder.

"I've got something," gasped Nick as his fingers closed around a rectangular object. "It's a book," he said, pulling it out into the daylight.

Standing up, Nick brushed the dust off his precious find and opened the cover.

"Look at this, Sam. It's someone's notebook or diary."

"Can you read it?"

"The ink has faded, but it's still legible."

"Is there a name on it? Do you know who it belonged to?"

"There is a name, on the front page here. It's old-fashioned copperplate handwriting, but I think I can make it out. It says, 'Lieutenant Edmund McDermott, officer of the New South Wales Corps.' How about that, Sam?"

31

Lois Myles and Professor Royston were kneeling on the cold stone floor of the old church. In front of them was the large stone slab.

"Well, I want to know what's underneath, Miss Myles, as much as you do," said the professor, "but how do you suggest we find out?"

"You've obviously tried to move it?"

"Obviously. It will take a long crowbar from the boat and all the strength of that Tongan deckhand to lift this slab."

"Have you tried shining a flashlight through this chipped corner?"

"The hole is too small. You'd never see anything," snapped Royston.

"I'd still like to try."

"Very well. Here's my flashlight."

Lois held the flashlight just above the hole, and then tried to peer in, her cheek brushing against the cold stone as she did so.

"Oh, there's a horrible odor down here," she exclaimed.

"We had already noticed that, Miss Myles. So far, you have discovered nothing new."

"I can't actually see anything … so far …" said Lois. She knew Royston well, and never responded to his sarcasm. "Hold on. There's a gleam of something. No, it's gone. Now, there's nothing. But that's very odd."

"What's odd?" asked Royston impatiently.

"It's impossible I know, but …"

"But, what, Miss Myles?"

"I could have sworn I saw a movement down there."

"A movement?"

"That's what I thought."

"Ridiculous. Impossible," blustered Royston, in a tone that nonetheless held a hint of uncertainty.

Lois sat back on her haunches and tore a page out of her notebook. She rolled it into a narrow tube and poked the end of it into the hole. For a moment she moved it about, probing this way and that, and then the expression of curiosity on her face changed to one of horror.

"What's happened?" snapped Royston.

"Something's got ahold of it," gasped Lois, with an odd mixture of amazement and alarm.

"Pull," said the professor. "Pull the piece of paper back. See if it hangs on."

For a second Lois glanced at Royston, aware that somehow this was less of a surprise to him than it was to her. Then she pulled. She gave the paper a sharp tug, and it immediately ripped free. She held up the torn end.

"Look at that," she said unnecessarily. The ragged edge of the paper was black, smeared with a thick, viscous substance.

"Don't touch that stuff," warned Royston.

"I wasn't intending to," replied Lois.

"We don't have the resources with us to do a chemical analysis," murmured the professor, "which is unfortunate. But let's seal that piece of paper in a plastic specimen envelope, and perhaps we can get it tested when we get back."

A voice from the doorway of the building called, "We're on our way back to the boat for lunch. Are you coming with us?"

Lois and the Professor rose from their crouched positions on the stone floor and turned toward the doorway, where Nick and Sam stood.

"Come and have a look at this," called Lois in response. As Nick and Sam approached, she told them about their experience.

"How could there possibly be something under there?" asked Nick.

"That's what we want to find out," replied Lois.

Sam knelt down beside the stone slab and slowly pushed the barrels of his shotgun through the hole in the open corner.

"Don't do that!" called Lois, but she was too late.

Sam tried to pull the gun back out, but it wouldn't come.

"Whatever's down there has ahold of my gun," grunted Sam.

"Does it have a strong grip?" asked Royston, his face lit up with interest and curiosity. By way of reply Sam gave a hard tug, but was unable to pull the gun free.

"Now, this is most interesting," continued Royston, rubbing his chin thoughtfully. "Most interesting indeed."

"It's not interesting to me," snarled Sam. "Whatever it is, it's got my gun." And with those words he cocked both hammers. Royston opened his mouth to speak, but before he could utter a syllable, Sam had pulled both triggers.

The massive explosion of the shotgun rolled and echoed around the tiny church. Nick raised his hands to his ears, but too late. Lois squeezed her eyes tightly closed. And with the blast of the gun came a scream, a wild, animal scream of agony—a death scream.

As the last echo of the blast and the scream died away, Sam tried again to pull the shotgun out of the hole in the floor slab—and it came free easily.

"You got a crowbar?" he asked.

Shaking his head to clear his ringing ears, Royston pointed at the crowbar lying on the stone floor a few meters away. Sam picked it up, inserted it in the hole, and applied pressure. The stone slab lifted easily, and he levered it to one side. As it shifted, the smell became overwhelming.

Nick, always the curious journalist, clamped a handkerchief over his nose and mouth and approached the open hole. He picked up the flashlight Lois had dropped and shined it into the opening.

The hole went straight down, the sides smooth like a well. Nick pointed the beam at the bottom of the well. There was some sort of black slime down there. Nick became aware that he had been joined by Royston, Lois, and Sam. As they watched, a large, viscous bubble broke the surface of the slime. And then, just for a moment, there was something else, a hand or a claw, that appeared above the surface for a second, and then disappeared again.

Then there was nothing. Nothing but the pit of slime and the unbearable, overpowering stench.

"Close it up again," gasped Royston. "Get a move on, man! Get that slab back in place. Shut it up again!"

Sam glanced at Royston, then grabbed the crowbar and levered the slab back into place. The stench began to fade, but much of it remained.

"Move the stone pulpit back," commanded Royston. "It was originally over the hole. Push it back where it was, so it covers the hole again."

Gasping for breath in the foul air, Nick and Sam did as the professor asked. Then all four of them made for the doorway of the church and the fresh air outside.

"Ah, I've never smelled anything so good," said Nick, as he walked toward the cliff top and inhaled lungfuls of fresh sea air.

"What was it, Professor?" asked Lois. "What was in there?"

"I don't know," replied Royston, almost too quickly. Lois looked at him suspiciously, certain that he had some idea of what it was they had just encountered.

"Some … some island creature, perhaps. I really can't imagine," continued Royston, unconvincingly.

"I don't care what it was," said Sam, as he wiped the barrel of his gun on the thick, dry grass. "I just want to get back to the boat and have lunch."

32

It was midday when Frank Gordon approached the front door of the modest suburban cottage and raised his hand to knock. Then he hesitated. He almost turned and walked away, but then he told himself, "Well, I've come this far," and knocked on the door.

A minute later the door was opened by W. H. Muir.

"Ah, good morning Mr. Gordon. You're very prompt, I see. An admirable trait. Come in, come in."

As Frank walked down the hallway, he noticed that this house didn't smell of stale meals and lingering memories as so many old peoples' houses seemed to. A fresh breeze blew through an open window, and the only smell was the aroma of freshly percolating coffee that wafted in from the kitchen.

"Please have a seat, make yourself comfortable," said Muir when they reached the living room. "I've just put on the coffee, would you like some?"

A moment later Frank was nursing a large mug filled with strong, black coffee. "Now," he said, "can you tell me what is going on at Cavendish Island?"

"Let me take you back one or two steps before that, if I may," said Muir, choosing his words carefully. He ran a gnarled old hand over his head, smoothing down the few wispy white hairs. "Mr. Gordon, has it ever struck you, as a newspaper editor, that this world is a battleground between the forces of good and the forces of evil, between light and darkness?"

"Sure. The good guys and the bad guys. If it wasn't like that, we'd have no news to print."

"But from what you told me earlier, I take it that you reject the possibility of there being a supernatural element in this conflict."

"I think this country is going to the dogs. In fact, the whole western world is going to the dogs. I'm sure the world was a better place when I was a kid than it is now. But maybe that just means I'm getting older. And even if my judgment is right, all that means is that human beings are sucking it up and going on."

"Consider the possibility that Satan attempts to exert his polluting influence on all aspects of social life and culture. When biblical ethics are portrayed negatively, or even sneered at, Satan has succeeded in spreading his evil influence a little wider. For instance, when pilfering from one's employer is rationalized, Satan has a victory. When revenge is regarded as the best response to someone who harms us, Satan has succeeded in twisting our moral conscience. In short, Satan can pervert society, morality, traditions and customs. In addition, Satan can work on an individual's inclination toward evil. If a person is naturally inclined toward anger and bitterness, in some way an evil spirit may directly encourage that attitude. If the malice continues and intensifies, demonic involvement in the person's life may become more direct."

"I still don't believe in these evil spirits of yours."

"Which is exactly what they intend, and it pleases them a great deal."

"What do you mean?"

"Their policy, at this point in history, appears to be to conceal themselves. Of course, this has not always been so. But, for the moment, they appear to be playing on the fact that devils are predominantly *comic* figures in the modern imagination. You know the sort of thing: figures in red tights with horns and tails. I'm sure their strategy is to suggest that since the current generation cannot believe in *that distorted image of the devil,* they therefore cannot believe in Satan."

For a long time Frank stared into his almost empty coffee cup. Finally he spoke, without raising his eyes.

"Supposing—just supposing—that what you have been telling me is true. Supposing that behind every horrible and bleak headline there are ... forces—"

"Beings," interrupted Muir. "Spirits who do not wish us well."

"Okay. Supposing—just for the sake of argument—that what you say is true, then how does Cavendish Island come into it?"

"Because of its history." Muir took a deep breath and continued, "Throughout human history there have been people who have not only believed in demons, but who have taken an unhealthy interest in them."

"Satanists?"

"Certainly some of them have called themselves Satanists. I imagine they believed they could make contact with these supernatural powers and harness them for their own use. A foolish belief. It was always they who became the slaves of the powers, not the other way around."

"And there's a history of this kind of thing on Cavendish Island?"

"There is. I sent your reporter a copy of an old booklet, published in Sydney in 1893, called 'The Dark History of the Secret Coven.' You may recall that I mentioned it in my first letter to you."

"I remember."

"According to that booklet, on the first fleet that came to Australia to establish the convict colony of New South Wales was a group of spiritualists. Some of them were officers, and some were convicts. The group was composed of both men and women. There were thirteen of them in all."

"Thirteen. A coven?"

"They called themselves the Secret Coven. They did their best to hide their activities and cover their tracks. But their evil influence and their bestial activities could not be entirely disguised. There are records suggesting that the first Christian minister in the colony,

Richard Johnson, knew of them and fought a bitter struggle against them. In retaliation, they burned down his church. His replacement, Samuel Marsden, knew the identity of some of these evil people and opposed their appointment to public office. For this he was called a bigot and clashed with Governor Lachlan Macquarie, who was completely duped by the smiling faces that concealed black hearts."

"What did they do?"

"Well, of course they conducted their secret rituals. Up to and including, so we are told, human sacrifice. They took pleasure in corrupting and degrading others. They sought, sometimes with success, to obtain positions of power and influence so that they could effect public policy."

"Why does all this history matter today?" asked Frank with a puzzled expression on his face.

"Because," said Muir, leaning forward in his chair, "because they still exist."

"Two hundred years later? Impossible."

"Not the same individuals, you understand, but the same secret organization. As one member died or, perhaps, became old and incapacitated, he or she was replaced by another. Each new recruit was carefully selected and indoctrinated and trained. In this way the Secret Coven is still alive—alive and active up to this very minute, Mr. Gordon."

"Harmless crackpots, that's all they are. They can't conduct human sacrifices nowadays. Perhaps in the early days with runaway convicts and general lawlessness they could do strange things like that, but not today."

"Nevertheless, they are dangerous. Some of the present members are lineal descendants of the first group."

"Such as?"

"Well, the commandant of the Cavendish Island penal colony, Commander Godfrey Black, was a member of the Secret Coven in his day. He had a child by his own daughter, a poor young woman by the name of Jessica. She, by the way, died in a lunatic asylum. One of the leaders of the expedition to Cavendish Island is a direct descendant of that child."

"Not Professor Royston?"

"No. His wife."

"How do you come to know so much?"

"There have been small groups of Christians over the years who have done their best to keep track of the activities of this group and to restrict and restrain them—by the power of prayer. It was out of this activity that 'The Dark History of the Secret Coven' was published. It is dangerous work. I am certain that, over the years, the coven has arranged for the murders of a number of its enemies."

"And Cavendish Island?"

"Commandant Black erected a building, modeled on a church but built for exactly the opposite purpose. The coven would probably call it a black chapel, I suspect. And I very much fear that the present expedition is just an excuse for members of the Secret Coven to go to the island, uncover the secrets of the building, and try to employ them for their own evil purposes."

"Look, I want to believe you, Mr. Muir, if only I could. But I'm a hardheaded newspaperman. This story of yours takes me outside of the categories I am used to."

"Perhaps to understand what is really going on, you need to learn to think outside of your established categories."

"Perhaps," Frank spoke the word reluctantly. "But even if everything you tell me is true, there is nothing that can be done about it."

"There is much that can be done. For a start, there is prayer."

Frank didn't exactly snort, but he made a snuffling noise that he tried to smother. And the expression on his face made it clear that he was unimpressed by prayer.

Muir ignored this response and continued, "Some friends of mine are meeting with me regularly to pray about this matter, and to pray especially for the safety of your Nick Hamilton. By the power of prayer a mantle of safety, a mantle of protection, can be cast over Mr. Hamilton and those close to him. Remember, Mr. Gordon, 'More things are wrought by prayer than this world dreams of.'"

"But what can I do?"

"Keep in close contact with Mr. Hamilton. Speak to him every day if you can. And at the first sign of trouble, try to encourage the members of the expedition to abandon their plans and return to Australia."

33

Nick, Sam, Lois, and Professor Royston stood side by side on the narrow beach. Sam raised his large right arm and waved vigorously. Toby, standing on the aft deck of the *Covenant,* saw the gesture and waved back. Then he climbed down the swinging ladder to the inflatable runabout, started the outboard motor, and began the run in to the beach.

"I'm going to check on Dr. Marshall and Miss Shaw," said Nick, walking down the beach toward the tent that stood some fifty meters away. Royston scowled but said nothing.

When Nick reached the tent, he lifted the flap and called out, "Anyone at home?" The tent was empty. Nick rejoined the others.

"There's no one there," he reported.

"Perhaps they've wandered off and got lost," sneered Royston.

"Or perhaps Captain Nagle has taken them on board to have lunch with us," said Sam, whose attention now seemed to be totally focused on food.

At that moment Lois tugged Nick's sleeve and asked, "Can you hear that?"

"All I can hear is the outboard motor of the runabout," he replied.

"No. Listen more carefully," insisted Lois.

Nick cocked his head to one side and listened. "You're right, there is something," he said.

"Up there," said Lois, shading her eyes with one hand and pointing up into the sky with another.

Nick followed the line of her gaze and saw a small black speck against the brilliant blue sky.

"It's an airplane," said Sam, squinting into the sky.

"What in the world is it doing here?" asked Royston crossly. "The last thing we want is visitors."

"I thought this island never had any visitors," said Lois.

"So did I," grumbled Royston.

The aircraft grew closer and lower. Toby in the runabout had also seen the plane and had throttled back his engine and was staring up at it.

"It's in trouble," said Nick.

"What do you mean?" asked Lois.

"Listen carefully. That engine is not running smoothly. It keeps cutting out."

"You're right, Nick," said Sam. "That pilot is in big trouble."

"This is the last thing we need," mumbled Royston to himself.

The aircraft was low enough then to be seen clearly, and the sound of its engine had become even more intermittent. Nick recognized it as a light, single-engine aircraft that would usually be used for short hauls.

"It's a long way from anywhere," he remarked.

By that time the aircraft was right over their heads, circling the island, its engine alternately roaring, coughing, and spluttering. At one moment it was thundering over the beach, directly above them, the next it was struggling to gain height to rise above the steep cliffs, and then circling back out over the water. Then the aircraft's engine stopped entirely.

The silence that followed was almost deafening. The plane looked to be a long way out to sea when the engine cut out. They saw the pilot bank steeply, then turn back toward the bay. Toby had cut his outboard motor, and his gaze was glued on the stricken airplane.

It slowly got bigger as it glided toward them, but at the same time it was losing height alarmingly. In the silence Nick imagined he could hear the screaming of the airstream over the wings. He prayed that the plane would have enough height to get the pilot back to the bay and relative safety before it came down in the drink.

It was larger now, its red and white markings standing out clearly. As it approached the bay, it appeared to be barely skimming the tops of the waves. The undercarriage was still up, Nick noticed, presumably to give the aircraft better lift and a few more meters before it came down. It passed the northern headland well below the cliff tops and turned toward the beach.

Then it touched the water for the first time. *It is like a skipping stone*, Nick thought. It touched, splashed, bounced, touched again, splashed and bounced again, then touched a third time. This time it came to a halt, sitting on the surface of the water, riding up and down with the small waves.

Toby started the outboard motor and turned the runabout toward the stricken aircraft. It seemed to sit on the surface for less than a minute, and then, with alarming speed, it started taking on water and sinking.

As the wings disappeared below the surface, a man could be seen scrambling out of the cabin. He was wearing a flotation jacket and carrying a canvas bag. He jumped into the water, and a moment later the cabin of the aircraft disappeared beneath the waves.

For a few minutes he was a brightly colored dot that could be glimpsed occasionally as the waves rose and fell, and then Toby was beside him, pulling him into the runabout, and heading back toward the *Covenant.*

"He's forgotten about us," complained Lois.

"No he hasn't," said Sam. "He'll take the pilot to the boat and them come back for us."

"I wonder where the pilot is from," said Nick. "Maybe there's a story in this."

"I wonder who he is," added Lois.

"As long as he is prepared to wait at Cavendish Island until we have finished our work," said Royston, "it doesn't matter who he is or where he's from."

"Maybe he's someone important," speculated Sam. "If so, we may have to raise anchor and take him somewhere."

"I don't care who he is, we are not doing that!" snapped Royston. "This expedition is not leaving this island until its work is done. Not for anyone."

34

There were only four men seated at the long table in the dark, wood-paneled boardroom. Before them were the remains of a seafood platter.

"Has there been any further contact from the island?" asked a large, solidly built man with the flattened nose and ears of a professional boxer as he reached for the whiskey decanter.

"There was another signal this morning," replied the slim, expensively dressed man at the head of the table, "but it hasn't been decoded yet."

"When do we make our move?"

"Not yet. Perhaps not for a long while yet."

"Why not?"

"Because my plan is to let our enemies do much of the work for us first. Let them do all the hard work. When the power source is fully operational, then we will act and not before."

"Is that wise?"

"Are you questioning my plans?"

"No, sir. Of course not, sir," muttered the big man, averting his gaze and pouring himself another finger of whiskey to cover his embarrassment.

"You are probably thinking," said the chairman, his voice husky and sinister, "that once the power source is operational, that will give our enemies the advantage. They certainly believe that. What they don't know is how thoroughly they are surrounded and how quickly we can act."

"Does anyone on the island know the whole plan?"

"Only one man. Our other agents don't even know about the backup forces. But that is for the best. When the moment for action comes, everything will fall our way."

"Thank you for agreeing to see me, Sharon," said Robyn Reed as she set a small tape recorder on the coffee shop table between them.

"You're not going to record this, are you?" asked the nervous, pale young woman sitting opposite the journalist.

"Not if you don't want me to." Robyn slipped the recorder back into her handbag. "This is not for an article. It's just so I can brief my editor, Frank Gordon. It was Frank who asked me to speak to you."

"What does he want to know?"

"About the Crimson Circle. I don't know why, he just asked me to find out what I can by way of background and brief him."

"Tell him not to bother." Sharon's fingers trembled as she lit a cigarette. "They're not nice people. In America they sue newspapers that criticize them. And they do other things."

"What sort of other things?"

"There was a district attorney in Florida investigating them. She had a nasty car accident."

"Arranged by them?"

"I guess so. I'm not happy about talking to you, Robyn. What if they found out?"

"But you've left the order now, haven't you?"

"Yeah. Except nobody ever really leaves. They keep an eye on people. For all I know, they could be keeping an eye on me now."

"Well, let's keep this brief then. How long were you officially a member of the Order of the Crimson Circle?"

"I dunno," said Sharon, running her fingers through straight, bleached hair, "eighteen months maybe. Maybe two years. Something like that."

"And what sort of things did they do at their meetings?"

"Oh, I can't tell you that."

"Why not?" asked the journalist, taking a sip of coffee.

"I promised. I swore an oath. If I broke that, there'd be consequences."

"Well, leave out all the details. Just tell me the *type* of thing that happened, in general terms."

"New Age-type things, I guess."

"Can you be just a little bit more specific?"

"Things like … white magic, they called it. Rituals. Spells. Healing things. Power things."

"And is that what the Order of the Crimson Circle is all about? White magic?"

"Well … they used to say … I dunno if it's true … but they used to say that the inner circle … the high initiates … well, that they practice the real thing."

"The real thing?"

"Black magic. Look, I shouldn't be talking to you, I really shouldn't. Thanks for the coffee, but I gotta go now."

"Okay, Sharon. But one last question. Was that it? Just rituals? Is that all there is to the Crimson Circle?"

"That's all I know about. Apart from their electronics, of course."

"I haven't heard about that. Tell me."

"Well, there's nothing to tell really. The Circle owns an electronics factory in California. They used to talk a lot about doing research into occult science. You know, finding electronic ways of enhancing occult power. At some of the meetings they had things that looked like radios to me, but they said they were wave amplifiers—or something like that. But I really don't know anything about that side of it."

"Thanks, Sharon," said Robyn. "You've been a great help."

"Thanks again for the coffee," said Sharon as she nervously rose from the table. "Look, don't take this the wrong way, but I'd rather you didn't call me again."

As she walked briskly away, Robyn took out a notepad and began to write rapidly. The first word she wrote was "terrified."

"Ladies and gentlemen," said Captain Nagle, "I'd like you to meet Alan Marchant."

All the members of the expedition party were seated around a lunch table set up in the main lounge of the *Covenant*—even Paul and Vicky were there, at Nagle's insistence.

Since his bedraggled and severely shaken arrival in sopping wet clothes, the pilot of the crashed aircraft had been checked out by Ingrid and provided with dry clothes by the crew. Now, he accompanied Nagle up the companionway, wearing jeans and a T-shirt borrowed from Vic.

"Take a seat, old chap," said Max. "We've saved places for you and the captain. I take it you'll have a bite to eat with us?"

"Delighted," said Alan with a shy smile. He was a solidly built man in his late thirties with curly black hair.

"You're very fortunate to be alive," said Cathy.

"Very fortunate indeed, and very grateful," Alan said. "I have a few cuts and bruises, but apart from that," he shrugged his shoulders, "I have come out of the accident unharmed."

"What's that accent I hear?" asked Nick.

"French-Canadian. I'm from Quebec."

"And what do you think you were doing flying such a small aircraft so far from anywhere?" demanded Royston.

"For the past ten years it has been used by a small inter-island airfreight company. Recently it was bought by a New Zealand businessman. I was ferrying it from Noumea to Auckland."

"What went wrong?" asked Nick.

"I don't know for sure. The electronics started playing up about an hour ago, interfering with the navigational equipment and the radio. That's why I strayed off my course. You can imagine my relief when I saw the island and this vessel in the bay."

"You realize you'll have to stay here," stated Stella.

"Pardon?"

"This ship is not leaving the island for at least a month. You'll have to stay here until then."

"Of course, of course. I'm just grateful to be rescued. I don't wish to interfere with your plans. In fact, I'd be more than happy to make myself useful—as a way of saying thank you for my rescue."

"That's all right then," Stella said firmly. "Just so long as there's no nonsense about the expedition being cut short because you've turned up uninvited."

"Actually," said Captain Nagle, clearing his throat, "that's a point that I wanted to raise."

"And exactly what point is that, Captain?" asked Professor Royston.

"The question of whether it is wise for the expedition to continue. I am concerned about Miss North's condition. It shows no sign of improvement. It is uncertain that even a major hospital or special treatment would help. Nevertheless, I feel that we have no choice but to try. My intention is to weigh anchor first thing in the morning, and to ship out on the morning tide."

"You don't seem to understand the situation, Captain," said Royston fiercely. "This is not your expedition, it is mine. I will decide if we leave, and when, and no one else. And I have decided that the expedition will continue as planned. That is my decision, and it is not open for discussion."

"I'm afraid it's not quite like that, Professor," said Captain Nagle quietly. "I am the captain of this vessel. Ultimately, the safety of all my passengers rests on my shoulders. It is the law of the sea, Professor. We leave tomorrow."

Royston went purple with anger as he hissed, "I am paying for this voyage. I am in charge. If you disobey me, I will complain to the owners. I will see to it that you are sacked. I will see to it that you never command another vessel. You will obey me or pay the consequences."

"I'm sorry you feel that way. You are welcome to use the radio to speak to the owners now if you wish. I have already done so. They trust my judgment and back my decision. Accept it professor: The expedition is over."

"Captain," said Stella, a quiet hatred filling her voice, "you don't realize the importance of what you are doing or what the awful consequences will most certainly be for yourself."

"Quite right. In fact, I'm not thinking about myself at all. I am thinking about my passengers: about poor Miss North in her bunk below; about Dr. Sommerville and her broken ankle; about the report from Sam and Nick that there's a dangerous creature loose on the island. The only responsible step I can take is to insist that we depart on the morning tide."

"So much for your precious expedition, Royston," chuckled Paul maliciously.

"I suggest," said Captain Nagle, rising from the table, "that you use this afternoon to do as much work as possible. Use everyone who can help. Make as thorough a survey as can be done in the time left. Because this afternoon is the only time you have."

35

C ome along, come along," urged Professor Royston. "We have to get a move on. Because of that wretched captain, we have to do all our work this afternoon."

Royston, his wife, Cathy, and Lois were once again in the old stone church.

"Cathy," continued Royston, "you've brought Miss North's photographic equipment with you?"

"I have it here."

"And you think you can work this equipment?"

"Both of her cameras look like standard SLR cameras, and I'm familiar with those. I've loaded one with color film, and the other with black and white."

"Fine, fine. Well, get on with it then. A full and complete photographic record of this building and all the decorations, that's what we need. Every detail, mind."

"Yes, Professor," said Cathy. She unpacked the photographic bag and placed one of the cameras around her neck. She felt a little strange taking over Holly's role, but she understood that it had to be done.

After working steadily for thirty minutes at photographing the front door and the strange carvings that surrounded it, she was startled to feel a cold hand touch the back of her neck. She instinctively flinched away from the touch, and turned around to see Stella Royston standing behind her.

"Did I startle you, child?" asked Stella. "I'm sorry. I didn't mean to."

Cathy recognized that it was the sort of "I'm sorry" that really means "I'm pleased."

"That's all right. I didn't hear you approach, that's all."

"I am particularly light on my feet," Stella agreed. "My husband says I have a cat-like step. How is the work going?"

"Very well, thank you. But there's quite a lot of it. So I'm not really confident all of this can be finished in one afternoon." Cathy hoped that Mrs. Royston would take this as a hint to leave her to get on with it. But she didn't.

"I wouldn't worry too much about that, child."

"What do you mean?"

"We will have more time than just this afternoon."

"But the captain said—"

"Never mind what the captain said. He is not the final authority."

"I understand that it's your husband's expedition. Nevertheless—"

"It's not my husband I'm thinking of."

"Then, I'm afraid I don't understand," Cathy said, a puzzled expression on her face.

For a long time Stella stared at Cathy, as if trying to make up her mind about whether or not to reveal a secret. Then she said quietly, "There are forces at work here that the captain doesn't even suspect. Powerful forces that can control the captain and his destiny. Forces that can manipulate and control any of us."

"Forces?"

"Beings."

"I'm afraid I don't understand."

Again there was a silence. But it was clear that Stella wanted to talk about this subject. "Then I will tell you. Before very long everyone will know anyway. So, it won't hurt for you to learn about it now."

"Learn about what?"

"There are beings, non-material beings—powerful sentient creatures of pure energy—who have found this building to be congenial to their purposes. They have resided on this planet for millennia. Most human beings don't even suspect their existence. But they have great power. One day they will emerge as the true rulers of this planet. And when that day comes, there will be certain people—certain human beings—at their side; people who have been selected and initiated into their circles of energy; people who will act as their channels of power."

"I'm afraid I still don't understand you, Mrs. Royston."

"Of course you don't, my child. This is all so new to you. But you will get used to it in time." As she said these words she reached out and stroked Cathy's cheek. Cathy had to stop herself from flinching away; she found the touch reptilian and repulsive.

"I will explain," continued Stella, seemingly unaware of the reaction she had provoked. "You will be one of the first outsiders to learn of the secret that has driven human history for thousands of years."

"I really should get on with this photography," Cathy ventured hesitantly.

"Later," Stella said with a sweep of her hand. "There will be ample time later. Now, where was I? Ah, yes. Over the millennia there have been sensitive human beings who have felt the presence of these Great Ones and have tried to contact them and draw on their power."

"I can't recall reading any historical accounts of that sort of thing," Cathy commented, genuinely puzzled.

"In primitive times, these sensitives used primitive language to describe their contacts. They didn't understand the true nature of the Great Ones. They thought they were dealing with demons and similar figures of mythology."

"I see. So that means that—"

"It means that people who called themselves Satanists and

witches," interrupted Stella, "people who performed black magic were in fact, although they didn't understand it at the time, making contact with the Great Ones. And the Great Ones responded to their primitive, low-level contact by granting them power. But now human knowledge has reached a point where we can understand the energy wavelengths on which the Great Ones function. Full contact can be made for the first time. Full power can be released for the first time."

Cathy stared at Stella, not knowing whether to feel shocked or to feel sorry for her. But Stella was evidently oblivious to this reaction, swept along by the word picture she was painting.

"This island," she was saying, "this very building, is at the conjunction of the ley lines the Great Ones have been using like a street map for many centuries. This building, Cathy my dear, is charged with the presence of the Great Ones. They are here. Now. All around us."

36

Nick Hamilton worked hard all afternoon alongside Paul, Max, Vicky, Sam, Toby, Vic, and the French-Canadian pilot, Alan. Only Captain Nagle and Ingrid stayed on the boat—the captain to monitor the weather and plot a course for the morning's departure, the doctor to watch over her patient.

By late in the afternoon they had uncovered the outlines of all the convict buildings. Paul and Max , assisted by Vicky, then began to hurriedly map these building outlines before the light faded. During the course of the excavations, several bags full of historical debris had been recovered, to be taken aboard the boat and examined later. Throughout the afternoon, Sam had stood watch with his shotgun at the ready, uneasily aware of the creature in the swamp.

With the light rapidly fading, Nick sat down on a large boulder to catch his breath. Alan, perspiration dripping from his face, lowered himself onto the grass near Nick's feet.

"I am no expert, but I would say that much has been accomplished this afternoon," said the Canadian.

"We haven't done too badly," agreed Nick. "This must be an unusual experience for you. What do you normally do for a living?"

"I am a pilot for hire. Usually I am based in Noumea, but for most of the past year I have been working for Burns Philp up in the Solomons."

"Interesting work?"

"I like to fly. And I like to live among the islands of the Pacific. It is the job of my choice."

"Have you ever crashed before?"

"Never. I have made one or two emergency landings, but never before have I crashed in the ocean."

"Do you have any guess about what was wrong with the plane?"

"I am not a mechanic. But I suspect the electronics had not been properly maintained."

By the time the historians had completed their surveying task, the tropical twilight was a deep purple, and the sun had almost set in the western ocean.

"All right, everyone back to the boat," shouted Sam. "Let's get a move on."

"I think there might be another building site, close to the old quarry," said Paul. "Let's go back that way and have a closer look."

"We stay away from that place," said Sam firmly. "Captain made me responsible for you. So you stay away. Now we all go back to the ship."

"You can if you want to," Paul said. "I'm taking a look around the rim of the old quarry. I have a powerful flashlight, and I'll be perfectly safe."

"Dr. Marshall," said Nick, "didn't you hear what Sam and I reported at lunchtime today?"

"I heard a lot of nonsense about impossible monsters. But I gave up believing in fairy tales a long time ago. Vicky, are you coming with me?"

"I'd rather not, Paul. If you don't mind, I think I'll go back to the ship with the others."

"Afraid the bogey man might get you? I'm disgusted by all of you." The American turned and headed in the direction of the swamp.

"I'll go after him," volunteered Nick. "You take the others back to the boat, Sam."

"In that case," Sam offered his shotgun, "you'd better have this."

Nick saw the others depart, and then, equipped with flashlight and shotgun, set off in Paul's tracks.

Because the sun sets so quickly in the tropics, it was already pitch black. The moon had not yet risen, and only the faintest starlight relieved the inky gloom. Nick kept the yellow glow of the flashlight focused on the ground immediately ahead of him. As he got closer to the swamp the ground became damp, and he could make out Paul's footprints in the mud.

"Dr. Marshall. Dr. Marshall," called Nick. "It's Nick Hamilton. Call out. Shout. Let me know your position, and I'll keep you company."

The response was a prolonged silence. Nick could hear the whispering rush of the wind in the low shrubs and tall grasses, and, from some distance away, the lonely night cry of a sea bird. But there was no sound from Paul.

"The idiot," Nick muttered as he resumed his forward progress. The night seemed to be getting blacker. Looking up, Nick noted clouds had blown up from the south and were beginning to block out even the feeble light of the stars.

There was a rustle in the undergrowth at Nick's feet. He flicked the flashlight beam in the direction of the sound. He saw nothing but stalks of grass quivering as if some small animal had just brushed past.

What was it? thought Nick. *A lizard? A rat? A snake?* And then he remembered being told there were no snakes on Cavendish Island. But a rat, that seemed quite possible. "After all," Nick told himself, "all those old sailing ships had rats in their holds. And while the convicts and their jailers were being disembarked, it might have been quite easy for some of the ship's rats to escape to the shore. Then all it would have taken was one male, one female, and a reasonable food supply, and this whole island could be crawling with rats by now."

The thought made him shiver. A picture formed in his mind of swarms of rats living in burrows under the long grass by day and coming out to feed at night.

"Dr. Marshall. Dr. Marshall," Nick shouted again to distract himself from thinking about hordes of hungry rats. Again there was no response to his call.

The cloud cover was getting thicker, and the night was becoming black as coal. A cool breeze was blowing in from the sea. Nick decided he would give the search for Paul another ten minutes and then and return to the boat. At the thought of the boat, images sprang into his mind of brightly lit cabins, a warm meal, and a hot shower.

Just then there was another rustle in the grass. Once again Nick swung the beam of light around, looking for the gleaming red eyes of the rats he knew were there. But once again they were too quick for him.

He pushed on toward the swamp, and a moment later found himself stepping into the broad trail of flattened grass left by the swamp creature—the same trail he and Sam had followed earlier in the day.

"Dr. Marshall. Paul," he called again.

This time there was a faint, distant reply, "Over here."

"Over where?" shouted Nick. "I can't tell where your voice is coming from."

"This way," came Paul's voice. "Over here."

"Stay there," Nick yelled. "I'll come to you."

Nick found that following the creature's trail was quicker and easier going than pushing through the long, entangling grass. Besides which, the trail seemed to be leading him in the general direction of Paul's voice.

"Paul. Paul! Call out again. Give me a sense of your direction."

"I'm here. Over this way." Paul's voice was stronger this time.

A few minutes later Nick rounded a bend to find Paul sprawled out on the ground, his face contorted with pain.

"What happened?" asked Nick as he knelt by the American's side.

"I caught my foot on a root and fell heavily. I think I've broken my leg," grunted Paul. "I've been hoping and praying someone would find me."

"Praying? I didn't think you were the praying type."

"I'm not," agreed Paul with a crooked grin, "but pain cures atheism."

"No," said Nick wryly, "death cures atheism. But pain sometimes helps. Here, take my arm, and I'll help you up."

As Paul lifted his hand, Nick saw that it was dripping with blood.

"What happened to your hand?"

"I don't know. As it got darker something came out of the grass and bit me. It hurts like the devil, I can tell you."

"Just lie still for a second," suggested Nick, "while I tear a strip off my shirt to make a bandage for your hand. We can't let it keep bleeding like that. And then I'll help you back to the boat."

Nick pulled up the edge of his T-shirt, tore at it with his teeth, and then extended the tear until he had a broad strip. As he bent over Paul, the American suddenly let out a terrifying scream. Nick spun around. There on the trail behind them was the creature.

The thing was gliding across the grass toward them like some gigantic caterpillar. A powerful stench came from it, as from slime that has long lain below water.

The shotgun! Nick had left it lying in the grass about two meters away. He sprang toward it, scooped it up in his hands, and raised it to his shoulder.

The thing before him seemed to have no head, but on the front of it was an orifice of puckered skin that opened and shut.

Nick cocked both barrels of the gun.

As the thing advanced, its front part reared from the ground, like a hooded cobra about to strike.

Nick fired. The blasts from both barrels of the shotgun tore into the soft, slimy flesh of the huge creature. It made no difference. It appeared not to feel the shotgun pellets, but lunged forward and fastened on Paul.

As the yells of Paul's agony rang in his ears, Nick tried to lay hold on the thing. But he could not: although something material was there, it was impossible to grasp it; His hands sank into it as in thick mud. It was like wrestling with a nightmare.

In a few seconds it was all over. The screams of the victim became moans and mutterings: Paul panted once or twice and was still. For a moment longer there came gurglings and sucking noises, then the creature began to slide away, paying no attention to Nick, and disappearing with amazing rapidity.

Gasping for breath, Nick fumbled in the dark looking for the flashlight he had dropped. He found it and flicked it on. Then he turned the beam in the direction of Paul's body. It lay on the flattened grass, no more than a rind of skin in loose folds over projecting bones. It had been sucked dry.

37

ois Myles and Vicky Shaw were sitting side by side on the single bunk in Lois's cabin on board the *Covenant*.

"How is Paul coping?" asked Lois.

"Not well," said Vicky bitterly. "It's just as well we're leaving. He seems to have lost all interest in the real reason for us being here."

"Well, that will be part of my report. You can be certain of that."

"Is there any chance that Captain Nagle might change his mind?"

"No. He's determined to leave. Mind you, the Roystons are equally determined to stay. Between now and the morning tide, anything might happen."

"Which would be better—to leave the island, or to stay?"

"The best thing that could happen from our point of view would be the shutting down of this whole expedition and our departure from the island as soon as possible. The Order is still considering the role this power source should play. And until they have decided, it's best that it not be reactivated."

"If for some reason we did stay," Vicky said slowly, "how close do you think the Roystons are to reactivating the source?"

"Very close indeed," replied Lois through clenched teeth. "They only need the right elements and the right ceremony and the connection will be made."

"Are we prepared for that? I mean, if that happens, what are we supposed to do?"

"Take charge," Lois said firmly. "That's what we will do in those circumstances. I have, concealed in my luggage, the latest model of the wave and oscillation amplifier. With the aid of that device, I believe we could take control of whatever forces the Roystons might succeed in awakening. But it won't come to that. The captain is determined that we will leave."

"If there's a debate at the dinner table tonight, about whether we should leave or not ..." began Vicky.

"Then we come down heavily on the captain's side. We answer every argument the Roystons put up. Getting those two off this island must be our first priority."

"But if they succeed in changing Nagle's mind?"

"Then I'll show you the new amplifier and teach you how to operate it."

As Nick staggered down the narrow path to the cliff top, he felt his hands and arms starting to burn. As a boy he had once splashed his hand with battery acid, and the burning pain caused by the creature's ghastly slime felt exactly the same.

He began to run faster, his feet pounding the rocky soil. His path took him past the old church, and as he ran he thought he saw out of the corner of his eye a large, dark shape moving alongside the building. But he couldn't stop to investigate.

The pain was increasing as he ran down the steep rocky path that led from the cliff top to the narrow beach that fringed the bay.

As soon as his feet hit the beach, Nick threw the flashlight and shotgun onto the sand and plunged into the waves. He swam several meters out into the bay, then dived under the water, pushing his body through the salty swell. He rose and gasped for air, and then he dived again.

The third time he dived, Nick could feel the saltwater washing away the thick, viscous saliva which had splashed over him, and gradually the burning eased, then finally stopped altogether.

Only then did Nick turn around and swim back to the beach.

He stamped up the sandy slope, shaking off the seawater and

looking for the flashlight. As soon as he found it, he flicked it on, and facing the boat, began to wave it backward and forward. For several minutes he thought his signal hadn't been seen, but then he heard the welcome sound of the outboard motor on the inflatable runabout. The sound assured him that someone was coming to pick him up.

Nick hoped that whoever it was would hurry. He was soaking wet, and the cool sea breeze was making him very cold, very fast. He beat his arms on his chest to keep warm, as the sound of the outboard got closer and closer.

Cathy stood on the aft deck of the *Covenant* peering into the darkness. She had seen the beam of the flashlight and had alerted the waiting Sam, who immediately set off for the beach to pick up Nick and Paul.

The sound of the runabout faded as it approached the beach, then Cathy heard the motor being gunned as it was turned around into the oncoming waves and steered back to the boat.

She waited impatiently, keen to tell Nick about her strange conversation with Stella. She pulled her coat closer to keep warm in the cool evening breeze. The little runabout seemed to be taking forever.

But then it was there, alongside the boat, and Cathy was leaning over the side, helping to steady the ladder as Nick and Sam climbed up.

As Nick swung himself over the side railing onto the aft deck, Cathy gasped, "Nick, what's happened to you?"

His face and arms were cut and bruised, his shirt was torn and dirty, he was soaking wet, and there were patches of blistered skin on his arms and hands that looked as though he had been burned.

"I finally caught a glimpse of that … that thing from the swamp," he replied. "In fact, I got closer to it than I ever want to be again."

"What about Dr. Marshall? I thought he'd be with you."

"He's dead."

"One of my passengers dead, and another one injured," snarled Captain Nagle. "That does it. If I ever had doubts about shipping out in the morning, that settles it."

"Aye, Captain," said Vic as he leaned against the instrument panel. The captain stared out to sea, his arms folded, looking toward the horizon that was invisible in the darkness.

"Foolishly," muttered Nagle, "I imagined this was going to be little more than a pleasure cruise."

"You can hardly blame yourself, Captain."

"Hmm … but if that idiot Royston gives me any more trouble, I swear I'll …" He didn't finish the sentence, but he clenched his fist as he spoke. "You know, Vic, there have been moments over the last few days when I've wished this vessel had a brig."

"Aye, Captain. Put a few troublemakers under lock and key and that would have cooled some tempers."

"It's a delightful thought, Vic. Now, what's the latest on that low-pressure system to the north of us?"

"It's deepening, Captain, so they've given it a name—Tropical Cyclone Jezebel."

"I suspected as much, so I've plotted a southerly course that should keep us well away from it. Tomorrow morning as soon as we clear the bay and are in deep water, I'd like you to come up and take the conn, Vic."

"Aye, Captain."

"I want to keep an eye on my passengers until we are well clear of this island."

38

Nick was sitting on his bunk when a knock echoed in his cabin.

"Come in."

"It's only me," said Cathy, as she entered.

"Take a seat," said Nick, waving her to the only chair in the tiny cabin. He was still badly shaken, and it was good to see her.

"There's something I wanted to talk to you about. Is now a good time?" said Cathy.

"Fire away."

"How are you feeling now?"

"Stiff and sore. Disoriented by what I've seen. But journalists are case-hardened; we bounce back. What's on your mind?"

"A very odd conversation I had with Mrs. Royston this afternoon."

Nick listened as Cathy told him about the powerful forces that Stella claimed were at work on the island; the "beings" that she referred to as Great Ones; the claim that these Great Ones had secretly controlled human history for thousands of years; the connection of the Great Ones with demons and witchcraft; and the place of the black chapel in all of this.

When she finished, Nick took a deep breath and looked thoughtful.

"So, what do you think it all means?" asked Cathy as the silence between them lengthened.

"I think the Roystons are engaged in what used to be called the black arts."

"Witchcraft? Satanism? That sort of thing?"

"That sort of thing precisely."

"She made it sound more … well, scientific than that."

"But of course. A scientific dressing is exactly what our age, and our culture, needs to make evil palatable. Hitler labeled some his most wicked deeds genetic experiments. When it comes to evil, cruelty, or a lust for power, if you call it science, it looks perfectly moral and upright. By talking that way, the Roystons can disguise even from themselves that they are playing the same silly, bestial games that have been played for centuries by those people who call themselves Satanists."

"But could it be real?" A frown crinkled Cathy's pretty forehead. "Could there be real forces or beings that the Roystons are making contact with?"

"Could be."

"Hmm. I'm a Christian, Nick, like you. But I have some difficulty in believing in a person, a being, like Satan."

"You obviously believe God is there, right?" asked Nick.

"Right. God is there. He is the Maker and Ruler of the world. He has made us and the world in such a way that relationships are the currency of the universe: our relationship with him and our relationships with each other. Of course, human beings reject the Ruler and rebel against the Maker and consequently make a mess of the world. Some rebel actively, but most passively, by just ignoring God. But God is still there. And he is still in control."

"Fine. All that we agree on. So since the supernatural world is real, as real as this table," said Nick, slapping the palm of his hand down on the small reading table beside his bunk, "why is it difficult to see a person, a being, as the prince of evil?"

"I don't know. It just is," Cathy said with a shy half-smile on her lips.

"Okay. That name Satan just comes from a Greek word meaning *adversary*. What the Bible says is quite clear. Satan is a malignant reality, always hostile to God and to God's people. But he has already been defeated in the life and death and resurrection of Jesus, and this defeat will become obvious and complete at the end of the age—at the end of history, when God sets all things right and eradicates the last traces of evil."

Cathy opened her lips to speak, but before she could do so the air was torn by a horrible scream. Nick leaped to his feet and threw open his cabin door, with Cathy close behind him. Then the scream came again—a heart-rending scream filled with agony of body and soul.

"That's Holly," said Cathy.

"You're right!" Nick sprinted down the corridor to Holly's cabin and tried the door handle.

"It's locked," he said, "apparently from the inside."

Just then they were joined by Ingrid. "What's happened to Holly?" she asked. "I left her heavily sedated and sleeping soundly."

From inside the cabin came the sound of soul-wrenching sobbing. Nick tried the door again. "It's definitely locked," he said.

"Break it down," urged the doctor.

But at that moment the captain arrived. Nick quickly explained the situation.

"Stand back," ordered Nagle. He drew a large key ring from his pocket and turned a key in the lock.

"There's something behind it," he said with a grunt. "Nick, give me a hand here. Put your shoulder to the door."

Both men pushed, but the door wouldn't budge.

"It feels as though there's something pushing against it on the other side," yelled Nick.

"You've got to get it open," urged Cathy. "Something's terribly wrong with Holly, I just know it is."

"Come on, Captain, let's try again," Nick said.

But this time the door flew open at their first push. All four of them rushed into the small cabin.

"The air in here is stifling," said Cathy.

"It's as hot as a sauna," Nick agreed.

Holly was lying on her bunk. There were long, deep scratches down her face, arms, shoulders, and neck. Ingrid hurried to her side and checked her pulse. She lifted Holly's wrist and then felt for a vein in her neck.

When Ingrid turned back to the others, her face was solemn. "She's gone," she said quietly. "Holly's dead."

"What killed her?" asked Captain Nagle.

"I don't know," Ingrid dispaired. "Something has killed Holly North, but I have no idea what on earth it was."

It was much later that night before Nick finally returned to his cabin. Having showered, he walked back to his cabin wearing a bathrobe, with a towel slung around his neck. He closed the cabin door, sat on the side of the bunk, and stared into space. So much had happened in the last few hours—so much.

The horrific death of Paul haunted him. As a journalist he had seen a great deal of the ugly, evil side of life, and he had taught himself to suppress it and carry on. But this time the horror kept breaking through.

Then there was the death of Holly. Even after a careful examination, Ingrid had been able to provide no explanation for Holly's death, or for the strange deep scratches that covered the exposed parts of her body.

As they had all sat around the main cabin after the somber evening meal, Sam had raised the question of the disposal of the bodies. He wanted both of them to be given what he called "a decent Christian burial." Stella laughed at this suggestion, saying it was the last thing Paul would have wanted. But her remark was ignored.

After much discussion it was decided that both bodies would be buried in the colonial cemetery, near the ruins of the troops' barracks, first thing in the morning. It would be a joint funeral. Nick and Sam had volunteered to recover Paul's remains immediately after sunrise and then to join the others at the cemetery for the service.

Following this agreement came the argument.

It began as a tense but quiet debate, and then became more heated, until it ended in a blazing row. On one side was Professor Royston arguing that the expedition should continue; on the other, Captain Nagle insisting on leaving the island at the first opportunity.

Royston called the deaths unfortunate, but added that once the bodies had been properly and decently buried, there was no reason not to continue. Nagle reminded the professor of the creature that had killed Paul, and that it clearly posed a threat to all of them. It ended with Nagle laying down the law and refusing to listen to Royston any longer.

After the argument the party broke up, people drifted off to take showers and retire for the night. Nick had been the last of them. As he sat on the side of his bed he knew it was late, but he also knew that he would have trouble sleeping.

He opened up the drawer in the small reading table beside the bunk looking for something to read. His eye immediately fell on the small notebook he had found earlier in the day. He picked it up and turned over its pages, dried and crackling with age.

He had intended to hand it over to one of the historians as soon as he returned to the boat but in the ensuing activity had forgotten. Nick remembered taking it out of the pocket of his jeans and slipping it into the drawer, telling himself he would hand it over later.

Well, he thought, *tomorrow will do. I'll give it to Max Taunton first thing in the morning. He's a historian, he'll know what to do with it.*

With that, he turned on the small reading lamp, turned off the overhead light, hung up his bathrobe, and climbed into the bunk. The journalist leaned back on his pillow, picked up the old notebook, and began to turn the pages.

The first page he flipped the book open to bore the date "July 7th, 1821." Nick began to read.

39

Wallace Humphrey Muir sat alone in the small living room of his suburban cottage. Spread out on the coffee table in front of him were the typed sheets that Frank Gordon had sent him—Robyn Reed's notes of her conversation with Sharon, the ex-member of the Order of the Crimson Circle.

Muir studied the notes closely.

"So, they call it occult science do they?" he muttered to himself. "That is a most interesting way of putting it."

For a while he sipped his tea in silent contemplation.

"I wonder what they imagine," he said at length, "they are tuning into with their wave amplifiers and other bits of electronic gadgetry. And do they really think, with their transistors and circuitry, they are doing anything different from an old-fashioned Ouija board? Dear me. Dress anything up with a bit of science, and the gullible always think it's something new. Ask a group of adults to pretend to murder and torture people, and they will be horrified by the suggestion. But make it a computer game, and they will relish every moment of it. Describe the ghastly spectacles the Roman emperors staged in the Colosseum, and modern adults say it makes them sick. But show them the same things in a movie full of special effects, and they find those horrors deliciously entertaining. Rather like scientists who do weapons research. They become so focused on their technology they manage to block out the horrible things their technology will one day do to flesh and blood and bone."

He finished his tea and slowly ambled out to his tiny kitchen to make a fresh pot.

As the kettle was boiling, he looked up at the calendar that hung over his sink. The photograph for the current month was a spectacular one: The photographer had caught an electrical storm—huge banks of dark clouds over a rocky coastline—with lightning branching out just as a massive wave was smashing against the headland. It was a powerful picture. Underneath was a scripture: "You will rule them with an iron sceptre; you will dash them to pieces like pottery."

"All this rebellion against the Almighty," sighed Muir. "It is so foolish. So petulant. So pointless. So doomed to failure."

Then his thoughts turned to those who had abandoned their rebellion, returned to the service of their True King—to the service of Almighty God, their Maker, Ruler, and loving Father. At this thought he smiled. It was a warm and loving smile that seemed to start deep inside and light up his whole face.

The smile faded as he thought of the grim times ahead. There were painful battles to be fought, and some would pay with their lives. But beyond the valley of the shadow of death were broad, sunlit uplands. The outcome was secure.

Whatever might happen in this or that battle, the Great War had been won on the day when God himself died—and then, in a dramatic reversal, had defeated death and darkness as the Author of Life, the one who had paid the Great Ransom to rescue his people from the captivity of darkness.

"*I am the good shepherd,*" the words of Jesus flashed into Muir's mind: "*The good shepherd lays down his life for the sheep ... I lay down my life—only to take it up again. No one takes it from me, but I lay it down of my own accord. I have authority to lay it down and authority to take it up again. This command I received from my Father.*"

Muir carried a fresh cup of tea back to his living room, sat it on the coffee table, and once again contemplated the report on the Order of the Crimson Circle.

After a while he said aloud, "This is serious. Perhaps even more serious than I thought at first." And with that he pulled out a list of names and telephone numbers and began to organize people to pray.

DARKNESS

"This is the verdict: Light has come into the world, but men loved darkness instead of light because their deeds were evil."
—John 3:19

40

All thought of sleep fled from Nick's mind. The journal of Lieutenant Edmund McDermott, officer of the New South Wales Corps, held him enthralled. The minutes ticked away unheeded as Nick read on. And then he reached the entry for July 31, 1821. As sentence followed sentence Nick could barely believe his eyes. He finished the page, put down the battered old book, and stood up.

Restlessly, feverishly, he paced the few steps his small cabin allowed, turned around and paced back again. His fists clenched and unclenched as he paced backward and forward, his mind racing. Eventually Nick muttered to himself, "It happened. It really happened."

A thousand questions shot uninvited into his brain, and he could find answers for none of them.

"So it wasn't a ghost ship then. It was real. I was real to him, and he was real to me."

Nick paced back and forth. He longed to go and talk to someone about his find. He glanced at his travel clock. It was 2:00 AM. He would have to wait until daylight to share this amazing discovery with Cathy.

"So," he said again, "it really happened. But how? If it was not just a vision, or a dream, or a nightmare, then it was … what?"

Perhaps the answer, he realized, would lie further on in the diary. Nick sat down on the edge of his bed, picked up McDermott's journal, and resumed reading.

An hour later he reached the last, hastily scrawled page, dated October 31, 1822. As he slowly closed the covers, the journalist thought, *There's a story in this, a terrific story.*

But also, he realized, a strange and puzzling story. And one that somehow involved him, Nick Hamilton. Like every reporter, Nick had a secret desire to write a book, something more permanent than tomorrow's birdcage liner. He began to formulate plans to research the background of Edmund McDermott and to write a book based on the journal.

It would be better than any novel, thought Nick. But then he paused. It would be a book full of questions, not answers. However, he would have to find out what had been going on in the colonial soldier's life and how his own life intersected with McDermott's before he could think about writing a book—or anything else.

Nick replaced the journal in the drawer of his bedside table, turned out the lights, and climbed between the sheets. But he couldn't sleep. There were too many thoughts turning around in a jumble inside his head.

❖❖❖

In the early hours of the morning, Cathy tossed and turned on her bed. In her feverish discomfort she pushed back the sheets and blankets. Her mind was tormented by strange images that seemed to penetrate her subconscious like hot needles going into butter.

Cathy moaned and mumbled aloud. Beads of perspiration stood out on her forehead. And as she slept, she dreamed.

In her dream she was a small girl again on the playground of her first school. She was playing hopscotch with her best friend. Suddenly her friend began to cheat, running away, laughing, and catcalling. When Cathy shouted her protest, the friend turned around, but it was no longer her friend's face beneath the familiar fringe of hair—it was a hideous, skull-like face.

In her nightmare, Cathy ran out of the schoolyard, terrified and hysterical. She ran all the way home, her heart pounding. As she approached her house, she could see on the front porch her father, dozing in his favorite rocking chair, his old gray felt hat fallen down over his face.

Cathy—a small, terrified child once more—screamed as she ran up the front walk, "Daddy! Daddy!" As she yelled, the figure in the rocking chair raised its head, but it wasn't her father—it was that thing again, that horrible, bone-white skull. Cathy turned and fled.

Exhausted, desperate, out of breath, she ran, then walked, and then staggered through streets that she no longer recognized. She was lost in the streets of some strange city. Adults brushed past her. They were speaking in a language she could not understand. When she tried to ask for help or directions, they ignored her or looked at her in silent scorn.

Then, just ahead, she saw a police station. Gratefully she ran as fast as her tired legs would carry her. Up the steps she ran and in through the front door. Behind the desk was a policeman in uniform, his back toward her, speaking on the telephone. She waited. At last he hung up the phone, and turned toward her. And then Cathy saw again—the death mask.

But at the moment of her final collapse, she seemed to fall not downward toward the floor, but upward. Before long she was float-ing above the strange city, drifting higher and higher. And as she rose, she could see that the city was at the center of a vortex of dark forces like black thunderclouds. It was a great and powerful center that controlled the countryside around it for as far as the eye could see, like a great, complex telephone exchange. Everything that hap-pened on the periphery was controlled by the center. And Cathy knew—how, she wasn't sure, but she knew—that the center was evil, and its influence was spreading infection everywhere.

But then in her dream, she was rising higher and ever higher. Until she saw that there was not one center, but two. There was, she saw, a Center of Darkness, and, opposed to it, a Center of Light. But then the perspective changed. As her flight carried her farther and farther from the surface, she could see that the Center of Darkness was really very small, and the Center of Light was vast and fathomless. The Darkness was no more than a speck, a mere fleck of soot, against the vastness of the cosmos-consuming light.

And then she fell into a deep, soothing, peaceful sleep.

She did not awaken until the world around her was jarred by a shattering explosion.

Nick lay in his bunk in his darkened cabin when it happened—sudden, loud, deafening, like a clap of thunder just centimeters from his ear. The boat lurched violently to one side, and then righted itself again. Everything seemed to shake and tremble. Nick's travel bag fell onto the floor. As the explosive echoes died away, he heard glass shat-tering in some distant part of the vessel.

Nick rocketed out of bed and flung open his cabin door. The deck was still swaying back and forth under his feet. The corridor was pitch black, and he could see nothing, but he caught an omi-nous whiff of acrid smoke.

Just then a flashlight came on, and Nick was aware of a pajama-clad Captain Nagle standing at his shoulder.

"Step aside please, Nick," commanded Nagle. Nick quickly let Nagle pass, and then followed the captain down the steep stairs. As they reached the engine room, they heard the sound of running water: not a trickle, but a roar.

Captain Nagle swung the beam of the flashlight around in an arc. The aft section of the engine room was awash. As they stood there, Nick felt the decking under his feet lurch and then settle a few inches deeper into the water. Nagle began wading through ankle-deep water toward the source of the problem.

"There it is." He pointed with the flashlight beam to a jagged hole ripped in the side of the hull about the size of a clenched fist. Water was roaring in through the opening with the strength and blast of a fire hose. The emergency lights flickered on. In the dim light they could see the water boiling around the diesel engine. Steam rose into the air as the seawater hit hot pipes.

"Only a bomb blast could have done that," declared Nagle grimly. "We've been sabotaged."

"Can it be fixed?"

"Not a chance."

"Then ...?"

"We abandon ship." There was a note of bitter disgust and tired defeat in the captain's voice.

Nick turned around and discovered that the narrow stairs were packed with passengers. The stunned silence was broken by a barrage of questions.

"What's happened?"

"Has there been an accident?"

"Who did this?"

"Can you fix it?"

"Are we safe?"

"Back to your cabins, ladies and gentlemen," bellowed Nagle. "You have two minutes to grab your essential belongings—just the essentials. You must be on the aft deck in two minutes. Two minutes!"

This command was greeted by a frozen hush.

"Did you people hear me? Move! Get going! Now!"

The babble of voices broke out again as the expedition members ran back up the stairs.

"Sam! Vic! Toby!" yelled Captain Nagle.

"Here, Captain," called Vic as he pushed through the fleeing passengers. Sam was close behind.

"Vic," ordered Nagle, "see what can be done to slow down the rate at which we're taking on water."

"Aye, Captain."

"Sam, launch the lifeboat."

"Aye sir."

"Toby. Where's that blasted Irishman?"

"Here sir!" Toby vaulted down the stairs.

"Toby, round up the passengers. Get them onto the aft deck in double-quick time. You are not to leave the cabin deck until it is fully evacuated. Jump to it."

"At once, Captain."

"You give him a hand, Nick," said Nagle, turning to the journalist at his side.

"Of course," said Nick, and took the stairs two at a time to the cabin deck.

"Where's Cathy?" Nick asked himself as he ran. She hadn't been in the group of passengers clustered on the stairs.

Nick rushed to Cathy's door and was about to pound on it when it flew open. A dazed, disheveled Cathy stood there, running her hand through her hair. "What's happened?"

"Explosion," explained Nick. "The boat's sinking. Put on some clothes, and stuff what you can into a bag, then meet me on the aft deck. You've got two minutes."

Cathy's face rapidly reflected disbelief, alarm, and anxiety. Suddenly she was wide awake and fully alert.

"Right," she said. "Two minutes. I'll see you on the aft deck."

Nick turned back to his own cabin. It took him less that a minute to tear off his pajamas and pull on jeans, a T-shirt, and a pair of joggers. He grabbed his canvas bag and in around thirty seconds had his clothes and other possessions stuffed inside. At the last moment he remembered the McDermott journal, rescued it from its drawer, and thrust it into the top of the bag.

He stepped out into the narrow corridor and found it filled with people, all trying to carry too many bags. Nick remembered Ingrid. She had also been missing from the cluster on the engine room steps.

He recalled that her cabin was next to Cathy's, hurried to the door, and pounded loudly. There was no response. He flung the door open. Incredibly, Ingrid was in her bunk, still asleep. He tried the light switch, but it wasn't working. With only the blue moonlight streaming in through the porthole to guide him, Nick grabbed the doctor's shoulders and shook vigorously.

"Whas the matter?" she mumbled groggily.

"Wake up, Doctor!" shouted Nick. "The *Covenant* is sinking. We have to abandon ship."

Ingrid's eyes blinked open, but she looked confused.

"Doctor," urged Nick, "you've got to wake up."

"It's my leg," replied Ingrid, shaking her head as she tried to clear it. "It was causing me pain last night, so I took a sleeping pill."

Nick turned back to the corridor just in time to see Cathy emerge from her cabin, struggling with a large suitcase.

"Here, I'll take that," said Nick, grabbing the case. "You look after Dr. Sommerville. Get her out of bed. Throw some of her clothes into a bag, and get her onto the aft deck."

"Right." Cathy strode into the doctor's cabin.

Nick sprinted up the companionway stairs to the main lounge, and then out onto the aft deck. The Roystons and Max Taunton were already there.

"Max, I also need my small travel case," commanded Stella. "Go back at once and fetch it. It's underneath my bunk."

"Yes, Stella. At once." The hapless Max turned and hurried back down below.

Nick dropped Cathy's suitcase and his own canvas bag onto the deck and followed him. On the way, Lois and Vicky pushed passed him, each struggling with a large case, closely followed by Alan Marchant with his small backpack over his shoulder. Just then the boat lurched sideways and settled deeper into the water. Nick recovered his balance and found his way through the darkness to Dr. Sommerville's cabin.

Cathy had managed to get the doctor dressed and was hastily pushing clothing into a battered old suitcase.

"My medical bag," said Ingrid. "I must have my medical bag. And my crutch. I won't be able to get around without the crutch."

Nick plunged into the cabin and found the medical bag, then he hunted around for the makeshift crutch that Vic had put together. He found it at last on the floor.

"Right. I've got those," he grunted. "Everybody out of here."

Just then Toby shouted urgently, "She's going under! Get a move on!"

Nick thrust the medical bag and Ingrid's bag into the Irishman's hands. "Take these up to the deck," he said. "Cathy, can you help Ingrid up the companionway, or do you need my help?"

"We're all right," grunted Cathy as the doctor leaned against her. Nick watched them start climbing the companionway stairs, and then he heard an ominous sound—the splashing of water. He turned around to discover the narrow engine stairwell was awash.

A large shadow loomed out of the darkness and pushed passed him. It was Nagle.

"Nick," he cried. "Are all the passengers out?"

"All out."

"Good. Get up to the galley and help Sam load food and essential supplies into the lifeboat. The *Covenant* is sinking fast."

41

*T*he first gray light of sunrise found a wet and bedraggled party of survivors on the narrow beach watching the *Covenant* slowly settle under the cold, green waters of the bay.

"Slightly less than thirty minutes," said Nick. "That's how long it took to sink. Sorry," he said, glancing at his wristwatch. "Journalist's habit: always check the time when things happen."

Several of the passengers stood on the beach, hands on hips, staring in disbelief and dismay. Others sat on the sand, huddled up, knees drawn up under chin, looking as miserable and uncomfortable as they undoubtedly felt.

"And now my rescuers are in need of rescue," said Alan Marchant very quietly. But in that early morning hush his voice carried up and down the beach.

"There is a curse on this island," said Max, with something like panic in his voice. "It has claimed the lives of Miss North and Dr. Paul. It caused the fall and injury of Dr. Sommerville. It snared you in its trap," he nodded toward Alan, "and now, we too are trapped."

"Eh? What is that you say, Dr. Taunton?" asked Alan.

"I said this island is evil. It is like a poisonous spider lurking in its lair, just waiting to entangle us and kill us all. And now we are caught in its web, and we will never escape."

"Come on, Max," said Nick, slapping the historian on the shoulder. "We've had enough gloom, doom, and despair for the time being."

Max looked down at his feet, shuffling his shoes in the yellow sand. When he looked up again, there was an embarrassed expression on his face.

"Sorry, Nick," he murmured. "Mustn't let my imagination get carried away." And with that he set off up the beach.

"Poor Max," said Cathy sympathetically.

"Why 'poor Max'?" asked Nick.

"Well, it must be a bit of a shock for a middle-aged academic who thinks he's going on a nice, safe, comfortable expedition to find himself in the middle of this horrible mess."

"Surely it is not just poor Max," offered Alan. "Surely it must be poor all of us."

"I guess so," agreed Cathy.

"But I think we have more good news than bad news, so far," he continued.

"How do you figure that?" asked Nick.

"Because all of us are still alive. When my aircraft developed mechanical problems, I thought I might die. I crashed, but I am still alive. I was rescued by Captain Nagle and the *Covenant*. Now that boat has sunk, but I am alive still. So far, I feel disinclined to complain."

"Good point," conceded Nick.

"Oh, that's good news all right," interjected Captain Nagle. "The problem is: How do we let anyone know?"

"What do you mean?" Cathy asked.

"Our radio is gone," said Nagle. "We have no means of contacting the outside world, no way of calling for rescue."

At that moment two different people on that beach both thought the same thing: *I have a radio. And I intend to keep it a secret.*

"You can lock up now, Sharon," said the owner.

The nervous young woman with the straight blonde hair

stepped out from behind the bar and walked around the pub, slipping the bolts into place on each of the doors.

"All done, Ted," she called out when she had finished.

"Thanks, love," was the reply. "You can go home now, if you like."

She fetched her jacket from behind the bar, draped it over one arm, and let herself out through a side door. As she walked down the darkened streets toward the railway station, she lit a cigarette with shaking fingers.

Ever since she had talked to Robyn Reed, she had been nervous. Even more nervous than usual. Each morning she tore open the newspaper, anxious that there might be some story about the Order of the Crimson Circle based on the information she had supplied. The journalist had promised her there wouldn't be, but Sharon had learned to trust no one. And she certainly didn't trust reporters.

At the station there was a cold, damp breeze, so she slipped on her jacket and hugged it close to her body. The railway car was almost deserted, and its rattling, swaying motion started rocking Sharon to sleep. She was so tired that she almost missed her station, waking up and leaping out of the train just in time.

As Sharon left the lights of the railway station behind and started the last long, slow trudge up the hill toward her apartment, she noticed that two of the street lights weren't working. *Funny*, she thought, *they were both okay last night.*

Just after this thought had passed through her mind, she heard a car engine start up behind her. She walked a little more quickly. Then it happened—very fast. Suddenly the car was gunning its engine, roaring up behind her, and, at the same time, the car lights came on. Sharon was caught in their spotlight. She was too tired to react quickly and stared like a rabbit on a country road as the big four-wheel-drive hit her with a sickening thud, and two wheels ran over her.

The car stopped a few meters away, its lights were turned off again. The driver came running back to look at his victim. He made sure she was dead. Then he slipped a silk bracelet around her wrist—a circle of bright crimson.

By the time Ern Daley had pulled on a bathrobe and come out of his front door, the car was speeding away. Ern saw the crumpled body in the middle of the rain-wet street and hurried toward it.

"Are you all right, miss?" he asked as he knelt. Gently he rolled her over. As he did so, a trickle of blood ran from the corner of Sharon's mouth and dripped onto the asphalt.

42

Vic, Toby, Nick, and Alan worked as a team erecting a row of seven two-man tents along the narrow beach that flanked the bay of Cavendish Island. While they did so, Captain Nagle and Sam made an inventory of stores and supplies.

"Well, Captain," asked Ingrid as she hobbled toward him, "how long before we starve?"

"As long as we husband our resources and are careful with our management, at least two weeks," was the reply.

"And if I catch fish," added Sam with a grin, "much longer."

"So supplies are not the problem," the doctor remarked with a thoughtful nod as Cathy strolled over to join them.

"What is this?" she asked. "Some good news at last?"

"We may be shipwrecked," said Ingrid, "but we won't starve— at least not right away."

"I call that good news," Cathy said with a smile.

"The problem," sighed Captain Nagle, taking his cap off his head and scratching his thinning hair, "is getting rescued."

"Will the charter company realize that we are in trouble?" asked Cathy.

"Oh, yes. They'll realize," Nagle said. "The question is, when?"

"What do you mean?"

"Well, when regular radio reports stop arriving, they will know we have a problem. What they won't know is whether the problem is simply a dead radio, or something more serious."

"But they won't wait a month before sending a rescue vessel, surely," exclaimed Ingrid.

"Quite right, Doctor. Quite right," agreed Nagle. "My best guess is that there'll be an Australian naval frigate here long before the month is up."

"Then why are you still so gloomy?"

"Doctor, I've just lost my vessel. As the ship's captain, I'm allowed a little gloom."

"It was hardly your fault. From what I've been told, it was sabotage."

"Oh, it was that, all right. And I intend to investigate that bomb blast to the very best of my ability. But that's not the worst of it."

"Then what is?" asked Cathy.

"In the first place, we shouldn't forget the creature that killed Paul Marshall. And second, there's the weather. At the last report there was a tropical cyclone building up just a few hundred kilometers to the north of us. If it decides to head in our direction ... well ... let's just say it won't be fun."

"What about the old church?" Cathy suggested.

"What about it?"

"Well, it's a solid stone building. Wouldn't it survive even the wildest cyclone? Wouldn't we be safe inside it?"

"Safe from the cyclone, yes," the captain said thoughtfully. "But don't forget what that building did to Holly."

"So that may be our choice," murmured the doctor, leaning heavily on her makeshift walking stick, "either death from a tropical cyclone or insanity in the black church."

With a skeptical look she turned and hobbled away.

Before long the work of setting up the camp had been completed, and Sam had brewed another pot of coffee.

As it was being poured, Professor Royston and his wife rather cautiously made their way toward Captain Nagle and Nick, who were standing somewhat apart from the others, talking quietly.

"If I may have a word with you, Captain?" the professor interrupted.

"What's on your mind?"

"The expedition ..." began the professor.

"What about it?" Nagle barked angrily. "If I thought you had anything to do with last night's explosion ..." He left the sentence unfinished, but his intentions were clear.

"Nothing," protested Royston. "Nothing at all. I swear to you. I had nothing to do with sinking the boat. It's the last thing I would have wanted."

"Really? If the boat was intact, we would have left Cavendish Island hours ago, and your precious expedition would be washed up. As it is, we're stuck here. So, the bomb seems to have achieved what you wanted, doesn't it?"

"Really, Captain, this is outrageous," an indignant Stella Royston said. "First you cancel our expedition on the flimsiest pretext—without, I might add, having the authority to do so—and then you accuse us of terrorism. Your company will hear about this."

"Eventually," Nagle said sourly.

"What do you mean 'eventually'?"

"We have to get off the island first."

"Which is exactly my point, Captain." Professor Royston turned to his wife and added, "You leave this to me, Stella my dear."

"So, what is your point, Professor?" asked Nick.

"Just that we are stuck on the island, as it were, and that we might as well ... well, get on with the task we came here to do. If you get my meaning."

"I certainly do," replied Nagle in disgust. "You want to take advantage of the terrorism by getting everyone back to work on your research. Is that it?"

"I simply want to take advantage of the *time*, Captain. That is all. We do, after all, seem to have a lot of time on our hands. And that time will hang very heavily upon us unless we have something to do.

Returning to the research project may be a way of keeping ourselves busy and our minds occupied until rescue arrives. Don't you agree?"

Nagle found it hard to disagree until he remembered Paul. "What about the creature?"

"Well? What about it?" demanded Stella. "There's no sign that it's been as far as the church. And that's where we'll be doing most of our work."

"And there's no sign that it hasn't either," suggested Nick. "It's more dangerous than you can imagine. I've seen it, and you haven't. And that raises another issue. We were planning to have funerals this morning for both Holly and Paul."

"There's nothing we can do for poor Holly," remarked Captain Nagle. "Her body went down with the *Covenant*. But there's still Paul."

"I'll go and recover his body," Nick offered. "I know where it is. But I'd like someone with me to keep a lookout."

"I'll come," volunteered Alan.

"That's settled then," said Nagle. "First thing after lunch you two will recover Marshall's body, and then we will all gather up at the colonial graveyard for the burial."

At this decision, Professor Royston opened his mouth to protest, but Captain Nagle headed him off. "And as for the professor's suggestion, we'll give that some more thought later."

As the Roystons walked slowly away from the group, Stella bent her head toward her husband and whispered harshly, "They will learn to do what they are told—or they will die!"

43

Shortly after lunch, in the blazing heat of the day, Nick and Alan trudged warily through the high grass in search of Paul's body.

Both spoke quietly, wary of advertising their presence.

"What is that?" asked Alan, stopping in his tracks.

"What's what?"

"Listen."

Nick listened carefully. There was a definite sound of rustling in the grass.

"Rats." Nick suggested. "My guess is the island is swarming with them."

"Are you sure it is just rats?"

"The creature that killed Paul makes quite a different sound," Nick assured the Canadian. "It's a heavy, slithering sound. Much more reptilian. Believe me, I'd know it if I heard it again."

Alan nodded doubtfully and resumed his forward progress, gripping the machete in his hand more tightly.

The grass was taller now—nearly two meters. After pushing through the long stems, Nick came across the path of flattened grass he had followed once before when searching for Paul.

"This is the way," he said over his shoulder, gesturing with the shotgun. "This path was made by the creature. See the way the grass has been pushed flat."

The flattened grass at their feet was brown and dead. Only the day before it had been green and lush.

"Look at this," said Alan. "Some sort of dried crystals all through this dead grass."

"I guess that's the dried-out slime of the creature," Nick surmised. Alan, who was bending down, about to touch the crystals, hurriedly withdrew his hand.

"Let's push on," said Nick, forging ahead.

Ten minutes later they reached the place where Dr. Marshall's body lay. It was still there. Much of the dried skin had been gnawed away, leaving the whitened skeleton exposed.

"That is horrible," exclaimed Alan.

"Right. You lay out that canvas sack flat on the grass," instructed Nick, "and I'll lift the shoulders, and see if we can slide the body in."

Alan nodded and laid out the sack with the opening just above the head and shoulders of the corpse. Then, with a shudder of repulsion, Nick bent over, took a grip on the exposed bone and withered fragments of flesh, and tried lifting. Immediately the joints parted, and the skeleton fell apart into separate bones.

"This is a most revolting task, my friend," muttered Alan.

"You're not telling me a thing," Nick said with a shake of his head.

There appeared to be no alternative, so Nick gritted his teeth, took a deep breath, and began shoveling the bone and dried-out skin fragments piece by piece into the canvas sack.

The Canadian stood back, looking green and ill, until Nick scowled at him, and then he joined in the grisly task. Between the two of them, they finished it as rapidly as possible. Then Alan hung his machete on his belt and picked up the bag. Nick kept hold of the shotgun. Several times he stopped to listen for the sound of slithering in the undergrowth as they walked. But they made it to the barracks site without incident.

"No problems?" Cathy anxiously rushed up to them.

"The corpse fell apart when we touched it," Nick replied.

"Oh, how horrible for you."

"But aside from that, no problems."

"I'm pleased," said Cathy, reaching out and touching Nick's arm. "I was worried about you."

Sam and Toby had dug a grave, and the body bag was lowered into it. Captain Nagle then pulled a battered copy of the *Book of Common Prayer* out of his pocket and read the service for the Burial of the Dead.

"Man that is born of woman hath but a short time to live ..." intoned the captain.

Nick looked around the watching circle.

The faces of both the Roystons seemed to carry expressions of irritation to what was happening. *Or am I just imagining that?* Nick thought.

Most of the others—Cathy, Sam, Vic, Toby, and Alan—simply looked solemn. Ingrid stood slightly apart, leaning heavily on her makeshift crutch and wincing occasionally with pain.

To Nick's mind, both Lois and Vicky seemed indifferent to the proceedings. *Now that's odd,* he thought. *Vicky was sweet on Paul Marshall. Shouldn't she be looking at least a little upset?*

"... earth to earth, ashes to ashes, dust to dust; in sure and certain hope of the Resurrection ..." continued Nagle.

But the Resurrection, thought Nick, *means judgment. Maybe the reason we are not good at dealing with death these days is because we can't cope with the prospect of final and ultimate judgment?*

Nick's gaze wandered to Max. The historian's eyes were red rimmed, as though he hadn't slept for several nights, and he rocked back and forth unsteadily on his feet.

He's drunk, realized Nick in amazement. *Max has got thoroughly sloshed. Great. We have two members of the expedition dead, the boat sunk, the doctor crippled, and now we have a drunk on our hands.*

44

Good afternoon. Muir speaking," quavered the old voice on the telephone.

"It's Frank Gordon, Mr. Muir. I'm afraid I have some bad news."

"Yes?"

"The contact that my reporter had with regard to the Order of the Crimson Circle ..."

"A former member of the Circle, I believe you said."

"Yes, well, that person is dead. Car accident. Hit and run."

"Was it really an accident?"

"The same thought had occurred to me, Mr. Muir," muttered the newspaper editor grimly. "And the truth is, we have no way of knowing. But that's not all. The news gets worse, I'm afraid."

"How much worse?"

"We have lost contact with the *Covenant.*"

"What do you mean by lost contact?"

"Well, I tried to call Nick by radio telephone an hour ago, and I was told that all radio contact with the vessel has been cut off."

"Dear me. That doesn't sound good, does it?"

"No, it doesn't. I spoke to the shipping company, and they confirm that their last contact was the regular report from the captain yesterday afternoon. Since then, he's missed two scheduled radio reports to the Sydney office."

"And how do they account for this failure?" asked Muir, after a thoughtful pause.

"They say their first assumption is that the boat is fine, but there is a technical problem with the radio."

"Why do they assume that?"

"Because the vessel was anchored in a safe harbor. If it had been at sea at the time, well, they would have feared the worst. But, seeing as how it was anchored … well, they insist that I shouldn't worry. They say they're not worrying."

"I see. And do they intend to do anything about it?"

"They say if it's just a routine technical problem, the ship's engineer, Vic Neal, should be able to fix it. So, they are expecting the *Covenant* back on the air within a few days."

"A few days? Hmm, I see. And if it isn't?"

"Then they'll call the authorities and report the vessel to be in difficulty."

"But in the meantime, we lose a few days," murmured Muir.

"Exactly," groaned Frank. "I'm not happy about it, Mr. Muir, but I can't see what we can do about it."

"We can pray. That's what we can do. I'll contact my people immediately. More than ever the folk on Cavendish Island need us to pray a mantle of safety over them."

"It frightens me, Nick. It really does," said Cathy, as she clung to her friend's arm.

On the way back from the cemetery, the party had stopped in front of the black church.

"I understand," said Nick. "It does kind of send shivers down the spine."

"That cursed thing," slurred Max, staggering uncertainly toward them, "that vile thing, it *bit* me. Can you believe that? It really did. It bit me."

"Here, let me have a look at that," murmured Cathy solicitously.

Max held out a bleeding forefinger.

"That's a nasty-looking nip," said Nick. "You'd better get Dr. Sommerville to clean and dress it for you."

"I will. I will. I fully intend to," slurred Max as he looked around uncertainly. "You never know what sort of infection you might get from that sort of … thing."

"What sort of thing?"

Nick's question went unanswered as Lois and Vicky joined the group. Both looked at the historian's bleeding finger and muttered something vaguely sympathetic.

"Do you think it could be poisoned?" bleated Max piteously, then added, "I'll pour some of my brandy on the cut. That will dis … disinfect it."

"It certainly can't hurt," agreed Nick. "It will clean the wound a bit. But you should still see Dr. Sommerville."

"I will. I will."

"Max, what bit you?" asked Cathy patiently.

"That … that … *thing*," slurred Max, waving vaguely in the direction of the church.

"What thing, Dr. Taunton?" snapped Lois impatiently. "Be more precise. Tell us exactly what bit you."

"Come here, and I'll show you," declared Max as he staggered toward the side of the church. The others followed, uncertain as to what he was trying to explain.

"There," announced Max triumphantly. "*That* bit me."

He was pointing at one of the carved stone monsters that decorated the walls of the church.

"It's an ugly brute all right," agreed Nick with a smile. "A cross between an eagle, a vulture, and a pterodactyl, I would say."

"*That* didn't bite you." Lois exploded. "Stop wasting our time."

"I tell you that … that *thing* there bit me. It really did."

"It's not real. It's stone." Lois angrily threw up her hands.

"If you don't believe me," said the drunk with a shrug of his shoulders, "then I'll just have to go and tell the doctor. She'll believe me."

"That's odd," Vicky quietly commented more to herself than to the others.

"What is?" asked Cathy.

"It's just that Paul also said that …" Her voice trailed away.

"Said what?"

"Nothing. No, nothing. It doesn't matter." With that, she hurried away.

"Cathy, come here," called Nick.

She joined him at the wall of the church where he was making a close inspection of the stone creature Max had accused of biting him.

"Look at its beak," said the journalist. "What do you see?"

"There is a smear of blood there. So that explains it. Max somehow managed to scratch himself on this thing, and in his drunken state thought it was a bite."

"Perhaps. You could well be right."

"Well, what other explanation could there be?"

"I really can't explain anything on this island, Cathy. So, for the time being, I'm keeping my mind open."

That night after Sam had managed to cook a meal on a barbecue grill he had set up on the beach, Nick joined Captain Nagle where he was sitting, some distance from the fire, nursing a mug of coffee.

"Deep in thought?" asked Nick as he lowered himself onto the sand.

"You could say that," agreed the captain. "I've just had the strangest conversation with Professor Royston."

"What about?"

"He was babbling on about the importance of that old building up on the cliff. According to him, and his hideous wife, that building has something to do with black magic, witchcraft, and secret rituals."

"He may be right."

"Not you too."

"Don't get me wrong. There's a universe of difference between what I believe and what the Roystons believe. But, as it happens, I've been reading something of the history of this island. And it appears that the commandant of Cavendish Island during its short period as a penal settlement was engaged in what the Roystons call the black arts. From what I've read, the commandant sounds like a thoroughly horrible piece of work."

"Yes, but that's just old superstitions. Nobody today believes in that rubbish."

"Tell that to the New Agers," replied Nick with a laugh. "All those astrologers and crystal gazers and channelers are playing the same foolish games as the old witches and Satanists."

"Ah, so you agree with me, Nick, that they are just foolish games?"

"Actually, I think I'm saying something a little different. When you talk about foolish games, you put the emphasis on 'games': You see it as childish and irrational. But I put the emphasis on 'foolish': And I see it as potentially dangerous."

"I'm a practical man, Nick. I have trouble with all that kind of stuff."

"Well, you'd admit that this world is divided between good and evil, wouldn't you?"

"Of course I would. The headlines in any newspaper, any day of the week, make that clear."

"So, if there is an active spiritual realm, what makes you think it is any different? Why shouldn't there be evil angels as well as good ones? Why assume that the great conflict between good and evil, between light and darkness, is confined to this world?"

"I guess my problem," said the captain quietly after a long pause, "is in believing in a spiritual realm at all. What I can see and hear and touch, that's my world."

"Well, that's where we part company, Captain," replied the journalist. "I'm a Christian. My worldview comes from the pages of the Bible. It gives me a perspective that is bigger than this planet, one that looks at the world from the broad standpoint of eternity, not from the narrow confines of time."

"This is all getting a bit heavy for me," Nagle said, setting his empty coffee cup down on the sand.

"But it matters," said Nick quietly.

"It's a bit strange finding a journalist who believes in all this stuff," remarked Nagle with a laugh.

"I'm a trained reporter, but I have also written some fiction. I've had a few short stories published. And I know the difference between the two. When I was a young journalist, I was an avowed atheist. But the guy at the next desk was a Christian. And we had some rousing arguments. They were good-natured debates, but they were solid. They used to start every lunch hour and be carried on in the pub across the street every afternoon. He wouldn't let up on me. Then the features editor asked me to write a piece about 'the building blocks of nature,' so I interviewed a professor at Sydney University. He painted this picture of atoms floating in space, of suns forming, of planets appearing, of life emerging from the chemical soup, and so on. After my piece appeared in the paper, my friend at the next desk said, 'If you can believe all that, what's so hard about the Incarnation and the Virgin Birth and the Resurrection?' And I didn't have an answer for him."

"So what did you do?"

"My friend challenged me to do what any good reporter would do—check out the sources. At the start of the New Testament there are four biographies of Jesus written by Matthew, Mark, Luke, and John. He challenged me to read at least one of them. I read all four. And I was appalled. What I was reading wasn't fiction, it was *reporting*. I was reading eyewitness accounts—written either by people who were themselves eyewitnesses, or who had spoken to eyewitnesses. Reporting has a *taste*, and I found that taste in what I read in the Bible."

45

The moon had finally risen, casting a pale blue light over the beach. When everyone had settled into their tents, Captain Nagle took his final patrol around the camp.

There was a line of seven two-man tents strung along the narrow strip of sand. The Roystons were in the first, Lois and Vicky shared the next, with Cathy and Ingrid in the third. The next in line had been allocated to Nick and Alan, then came the tent that Nagle shared with his engineer, Vic. Next to it was the tent occupied by to his two crewmembers, Sam and Toby. Finally, at the end of the line, was the tent that historian Max Taunton had to himself.

All the tents were in darkness except for the last. Nagle walked over to it and lifted the flap. Max was in his sleeping bag, but his eyes were open, or, at least, half-open. He was clutching a half-empty brandy bottle against his chest, and a hurricane lamp was sitting on the sandy floor of the tent, burning brightly.

"Shall I turn off the lamp for you, Dr. Taunton?" offered Nagle, "to save you getting out of your sleeping bag?"

"Leave it alone," he slurred in response. The captain couldn't help noticing a note of rising panic in Max's voice.

"It's time we all got some sleep, Max," Nagle said soothingly. "It's been a long and lousy day. We all need to get some sleep if we're going to cope with tomorrow."

"Light," whispered Max. "I must have light."

"Why?" asked Nagle, squatting down on his heels and looking directly into the other man's face.

"It doesn't like the light. It prefers the dark."

"What does?" asked the captain, knowing it was a mistake to argue with a drunk.

"It. That thing up there. The thing that did this," hissed Max, holding up his bandaged finger.

"What thing?"

"That creature, that gargoyle, or whatever it is that bit me."

"I heard all about that, Max. You scraped your finger on the stone, that's all that happened."

"That's all you know. It's all right for you. It's not after you. But it's coming after me. I know it is. But I won't let it get me. The light will keep it away."

"You won't sleep if you keep the lamp burning all night."

"I don't want to sleep. After sunrise, I'll sleep. It'll be safer then."

"If that's what you want," Captain Nagle began to leave.

"It's *my* blood it's after. So I have to take measures to protect myself."

Max was still mumbling to himself as Nagle left and walked the length of the beach to his own tent. He crawled inside and settled into his sleeping bag. His mind was whirring, and he wasn't sure he would be able to sleep. But it had been a long, tiring day, and he found himself tumbling into the realms of sleep much quicker than he had expected.

And as he slept, he dreamed. In his dream he was on the bridge of the *Covenant*. He was slowly navigating his way through a pitch-black night. He had the boat's fog lights turned on, and every so often he sounded the foghorn. The deep rumblings of that horn reverberated and echoed back again, sounding like some ancient sea monster. Nagle found himself gripped by an irrational fear that the foghorn would awaken some sleeping giant, a creature that had been hibernating in the deep mud at the bottom of the ocean since the dawn of time. He reached for the switch that would activate the blast of the horn, and found his fingers trembling. He couldn't do it. He was afraid of the monstrous power it might awaken.

Nagle glanced down at his navigational instruments: They were going crazy. The compass was spinning wildly, and none of the readings on any of the dials made any sort of sense. He peered ahead, trying to discern something, anything, ahead in the darkness. Then he seemed to see a shape, a deeper blackness that rose against the darkness of the night. The shape loomed and moved around the ship. And what was the shape? Nagle thought he could vaguely make out spreading wings. And talons. Were those talons reaching out toward the vessel?

Just then the shape seized the ship and began to break it apart with a crushing, shattering noise.

Nagle found himself lying awake in his sleeping bag, sweating profusely. It took a moment to remember where he was and what he had been dreaming. Vic was still asleep and snoring quietly beside him in the next sleeping bag.

Then Nagle heard it again: a crashing, shattering sound. That was what had awakened him. It had not just been in the dream—the noise had been real.

The captain crawled out of his tent and stood up. There was nothing to be seen except for the tents, the strip of sand, and the blue moonlight. Small waves lapped noiselessly up to the high-tide mark, then trickled away again. The waters of the bay were so calm as to be almost motionless.

Then Nagle saw a light, in fact two lights, weaving unsteadily down the stone steps from the cliff top. He walked briskly toward the lights.

When he reached the foot of the steps, he could see Max lurching toward him, a hurricane lamp in one hand and a flashlight in the other.

"I've dealt with it," shouted Max as he approached. "Attack is the best form of defense, so I've dealt with it."

"Dealt with what?"

"I remembered there was a sledgehammer in the tool box. I saw your men using it to hammer in tent pegs. And I remembered it."

"Well?" asked Nagle impatiently.

"I remembered the hammer. And I thought, 'I'll get the gargoyle before it gets me.' That's what I thought. So I took my lights, and I went up to it, and I smashed it. I knocked it off its pedestal, and smashed it into pieces. And now, Captain, if you don't mind, I'm going back to my tent, and I'm going to sleep."

With that, he began to stagger away.

"Dr. Taunton," called out Captain Nagle, "may I borrow your flashlight? I'd like to take a look at this thing you've been attacking."

In the cold, sapphire moonlight, the dark chapel looked even more sinister than it did by daylight. Nagle shuddered involuntarily and wondered if he was doing the right thing. Should he have come up here? In the middle of the night? On his own? "Yes, of course I should have," he told himself, "to do otherwise would be to give in to superstition."

He stood in the small clearing in front of the old stone building for some time, playing the beam of the flashlight over the facade. As far as he could see, all was in order, and exactly as he remembered it from previous visits.

He circled slowly around the building, and as he rounded the corner he caught sight of a stone plinth or buttress, which was empty: The statue it had held was missing. The captain directed the flashlight beam toward the ground, and there it was.

Max had told the truth. He really had attacked the thing with a hammer. Nagle knelt down and examined the broken remains of the statue. It had been shattered into four large pieces and a number of smaller pieces. It was, he recognized, an irrational thing to do, but perhaps it would mean that Max would get a good night's sleep.

As he stood upright again, he wondered what the Roystons would say about the damage when they saw it in the morning. "They will be hopping mad," the captain said aloud with a grin.

"Well, let them be." Nagle was pleased by the thought that the statue's destruction would comfort Max while, at the same time, discomfort Professor and Stella Royston. That was the kind of equation he liked.

Turning his back on the building, Nagle made his way back down to the beach. As he passed Max's tent, he noticed that the lamp was extinguished and the sound of loud snoring was coming from within. He smiled to himself and proceeded up the beach to his own tent and the warmth of his own sleeping bag. As he settled back down again, a deep weariness crept over him, and he fell asleep almost at once.

He felt as though he had slept for no more than a few minutes when he was aware of being violently shaken.

"Captain. Captain. Wake up," a voice was urging.

He opened one eye, and found Cathy's face just a few inches from his own.

"Captain, something terrible has happened," she said breathlessly. "I've already awakened Nick, and he said I should wake you up as well. It's poor Max," Cathy explained. "He's dead."

Nagle crawled out of his sleeping bag and out of the tent. The air was chill, and there was the first gray light of dawn filling the bay. He must have slept for longer than he realized.

"Now, back to the beginning, please, Miss Samson," he said.

"I woke up early," said Cathy. Her face, he noticed, was white, and her hands were shaking. "Actually it was Dr. Sommerville who woke me up. Her leg was hurting her, and she was groaning loudly in her sleep. I got her some painkillers, and then I realized that I couldn't get back to sleep myself. So, I got up and went for a walk along the beach, away from the tents. I didn't want to disturb anyone else. And when I got to the rocks at the far end of the beach, I found him."

"Found who?"

"Max. He's dead, and it's … it's just … horrible." Cathy sobbed these last words.

"Has she told you?" asked Nick as he grimly approached.

"I gather Taunton is dead," said Nagle hesitantly. "But I can't make sense of anything else so far."

"On the rocks, you said?" Nick addressed Cathy.

She nodded.

"Come on, Captain," urged the journalist. "Let's see for ourselves."

The younger man took the lead. As they reached the jumble of boulders at the end of the beach, Nick stopped. "There," he pointed, "up on that jagged point of rock."

The journalist began climbing over the intervening boulders, with the captain close behind. A minute later they were standing on a narrow ledge of rock, looking down on the battered body of Dr. Max Taunton.

"I can't believe it," Nick breathed quietly. "What on earth can have done this to him?"

"That's quite a mess," agreed Nagle in a voice that was little more than a whisper. "He's been ... disemboweled."

Max's body was flung backward over an edge of rock. It looked as though sharp talons had ripped him open from chest to pelvis. His internal organs had fallen in a tangled mess out of the body cavity. The blood was congealed and starting to blacken.

"Not just disemboweled," continued Nick, "but something ... whatever it was ... has taken bites out of him."

Trying to make sense of the mangled human flesh in front of them was difficult, but as he looked more carefully, Nagle could see that the journalist was quite right: In addition to the tearing, there were deep bites into one side—splintered and crushed fragments of bone and flesh marking the wounds where part of the body was missing.

Both men climbed back down from the rocks and stood somewhat shakily on the beach, trying to make sense of what they had seen.

"What sort of animal could do that?" wondered Nick.

"I have no idea," replied Captain Nagle. "It's like the sort of damage I'd expect from something large and ferocious. A lion perhaps? Or a crocodile? But there can't be anything of that sort on the island, surely."

"A lion, no. But if that swamp creature is a reptile, well, there may be other reptiles around."

"Could the swamp creature have done this?"

"I don't think so. Judging from the way it attacked Dr. Marshall, this is not its work."

"Then we have at least two killer beasts on the island to contend with," Nagle concluded darkly.

"It looks like it," Nick agreed.

46

*L*ater, several of the men gathered around Max Taunton's tent, trying to reconstruct the course of events that had led to his death.

"Look at those slashes in the canvas," said Sam. "Made with a knife?"

"Or with claws?" Toby leaned down to look closer, pale and shaken by the horror of the morning's discovery.

"What do you mean?" asked Nick.

"Look at these marks in the sand." Vic pointed. "It's as if something heavy has been dragged from the tent down into the water. That could have been Dr. Taunton's body."

"In that case," asked Nick, "why didn't he wake up?"

"I think I can answer that," said Captain Nagle. "Max wasn't just asleep, he was dead drunk."

"The poor man," muttered Toby.

"Toby, I want you and Sam to fetch Dr. Taunton's corpse. Place it in his sleeping bag, and we'll bury him beside Dr. Marshall."

"Not me. I don't want to touch him. I'm not superstitious, but Max brought some sort of curse on himself, and I'm not touching him. And that's final," Toby declared.

"I'll go with Sam," volunteered Vic.

"Thanks, Vic," said the captain. "You'd better get it over and done with as soon as possible."

As the others drifted away, Nagle stood there looking at the ripped shreds of the tent and thinking about the events of the previous night. So far he hadn't mentioned them to anyone. Had they really happened? Or had he dreamed them?

Determined to find out, he turned around and began the climb up the stone steps to the cliff top.

At the top of the steps he turned toward the black chapel, pushing his way through the low tangle of undergrowth. When he reached the clearing in front of the old building, he stood, and placed his hands on his hips. "Was I really here in the middle of the night?" he asked himself, "or was all of that just a horrible nightmare?"

The captain made his way slowly around the side of the building. He pushed away a bush that was obscuring his view, and there it was. There could be no doubt about it. It was the gargoyle that had obsessed the drunken man. But instead of lying on the grass, broken into pieces, it was sitting on its buttress just as it always had.

"Then I must have dreamed it," muttered Nagle to himself. "But it seemed so real. It didn't seem like a dream at the time. However, now I'm not so sure."

He walked right up to the statue and ran his fingers slowly over its carved lines. There were no signs of any breaks or fractures. It was just as whole, and just as ugly, as ever. Its body looked sleek, and fat, and—yes, well fed. Nagle even imagined there was a smirk of triumph in the lines of its horrible, curved beak.

"I've got to stop letting my imagination run away with me," he said firmly and walked decisively back to the camp on the beach to organize breakfast.

Max was buried immediately after breakfast. With the ceremony completed, the remaining members of the expedition stood in the colonial cemetery, as if reluctant to be parted from each other.

Already the sun was high in the sky, and its heat was beating down mercilessly. Moisture was steaming up from the ground and from the undergrowth. The slightest effort raised a sweat in that hot, tropical weather.

A heaviness and lethargy hung over the group. It was Alan Marchant who broke the pall of silence.

"Well," he said, "what do we do? How do we go about getting ourselves rescued?"

"Perhaps we could light a signal fire on the beach," suggested Vicky.

"We're too far away from regular shipping lanes for that to help us," Nagle informed her.

"What about airlines?" she persisted. "Do any of the airlines fly over the island?"

"None of the airline routes are anywhere near here," replied Alan. "If someone else in New Zealand buys an aircraft that is based in Noumea, and if the pilot ferrying it to New Zealand is blown off course, then someone will fly over. But otherwise ..." He shrugged his shoulders.

"What do we do then?" asked Cathy.

"We wait," proposed Nick. "That's all we can do—wait. When will your company become alarmed by the radio silence, Captain?"

"In another day or two. At first they will assume equipment failure, and they will also assume Vic will be able to fix it. They will allow two or three days for that."

"And then?" questioned Nick. "When they decide it is more serious, then what?"

"They will alert the authorities."

"And what precisely will the authorities do?" asked Alan.

"All shipping and aircraft will be alerted to keep a lookout for us. The Australian navy will send out a search aircraft. They will fly low over the island as well as search the sea in the general vicinity."

"And when they make their low overpass, they will see us, correct?" continued Marchant.

"Quite correct. Then a ship will be dispatched to pick us up.

They will probably parachute a radio down to us immediately, so they can know what sort of condition we are in and how urgent our rescue is."

"So," said Professor Royston. "We have another two, or perhaps three, days before we have any contact with our potential rescuers. How are we going to fill that time?"

"I know what I'm goin' to do," declared Sam quietly but firmly.

"And what's that, might I ask?" Royston asked, in condescension. "What entertainment do you have planned for yourself?"

"I'm goin' huntin'. Whatever killed Dr. Marshall, I kill it," replied the big Tongan. He said it with such seriousness and determination that no one doubted his ability to do just that.

"Sam and I together will hunt for the swamp creature," added Captain Nagle. "We'll take Sam's shotgun, my rifle, and a machete. We'll find a way to deal with that … thing."

"And what about the rest of us?" asked Lois. "What are we supposed to do? Just sit around for three days?"

"Why not?" proposed Alan. "That would be the sensible thing to do."

"It would not," snapped Stella. "It would be a stupid thing to do. After all that has happened, we need to keep our minds occupied. We need to keep busy."

"Quite right, my dear," her husband agreed. "And to that end, I propose that we resume our research. The expedition members are still on the payroll of the university. We might as well earn our money. And keep ourselves usefully occupied at the same time."

"I agree with the professor," said Lois. "What he says is perfectly sensible."

"Thank you, my dear. And what about everyone else?"

"I suppose so," said Cathy doubtfully. "I guess I might as well, if you are all going to."

"Excellent. Excellent."

"I'm afraid I'm of no use to man or beast," grumbled Ingrid. "All

I can do is to hobble back to the beach and try to make myself useful at the camp."

"You shouldn't go by yourself," advised Vic. "I'll come back with you. And since Sam is going hunting, I'll make a start on lunch."

"What about you, Mr. Hamilton? What are your plans?" asked Professor Royston.

"Well, if everyone else is going to be busy, I'll go back to the caves," he replied.

"What caves?"

"The caves that Dr. Sommerville fell into. There seems to be a whole system of caves underneath the island, and I promised myself that I would check them out."

"I will keep you company, if you wish," offered Alan.

"If you'd like to come along, you're more than welcome."

"Fine. That's just fine." Royston was more than satisfied. "Now Lois and Vicky, why don't you two take over the historical work here at the barracks. Stella and I will go back to the church. And Cathy, you can help us there."

"If you wish," said Cathy in a quiet voice, beneath which was a hint of fear.

"Excellent. Excellent. Well, let's all get moving again." The professor was in high spirits, perhaps because he had at least temporarily succeeded in taking over the direction of the expedition again.

"Let's synchronize our watches," said Nagle. "And we'll all meet back on the beach for lunch at one o'clock."

47

I'll go down first," said Nick, "and then you can follow."

"As you wish," replied Alan.

The two men were standing over the hole into which Dr. Ingrid Sommerville had fallen. Before beginning their expedition they had returned to the beach to obtain a length of stout rope from the *Covenant's* lifeboat, two high-powered flashlights from the emergency supplies, a small axe, and a large hunting knife, which now hung from Nick's belt. Nick had also slipped a notebook and pen into his top pocket—the reporter's instinct.

"We might need the rope once we get down there, so if we tie it to this bush with a slip knot, we can pull it down after us," Nick suggested.

"If you say so."

As well as jeans and a T-shirt, Nick was wearing his solid bush-walking shoes. With the aid of this footwear he was able to get a grip on the rock with his toes as he lowered himself, hand over hand, into the darkness.

When his feet finally touched bottom, it was on the slope of loose shale he had come across before. As soon as he let go of the rope, he began to slip and slide.

"I'm down, Alan," he called. "You next."

For a moment the light from above was blocked as Alan's body filled the opening. A moment later he was swinging lightly down on the rope and landing beside Nick.

"You've done this before," Nick observed appreciatively.

"I have done a little rock climbing in my time," said Alan dismissively.

Nick tugged at the rope, the slip knot came free, and the full length landed with a clatter at his feet. He picked it up, wound it into a coil, and slipped it over his shoulder.

"Right, let's get going then."

"You've been here before," remarked Alan. "You lead the way."

They slid more than walked down the steep slope of shale and gravel. At the bottom both men switched on their flashlights and shined the beams around the walls of the cavern.

It was a large, high-roofed natural cavern, and at the far end was an almost round opening, which clearly led into another cave or tunnel beyond.

Nick walked directly to the opening.

"Shouldn't we look around here first?" asked Alan.

"It's pretty bare," remarked Nick. "I didn't see much of interest last time I was here. No, I think we need to push on and find out how far this complex runs and where it leads to."

"If you wish," said the Canadian with a shrug of his shoulders.

When they reached the opening on the far side of the cavern, Nick paused. Beyond was a vast hollow blackness that his flashlight couldn't penetrate.

"This next chamber must be huge," he said.

Then he remembered the small skeleton he had seen on his first visit and directed the beam of his flashlight to the rocky floor.

"There, Alan. Take a look at that. What do you make of it?"

Alan crouched down and ran his fingers lightly over the dry, whitened bones. It was just as Nick remembered it: about the size of a large dog, but with greatly extended jaws. And embedded in those jaws were sharp, curved, vicious-looking teeth. Its feet ended in sharpened claws, like talons.

"Three days, my dear," said Professor Royston as he walked slowly around the cool, dark interior of the old stone building. "Will that be enough time?"

"More than enough," whispered Stella harshly. "We are almost there. Why do you imagine there have been so many deaths, Earl my love? The powers embedded in this place have already awakened. They have already started to *feed*. I have no doubt they have claimed the soul of Holly and of our own dear Max."

"Max's death means we will have to elect a new member to the coven when we get back," Royston realized.

"That is the least of our concerns now," snapped his wife abruptly. "I am also inclined to think that this place was involved in the death of Paul as well."

"But how could that be? Paul was killed by that creature from the swamp."

"And do you really imagine, Earl, that beams of power do not reach out from this center? Of course they do."

Just then the door of the black chapel opened, and Cathy entered.

"Here is your bag, Professor," she said, "the one you asked me to fetch from the beach."

"Ah, good. Thank you, my dear. Just put it down over there, beside the altar."

"Tell me, Miss Samson," said Stella, in a voice that was sinuous and oily, "have you ever, in all your studies of convict stone masonry, come across a building quite like this one?"

Cathy looked around at the horrible, grinning faces of the gargoyles and at the strange, disturbing patterns that caught the eye in every direction. "No, I never have. In fact, I've never come across anything even remotely like it."

She ran her eyes around the room once more. There was something disconcerting about the proportions of the room, as well as the decorations. Lines and angles did not seem to meet in quite the right way. Carvings on lintels and around the doors and the narrow windows seemed to hint at more than they portrayed. The effect was constantly disorienting.

"But," continued Stella, "this is not just a building to be observed and studied. This is a building to be *experienced.*"

There was a hunger, almost a lust, in her voice as she pronounced that last word.

"Experienced?" Cathy's voice trembled.

"Yes, exactly, experienced. And that is what we are about to do—you, and us together, my dear. We are about to experience all this building has to offer."

The closer they got to the swamp, the slower, and the more cautiously, Sam and Captain Nagle walked. The grass in the immediate vicinity of the swamp was shoulder high on both men and broken at intervals by short bushes covered in sharp thorns. The heat, the humidity, and the stillness of the air were oppressive. Nagle, who was in the lead, stopped to mop his forehead with a large white handkerchief.

"Not nice weather, is it, Cap'n?" asked Sam in a low voice.

In reply, Nagle glanced up at the sky that was slowly building up with banks of clouds.

"We might get some relief if that storm breaks," he said. Then he stuffed his handkerchief back into his pocket, lifted his rifle to the ready position, and pushed forward through the long grass and undergrowth.

Nagle was carrying a slide-action Remington M760 "Gamemaster," loaded with centerfire .22 Long Rifle ammunition in a tubular magazine. In the captain's hands, it was almost as fast as a semi-automatic weapon.

Sam was armed with an Ithaca single-barrel, pump-action, twelve-gauge shotgun with an extended ten-round magazine. It had a fully-choked barrel, which meant that he could get a deadly tight spread of pellets at maximum range. Sam knew that he could get off all ten rounds and still be far enough away to turn and run if the creature refused to fall.

A few meters farther on, Nagle stopped again to listen. Apart from the distant cry of a lone sea bird there was nothing—no stirring of wind, no rustling of leaves. The captain rebalanced his rifle across his arm and moved on.

Several minutes later they stepped through the last of the long grass and stood on the edge of the swamp, the body of water that had once been the Cavendish Island rock quarry. Sam nudged the captain's elbow and pointed. Some ten meters away, a half-dozen dark gray rats were swarming over the carcass of a large sea bird. Sam picked up a stone from near his feet and threw it with precise accuracy.

"Ignore them," said the captain. "Keep your eyes on the water."

The surface of the swamp was filled with floating masses of weed and the broad leaves of water plants. There was no ripple, and no sign of movement. It was so still it could have been a painting. In the few gaps between the weeds, the water looked to be inky black.

There was no breath of wind in those oven-like temperatures to stir the water and no sign of movement from beneath.

Nagle ran his eyes over the edge of the swamp. In several places there were the distinct signs of flattened grass indicating that the creature had, at some time, left or reentered the water at that point. The captain knelt down and peered into the black water, trying to catch some glimpse of movement below.

Having stepped through the almost circular opening into the larger cavern, Nick felt a gentle breeze blowing against his cheek.

"Can you feel that?" he called over his shoulder.

"There's a bit of air movement, isn't there?"

"So, you feel it too. It's not just my imagination?"

"What does it mean?"

"It probably means that at some point, perhaps a long way from here, this cave system opens out over the sea, perhaps in one of the high cliffs around the island."

A sudden scurrying sound attracted Nick's attention, and he flicked the beam of his flashlight in the direction of the sound.

"What's that?" asked Alan.

The light caught a swarm of a dozen or so rats scurrying across the floor of the cavern. Their eyes gleamed red in the flashlight beam.

"I do not like rats," Alan said with a shudder. "Those sharp yellow teeth spread horrible diseases."

"I must admit that I'm not a big fan of them."

"I take it that is an example of Australian understatement?"

"Yeah. Something like that."

They were moving forward, keeping their flashlights shining on the uneven floor surface.

After a while Nick paused and directed his light toward the roof of the cavern. It was barely visible many meters over their heads.

"What a strange natural formation," he remarked.

"This island had a volcanic origin, did it not?" Alan asked.

"Yes, I believe it did."

"Then perhaps we are in the hollow chamber created by the central vent."

"Could be. That makes sense. And perhaps the rest of the caverns and tunnels that open off this were the side vents back in prehistoric times."

"That seems likely, does it not?"

They walked on in silence for several minutes.

"If what you suggest is correct," said Nick at length, "then this floor we're walking on is the level the lava settled at when the volcano ceased to be active."

"Yes, I guess you are right."

Nick veered away from the straight course he had been taking and began heading toward one of the sides of the cavern.

"What are you looking for?" asked Alan.

"A way out of this main chamber. Look over there. Come on, this way."

A moment later they arrived at a side of the cavern. It curved away into the darkness high over their heads.

"I thought I saw an opening here," Nick said. "Ah, yes. There it is, just ahead."

He led the way to a tall, narrow slit in the rock.

"Come on, Alan. Let's see where this leads."

The opening was just wide enough for the journalist to squeeze through. On the other side he found himself in a natural tunnel with close sides and a high roof. The Canadian also squeezed through the opening and was soon standing beside him.

They took several steps forward, when Nick suddenly stopped.

"Look, Alan. Look down at the floor."

"What is it?"

"This is not natural rock we're walking on. This is a level cement floor."

"But that is impossible."

"Impossible or not, it's here." Nick crouched down and ran his fingers over the cement surface.

"No doubt about it," he said, "this floor was laid here by human beings. Someone has occupied Cavendish Island—and lot more recently than 1822."

48

"One of the best ways of doing historical research," Professor Royston was saying to Cathy, "is by entering imaginatively into the world we are seeking to understand."

"I suppose so," she replied dubiously.

"No 'suppose' about it," snapped Stella Royston. "It is by far the best way of understanding the past."

"Now we know," continued the professor, "that Commander Black, who erected this building, was a Satanist."

"Do we?" gasped Cathy. "I had no idea that—"

"Well, that just shows that you haven't done your homework," responded Royston smugly.

"You really should have done some reading about this settlement before you came, child," added Stella severely.

"But I thought I was employed to report on the convict stonework …" Cathy's voice trailed away.

"The stonework?" muttered Royston vaguely. "Oh, yes. To be sure. I'm certain you could write a very interesting paper on the convict masonry. And perhaps we'll think about that at a later date. But for the time being, let's focus on the function of the building."

"The function?" Cathy felt even more confused.

"Oh, don't be so dense, child," Stella said impatiently. "The function. Why do you imagine that a man like Commandant Black would expend so much time and energy on a building such as this?"

"Well, if he really was a …"

"Yes—say it, Miss Samson, that's what he was—a Satanist,"

Royston remarked. "Hence, the main function of this building, in the eyes of the man who designed it and built it, was for the purpose of conducting the notorious Black Mass."

"Black Mass?" Cathy swallowed hard.

"That's right, child," interrupted Stella. "So that is what we will do. We will enter imaginatively into the world of Commander Black in 1822 by reenacting a Black Mass."

"A Black Mass?" repeated Cathy increduously.

"Of course. Of course. This is an excellent approach to historical research," said the professor.

"The very best," added his wife.

"Quite so, my dear. As you say, the very best. We have the necessary implements to conduct a Black Mass, and that is exactly what we intend to do."

"Look, I don't really think I want to have any part in—"

"Oh, but you *will* have a part in this," murmured Stella with a sinister smile. "You will have a central and a most important part in this."

"That's very kind of you to think of including me, I'm sure," muttered Cathy as she backed toward the door of the building. "Why don't I continue my survey of the exterior masonry while you do … whatever it is you want to do?"

"But it wouldn't work without your help, Miss Samson," said Royston ingratiatingly. "I'm sure that you want to give as much help as you can to historical research. Surely you wouldn't want me, as a full professor, and one of the leading historical researchers in the country, to spread the word that you are incompetent and unhelpful."

"No, of course not. It's just that I can't possibly—"

"Good. It's settled then. You will assist us with our Black Mass."

Nick crouched down, examining the concrete floor. After swinging his flashlight beam around in an arc, he said, "These are oil spots here. At least, I think they're oil spots."

"I do not believe it," announced Alan.

"You can believe what you like," replied the journalist, "but I've owned too many old clunker cars not to recognize oil on cement when I see it."

He rose slowly to his feet and began to cast the light beam back and forth, up and down the tunnel.

"Which is the best way to go?" he said, thinking aloud.

"I would suggest that direction," said Alan with a gesture.

Nick looked in the direction Alan was indicating and swept his flashlight over the floor and the walls.

"No, not that way," he said at last.

"Why not?"

"Because the cement floor ends just a few meters farther on in that direction. I want to go the other way and see just where this level cement pathway leads."

"If you insist," said the Canadian casually.

Once again Nick took the lead, moving ahead more slowly, stopping often to examine the cement under their feet. After ten minutes or so he stopped again and drew Alan's attention to deep parallel scratches in the rock wall, high above their heads.

"Those are not natural," commented Nick.

"How do you account for them, then?" Alan asked.

"How about this: Say that some equipment was being moved down this tunnel—large, heavy equipment—and as it was being moved, it bumped against the rock wall and made those deep scratch marks. How about that for an explanation?"

"Most ingenious."

"Okay then, how would you explain the marks?"

"I can't. However, I am certain there is a natural explanation. What we are looking at—whether we realize it or not—is a natural phenomenon of some sort."

"Of an entirely human sort, if you ask me. All right then, we'll agree to disagree. Let's push on and see what else we find."

Their voices set off rolling echoes that reverberated through the tunnels and caverns long after they had stopped speaking.

With Nick still in the lead they resumed their cautious, searching progress. Suddenly there was a sound ahead—a hissing, slithering sound. Both Nick and Alan directed their flashlights toward the noise. For a moment there was the flash of something moving in the beams, then it was gone.

"What was that?" asked Alan.

"I'm not sure. I only caught a glimpse of it. What did it look like to you?"

"Was it a rat?" suggested the Canadian.

"If so, it was a very large rat. And it was the wrong color. And it didn't move like a rat. It moved more like a ... well, I once saw a monitor lizard, when I was in Indonesia, it was about that size," explained the journalist.

"Perhaps that's what it was then."

A few paces farther on they came to the place where the creature—whatever it was—had crossed the tunnel. They found small openings—about the size of storm drains—on either side of the tunnel.

"That's were it came from," said Nick.

"And where it went to," added Alan. "It came out of that opening there, dashed across the tunnel, and disappeared through the opening on the other side."

"I agree."

Nick crouched down and shined his flashlight into the openings. Both ended in corners a short distance away.

"I can't see anything," he said, rising to his feet. "Come on, let's keep going."

A few minutes later they rounded a corner in the tunnel and saw something that took their breath away: Set in the tunnel wall, just a few meters away, was a solid steel door.

"There's another *natural phenomenon* for you," said Nick in a startled whisper.

❖❖❖

"So you see, Miss Samson, there is really nothing to worry about. There is nothing to alarm you." Professor Royston was trying hard to sound warm and friendly. "It's not as though we are suggesting a *real* Black Mass. No, this is just a sort of historical re-creation, if I may put it in those terms."

"Still ..." said Cathy, not wanting to be difficult, but feeling extremely uncomfortable, "still, this is not how I was trained to approach history. So, if you don't mind, I would still rather have nothing to do with it."

"But we do mind," said Royston, all pretence at warmth and friendliness gone from his voice. "We mind very much."

"The reenactment cannot take place without you," Stella said coldly. "So stop being a foolish, empty-headed girl, and we will explain what's involved."

The professor began to babble about ancient traditions, superstitions from the Dark Ages, English folklore, occult practices of the ancient Egyptians, and many other things. Cathy wasn't really listening. She wanted no part of this activity, but both Professor Royston and his wife were standing between her and the door. If they hadn't, she would have made a run for it.

Stella Royston was a big, beefy woman who would have been close to twice Cathy's weight. *I'll never get past her,* thought Cathy. *I have to talk my way out of this situation somehow.*

As he kept talking, Professor Royston started unpacking a canvas bag he had carried up from the beach. He produced two long, elaborately carved candlesticks, each with a yellow, greasy candle. These were followed by a silver chalice with strange markings engraved on its side. Finally, from the bottom of the bag, he produced several black garments.

At first Cathy thought these were academic gowns, but when Royston held one up and shook it out, she saw that they were, in fact, monks' habits complete with hoods.

"Here you are, girl, this one is yours." Stella tossed one of the black monks' robes at Cathy. "Put it on."

Cathy held up the garment and looked at it, uncertain exactly what she was supposed to do with it.

"You are such a young fool!" snarled Stella. "What you do is take off all your clothes, then put on the robe. Do it now!" And with that, she turned back to watch what her husband was doing.

Cathy didn't move. She was frozen with fear.

The professor arranged the candlesticks on the altar and then lit them. The chalice was then placed exactly between them.

"Not like that," corrected Stella as she marched toward the altar.

Cathy recognized her chance and sprinted for the front door of the building. She flung it open—and there was blessed fresh air and sunshine. And there was Toby.

"Oh, Toby!" she exclaimed. "I'm so glad to see you. Those two in there are … quite strange. Come with me back to the beach, please."

"I'm sorry, Miss Samson, but you don't quite understand."

"What do you mean?"

"What he means, my dear," said Professor Royston, over Cathy's shoulder, "is that he works for us."

"I'm afraid that's quite right, Miss Samson. I am a member of their group. My job is to stand guard and make sure that you three are not disturbed. So you be a good girl, Miss Samson. You go back inside and do exactly what Mrs. Royston and the professor tell you to do."

49

Sam picked up a rock about the size of his fist and heaved it into the middle of the swamp.

"That'll wake him up," he said with a chuckle.

Nagle lifted his rifle to the ready position and began to pace warily around the edge of the water.

"If we split up," he said to Sam as he began to move, "that will mean the creature has two targets instead of one. So, let's make it as hard as we possibly can for it."

"And easier for us—give us more chance, eh?" said Sam with a grin.

"Exactly. Let's give ourselves as many chances as we can."

Soon the captain stood on one side of the body of water, Sam directly opposite.

"What did Nick say about the effect of the shotgun on the creature?" Nagle called. "Can you remember?"

"Sure," Sam shouted back. "Nick said, no effect. But I think he only fired once. Ten rounds of shot, that will have effect. I promise you, Cap'n."

"I hope you're right, Sam."

There was a long silence in the still, shimmering air. Then Sam picked up another large rock and heaved it out into the middle of the water. The thickness of the weeds caused it to land with a dull, unhealthy, squelching sound. Sam thought he would have felt better if there had been a nice, sharp splash.

"Still nothing," said Nagle after another long wait. He quickly added, "Hold on. There's some movement, I think."

Sluggish oily ripples were starting to spread out from the center. They heaved the weed bed up and down, like the beating of a dying man's pulse until, at last, they fell against the banks like dead waves from a dead sea.

"Something big is moving under there," Nagle said quietly.

Both men stood and stared, their eyes riveted on the stagnant surface of the swamp.

A moment later, lily pads in the middle began to lift, and then settle again. A large floating mass of weeds lifted and shifted, as if pushed from beneath.

"It's moving, Sam. Keep your eyes peeled," shouted Nagle unnecessarily.

Then the weeds lifted again, and for a moment there was a glimpse of a smooth, gray-green back—a rounded hump. It was there for just a second, and then it slid back into the water again.

"Wait until it's well out of the water before you try a shot, Sam."

"Aye, Cap'n."

A seagull flew overhead and called loudly. Both men had their gunstocks to their shoulders; both were ready to shoot.

Suddenly the weed bed began to turn, as if stirred from beneath. It broke the surface again—a gray, slug-like shape—only to plunge out of sight again almost immediately.

As the ripples ran across the surface, both men waited tensely.

Then it broke the surface again. This time the whole forepart of its body was raised up, like a cobra preparing to strike.

It turned toward Sam.

The door was embedded in the side of the tunnel. It was actually a set of double doors about three meters high and four meters across.

Nick walked up to them and ran his fingers across their surface.

"How's that for a *natural phenomenon?*" he repeated.

"That is enough sarcasm for one morning," Alan snapped. "You were right, and I was wrong. There have been men here."

"In secret."

"As you say, in secret."

The hinges were cemented into the rock, and the doors were bolted and padlocked.

Nick shook the bolts and rattled the padlock.

"Solid," he said.

"Perhaps even more solid than when they were put there," proposed Alan.

"What do you mean?"

"Just that they might be rusted into place and, hence, impossible to open."

"Oh, I'll find a way," Nick declared. "I'll find a way to get these doors open and find out what's behind them."

He leaned his weight against the double steel doors and pushed.

"Not even the slightest movement," he puffed. "If the *Covenant* had not sunk, we might have access to powerful tools and perhaps even explosives."

"But the *Covenant* has sunk. And all we have are those things that were rescued or were already in the lifeboat."

"But that includes some tools," persisted Nick. "I'm not giving up on this."

"That is admirable determination. But determination alone will not open those doors."

"I wonder who installed them—and why." The sound of Nick's last words rolled and echoed up the tunnel and back again.

"I have just had a thought," said Alan.

"Yeah?"

"Is it possible that the Japanese built these doors?"

"The Japanese?"

"During World War Two, I mean. Could they have used Cavendish Island as a secret base during the war in the Pacific?"

"I suppose that's possible," agreed the journalist. "They certainly had vessels in the South Pacific, submarines and lone raiders. Perhaps this was a supply depot for them."

"That is what I am thinking."

"Hey, it would make a great story: the last untold story from World War Two—war mystery revealed at last."

"Do you always think in headlines?" asked the Canadian with a laugh.

"I'm a journalist," replied Nick simply.

"What I am holding in my hand is an M52 automatic pistol with a fully loaded eight-round magazine. I have loaded it with powerful 7.62-millimeter bottleneck cartridges, although their usual muzzle velocity of 1,600 feet per second will be somewhat reduced by the silencer fitted to the barrel," said Toby.

"You wouldn't dare," said Cathy, in disbelief.

"We would dare," said Royston. "The whole point, Miss Samson, is that we would dare. We have already dared much more than merely disposing of the body of a young woman on an isolated island. Nothing will stop us from tapping into *the power* that lies all around us in this place—nothing."

"Don't make me hurt you, Miss," said Toby, jabbing her in the ribs with the barrel of the automatic.

Dazed and disbelieving, Cathy staggered back into the dark interior. She felt hot tears begin to trickle down her cheeks, then she was annoyed with herself for crying.

As Cathy entered the dark chapel with the Roystons at her side, she heard the doors being closed behind them and a bolt sliding into place. Toby had again taken up his guard station outside.

The altar was now more elaborately decorated than it had been before Cathy's abortive attempt at escape. It was dominated by a small statue carved out of highly polished ebony. It depicted a hideous dragon, in the style of one of the Asian countries.

"Charming, isn't he?" remarked Professor Royston, noticing where Cathy's eyes were focused. "I call him Belial. He is centuries old and has been used in the Great Ritual many, many times. As a result, he contains much stored power. It is his power that will enable us to fashion and control the power in this building."

"Now," commanded Stella imperiously, "take off all your clothes, girl, and put on this robe."

"I refuse," Cathy declared firmly.

Stella stepped up to Cathy, and with her eyes only a few inches from Cathy's face said, in a surprisingly deep voice, "You will obey."

"No, I refuse."

"She has a surprisingly strong will, this one," said Stella, turning away. "That will make breaking her will all that more pleasant." Then she turned back to Cathy and snarled, "For I will break your will, girl. You may be sure of that. And the more power I have to exert to do it, the less you will like it."

Stella stood back and stared at Cathy with a cold curiosity, like a scientist staring at a specimen in a bottle. "For the time being, Earl," she said, "tie the girl up."

And before Cathy could utter a word of protest, she found her hands being pulled behind her back and tightly bound with rope around one of the stone pillars of the chapel.

The thing that reared menacingly over Sam was like some gigantic caterpillar. It seemed to have no head, but on the front of it was an orifice of puckered skin, which opened and shut and slavered at the edges.

"Shoot man! Shoot!" yelled Nagle. As he spoke, he raised his own rifle to his shoulder and fired three shots in rapid succession.

The explosive cracks from Nagle's rifle seemed to wake Sam from his dazed state, and he began to fire his shotgun. He fired again and again, but it had no visible effect as the creature swayed over him.

"Five rounds rapid," muttered Nagle to himself, remembering his early military training. Five sharp cracks followed in rapid succession.

The thing appeared to be feeling the blasts. It wavered uncertainly and began to slide back into the water. Sam fumbled in his pockets for the box of spare cartridges he was carrying. Taking his eyes momentarily off the creature, he rapidly slid ten cartridges into the extended magazine.

This was a mistake, for as he looked up again, the thing leaned toward him and struck swiftly. As the creature fell on his arm, Sam heard obscene gurgling and sucking noises and felt a burning pain pulse through his body.

A series of rapid explosions next to his ear told him that Captain Nagle was firing at the thing from close range. The creature broke off contact, and Sam fell back exhausted.

The big Tongan's face contorted with pain, but he didn't make a sound as Captain Nagle dragged him to safety, well away from the dying swamp creature. Nagle then returned to the thing, picked up the machete and began hacking away, severing the forepart from the rest of the body. By the time he had finished, there was no sign of life left in the monster.

For the next minute or so the captain examined Sam's wounds in silence.

"It's that large wound on your left arm that has me worried," he said at last.

The next few minutes were spent cleaning and binding up Sam's wounds.

"That's all I can do here," said the captain. "Now, let me help you up. You lean on me, and we'll get back to the camp as quickly as possible, back to Dr. Sommerville and her emergency kit."

❖❖❖

The tunnel curved slowly around, restricting the view both forward and backward. The echoes caused by the men's boots seemed to reverberate and roll through the caverns and tunnels in all directions around them.

Although the flashlights they carried were large and powerful, much of the light they projected was absorbed by the rock itself, which was the same black basalt as the rest of the island.

"I should have spent more time on those steel doors," muttered Nick, complaining to himself. "There must be a way to open them. If only I'd tried harder, I might have found it."

"We can try harder later," suggested Alan. "What I don't understand is why you insist on continuing when we have already found enough mystery for one day. We should have returned to the beach, picked up a tool kit, and then returned to work on the doors."

"You can go back if you want," Nick replied irritably, "but I'm not finished here yet."

As they rounded the next curve in the tunnel, the path straightened ahead of them, and it appeared to come to a dead halt a hundred meters ahead.

"There. What did I tell you," Alan said. "Now can we go back?"

"Do what you like," said Nick calmly, "but I'm not done."

Marchant stood still and folded his arms, like a teacher waiting for a noisy class to pay attention. Nick pushed on down the final hundred meters of the narrow rock tunnel. "Alan, come here," he called.

Alan hurried to the journalist's side.

"Take a look at that," said Nick, triumphantly.

He was pointing to another door set into the tunnel wall only a few meters short of the end of the passage. This door was made from wood and was damp and rotted.

"Stand back," said Nick, "I'm going to break it down."

"Is that wise? We don't know what's behind there."

"Exactly. Stand back."

Nick kicked at the door, and it splintered under the savage

blow from his boot, swinging back crazily on its hinges. Nick kicked again, and the whole door collapsed into the dark cavity beyond.

"Now, let's go exploring, shall we?" puffed Nick, slightly out of breath.

They found themselves in a large cavern or chamber. Both swung the beams of their flashlights in wide arcs, exploring the area. It was smaller than the main central cavern they had come through, but it felt large and spacious after the confines of the tunnel. On the far side there appeared to be an opening leading into another cave or tunnel beyond.

Scattered across the level floor of the chamber were old pieces of wooden furniture—tables, chairs, and filing cabinets.

It was the filing cabinets that Nick headed for first.

"Empty," was his disappointed comment after sliding open all three drawers on the first. "They're all empty. They must have cleaned the place out when they left."

"Could they be World War Two vintage?" asked Alan.

"I guess so," said Nick. "It's not impossible. Hey, what's that over there?"

Nick was pointing with his flashlight toward a long desk set against the far wall. He hurried over to it. Set into the desk was a complicated array of dials and switches.

"This looks more like a scientific research setup than a military base," he remarked.

Nick pulled up one of the old wooden chairs and sat down at the control desk "Now, are any of these dials and switches labeled? Yes, they are. Good. Ah, no, that doesn't help—all the labels are numbers and letters. What does switch QF-44 do, I wonder? And what readings does dial KT-102 show?"

"As I said, we will probably never know."

"Stop being such a defeatist, Alan. Look, this panel here has some sort of faded map on it."

As he spoke, Nick wiped away the layers of dust.

"It's a map of the island," said the journalist excitedly. "Come and have a look at this. See, the black lines show the coastline and the sur- face features of Cavendish Island, but the thin red lines indicate some- thing else—probably the network of caves; that would be my guess."

"Quite possibly. It still tells us nothing."

"Oh, yes it does. There are red dots with small numbers beside them at several places. They might indicate storerooms, or other experimental stations like this one or ... well, almost anything."

"Exactly. They could represent almost anything."

"I'm going to copy this map of the cave system," announced Nick, taking out his notebook and pen. "And I'll mark all the places that are marked on the original. Then we can use this map to find our way around underground, and we can check out each of these places."

For some minutes Nick sketched in silence, while Alan paced nervously around the chamber.

"Map complete," Nick said. "Now, I wonder if any of these switches or controls still operate."

"Of course not. They would require electrical power to func- tion, and there is no electrical power on the island."

"Well, there once was. I wonder what they used. A generator, I guess. Perhaps with battery backup. Look, the cables from the desk run up toward the roof, and then into the next cave," said Nick, tracing the cables with his flashlight as he spoke. "Now, depending on how big the battery backup was and what sort of chemistry it operated on and how long it has been here ... well, there might be some power left."

"That's a lot of conditions to be met," said the Canadian sar- castically.

"Let's find out," Nick suggested. He leaped up and walked the length of the control desk, flicking every switch as he did so. Then he stood and waited.

For a long minute there was silence.

"See," said Alan. "What do you expect—"

But he stopped abruptly as a distant hum began. A moment later, small red and green indicator lights flickered into life across the desk.

From where Cathy was tied up, she could see the Roystons in the center of the building and the altar. It had become very overcast outside, and the little light that struggled in through the narrow windows had been even further diminished.

She watched as the Roystons proceeded to remove all their clothing. Then Stella produced a small jar of ointment from her handbag. She dipped her finger into it and used it to paint strange marks and signs on her body and on her husband's body.

She then approached Cathy and, dipping her finger once more into the pungent ointment, smeared some on Cathy's forehead and on her temples. As it began to burn into her skin, Cathy almost cried out loud at the pain, but she bit her lip and choked back her tears.

As the strange ointment began to take effect, Cathy found her mind starting to wander, and she became dazed and confused. Summoning all her concentration, she closed her eyes and prayed. She didn't ask God to release her from her terrifying captors, but rather that his will would be done in the situation—whatever that will might be. If she was meant to glorify him by dying faithfully and courageously, then she was ready to do so. She only asked that she would not fail him, or dishonor him, whatever the trial she had to face. She prayed for the strength to do so like a Christian.

The praying cleared her mind, and she found herself feeling calm and able to watch what was happening in a disinterested way—almost like a spectator. What Cathy didn't know was that at that very moment Wallace Muir and his friends were praying at his house, and their prayers were being added to hers.

Stella next produced a thick piece of chalk and proceeded to draw a pentagram on the stone floor. Around this figure she drew a large circle and wrote a number of strange runic symbols in the corners of the pentagram.

Both Roystons squatted in the lotus position inside the chalk circle with their eyes closed, while Stella began chanting in some ancient language.

With the black stone absorbing so much of the light, the small building was as dim as twilight. While the Roystons were preoccupied, Cathy struggled with the ropes that bound her. They were very tight, and freedom seemed impossible.

Stella was rocking slowly back and forth as she chanted in a strange guttural language that sounded like nothing Cathy had ever heard before. Between the two Roystons, right in the middle of the chalked pattern, was the silver chalice from the altar.

"Now, how did that get there?" Cathy asked herself. "Did Professor Royston place it there while I was watching his wife?"

Stella picked up the chalice and smeared some of the pungent ointment around the inside of its lip. A moment later she was holding a small silver knife in her hand. She gripped it firmly with her right hand, and then, much to Cathy's horror, plunged it firmly into the palm of her left hand. She held the bleeding wound over the chalice into which her blood dripped.

In the dim light it was difficult for Cathy to see everything that was going on. But it looked to her as if Stella Royston had rubbed some of the strange ointment onto her left palm, and the bleeding had miraculously stopped.

Then both the Roystons held the chalice together in their cupped hands as Stella chanted even louder. They rocked the silver cup back and forth in their joint grasp and swirled its contents around. After the chanting had reached a climax, Professor Royston surrendered his grip on the chalice, and his wife splashed its mixture of blood and ointment around the chalk circle.

"How repugnant," muttered Cathy to herself.

Once again she strained against the knots that held her as the light in the black chapel grew even dimmer and somehow—Cathy didn't understand how—seemed to take on a reddish hue.

Something seemed to be happening in the center of the circle, in between the two crouching figures. A mist appeared to be rising from the black paving stones, and something strange was happening to the light—it was shimmering and distorting and changing in peculiar ways.

A moment later, there was something there. Where there had been only the two human shapes, a moment before, now there were three shapes. And the third one was definitely not human. Cathy squinted through the darkness, trying to make out what it was.

It looked, vaguely, like a giant lizard. In her calm and detached way, Cathy remembered having seen a giant monitor lizard from Indonesia at the zoo when she was a child. The third shape in the circle could have been that, the giant lizard called the Komodo dragon.

But then she thought again. The shape wasn't quite right. It was moving now, twisting and turning in a sinuous way. It turned toward Cathy, and she saw its reptilian green eyes. They were disconcertingly intelligent eyes. The movements of its long neck and its strange limbs were darting and quick. If it had been an ordinary animal, Cathy would have described its behavior as disoriented and confused.

Both Roystons were staring at the thing that crouched on the stone between them. The professor looked amazed, and white with terror. His wife was smiling smugly and looking triumphant.

Still Cathy did not give way to the terror that was building up inside her. She made herself contemplate the strange reptile in a calm, uninvolved way, as if she was a mere observer to all that was going on. On second thought, she decided that it did not look so much like a Komodo dragon, but more like a museum model of one of the smaller dinosaurs.

Its muscular neck was thrust forward, and its jaws were wide open. The muscles were tense, the skin tight. Out of that long neck came a sound—a threatening, hissing, snarl. Its front limbs had gigantically developed central toe-claws. It looked every inch a predator.

I know what it is, thought Cathy. *Or, at least, I know what it looks like. It's just like that museum model of a small, carnivorous, dinosaur.*

At that moment Stella opened her eyes wide, pointed toward Cathy, tied tightly to the stone pillar, and issued a command, "Feed!"

50

---

*J*ust look at that," cried Nick excitedly, as row after row of small red and green lights began blinking.

"Be careful, Nick," warned Alan. "You don't know what you're doing there."

"I'm a journalist. Not knowing has never stopped me before," replied Nick with an impudent grin.

"I'm serious. Be careful."

Nick went back to the chair in the center of the long control desk, sat down, and watched what the panel was doing in front of him.

"The needles on all of these dials are starting to move, Alan."

"That's what I meant when I said to be careful. You don't know what any of that means, and what it could do."

"Some lights have come on underneath this map of the island."

"What do you mean 'underneath'?"

"As in underneath the frosted glass that the map is on. Some small white lights have come on, probably marking other important sites in the cave system."

Nick pulled out his notebook and added these places to the markings he already had recorded.

"Now, the large knobs beneath the dials must have some function. I wonder what it is." As he spoke, his right hand moved toward the nearest of the knobs.

"Stop it, Nick. I am not joking. This is serious. What if the island was land-mined by the Japanese when they left? What about that possibility, eh? I will wager that possibility never occurred to you. You might set off mines all over the place if you keep on fiddling. You might kill some of your friends on the surface. So do what I say, and leave it alone."

"You are really sounding like an old woman, Alan. In the first place, land mines would not be detonated from here: They'd detonate when we stepped on them. And so far that hasn't happened. So I don't believe the island is mined. And in the second place, there may be enough power left to run this console but there won't be enough for any major activity."

"You cannot be sure of that."

"No, you're quite right, I can't be sure. But it seems more than likely."

As he spoke he began turning the row of knobs he could reach up to their maximum. Within a few seconds there was a response: The distant humming that had accompanied the switching on of the machinery increased, slowly building to a higher note.

"You hear that?" cried Alan in exasperation. "Everything you touch has an effect."

"I can hear it. And I am coming to a conclusion."

"What conclusion?"

"That none of this equipment is as old as the Second World War. It couldn't be that old and still be in operating condition."

"Perhaps you are right. And if so, that is all the more reason not to play around with it."

"I'm not playing around. I'm investigating."

Nick rose from the chair and began walking up and down the long console-like desk. Every meter or so he stopped to examine the dials, switches, and knobs. Alan stood back, hands stuffed in his pockets, looking nervous.

At the far end of the console was a large red button, set in a metal sleeve as protection against being accidentally pushed. Underneath it was a small plate marked "AAA." Nick stood back and thought for a moment. But not for long. He leaned forward and pushed the button hard.

The whining from the next chamber increased rapidly in volume and pitch. Then, like the crack of doom, came the explosion. It was like the sharp, ear-shattering clap of thunder that comes when lightning strikes very close. Simultaneously came the flash of light. It came from the opening into the next chamber, and was so strong as to be almost physical. It was a blindingly brilliant, blue-white flash.

It was all over in an instant. As the echoes rolled away into the distance, Nick and Alan found their ears ringing.

There was an ugly look of triumph on Stella's face as she pointed toward Cathy.

When the strange, diabolical creature did not instantly obey her command, she repeated it.

"There is your sacrifice—feed upon it!"

Cathy understood that she was the "it" Stella referred to. She pulled again on the ropes that bound her, but it was no use. Professor Royston had secured her too tightly for escape to be possible.

The creature turned its head and looked in Cathy's direction. She was struck by its look of intelligence, or possibly it was raw cunning. Their eyes met, and then the creature turned away again and looked at the person who was speaking to it.

"You will obey my commands," snarled Stella, in a strangely deep, guttural voice. "You will kill the sacrifice and feed upon it."

The great lizard seemed more interested in Stella than in Cathy. The next moment it happened. Faster than a blink, the creature struck. It lifted one of its front claws and sliced open Stella's thigh, from the hip to the knee.

Stella stared, wide-eyed and open-mouthed, unable to make a sound, unable to move. The creature knew a victim when it saw one. It reached forward and gripped Stella with its front claws and swiped at her with one of its large back claws—slicing her body open from the chest to the pelvis.

Still the woman said nothing and made no sound. She simply sank to the floor in shock, rapidly bleeding to death. That was when Professor Royston began screaming. He didn't move. He didn't run away. He just screamed—a wild, inarticulate scream of pure terror.

The creature paid no attention to this noise. Perhaps it was the sort of noise it expected its helpless victims to make. It just leaned forward, took a deep bite out of Stella's shoulder, and began to chew.

With a loud rattling, the double doors of the church flew open, and Toby was standing there, pistol in hand.

"Kill it!" screamed Royston. "Kill it, you fool! Kill it now!"

But Toby didn't shoot immediately. Moving calmly but quickly he unscrewed the silencer from the gun's barrel. Only then did he take aim and fire five shots in rapid succession.

The reptile felt the blows of the bullets. It staggered and turned, with a stream of blood running down one flank. Then it moved toward Toby. Cathy was astonished at how fast it moved. But Toby moved even faster. The creature crashed heavily against the wooden doors as Toby pulled them closed behind him. Then came the sounds of bolts sliding into place.

"No!" cried the professor, who then curled up in a tight fetal position, sobbing to himself.

Royston's cry attracted the creature's attention. It stalked over to him and began to sniff his body. Cathy couldn't understand why it didn't attack at once. *Perhaps,* she thought, *it only kills moving prey.* She decided she was correct when the professor uncurled his body and staggered to his feet. The thing responded by snarling and crouching into an attack position, ready to spring.

"No," quavered the old man, his body looking white and shrunken. "No. Please. We have served you. You and your kind. For much of our lives we have worked for you. We have done the rituals. We have initiated others into your secrets. We are your servants. We are your slaves. We have lied for you. We have killed for you. Please …"

This last word was a feeble, trembling, fading note as the great lizard raised its razor-sharp front claw ready to strike. Cathy turned her head away. She couldn't watch any more.

51

We can't stay here much longer," Lois looked up at the sky. "There's a storm coming on. And I think it's coming on quite fast."

"I should update Paul's map of these buildings first," said Vicky.

"You've got his map there?"

"It's in my backpack."

"All right, do it then. But be quick about it."

Vicky fumbled with the straps of her backpack, and then produced the notebook she had worked on with Paul Marshall at the barracks site.

"I'm assuming," she muttered as she wrote, "that the more information we have about this island and its history, the better."

"We will certainly be expected to submit a very detailed report," agreed Lois, pacing impatiently. "The more detail in our report, the happier Master Control will be with us."

"And we know what happens when they are unhappy," added Vicky.

"Stop talking then, and get on with it."

For some minutes Lois paced restlessly while Vicky hurriedly scribbled notes and added details to the sketch map of the area she had drawn earlier.

"What's that?" asked Lois.

"What's what?"

"I thought I heard a noise."

"What sort of noise?"

"Rustling, in the grass. Didn't you hear it?"

"No. I heard nothing."

"Perhaps I imagined it then," concluded Lois.

"Isn't it dangerous?" Vicky asked as she wrote.

"Isn't what dangerous?"

"Allowing the Roystons to make contact with the Dark Powers before we do?"

"It will make no difference in the end."

"Why?"

"Because," replied Lois irritably, "we have resources available that you haven't been told about yet."

"Why haven't I been told? I'm a member of the Order, aren't I?"

"Yes, you are. A very low-ranking member. You are told what you need to know. And at this moment you don't need to know about all the resources Master Control is employing in this operation. When the time comes, you will be told."

Vicky looked sulky, but she kept on writing.

"There, I heard it again," said Lois a moment later.

Vicky snapped her notebook closed, cocked her head to one side, and listened carefully. "Yes, I can hear it now," she said, as she slipped the notebook into her backpack..

"It seems to be all around us," Lois whispered.

And then they began to appear out of the long grass: rats—large, sleek rats with long, gray snouts and sharp yellow teeth.

"Ugh," gasped Lois. "I hate rats. I can't stand them. They make my flesh crawl."

"I don't like them much myself," agreed Vicky. "Let's get out of here."

But when the two women turned to leave, they found the rats surrounding them in a wide circle. More and more of them kept emerging from the long grass.

"There are hundreds of them," whimpered Lois. "Hundreds and hundreds."

Vicky turned and started to walk toward the trail that led back to the beach. But instead of moving away, the rats turned in her direction and started to creep toward her.

"They're very aggressive," murmured Vicky. "It's almost as though they're ambushing us."

"Vicky." Lois gripped her companion's arm. "I have a phobia about rats. If one of them so much as touches me ..."

Again the two women tried taking some tentative steps toward the path back to the beach, and again the rats responded by moving closer to them. There were more of them now—and they looked very hungry.

"Do we have a weapon of any kind?" asked Lois cautiously.

"No. The others took all the weapons. Hold on ..."

"Yes? What is it?"

"I wonder how dry this grass is."

"Why?"

"I have a cigarette lighter in my pack."

"Yes! Yes! Try it. Try anything."

Vicky slipped her pack off her shoulders and fumbled around inside it.

"Quickly, quickly," whimpered Lois. "They're getting closer."

Vicky found the cigarette lighter. It was almost full of lighter fluid. She flicked the lighter into flame and inched toward the tall grass.

As she moved, one of the largest rats made a dash toward her. It sank its teeth into her wrist. She screamed, dropped the lighter, and staggered backward. She lifted her hand, the rat still dangling from it. She shook the savage rodent off her hand and kicked at it savagely. It scampered back a safe distance. Vicky held her bleeding right wrist with her left hand. It was burning with pain.

"Give me your handkerchief," said Vicky.

Still keeping her eyes on the steadily encroaching circle of rats, Lois produced a white handkerchief and tied it around Vicky's wrist.

"Now we've lost our only weapon," moaned Lois.

"No. Look," cried Vicky excitedly. "Where I dropped the lighter, the grass is burning."

Red and yellow flames were leaping from a tuft of long grass and starting to spread rapidly. Low, hungry flames burned quickly through the dry grass, spreading out in a circle. Soon there was a burned, blackened patch, surrounded by leaping flames.

"Come on," urged Vicky. "Into the center of the fire. If we stand on the blackened grass, we should be safe."

Frozen with fear, Lois stared at the closing circle of rats.

"Come on, Lois, get moving."

Vicky forced her terrified companion to run forward, jump over the low wall of flames, and take a stand in the burned circle.

"Now we should be safe," said Vicky, catching her breath.

But the rats seemed strangely reluctant to retreat. And there were so many of them—waves and waves of them in a tight circle now—that the front rows were being pushed forward by the aggressive, hungry rats behind them. As the flames approached, the rats rose up on their hind feet, but they didn't retreat.

The fire reached the first ranks of the densely packed circle. The savage creatures squealed as the flames engulfed them. There was a sharp crackling sound and a horrible stench as the rats began to burn.

At last the outer circle of hungry rats started to break up and retreat.

"Now," cried Vicky. "Come on, Lois. This is our chance. Can you do it?"

"I ... I think so."

"Come on then. Let's go."

Vicky took the terrified Lois by the hand and led her over the charred bodies of their small attackers. The bones of the burned rats crunched beneath their shoes. Then the two badly frightened women leaped over the flickering flames at the edge of the fire—and ran for their lives.

52

---

strong odor drifted through the cavern. Nick sniffed thoughtfully.

"I can smell ozone," he said.

"What?" asked Alan.

"The heavily ionized air you can smell after a lightning strike."

Nick picked up his flashlight from the strange electronic console, its beam looking very dim and yellow after the brilliant flash of a moment before. He led the way toward the opening on the far side of the cavern, the opening from which the flash and explosion had come.

"Come on, Alan," he urged, "this way."

"I think that is unwise."

"Well, you can stay here if you like. I'm investigating."

With that, Nick stepped though the opening and disappeared from sight. All that remained was the reflected glow of his flashlight. After a moment, Alan followed.

The chamber was smaller than the first. Lying on the floor, against one wall, was a very large metal pipe, some half a meter in diameter and three meters long. Its outer skin was a dull, burned black, and it was connected to heavy cables at both ends.

As Alan entered the chamber, Nick was crouched over the pipe.

"Don't touch that," warned the Canadian. "Haven't you done enough damage already?"

"This is where the humming is coming from," said Nick. "It

sounds as though it holds some sort of storage facility, and it's slowly building up a massive electrical charge."

"Then stand back before you are electrocuted," snapped Alan impatiently.

Nick rose and ran his flashlight beam around the small cave.

"There's nothing else here," he announced. "But there is an opening on the other side. Let's keep moving."

Without waiting for a reply from Alan, Nick disappeared through the opening into the tunnel beyond.

"Look down toward your feet," called Nick over his shoulder. Alan saw several thick, heavy-duty cables snaking along the floor of the tunnel in the direction in which they were walking.

The tunnel was so narrow that they had to walk in single file, and, occasionally, had to duck as they passed under bulges in the rocky roof of the passageway.

After walking a hundred meters or so, they came upon another steel door set into the side of the tunnel.

"This one's locked too," said Nick. "I've been struggling with it, but it won't budge. However, look at that."

With his flashlight beam Nick indicated the cables that ran into the steel door.

"See, there are networks of cables on both sides. Some of them run back the way we have come, and some run on ahead of us. And listen."

Both men stood and listened for a moment.

"I'm right, aren't I?" Nick continued. "There is a buzzing electrical sound coming from behind that door."

Alan nodded in agreement.

"So, whatever power supply system was left in place when these caves were deserted is in there—and still working. It's a pity we can't get at it. Anyway, let's keep following these cables and see where they lead. Follow me."

For some minutes they walked in silence, the only sound the

echoing scrape of their boots on the rock. Then the tunnel opened out, and they were in another large cavern.

The cables snaked across the floor of the vast cavern in several clusters. One cluster ended at the far wall at what appeared to be another console of electrical switches set into the rock face. In front of the console were two high-backed chairs.

"I'll check that out." said Nick nodded toward the console. "You check the other cables."

"I certainly will not," protested Alan. "I have learned not to trust you, Nick, in the presence of electrical equipment. We will both check out the console."

"As you wish."

Their footsteps echoed from the high ceiling and the surrounding tunnels. Alan was the first to reach the console, as Nick kept stopping to look around. When he caught up with him, Alan was staring down at the two high-backed chairs, his face as white as a ghost, his eyes wide open, his jaw sagging. He seemed to be incapable of speech.

There, seated in each of the chairs, was a corpse. Each was little more than a skeleton, with skin like the dried, mummified flesh of an Egyptian pharaoh stretched tightly over the bones. The journalist reached out a hand to touch one of the bodies.

"Do not do that!" cried Alan in alarm.

"Why not?"

"We do not know what killed them. You might become infected. Or something. I do not know. But you should not touch them."

Nick ignored Alan's warning and lightly touched one corpse on the cheek. Immediately the dried, taut skin crumbled to dust. It gave him a start, and he stepped back.

"See. I told you not to touch them."

"Well, they are not Japanese," said Nick after a thoughtful pause. "So this is no leftover World War Two base. That's one theory out the window. But the big question is: How did they die?"

"We will never know that."

"Perhaps. However, I can tell how they appear to have died."

"Then tell me. How?"

"From old age."

"That is ridiculous."

"Quite possibly. But that's what it looks like. Dried, wrinkled skin; thinning hair; wasted muscles. If the corpses weren't so well preserved, I'd assume that's what it is."

"And you would be wrong," said Alan firmly, "quite wrong."

The corpses sat in their high-backed chairs as if waiting for an order to operate their console. Both were dressed in the traditional white coats of laboratory assistants.

"Some sort of scientific research was going on here," said Nick at last. "At the risk of pointing out the obvious, highly secret scientific research. Someone was doing something here they didn't want the rest of the world to know about."

"Then where are they now?" challenged Alan.

"Something went horribly wrong with their experiments or tests," replied Nick quietly. "Everyone else fled—leaving their dead behind."

Cathy kept her eyes squeezed tightly shut. She could hear the diabolical creature eating, but she didn't want to watch it. She could hear the sickening crunch of bones and smell the sickly, coppery aroma of fresh, warm blood. But she didn't want to see.

Hidden behind her eyelids, she prayed desperately and repeatedly, "Please save me. Save me. Save me. Save me." Gone was her sense of distance and detachment. Now her nostrils and her mind were filled with the stench of death, and all she was able to do was cry out to God in despair and desperation, "Please save me. Save me. Save me."

She could feel hot tears coursing down her cheeks; her breath was coming in shallow gasps as she sobbed quietly. She knew sound and movement attracted the reptilian thing that was eating the Roystons, and she was determined not to move and not to utter a sound. She was helped by the ropes that bound her so tightly. She knew that without them she would have trembled, run, fled—and been caught and killed. But the ropes held her in place, and kept her still. All she had to do, Cathy told herself, was not to cry out—not to make a sound—and perhaps that thing would ignore her.

Where is Toby? Cathy asked herself. The question kept turning around in her mind: *Why doesn't he reload, come back, and kill that creature?*

She took deep breaths and tried desperately to calm her mind.

I need to remember something calming. Something encouraging, Cathy thought. *What words of the Bible can I remember?*

She squeezed her eyes even more tightly shut, and concentrated. The first words that came into her head were those of St. Paul: "To be absent from the body is to be present with the Lord." As she remembered these words, a little of the tension started to drain away.

Cathy was not afraid of death. She knew that once her body was dead, she would be in the hands of God. She would stand before him as someone whose failings and wrongdoings, whose willful rebellion had been paid for by Jesus as her substitute in his death on the cross. She would stand before God as one of the Ransomed Ones: as one of God's own family.

Being dead did not frighten Cathy. She knew the Bible promised that on that day Jesus would wipe away every tear. She knew with utter certainty that those who knew him in this world would be with him in the next and that she would hear him say, "Enter into the inheritance of your Lord."

Being dead did not frighten Cathy. But the business of dying did. *Would there be much pain?* she wondered. When the creature finished its meal and attacked her, would she die quickly? Or would she feel every hideous slash, every painful bite?

Cathy opened her eyes. As she did so, the creature turned slowly toward her. Blood was dripping from its jaws. It opened its mouth and snarled, displaying rows of sharp, curved teeth. But still it didn't move toward her.

Cathy blinked. She was finding it hard to see inside that somber chapel. And not just because of the darkness.

There seemed to be a mist building up.

Then the little light there was seemed to shiver uncertainly. The creature appeared to be quivering, and its outline was no longer so clear. The shimmering in the air became more pronounced, and a moment later, the creature was gone—vanished.

Cathy fainted.

53

Captain Nagle and Sam staggered down the steep stairway that led from the cliff top to the beach. Sam was leaning heavily on his captain and gasping for breath. Although he never complained, his face was contorted with pain.

"Nearly there, Sam," said Nagle. "Hang on."

"Aye, Cap'n," was the grunted reply.

As they reached the foot of the steps, Vic and Ingrid caught sight of them.

"Come on, give me your other arm, Sam," said Vic. "Lean on me. We'll get you to the camp, and the doctor can take care of you."

Ingrid had already summed up the situation and, leaning heavily on her walking stick, had hobbled back to her tent to fetch her emergency kit. By the time the two men had brought their colleague down the beach, the doctor was sitting on a ground sheet spread over the sand, her medical kit open beside her.

"Sit him down here," she instructed, "beside me."

Nagle and Vic lowered Sam onto the ground sheet, and he lay back with a groan.

"What did this?" asked the doctor.

"That swamp creature," explained Nagle. "It attacked Sam as it was dying."

"So, hmm," muttered Ingrid, as she peeled off the makeshift bandage and examined the wound underneath, "there's something in that beast's saliva that has infected this wound. I'll give

Sam an injection of broad-spectrum antibiotics, clean out the wound with antiseptic, and give him some sulfa tablets to take. That should do it."

"How bad is it?" asked the captain.

"It's a large wound, but not a deep one. I've seen worse. He'll live."

"Thank God for that," muttered Nagle.

"Amen to that, Captain," added his engineer.

"You can thank whomever you like," said Ingrid as she worked. "Personally, I'm an atheist. Sam is a fit young man, and the body has remarkable recuperative powers, so I think he'll be fine."

Nagle and Vic walked slowly down the beach, leaving Ingrid to her work.

"That's good news about Sam," Vic said quietly, "but we have another problem."

"Yes?"

"Cyclone Jezebel. Have you noticed how dark the sky has become? And how much the wind has whipped up?"

"Yes, I have, Vic. So far, I've avoided worrying the others, but I know what you're saying. We can't stay on this beach; it won't be safe."

"I've been planning ahead, Captain. This morning, while you and Sam were hunting, I've been packing up our gear, getting it ready to move out to a safer place."

"Good man." Nagle slapped his engineer on the back.

Just then they heard five gunshots, fired in rapid succession.

"Where did that come from?" demanded the captain.

"From up there," replied Vic Neal, pointing. "From inside the old church."

The two men arrived at the clearing in front of the church to find the doors to the old stone building bolted shut. Nagle slid back the bolts and threw open the doors. He was greeted by the sight of the mangled, butchered bodies of Professor Royston and his wife.

Vic swore under his breath; the captain was silent. For a long moment both men stood frozen on the doorstep, then the captain advanced.

"Dead." Vic was unable to restrain himself from stating the obvious.

"And partly eaten, by the look of it," added the captain.

"But ... Who? How? Why?" stammered Vic.

"Perhaps there's another of those swamp creatures—or its smaller cousin—around somewhere."

"Captain, over here," shouted Vic, who had dragged his eyes away from the bloodied corpses and seen Cathy, bound by ropes to one of the stone pillars.

"She's unconscious," said Nagle, hurrying to her side. "Come on, Vic, get her untied and out of this wretched place."

Vic struggled with the knots for a minute, then pulled out his sailor's knife and sliced through the ropes. Cathy sagged forward, and Captain Nagle caught her in his arms. With Vic holding her shoulders, and the captain her feet, the two men carried the unconscious girl outside and laid her on the grass in the clearing in front of the dark chapel.

As they stood there, taking deep breaths of the fresh air being whipped off the ocean by a strong wind, the two men looked at each other. Then, without exchanging a word, Nagle walked over and closed and bolted the door. Neither of them felt as though they could cope with the horror inside.

Cathy groaned, and Nagle dropped to one knee by her side.

"Nick?" she murmured.

"It's Captain Nagle, Miss Samson. Have you been hurt? Are you all right?"

"All right? Yes. I think so," she replied weakly. And then, with a rising note of panic in her voice, she said, "The professor. And Mrs. Royston ..."

"We've found them, Miss Samson. They are beyond help and beyond hope. You saw what happened?"

"Yes, I did ..." began Cathy, and then she started to sob.

At that moment Toby stepped out of the bushes. "I heard some shots. What's going on?"

"We heard those same shots," answered Vic, "and we came up here to find the Roystons dead and Miss Samson tied up inside."

"Dead? How did they die?"

"You saw them die," said Cathy breathlessly, restraining her tears. "It was you who fired those shots."

"Me?" protested Toby. "That's nonsense. I was around the cliffs, looking for somewhere safe for us to move to for protection from the cyclone. The girl's delirious."

"It was you," whispered Cathy, with a vehemence that sapped her strength. "I saw you. I know you were there. You were part of it."

"You're not going to believe the ravings of a delirious woman, are you, Captain?" Toby appealed to Nagle.

"At the moment I don't care what happened," snapped Nagle. "We can sort that out later. For the moment, Miss Samson has to be seen by the doctor. And then we need to move the camp."

There were several large tunnels leading out of the vast underground cavern. Having temporarily abandoned the mystery of the dead scientists, Nick checked each opening. Then he turned to Alan. "This way Alan. I can feel a breeze here. This one probably leads to the surface."

Without waiting for the Canadian to reply, Nick walked briskly into the tunnel. Alan had to hurry to catch up.

"Do you understand what is going on down here, Nick?" asked Alan.

"Understand is the wrong word, my friend," replied Nick, "but I'm starting to develop a few educated guesses that won't be too far from the mark."

"And what are those guesses?"

"For the time being I intend keeping them to myself," replied Nick.

That remark closed the possibility of further conversation, and for several more minutes the two men walked in silence, their ears echoing to the sounds of their footsteps.

"Hold on, what's this?" said Nick as he rounded a bend in the tunnel.

"What is it now?" asked Alan, an uncertain tone in his voice.

"It's a nest. At least, I think it is. That's certainly what it looks like."

Alan drew level with Nick and looked over his shoulder. Immediately ahead of them was a low, thick-walled cylinder of mud, in the center of which were a number of extremely large eggs.

Nick moved forward slowly, his flashlight trained on the gray, mottled surface of the eggs.

"They are huge," he said, breathlessly. "I've often seen emu eggs, and someone once showed me an ostrich egg, but these are much bigger. And there are, let me see ... five, six, seven of them."

Nick approached the sloping mud wall of the nest and crouched down. Tentatively he reached out and touched one of the eggs. Then he ran his fingers over another, and yet another.

"Cold," he remarked. "These aren't being cared for any longer. But I'd very much like to know what bird, or reptile, laid them."

"Why?"

"Because whatever it was, it was very big. And I don't fancy walking around a maze of tunnels that I share with some very large, unknown creature."

Alan looked nervously over his shoulder. "Perhaps we had better press on."

But Nick was not interested in leaving at the moment. He was busy examining the area surrounding the nest with his flashlight.

"These, I take it," said Nick, "are the footprints of Momma and Poppa."

He indicated imprints in the mud on the floor of the cave made by a large, three-toed claw.

"Have you ever seen anything like that before?" asked Alan.

"Never. And I would be quite happy if I never see the animal whose claws fit these tracks. Look at that long, curved center toe. That is a talon that could rip a horse to pieces. And judging by the depth the prints have sunk into the mud, I would guess this creature has a fair amount of weight to put behind its attack."

"You are making me nervous, Nick. I would like to leave these caves, and I would like to do so very quickly."

"Yeah, I don't feel all that comfortable myself. Let's move on."

The two men continued down the tunnel, the breeze growing stronger all the time. After a few minutes Alan said, "Listen. Can you hear that?"

"Yes. It's the sound of the sea," agreed Nick. "We must be getting close to the cliffs."

"And to a way out of here," added Alan.

STORM SURGE

Darkness was over the surface of the deep, and the Spirit of
God was hovering over the waters.

—Genesis 1:2

54

*T*he first treatment Ingrid provided for Cathy was simply to
hold her in her arms and let the young woman sob on her
shoulder.

"You're suffering from shock," said Ingrid, patting Cathy's back
gently. "And from what I've been told, that's hardly surprising."

"I don't know for sure exactly what happened up in that old
building," said Captain Nagle, "but whatever it was, it was pretty horrible."

"Do you want to talk about it?" Ingrid asked Cathy.

"The Roystons," began Cathy, in a quiet voice, "they were …
they were devotees of witchcraft and Satanism and—"

"Never trusted either of them," interjected Nagle. "I wish I'd realized what they were up to, Miss Samson. Then perhaps you wouldn't have had to go through …"

"You weren't supposed to know, Captain," said Cathy. "None of us were. We may not have liked them particularly, but none of us realized just how strange and evil they were."

"What did they do?" asked Ingrid, her curiosity aroused.

"They conducted a ceremony, a ritual, of some sort," Cathy replied, trying to sound casual as the horror of it all came flooding back.

"Some sort of hocus-pocus nonsense?"

"Something like that. Only it wasn't nonsense. It worked."

Ingrid snorted in derision. "That sort of thing doesn't work," she huffed. "It's all impractical, immaterial nonsense."

"Well, you may need to rethink your philosophy of life," responded Cathy with a weak smile. "This time it worked."

"So, what happened?" Ingrid inquired skeptically.

"It was a summoning ritual they performed. They held me there, tied up, to be a sacrifice to the being they called up. And it appeared. A creature. A beast."

"You must be in shock," Ingrid murmered. "You're delusional."

"Don't be so narrow-minded. Toby saw it too. He fired his pistol at it."

"He's still denying that, you know," muttered Captain Nagle.

"Of course he is," Cathy snorted angrily. "He was part of their weird cult, or coven, or whatever it was. He stood guard at the door and prevented me from escaping from their clutches. That's why he denies it."

"Really? Did he indeed?" Nagle raised his eyebrows.

"Please believe me," pleaded Cathy. "I know what I saw. I know what happened."

"I don't disbelieve you, Miss Samson," said Nagle. "But, for the moment, there is very little I can do about it. However, I will keep Toby under very strict observation from now on."

"Thank you, Captain, for not dismissing my experiences as the ravings of a weak-minded female."

Ingrid spoke bluntly, "They must have given you an hallucinogenic drug if you imagine that their ritual actually worked."

"Ingrid, please don't have such a closed mind," pleaded Cathy. "How do you explain what happened up there? The Roystons weren't just killed—their bodies were torn to pieces, and partly eaten."

"The girl's telling the truth there, Doctor. I saw it. Just utterly, indescribably, horrible."

Cathy went a pale green color as she remembered the horrors she had seen, and heard, and smelled. For a moment, she buried her face in her hands. Then she recovered her composure.

"The doors of the building were locked," she resumed.

"That's true," said Nagle. "I unlocked the doors myself."

"And I was tied to a stone pillar. I couldn't move at all. So what attacked the Roystons? What inflicted those horrible wounds? What *ate* them? How did they die?"

"I can't explain any of that," dismissed Ingrid brusquely.

Just then the distant figures of Nick and Alan appeared, climbing over the tumbled rocks at the far end of the beach. As soon as Cathy recognized them, she stood and ran toward them.

Nick and Cathy met in the middle of an open expanse of sand. She threw her arms around his neck and began to sob uncontrollably.

"Oh, Nick, Nick, it was horrible," she managed to say in between the tears.

Nick led her back to the encampment. After he sat her down and dried her eyes, he insisted on hearing the whole story. Cathy told him everything that had happened, slowly and in detail.

When she finished, Nick's face looked cold and angry. "For a start," he declared, "for a start—Toby O'Brien. He will explain his actions, or pay. Probably both."

"That will have to keep for later, Nick," interrupted Captain Nagle. "For the moment we have a more urgent danger to deal with. Tropical Cyclone Jezebel is approaching. If we stay on this beach, we won't survive. We have to move all our things to someplace safer."

"Where do you suggest?" asked Nick. But before Nagle could

reply, Lois and Vicky came stumbling hurriedly down the steps from the cliff top.

"What happened to you two?" asked Ingrid.

"Rats!" said Lois, resting her hands on her knees, gasping for breath. "Horrible, filthy, crawling rats. There were hundreds of them. Perhaps thousands. They surrounded us. Up at the old barracks site. They wouldn't let us through." She collapsed on the sand.

"Were either of you actually bitten?" asked the doctor.

"I was." Vicky held up her right hand.

"Come over here to my 'clinic,'" said Ingrid. "I'll need to clean that wound and give you a tetanus shot."

As the doctor led Vicky away, Nick turned back to Captain Nagle.

"Where do you suggest we move to for safety?"

"Well," replied Nagle cautiously, "bearing in mind the hurricane-strength winds and the rain and the electrical storms, we need to be in a very secure place. I hesitate to suggest it, but nowhere I can think of would be as safe as that old stone church."

"No!" said Cathy emphatically. "I can't go back there. Anyway, the bodies are still there."

"True. But where else is there?" asked the captain.

"The caves," suggested Nick. "There's a deep network of caves and caverns and tunnels. We would be safe from the worst weather there. And, as Cathy says, the caves would be a lot more ... acceptable ... than that black magic center on the cliff tops."

"Right. It's a good thing you and Alan explored those caves," said Nagle. "Let's get everything packed up and start moving."

"There's an entrance just above the boulders at the far end of the beach," explained Nick. "It's not far."

55

_M_ost of the packing up had been done by Vic Neal. He had pulled down the tents and tied them up into neat bundles and put the provisions into boxes and cases.

Captain Nagle, Nick, Alan, Vic, and Toby carried the heavy supplies over the rocks and into the cave. Cathy, Lois, and Vicky carried the lighter items. Sam was still too weak to help, and Ingrid was dependent on her walking stick.

Nick took care to keep well away from Toby. He was still angry and fearful that he might do the wrong thing if he attempted to deal with Toby before he had calmed down.

The wind was rapidly growing stronger, blowing stinging sand into their arms and legs. The sky was a boiling cauldron of black thunderclouds. Even in the protected bay, the waves were larger and white crested.

"How strong will the winds be?" grunted Nick as he lifted a heavy load over the boulders and toward the mouth of the cave system.

"More than two hundred kilometers an hour," replied Vic. "That would be about right, wouldn't it, Captain?"

"Quite right, Vic. In fact, sometimes closer to three hundred kilometers an hour. And we should expect violent rain, thunder, and lightning. This sort of cyclone is what the old-time clipper captains used to call a typhoon or a hurricane."

"What's the biggest risk we face?" asked Alan, standing in the cave mouth.

"Most deaths in cyclones come from drowning," replied Nagle. "So as long as we are well inside the cave system, protected from the winds and storms, the only real danger will be if there's a storm surge."

"What's that?"

"That's when the wind and the rain, combined with the force of the sea, produce a huge wave. There is a risk that such a storm surge will flood the cave system. If you want to worry about something, Mr. Marchant, worry about that."

With that ominous comment, Nagle returned to the beach for another load.

By sunset all the remaining members of the expedition and the supplies they had salvaged from the *Covenant* were in the cave above the beach. Hurricane lamps were lit, and Cathy and Vicky were busy preparing a quick-fix meal.

"I should be doin' that," sighed Sam as he lay shivering in his sleeping bag.

"You need to rest," said Ingrid firmly. "We will miss your wonderful way with food, but if you rest now, you will be cooking for us again in a few days."

Sam smiled weakly and a few minutes later was asleep again.

"We can't stay here," explained Captain Nagle as they ate. "We will have to move much farther into the interior of the cave system if we are to be safe from Cyclone Jezebel."

"Can't that wait until morning, Captain?" whined Lois.

"No, I'm afraid it can't. Do you feel the strength of the wind that is blowing in through that cave entrance? It's twice as strong as it was an hour ago. We may well get the worst of the cyclone during the night."

"There's a very large cavern deeper in and higher up," suggested Nick.

"Sounds ideal. We'll take all our gear and head there as soon as we've eaten."

❖❖❖

Frank Gordon sat at his desk impatiently tapping a pencil on his thumbnail.

"Rhonda," he bellowed through the open door of his office. "Try that number for me again. Please."

"Yes, Mr. Gordon." Rhonda had become used to the fact that her boss never bothered with the intercom.

"The number's ringing," she called out.

"Put it through." Frank picked up the handset on his phone.

"Blue Water Shipping Services," said a cheerful voice on the end of the line.

"Have you people found your lost boat yet?" growled Frank.

"I beg your pardon, sir?"

"The *Covenant*, girl, the *Covenant*. Has there been any word from it?"

"I'll put you through to our Mr. Patterson. He should be able to help you, sir."

There were several loud clicks on the line, a lengthy pause, and then a male voice: "Patterson speaking. What's the problem?"

"This is Frank Gordon, editor of the *Mirror*. You've lost a boat, Mr. Patterson. One of our reporters is on it. So I'm calling to ask if you've managed to find it yet."

"As I explained last time you called, Mr. Gordon, the *Covenant* is not lost. It is anchored in a very safe harbor at Cavendish Island. It is true that the crew has a problem with the radio, but I'm sure that problem will be corrected shortly."

"And if it isn't?"

"None of this is new to us, Mr. Gordon," said Patterson wearily. "As I told you before: Right now they have another twenty-four hours. If we haven't heard from them by then, we will call in the proper authorities."

"If anything happens to my reporter, Mr. Patterson, your name will be on the front page of the paper in large black letters. And we won't be saying anything complimentary about you or your company."

Frank slammed down the telephone and sat in a sulky silence, staring at his desk pad.

"Who is it?" he growled at the tap on his door.

"It's me, Frank."

He looked up to see Robyn Reed.

"Ah, Robyn. Come in. Have a seat. What have you found out?"

"The police are treating young Sharon's death as a routine hit and run. They're not interested in any possible connection with the Order of the Crimson Circle."

"And what about you? What do your reporter's instincts tell you?"

"I'm not sure, Frank. She was certainly terrified when we met, so anything's possible. And this Crimson Circle is a weird bunch."

"What's the latest you have on them?"

"Well, I'm not certain about this, but it seems their leader and founder might be in Australia. There's certainly something stirring up the members of the Order at the moment, some great wave of excitement. And from the hints I've picked up, it seems likely the big man has slipped quietly into Sydney. For what purpose I don't know."

"That's very interesting, Robyn. Good work. Keep on it. Let me know anything else you find out. If the boss man's in town, that means they're cooking up something pretty big."

56

Two hours later, the whole camp had been transferred to the large cavern Nick and Alan had found. Supplies were carried in, sleeping bags had been rolled out, and the group was trying to settle down for the night.

Nick was sitting by the one hurricane lamp still burning, lost in thought. He could feel only slight stirrings of wind on his face, but he could hear it clearly. It was a ghostly, hollow moaning that roamed and rattled through the caves and tunnels. It rose and fell like the wail of a soul in agony.

"Eerie sound, isn't it?"

Nick turned around to find that Captain Nagle had quietly slipped up beside him.

"I couldn't sleep either," the captain explained.

"It's the sound of the wind," Nick said. "If we were up on the surface, I assume it would be a savage, howling, scream. But down here, it's that strange, awful moaning."

"Like the groanings of dead men in Davy Jones's Locker. Yes, I know what you mean."

They fell silent as they both listened to the wind as it rose and fell, echoing through large caverns, small chambers, and narrow tunnels. Sometimes it sounded like a sob, like a woman crying in the night for her lost child. Sometimes it rose to the furious roar of a caged animal. But it never stopped.

"They call this one Cyclone Jezebel," resumed Captain Nagle.

"Now, that's a biblical name, isn't it? Who was Jezebel? You're a Bible reader, so I assume you know."

"She was a pagan queen married to one of the kings of ancient Israel. It was one of those political marriages to cement an alliance. Instead of worshiping the Living God, she worshiped various pagan weather and fertility gods. She killed prophets and persuaded her husband to become a tyrant and impose her religion on the people. She also persuaded her husband to have a man named Naboth killed so he could take over the man's vineyard."

"Not a nice lady."

"Not a bad name for a cyclone."

"I guess so. Talking about pagan religions: That's what the Roystons were doing, wasn't it? Bringing back pagan religion, I mean."

"Yes. They would probably have called themselves neo-pagans," said Nick.

"And that has me wondering," continued Nagle quietly.

"About what?"

"Well, I've always said it doesn't matter what people believe, as long as they're sincere. But the Roystons kind of prove that isn't true, don't they?"

"Quite correct," Nick began.

"Sshh!" hissed Nagle suddenly. He cocked his head to one side as though he was listening for some distant sound.

Nick waited.

"Can you hear that? It's not just my imagination, is it?"

Nick listened. Then he heard it too. The sound of water, of rushing, gurgling water.

"It's the storm surge," yelled the captain. "It's coming. We've got to get out of here."

Nick and the captain ran around the cavern waking the sleepers.

On the rock floor no one was sleeping deeply, and within seconds all were awake and trying to gather their thoughts and possessions.

"On your feet," shouted Nagle. "Gather up your things, but only what you can carry in your arms. We have to move fast."

Nick could hear the water in the lower tunnels. It was louder now—not sloshing or surging, but roaring. He hurried to Sam's side.

The journalist slipped his arm around the big man's shoulders and hoisted him to his feet, then half shuffled and half dragged him toward the exit on the far side of the cavern.

"We have to get higher," called Nick. "The cave that Dr. Sommerville fell into is the highest I know, so we'll head for that. Alan, you know the way—you take the lead."

At that moment, the first rush of water surged into the vast cavern. It came out of the narrow tunnel in a gush and spread rapidly over the wide, flat, rocky floor. Nick found himself and Sam in water up to their ankles.

Everyone was making good progress with Alan in the lead. Captain Nagle urged them to follow quickly, running around them like a sheep dog. Nick and Sam fell farther and farther behind.

"Help me all you can, Sam," said Nick as a fresh wave of water surged up to their knees.

"I'm tryin', Nick, believe me, I'm tryin'."

With his right arm around Sam, a flashlight in his left hand, and his canvas bag slung over his shoulder, Nick was struggling—and the roar was getting louder as the main wave of water surged toward them up the tunnels.

"Captain," called Nick, "Take this for me."

He threw his canvas bag to the captain.

"Got it," yelled Nagle, over the roar of rushing water. "I have to watch the main group. Follow us as quickly as you can, Nick."

"We will."

The others disappeared into the tunnel mouth on the far side of the cavern. Sam was very weak, almost close to a dead weight leaning against Nick. The thigh-deep water they now were wading through also slowed them down.

Just as they reached the tunnel that would take them to the

higher cave and to safety, the roar of the water became a thundering cataract. Nick turned around and saw a three-meter-high wave surging toward them.

"Look out, Sam," he yelled. "Here it comes."

A second later they were picked up by a giant hand and hurled forward into the tunnel. Nick held his breath as they were submerged in the roaring, rolling surf of the storm surge. He was vaguely aware of the rock walls of the tunnel rushing past them as his lungs began to ache and burst for lack of air.

Just as he thought he would have to breathe or die, Nick's head burst through the surface of the wave, and he greedily sucked in air. The water was still up to their chests, and was still pushing them along.

"Sam! Sam! Are you okay!"

"Okay," came the breathless reply. "Okay."

Then another surge front caught them. It swept over their heads and pushed them along even faster. Nick managed to gulp in a lungful of air before he was submerged again.

As the tunnel curved around, the water pushed the two men against the rocks in a series of painful collisions. *This is it,* thought Nick. *I can't hold my breath any longer—I'm about to die.*

Suddenly the water was falling. It was sinking back down toward the rocky floor almost as quickly as it had risen. With his lungs burning, Nick gasped hungrily at the air.

"You still with me, Sam?"

"I got better lungs than you, Nick," sputtered the big man, but he sounded far from well.

Nick had dropped the flashlight in the first surge. They were now standing in a pitch-black tunnel with water slopping around their knees, cut off from the others, and with no idea of where they were.

Nick tightened his grip around Sam's shoulders and said optimistically, "We've made it, big fella. We're still alive."

Sam began to cough. "I think I swallowed some of that water."

"Which way do we go?" Nick asked himself aloud. He leaned

forward and felt the direction in which the water around his feet was flowing.

"Okay," he said, "the water's flowing downhill, so we go in the opposite direction."

Pushing their feet through water that was swirling rapidly in the opposite direction made it hard going. Their muscles strained, and they tired rapidly as they pushed forward. Several times they bumped into the rock wall as the tunnel turned in unexpected directions.

"I would have expected to be in the main chamber by now," muttered Nick. He was thinking of the chamber that he and Alan had walked through the day before, the hollow core of the dead volcano. Still they could not find it, but struggled on through one narrow tunnel after another.

The water around them was now little more than a rapid trickle, no deeper than their boots. Nick groped toward the sides of the tunnel, trying to find their way in the utter and complete darkness, and trying to avoid collisions with the hard rock face.

"We are going to have to face it, Sam old friend." He paused after some minutes of struggling on in this way.

"Face what, Nick?"

"The fact that we are lost. Thoroughly and absolutely lost."

57

*B*y the dim, yellow light of a rapidly failing flashlight Vic hunted through the Velcro-sealed pockets of his waterproof jacket for a box of matches. When he found it, he struggled to light the only hurricane lamp they had brought with them. The wick was damp, but after a dozen or so attempts it finally lit, and the cave was illuminated by the warm, yellow-white glow of the lamp.

They were in the small, high cave into which Ingrid had first fallen. Behind them was the steeply sloping bank of shale and gravel she had landed on. In front of them was a flat open space, which ended in an almost circular opening into the large central cavern beyond.

The rocky floor on which they sat utterly exhausted was dry—but the water had reached as far as the central chamber. Even as they sat there, they could hear it draining away.

Captain Nagle began a head count. He saw Alan, Cathy, and Ingrid, side by side; Lois and Vicky on his left; and, at his right hand, Vic and Toby.

"Nick's missing," he said quietly.

"And Sam," added Vic.

At the same moment Cathy was struck by the same realization.

"Where's Nick?" she asked apprehensively.

Nagle turned and looked at her. "I was about to say that he's still on his way, that he's right behind us. But that would be an optimistic lie. In reality, I have no idea where he is."

Cathy looked ashen-faced, and her breathing became shallow. At that moment she realized, consciously for the first time, how much Nick meant to her. There was a hollow feeling in her stomach as she contemplated a life with no Nick in it.

"Are you that fond of him?" Ingrid reached out and patted Cathy's hand.

"Yes. Yes, I am," whispered Cathy. "I'm desperately fond of him. I hadn't realized how much until this minute."

"Have you rested enough now, Sam?" asked Nick.

"Yeah. I'm feelin' much better. You want to push on?"

"I think we should."

"You got any idea where we are?"

"No idea at all. I'm afraid it's a case of you makes your choice, and you takes your chance. But we will accomplish nothing by sitting here cold and wet. If we keep moving, that will at least warm us up, and it might even dry us out a little. And we have more chance of finding our way out by moving than by keeping still."

Nick helped Sam to his feet, and, keeping the fingers of his right hand lightly trailing the rock face so as to be able to follow the curve of the tunnel, they set off.

How long they walked, neither of them could tell. At times it felt as though they had been walking for hours, and they stopped and rested for a while. But if they rested for too long they started shivering, and Sam in particular began to cough and tremble. Then Nick insisted they get back on their feet and keep moving again.

Nick assumed they were in a part of the cave system he and Alan had not explored the day before. If he had his notebook, with its sketch plan of the caves, he was sure he could find his way out. But, the notebook was in his canvas bag, and that was with Captain Nagle. And even if he had it, there was no light to read the notebook by—they were in total darkness.

Although moving was keeping them warm, Nick could feel the

energy draining out of his body rapidly, and he knew that Sam was making a heroic effort to keep moving at all—even though Nick was supporting much of his weight.

Then they rounded a curve in the tunnel, and Nick thought he could see a dim glow. At first he dismissed it: His eyes must be deceiving him. But as they moved on a few more paces, he saw a faint but definite glow ahead.

"Sam, look at that," said Nick.

Sam raised his eyes from his boots, which he was dragging along with much effort.

"Hey, Nick. Am I goin' crazy, or is that a light up ahead?"

"It's a light all right. Come on, Sam. One last effort, then you can lie down again and rest for a while."

They pushed on, and a minute later found themselves standing at a round opening into a vast cavern, which was dimly lit by some sort of electrical glow. They entered and found the floor of the cavern damp but free from running water.

Nick lowered Sam to the floor, and propped him up against the wall.

"Stay here while I look around," he said.

On the opposite side of the cavern was a long, console-like desk covered with electrical dials and switches. The dials were lit up, and it was their dim glow that enabled them to see.

"We're back!" called Nick in surprise. "We've come full circle and ended up in the cavern we started from."

A sudden shower of sparks made Nick step back a safe distance from the console.

"The water appears to have short-circuited something in the desk and has started the machinery operating."

As he said these words, Nick heard a low electrical hum coming from the next chamber, a hum that was gradually increasing in volume and pitch. He knew what that meant.

"I should warn you, Sam ..." he began, but before he completed his warning there was a violent, ear-splitting crack of thunder and a brilliant blue-white flash of light that lit up the whole chamber for a fraction of a second.

"Does anyone have a wristwatch that's still working?" asked Captain Nagle.

"I have," volunteered Alan. "I wear a diver's watch."

"Excellent. Bring it over here to the hurricane lamp, please. What time do you have?"

"Just a little after midnight."

"Is that all?" Toby cried out, the stress he was under making his Irish accent thicker than ever. "It feels as though we've been in these caves for a whole night."

"Well, we now know that most of the night is still ahead of us," said Lois, sourly.

"What can't be cured must be endured, as my old mother used to say," commented Vic.

"Spare us your trite clichés," she snapped.

"What will happen to us?" Vicky's voice trembled, on the verge of tears.

"What should we do, Captain?" asked Ingrid briskly.

"We wait," replied Nagle.

"I think the storm has passed," called out Cathy. She had clambered up the steep slope of shale and gravel and was underneath the hole that Alan and Nick had climbed down the day before. "I can see a few stars," she added, "and there's almost no wind. I can't hear it or feel it."

"We wait," repeated Nagle.

"What are we waiting for?" asked Lois skeptically. "Some mythical rescuer?"

"No. We are waiting for the rest of the cyclone."

"What do you mean?" inquired Vicky hesitantly.

"I mean that we are in the eye of the storm."

"I can see more stars now," called out Cathy excitedly. "The clouds must be breaking up."

"There you are, Captain," Ingrid said confidently. "Doesn't that mean the cyclone is gone completely?"

"Far from it, I'm afraid. The eye of a severe storm is often surrounded by a wall of clouds with a clear center. Those stars Cathy can see will disappear soon as the eye passes over us. First will come the wall clouds, and then the rain clouds, and then we'll be back in the thick of it again."

"Should we send out a search party to look for Sam and Nick?" asked Vic.

"Not yet, Vic," responded his captain. "There might be a second storm surge when the rest of the cyclone hits. We will search for them, but not until morning. Are any of the flashlights still working?"

"One of them still is, Captain," replied Toby. "But its batteries are almost dead."

"The stars are disappearing again," called Cathy from her vantage point. "The clouds are coming back."

"That's not good, is it, Captain?" Vic asked dolefully.

"No, it's not good at all."

"What does it mean?" asked Ingrid.

"It means that Tropical Cyclone Jezebel is moving very fast," explained Vic.

"Cathy," called Nagle, "come down from there. We need to make ourselves as comfortable as we can—and just wait."

The brilliant flash of artificial lightning temporarily blinded Nick and Sam. Then came another crash of thunder that sounded like the crack of doom, and another brilliant, powerful electrical flash. The two men became aware of the sharp smell of ionized air, generated by the massive electrical discharges.

"The water seems to have put this system into overdrive," said Nick over another ear-splitting, blinding crash.

Each brilliant flash seemed longer and stronger than the one before. Each one cast the entire area of the vast cavern into sharp relief, with strong white light contrasting with dense black shadows.

"I'm going to try to stop this," said Nick, making his way to the console. As the artificial thunder and lightning came again, he began flicking off switches and turning down knobs to the zero position.

Turning around to see what, if any, effect he was having, Nick noticed the cavern beginning to fill with a kind of mist. Then the air seemed to shimmer. It was as though the molecules of air were so heavily charged they were trembling.

The next time the electrical discharge flashed and filled the cavern with light, Nick blinked and couldn't believe his eyes—there was something standing in the middle of the cavern. In the same spot where a moment before the air had shimmered in a mist, there was now an animal. It was roughly two meters tall, and looked like a large, bad-tempered lizard standing up on its hind feet. Nick recognized it as exactly fitting Cathy's description of the animal that had killed the Roystons.

It had a dark body, with reddish stripes, like a tiger. In the silence between the thunder crashes Nick heard it making a noise: a hissing, snarling sound.

In the next flash, Nick saw that the reptile's mouth was smeared with dried blood, and that on its flanks were the crisscrossed marks of healed scars. Whatever it was, this thing was a fighter.

The flashes seemed to be coming closer together now. And they seemed to be upsetting the creature, which threw back its head and let out a savage howl, pawing at the air with its long, sharp fore-claws as it did so. Then came a period of quiet and darkness, and Nick wondered where the thing was. Had it moved? Was it coming toward him? Or toward Sam?

The lightning flashed again, and Nick was relieved to see that it was still standing in the center of that vast space, but it was no longer alone. There seemed to be several of the creatures there now, standing side by side, all snarling and hissing. At the next flash Nick counted eight.

"Sam," he called out, "whatever you do, don't move and don't make a noise."

But the sound of his voice had attracted the attention of the pack of reptiles. They turned and looked in Nick's direction. In the next flash Nick could see the leader of the pack staring straight into his eyes. And its stare was disconcertingly intelligent, cold, and cunning.

58

*F*irst came the wind. They heard it rustling and shaking the bushes outside the cave entrance. Then it started to build. Within minutes, so it seemed, it had reached a pitch where it was screaming like a banshee.

Inside the cave, they had to shout to be heard. The hurricane lamp rocked unsteadily on its base.

"Move that thing to a safer spot," shouted Nagle.

"Aye, sir." Vic, lifted up the lamp and carried it to a far corner, where he wedged it between two jutting pieces of rock. His action reduced the amount of light in the cave, creating a circle of brightness around the lamp, and a dim yellow glow everywhere else.

"When will all this end?" howled Vicky.

"Stop being such a child. Pull yourself together," chided Lois. "You're an adult. Behave like one."

"Really?" replied Vicky sharply. "The way you behaved when we were surrounded by rats? Is that the model you want me to follow?"

"Just shut up," growled Lois.

"The weather is bad enough," yelled Captain Nagle over the wind. "We should do our best not to get on each other's nerves as well."

Cathy was sitting quietly by herself, at little apart from the others. She was staring into the distance when a blazing stab of lightning, followed by a vicious crack of thunder, made her jump.

She realized that the surface of Cavendish Island was now being pummeled by a savage electrical storm.

She huddled down into her damp jacket, trying to keep warm. As she stared across the cave, her eyes came to rest on the circular opening that led into the large central chamber. She stared because there was something wrong with the air at the opening. It was filled with mist and was starting to shimmer uncertainly.

With a sinking feeling in her stomach, Cathy recognized it: She had seen it once before—in the dark chapel just before the Roystons died. She started to feel frightened and nauseous, but she couldn't drag her eyes away.

Still the air trembled uncertainly. Then she saw it, at the very edge of the dim yellow glow that filled the cave. The creature was there. It crouched like a marauder ready to strike, ready to kill. She tried to call out, to warn the others, but nothing would come out of her mouth. She could barely breathe. Then came another flash of lightning, and another crash of thunder. And the creature was gone.

Cathy stared hard at the place where it had stood a moment before. It was definitely gone. The horrible reptile that had crouched down on its haunches just a moment before had vanished.

"I must be imagining things," she told herself. "My nerves have been so shaken by everything that has happened that now I'm hallucinating. I must stop this. I must think of something else. I will make myself think about Nick."

Cathy closed her eyes and tried to block out the storm.

Then came the rain. It thundered down in buckets. It poured through the entrance to the cave and turned the slope of shale and gravel into a waterfall. Everyone had to move to one side of the cave, away from the river of rainwater that ran down past them and through the opening into the large central chamber beyond.

"Will there be another storm surge?" shouted Cathy.

"I wouldn't be surprised," replied Nagle at the top of his voice.

"What about Nick and Sam? If they are still alive somewhere, they may be caught by it."

"If they've survived the first storm surge, then they can survive a second."

The artificial lightning came again—a sharp electrical crackling, even more brilliant than before. The creatures in the center of the large cavern didn't like it. They reared up, snarling and snapping. Then, within a second, the cavern was plunged back into darkness.

Nick seized his opportunity to run around the edge of the cavern wall, putting as much distance as possible between himself and the pack of hunting reptiles—because he was quite convinced that hunting was exactly what they were doing.

The next flash of lightning showed the animals to be spread out, hunting in a pack. But, Nick was relieved to notice, they were creeping toward the spot he had occupied a moment before. His movement in the dark had confused them. And, he was pleased to notice, they appeared not to have discovered Sam at all.

The flashes and crashes were growing further apart. *Perhaps I achieved something when I turned off all those switches,* thought Nick. As the period of darkness lengthened, Nick's eyes began to adapt, and he found he could see again by the dim glow from the dials on the console.

In the dim light the predators were harder to see. The leader of the pack was standing very still, its head in the air, sniffing. *It's trying to smell me,* thought Nick.

Then one of the reptiles struck another a savage blow on the flank. The victim of this attack spun around—Nick was astonished at how quickly it moved—and faced its attacker, growling fiercely. The two combatants circled each other warily. When the other predators realized what was happening, they abandoned their hunt and turned their attention to the fight.

Razor-sharp claws were waved menacingly in the air, and the hissing, snarling, and growling increased in volume. Then one of the two combatants made a lightning-fast lunge at the other. The victim of the attack leaped in the air, raising both of its rear claws, with their long, hooked, talon-like central toes. The twin claws curved high in the air and then slashed down upon the back of the opponent. The air was split by a hideous shriek, and the victim fell on one side, snarling and spitting.

The rest of the pack gathered around as the victor began to snap its hideous yellow teeth toward the victim's neck. On the third or fourth attempt the teeth connected, and the reptile bit down hard. The hurt creature thrashed desperately for a minute or two, and then was still.

Then, to Nick's disgust, the rest of the pack gathered around, and all began to eat the dead animal. In the middle of the cannibalistic feast, the massive electrical discharge fired again.

As the lightning flashed, the leader of the hunting pack raised its head—and spotted Nick. Its jaws were now dripping with blood as it turned and stared directly at the spot where Nick was standing.

The rain was now coming in torrents. Unbelievably, it just got heavier and heavier.

"I've seen pictures of cyclones and hurricanes on the television news," shouted Cathy into the ear of Vic, who was seated right beside her, "but I've never been this close to one before. The television doesn't give you any idea how noisy they are."

"That's quite right, Miss," agreed Vic. "I've only been on the edge of one in the past. I've never been in the center before. And I don't think I ever want to again."

It was hard to estimate passing time in that dimly lit cave, but the howling of the wind and the torrential rain was starting to ease. It was still savage in contrast to normal weather, but it was a relief to the occupants of the cave. It became possible to hold a normal conversation again.

"How are you feeling?" asked Captain Nagle as he sat down on Cathy's other side.

"I recommend a cyclone as an effective and rapid cure for shock, Captain. It takes your mind completely off whatever you've been through."

Nagle laughed. "You're a very courageous young woman. You're pretty tough, and that's meant as a compliment."

Nick feared the predator had caught his scent. It was turning away from the kill and moving stealthily toward him. Then there was an electrical spark in the console, and the reptile leaped toward it, snarling.

Good, thought Nick, *this must mean they depend on eyesight more than sense of smell. And it's not going to be easy to see in this cavern.*

At that moment, the electrical discharge fired again, filling the air with the tang of ozone, and in that second the leading predator caught a glimpse of Nick and sprang in his direction. As the darkness descended, Nick ran as hard as he could in the opposite direction. He heard the creature thump hard into the rock wall, not far behind him, and he kept on moving. As he reached Sam's side, the humming from the next chamber was building again toward its massive discharge as an artificial electrical storm.

"How are you?" Nick knelt beside Sam.

"I'm fine. Those things don't seem to have noticed me yet."

"Noise and movement attract them. Keep still and quiet, and you should be okay."

Then came the crash and the flash of light. Nick stayed very still, crouching as low as he could against the rock wall beside Sam. The predators, he was pleased to see, were still looking for him in the wrong place.

As the echoes of the last crack of thunder died away, Nick noticed another sound. It was water—a rushing, surging, roar of water. He recognized it at once. For reasons he couldn't understand, there was a second storm surge on its way.

"Hang on tight," Nick whispered into Sam's ear. "There's another flood coming."

"Oh, great," murmured Sam.

Unable to find Nick, the reptiles had gone back to devouring the carcass. With swipes of their huge jaws they were tearing strips of flesh from the hide of the dead animal.

The thunder of the approaching water was getting louder.

"We are in for another drenching," whispered Nick. "There's nothing we can do, Sam, except hang on and wait for it to pass."

"I don't know if I can hold my breath for that long, Nick."

"We'll have to try."

A moment later it thundered toward them. It hit the reptiles first. They screamed and snarled as the water flung them off their feet and battered them against the rock wall.

Nick and Sam clung to each other tightly as they were picked up in a giant, watery hand and carried toward the roof of the cavern.

59

Captain to the bridge! Captain to the bridge!" The first officer of the patrol boat held down the button on the intercom.

A minute later the captain appeared, buttoning up his jacket and pulling on his cap. He had to stand for a few moments at the entrance to the bridge, steadying himself, as the ship pitched and rolled wildly.

"Yes. What is it, Number One?" he asked his first officer.

"Permission to put the ship into the bay, Captain," replied his subordinate, saluting smartly.

"Permission denied, Number One."

"But sir. We can't survive much more of this. And the radar shows that we haven't hit the worst of it yet."

"How wide across is the cyclonic depression?"

The first officer grabbed a chart and read off the figures.

"Almost 350 kilometers, sir."

"And you say it will get worse?"

"Take a look at the radar screen for yourself, sir."

The captain stumbled as the ship pitched wildly, and then, hanging on carefully, made his way across the bridge to the radar screen.

"I see what you mean, Number One," he said a moment later.

"May we put into the bay then, sir? It's the only protection for a thousand kilometers."

"Our orders are to stand off until we are called in. Have you contacted regional headquarters, Number One?"

"I tried to, sir. But this storm is interfering with all communications."

"Even satellite links?"

"Even those, sir."

There was a long, tense silence while the captain considered his position.

"Our orders were quite clear. But given the weather, we have no choice. You have permission to make for the bay, Number One."

"Thank you, sir."

All Nick knew was that he was under water. He could not breathe. He was being tossed and tumbled around. But he still held tightly to Sam.

He would have swum for the surface, but he had been so tumbled about he that no longer knew which way was up. Then the surging and buffeting ceased. In the moment of stillness that followed, Nick felt himself drifting upward. As soon as he was clear about the direction, he began to swim strongly, still keeping a tight grip on Sam with one arm.

The big man was heavy. Nick's lungs were bursting. He knew he would die if he didn't breathe within seconds. At the last moment—or what felt like several moments *after* the last moment— his face broke the surface, and he gasped in air. Then he pulled Sam to the surface.

"Breathe! Breathe!" he yelled at his friend.

To Nick's relief, Sam released the breath he had been holding and gulped in air.

As the two of them bounced and floated over the surface of the floodwater, close to the ceiling of the high cavern, they were pushed back and forth by the rhythmic waves set up by the storm surge. One moment they were bumping against the rock wall, and the next they were being pushed away again.

The darkness was total. Nick wondered where the reptiles were. Had they been drowned? Or were they also floating on the top of the flood surge, not far away?

Then Nick noticed something strange: With his ears above water he could hear nothing but waves—slapping rock, surging and sloshing about. But when his ears dipped under the water he could hear something else—a deep humming sound that seemed to be getting louder.

With a chill, he realized what it was—the massive electrical machinery was building up another charge. Part of his mind wondered how this could be possible. Obviously the key working parts of the system were heavily waterproofed. But when the discharge was released, tens of thousands of volts would electrify the water—the same water that he and Sam were swimming in. It would mean instant death.

"We've got to get out of this water, Sam," sputtered Nick.

"Good idea," gasped Sam. "I approve. How we gonna do it?"

Beside Nick was the rock wall of the vast cavern. As he touched it with his fingers, it felt as though it was slipping past. But that couldn't be. Then Nick realized what was happening: the water level was falling.

While still supporting Sam, Nick groped toward the wall with his free hand and his free foot. As he desperately searched for a handhold or a foothold, he heard a sound that made his blood run cold—a hissing snarl, only a few meters away in the watery darkness.

At least one of the creatures had survived the flood. As a sense of rising panic threatened to overwhelm him, Nick felt his foot hit a rock ledge. He dragged Sam in the direction of his find. Then came the snarl and the hiss again. The predator was getting closer.

The rock ledge was just under the surface of the water. It felt to be a least a meter wide and several meters long.

"Come on, Sam," he urged. "Swim a few strokes if you can. I've found a place where we can rest."

"Rest," gurgled Sam, his mouth half under water. "I need rest."

"Help me, then. Just a few strokes, this way."

With Sam's help, Nick got them onto the rock ledge. It was covered by several centimeters of water, but they were able to crawl onto it. Fortunately, it supported the weight of the two men. They leaned back and breathed deeply.

Nick ducked his head underwater. The hum was still building up. When he raised his head again, he heard the other sound—the snarling hiss of the predator. It seemed to be very close, but in the dark he couldn't see a thing. And then he remembered that neither could the predator. *Keep still, make no sound*, Nick told himself, and he prayed that Sam would do the same.

The level of the floodwater continued to fall. Soon it was down to the level of the rock shelf, and then it was just a little below it. Nick dragged Sam's legs up onto the shelf and made sure that he was completely out of the water. The electrical discharge—tens of thousands of volts—must be very close now, Nick realized. He and Sam were soaking wet, and they might still be electrocuted. But at least on the rock ledge, just above the water, they stood a chance.

Something rough brushed against Nick's leg. With a shudder of horror, he realized it was the scaly hide of the reptile. He twisted his body around to keep his leg as far from the water as possible. The creature growled again. Nick could have sworn it was right next to his ear.

Then came the crash and flash of the electrical discharge. Nick was looking straight downward, and he saw a massive blue spark arc through the water. In its ghostly light he saw the predator, floating on top of the floodwater, only a meter away. In that same moment it saw Nick, and with its hunter's instinct, raised its sharp, talon-like claws to strike.

The creature screamed in agony as thousands of volts of electricity surged through its body. The water, less than half a meter below the ledge on which they were balanced, began to boil and steam.

Nick and Sam instinctively pushed themselves against the wall of the cavern, as far as they could from the water. But by the time they had done so, it was all over. The gigantic blue spark was gone, and the pitch-black darkness had returned.

60

---

*D*awn appeared as a dim, gray circle of light in the overhead entrance to the cave. Alan scrambled to the top of the slope of shale and gravel.

"The rain has gone and so have the clouds," he called to his companions below, "but the wind is still strong."

"Captain, can we start looking for Nick and Sam now, please?" asked Cathy.

"Yes, now that there's some natural light coming into this cave we can take the hurricane lamp and make our search. Alan, you explored these caves with Nick yesterday. I want you to come with me."

"Certainly," said the Canadian.

"I want to come too, Captain," declared Cathy.

"Well, I'm not sure that would be wise."

"You mean, would I be able to cope if we found Nick's body?"

"Yes … yes … to be honest, that's what I was thinking."

"Captain, during the night you told me I was tough. You were right. Let me come."

"Very well. If you insist. The rest of you wait here until we return. Alan, you take the lamp and lead the way."

Alan led them through the almost perfectly circular opening into the large central chamber beyond.

On the other side he stopped for a moment to get his bearings, then said, "This way."

He led them across the chamber that had once been the core

of the volcanic heart of the island and through a small opening on the far side. All the tunnel surfaces around them were dripping with water, and the rock was slippery underfoot.

"Just be careful where you step," warned Alan. "Where the rock is uneven, there are pools of water."

They walked down the long, high, narrow tunnel that weaved through the rock. They passed the steel doors that had so intrigued Nick the day before, but they didn't stop to examine them.

"Is this the way you led us last night?" asked Cathy, "when we were escaping from the storm surge?"

"Yes, that is correct. This is the way we came," replied Alan.

"I didn't notice any of these things at the time."

"None of us noticed anything," remarked Nagle. "We were running so hard to keep ahead of the water."

Their progress was slow as they stopped to examine every pool of shadow, fearful of finding a drowned body, but knowing they had to look.

"This is the entrance to the big cavern," said Alan at last. "Follow me, through this way."

As Nagle and Cathy followed, they were aware of stepping into a vast space that swallowed up most of the light from their one lantern.

"This is where we set up camp before the flood, isn't it?" asked Cathy.

"This is the place," confirmed Nagle.

"Well, there is a lot of floor space to be covered, so I suggest we start looking," ventured the Canadian.

Their voices rolled and echoed around the vast chamber. Suddenly, a voice called out from above their heads, "I suppose you didn't think to bring a ladder, did you?"

"Nick!" cried out Cathy in delight and relief. "Where are you?"

"Up here. Rock ledge. Just opposite you."

"And is Sam there with you?" called out Nagle.

"Aye, sir. I'm here," replied the big Tongan.

"That's wonderful," laughed Nagle. "Simply wonderful."

"How on earth did you two get up there?" inquired Cathy.

"It's a long story," began Nick.

"We swam," added Sam. "But we can't swim back down."

"Bring the light closer," called Nick. "Let me see how far up we are."

A moment later Alan was standing directly underneath the ledge.

"It's not too far," said Nick. "I can jump down. But Sam will need help. I'll help him over the ledge and lower him toward you. Captain, can you and Alan be standing by to grab his feet and support his weight?"

"We're ready," replied Nagle.

Ten minutes later, both men were back on the floor of the cavern, and Cathy was hugging Nick.

"I'm so glad you're safe," she said. "Now everything's all right again."

"There are still a few problems, Miss Samson," said Captain Nagle.

"Such as?"

"We have no tents, no sleeping bags, no dry clothes, and about one day's supply of food."

The dark-haired man in the expensive business suit sat alone in the long boardroom. His eyes glittered strangely as he stared unblinkingly down the length of the polished, dark wood table.

Behind his head was an oil painting of leaping flames and blazing fire, a painting so real that to the observer it seemed to flicker and burn. However, although it depicted fire, it was not a picture of destruction, but of triumph—of crushing, self-glorying, terrifying triumph.

The atmosphere in the room was heavy with an exotic incense that rose in a trickle of heavy blue smoke from a carved Asian jar in the middle of the table. The carvings on the jar showed a figure that was halfway between a lion and a dragon. The same motif kept recurring around the room—carved into the armrests of the chairs and woven into the fabric of the drapes.

The man held a large, flame-red crystal in his hands and turned it over slowly as if watching the changing lights it reflected or, perhaps, something deeper within the crystal itself.

There was a quiet knock, and the door opened. A beautiful young woman stepped into the room and closed the door. Then she stood and waited, her hands by her sides.

"Well?" asked the man at last.

"There was a radio contact late yesterday."

"From whom?"

"Agent Phoenix."

"And what did he have to report?"

"He said he sank the boat in the bay of the island."

"He did what?" The anger in his voice was all the more apparent because of the quietness of his tone.

"Sank the *Covenant*. In the middle of the night. With explosives." The young woman looked extremely nervous as if she half expected to be punished for bringing bad news.

"Did he give a reason for this action?"

"He said the captain had announced his intention to depart in the morning. Agent Phoenix felt he should keep the party on the island. He said he knew we had additional plans, and he thought it might be best if ..." Her voice trailed away.

"The man is a fool. He will be dealt with. Was there anything else?"

"Yes. He reported that the Roystons are dead."

"Dead? Both of them?"

"Yes, Master."

"How did they die?"

"Agent Phoenix says they were killed by the Dark Power they summoned."

"Of course. We should have known that would happen. They did not know what they were playing with. They were trying to control the powers of the cosmos with the tools of the Dark Ages. Idiots! Then all is not lost. The Dark Powers will fall into our hands. And we will know how to control them. And how to use them."

"The question now is," said Captain Nagle to the group in the cave, "how to get out of here."

Nick and Sam had been reunited with the others, and now they were gathered under the glimmering of daylight that crept in through the entrance hole in the roof of the cave. Outside they could still hear the wind howling at gale force.

"Tropical Cyclone Jezebel has passed," continued Nagle. "These winds are just the aftermath, and there's a good chance they'll be gone by sunset. So we should think about leaving the caves and re-establishing some sort of camp on the beach. On the whole, that's the best place to be, sheltered by the arms of the bay. So, what's the best way out of here?"

"Not up that way." Alan pointed to the steep slope of gravel and shale and the opening in the roof above. "We should go back through the caves, the way we have come, and out on to the beach through the cave in the cliffs above the rocks. Anyone disagree with that?"

No one did.

"Right, then," Nagle said. "Let's gather up what belongings we have and set off before this hurricane lamp runs out of fuel. Bring everything we have here. On the way we may find some of our things that were scattered by the flood. If they are usable, pick them up and bring them along. Food, for example. Anything in cans will still be edible, so keep your eyes open as you walk."

Cathy fell into step beside Nick at the head of the party.

"Nick, could the rituals the Roystons were engaged in—the

Satanism, or the witchcraft, or whatever it was—have anything to do with all the things that have happened to us?"

"What do you mean, Cathy?"

"Well, we seem to have brought some sort of terrible curse down on our heads. Could that be related to the Roystons' Satanism?"

"What you're asking me is if there really are evil spiritual powers, and just how powerful they are?"

"Yes, I guess so."

"Well, for a start, remember what the Bible says. When he wrote to the church in ancient Ephesus, Paul said, 'Our struggle is not against flesh and blood, but against the rulers, against the authorities, against the powers of this dark world and against the spiritual forces of evil.' That tells us there is a real warfare going on, a genuine conflict, on the spiritual plane."

"But I had someone say to me once that because the forces and laws of nature have been discovered, we can no longer believe in spirits, whether good or evil."

"Was the person who said this to you a Christian?" asked Nick.

"Yes, he was. One of my ministers, in fact," replied Cathy.

"Oh, brother," muttered Nick, shaking his head. "Belief about supernatural interventions is not necessarily primitive or prescientific. To accept that notion is to accept the very narrowest kind of materialism. And quantum physics has already shown that even the material world is a far stranger place than we could ever have imagined. A universe that can contain quarks, pulsars, quasars, black holes, and antimatter can contain far more than the cynics and skeptics will ever admit."

As they talked, they reached the vast cavern in which they had first camped.

"What's this over here?" asked Captain Nagle as he caught up with Nick and Cathy. He pointed to a pile of bones, already white and clean of flesh.

Nick knelt down and examined them.

"This is all that's left," he concluded, "of the predators, the reptiles that attacked Sam and me in the early hours of this morning."

"Reptiles?" said Cathy. "You mean like …"

"Yes. They exactly matched your description of the creature that killed the Roystons."

"So, now you believe me."

"Cathy, I always believed you," said Nick quietly.

"But I don't understand," Nagle said, lifting off his cap and scratching his head. "If they died only a few hours ago, how come there's nothing but bones left."

"It makes no sense to me either, Captain," responded Nick.

Ingrid hobbled over to the scattered bones, leaning heavily on her makeshift walking stick. "I'm no expert in forensic medicine," she said as she bent over and picked up a jawbone, "but if you'd asked me to guess, I would have said this creature had been dead for months, not hours."

"We saw them," argued Sam. "Nick and me, we saw them, just a little time back."

"I'm not doubting your word, Sam," said Ingrid. "I just don't understand it, that's all."

"Look at the teeth in that jaw," exclaimed Alan. "This thing must be a fearsome killer when it's alive."

"It is," said Cathy quietly, as memories came flooding back. Nick slipped an arm around her shoulder and hugged her.

"This is identical to the skeleton I found in that first cave, on the day of your fall, Doctor," Nick remarked.

"Which means these things have been around on this island for some time," said Nagle thoughtfully.

"And there may be more of them," added Vicky faintly.

"We should keep moving," said Lois briskly.

"She's right, folks," agreed Nagle. "Let's get a move on."

As they got closer to the cave that opened out over the sea, they started finding seaweed and fish deposited by the storm surge.

Most of the fish were dead, but some still flopped about feebly in puddles of water.

Rounding a corner, they found their way barred by the carcass of a two-meter bronze whaler shark. Nick nudged it with his foot, and its tail twitched, but clearly its life was almost extinct.

"It's safe, I think," he said to Cathy. "Just step over it." He went first, and then held her hand as she followed.

All the time the strength of the wind was building up. At last they reached a point where daylight could be seen gleaming around the next bend, the breeze was brisk, and the sound of the wind and the sea was very loud.

"I think we should stop here, Captain," proposed Nick. "If we go any farther, we'll feel the full force of the wind."

"Okay, folks, we'll camp here until the wind dies down. And that won't be, probably, until sunset, so we'll have to spend the day here. Make yourselves comfortable."

"Or as comfortable as we can," said Lois sourly.

"Precisely, Miss Myles," responded Nagle cheerfully, "as comfortable as you can."

Their temporary campsite was the corner of a broad, low-roofed cave. There were boulders scattered about on which they could sit, or place their pitifully few belongings out of the puddles of water that still remained.

Vic found a piece of driftwood and used it to clear the clumps of damp seaweed out of the way. Both the flashlight and the hurricane lamp were turned off to save their limited batteries and kerosene.

Nick, Vic, and Captain Nagle walked fifty meters from the campsite, around two more bends, until they reached the cave mouth in the cliff tops. Here the wind was powerful, lashing at their hair and clothes. If they had stood too close to the cave mouth, they would have been drenched in sea spray.

From where they were standing they could not see the bay, only the open sea and the distant horizon.

"I wouldn't like to be sailing in that mess." Nagle gestured to the six-meter swell that was rolling across their field of vision and crashing into the rocks below them.

"I think we've picked the best campsite—for today, at least," Vic commented. "There's less daylight back there, but at least there's no wind and spray, and we can hear ourselves think."

They returned to find the others beginning to unpack their soaking wet bags and spread their remaining clothing over rocks to dry.

"One good thing about this strong wind," said Alan, "is that it should dry our clothes quickly."

"Even the ones we're wearing," Cathy smiled. "This sweater of mine is stiff but almost dry already."

As he hunted through his canvas bag, Nick found that only the outer layers were wet, and in the middle were some dry clothes.

He pulled out dry underwear, socks, and a sweater, but he would still have to wear his damp jeans. He dug into his bag to see what else had survived the flood.

Right in the middle of the bag, wrapped up in several pairs of socks, he found a small booklet that he had carried all the way from Sydney but had, until that moment, forgotten. It was "The Dark History of the Secret Coven." He sat down on a boulder some distance from the others and began to read.

61

Extracts from "The Dark History of the Secret Coven." First published in Sydney, Australia, in 1893.

*I*n these enlightened closing years of the 19th century, with one great scientific discovery following rapidly upon the heels of another, there is a large percentage of the populace that no longer believes in witches. However, it is well to remember that millions of our ancestors did. It is also well to understand that while we relax in the material comforts of the advanced age in which we live, there are still those who believe in and practice witchcraft, magic, and the occult.

Even today there are those in our midst who believe themselves to be the possessors of magical powers beyond the imagination of the rest of us; in many cases, powers inherited from mothers who were witches and fathers who were warlocks. These same people believe themselves capable of casting powerful spells and of raising evil spirits to wreak all kinds of terror in people's lives.

Regrettably our Christian colony, soon to be a nation, has not been well served with materials dealing with a well-informed perspective on demons, principalities and powers, and the nature of our Christian society's conflict with the powers of evil. Tragically there are many who, even now, do not know that this conflict goes back to the very earliest days of the colony …

… there are dark and secret pages to the history of this colony, pages which, until this time, have never been revealed.

*Many modern citizens of this proud, young land would be shocked
and disgusted to learn that on board the eleven ships of the First
Fleet in the year of Our Lord 1788, among the 700 convicts and
the officials and marines of the New South Wales Corps, was a
complete coven of thirteen witches and warlocks. Some of this
group of thirteen were convicts, and others were guards; some
were males, and some were females. All were capable of the
grossest forms of indecency, perversion, wickedness, and evil.*

*This malevolent and malicious group called themselves "The
Secret Coven." They exercised a great power over the fearful and
superstitious minds of the convicts, and succeeded in terrifying
those few marine officers who learned of their existence. In this
way their horrible secrets were kept securely locked by the key of
terror. Membership in The Secret Coven was for life, and when
one of the thirteen members died or became permanently incapacitated due to severe illness, another was selected, prepared, and initiated to replace the departed one. In this manner The Secret
Coven perpetuated and continued itself, year after year, and generation after generation. The shocking and horrible truth is that
The Secret Coven continues to exist and to thrive in this year of
Our Lord 1893. ...*

*... much of the history of this highly secretive and malevolent
group has come to light only in recent times when one of its members was rescued from the darkness and brought into the light by
the power of the Gospel of God's Mercy, Grace, and Compassion.
Mr. Jonah Ebenezer Locke was inducted into the mysteries of The
Secret Coven by an aunt and uncle when he was still in his teens.
For more than a decade he indulged in their horrible practices.*

*However, the Christian morality he had learned at the knee of
his widowed mother made his conscience difficult, and this led him
to drink. When he was deep in the grip of alcohol, he was rescued
by a missioner from the Kent Street Mission Hall of the Sydney
City Mission. In this way he heard and understood for the first time*

the forgiveness that is available in Christ and the glorious liberty
that only the children of God can know ...

... since this occurrence he has provided to the author of the
present pamphlet such information as he knew about the dark and
evil history of The Secret Coven. From his disturbing narrative it
becomes clear that certain figures have played key roles in the
coven as it has infected the Colony of New South Wales.

One of these was a certain Commandant Godfrey Black,
who, in the year of Our Lord 1821, was appointed commandant
of a new penal settlement at Cavendish Island. This settlement
failed after only two years, but those years were a time of hell on
earth for the poor unfortunates who accompanied Commandant
Black to that benighted place ...

... according to the information supplied by Mr. Locke,
Commandant Black built a mockery of a church in compliance
with certain very ancient plans drawn up by masters of the black
arts. In that building he conducted human sacrifices and sought to
summon up the Prince of Darkness, Beelzebub himself. Of the
handful who survived those horrors and who were eventually
returned to Sydney Cove, terror closed their mouths, and nothing
was ever revealed of the level of indecency, perversion, and horror
they had suffered at the hands of Black.

... this evil man drove his own wife to an early grave and
cast out his daughter, according to Mr. Locke, when she became
pregnant as a result of Colonel Black's own horrible incestuous
practices. This poor young woman died shortly after giving birth,
and, tragically, The Secret Coven obtained the baby and raised it
from infancy to be thoroughly degraded in the practices of witchcraft, Satanism, and the occult ...

... other horrific examples of black magic revealed by Mr.
Locke included the following rite for inflicting great harm on an
enemy: "Take a thin lead plate and inscribe on it with a bronze
stylus the name of your enemy, and, after smearing it with the
blood of a bat, roll up the plate. Cut open a frog and put it into its

stomach. After stitching it up with Anubian thread and a bronze needle, hang it upon a reed from your property by means of hairs from the tail of a black ox, at the east of the property at the rising of the sun. Then you are to recite the following invocation—'I invoke and conjure you evil angels, just as this frog drips with blood and dries up, so will the body of (insert the name of your enemy).' This is to be done immediately before sunrise for thirteen consecutive days." ...

... *after passing on these things, and much other information besides, Mr. Locke died after being struck by a runaway carriage in Pitt Street. Based on the information he had provided, there are some who believe that his death was not an accident, but the revenge of the coven whose secrets he had, in part at least, revealed. However, at the inquest it proved impossible to persuade the magistrate that a full investigation should be conducted* ...

... *not only in St Paul's epistle to the Ephesians, but throughout the New Testament, Our Lord Jesus Christ is portrayed in terms of a struggle with the powers of darkness. Jesus confronted the demonic in His earthly ministry, dealt a decisive blow to the kingdom of evil on the Cross, continues to wage war against the hosts of Satan through His church, and will finally vanquish Satan and his forces once and for all after His Second Coming* ...

62

What are you reading?" asked Alan as he walked up to Nick.

"Oh, it's just an old booklet that someone gave me before I left Sydney. How is morale among the troops?"

"Troops? Oh, you mean the expedition party?"

"Yes. Or what's left of it."

"Morale is remarkably high. Perhaps the fact that we have passed through many horrors and have survived gives us a feeling of comfort and confidence."

"Perhaps. That would make sense." Nick slipped the booklet into a top pocket as he spoke. For some reason he felt reluctant, at least for the present, to share what he had discovered about the background that lay behind the Roystons and their strange mentality.

"Well," said Alan, "I have managed to find one dry cigarette in my last packet, and I intend to borrow a match from Vic Neal and smoke it. That will raise my morale." With these words he wandered off.

Nick pulled the booklet back out of his pocket and began leafing through it, picking up words and phrases here and there. And all the time his mind was racing rapidly.

"A penny for your thoughts," said Cathy as she approached.

"Vastly overpriced at a penny," laughed Nick.

"Come and look at the sea and the sky with me," she said, holding out her hand. Nick gladly took it, noticing how small and soft it was. Together they walked around the last two corners that took them to the cliff-top opening.

"Ah, it smells so clean and fresh," sighed Cathy as the wind whipped through her dark hair.

"Compared to the smell of rotting fish and seaweed, it is glorious," agreed Nick.

"You always manage to sound like such an old cynic," she laughed in reply. "Are all journalists cynics?"

"Actually we tend to divide ourselves into two categories: the cynics and the skeptics. When you join a new paper, they always ask you: 'Which group would you like to belong to? The cynics or the skeptics?' That's how it's organized."

"Now you're making fun of me."

"That's something I would never do," said Nick gently, as he took her in his arms.

For a long moment they looked into each other's eyes, and then they kissed.

"Cathy, there are things that we should—"

"Later." She pressed her finger on his lips. "When we have left the island. There'll be time enough then."

She buried her face in the warmth and comfort of his chest, and, shortly afterward, they kissed again.

"Is there any sign of the wind dying ... oh, sorry. Didn't mean to interrupt," said Ingrid as she hobbled around the corner.

"Don't be sorry." Nick released Cathy from his embrace. "I think the wind is dying a little, but it's still howling out there."

"Pity. The sooner we get out of these wet, dark caves the better it will be for all of us. Even under an overcast sky and in a strong wind, the beach would be a healthier place for all of us."

"I agree," Nick said. "But I still think it's best not to make the move until the captain gives the word."

"Quite right," she nodded. "Survival depends on having a clear chain of command. If we each went our own way, we'd all be dead in a week."

"Cheerful thought," Cathy remarked.

"Sorry. I tend to be a bit gloomy."

"Let's get back and see how the others are getting on," proposed Nick. "We can ask the captain how long we'll have to stay in here."

The temporary campsite was now looking more comfortable and more settled. Vic had found enough dry driftwood to build a fire.

As time passed they tried to rest, but too much of the floor of the tunnel was covered with puddles of water, and all the boulders had sharp, uncomfortable edges. It was a great relief to finally hear Captain Nagle say, "Well, the wind is still strong, but I think it's died down enough for us to return to the beach. Gather up your things and follow me."

Bags were hastily repacked. There was not much to carry, and the group was ready to move within minutes.

Captain Nagle and Vic led the way, clambering down from the cave mouth over the large boulders and tumbled rocks, around the corner of the cliff, and toward the narrow beach that had been their first campsite.

Nick, Cathy, and the doctor brought up the rear. As person after person rounded the corner of the bay, they fell silent. Nick knew something was going on. Cathy's anxious glance told him she had realized it too.

As they helped Dr. Sommerville maneuver with her crutch around the last pile of rocks, they saw what was causing the stunned silence. There, anchored in the middle of the bay, was a vessel. It was painted light gray, and it had the lines and shape of a patrol boat.

The final three joined the others on the beach, staring at a sight they had not expected to see.

It was Sam who broke the silence. "We're saved," said the big Tongan with a huge grin.

"No. I'm afraid not," said Alan, producing a small pistol from his pocket. "You are all under arrest."

DAWN

"The people living in darkness have seen a great light; on those living in the land of the shadow of death a light has dawned."
—Matthew 4:16

———❖———

63

*M*ove toward the middle of the beach." Alan waved his pistol.

Reluctantly everyone obeyed his order, watching as an inflatable zodiac runabout was lowered from the patrol boat, and men in uniform carrying guns jumped into the zodiac and started the outboard engine.

"Where are your weapons?" demanded Alan.

"Lost in the flood," replied Captain Nagle.

"You will sit there, on the sand, while I deal with my colleagues," Alan said, as he walked toward the approaching zodiac.

"Who is he?" asked Cathy. "And who are they?"

"Look at the flag on the patrol boat," replied Nick. "And the name on its bow. That vessel is called the *Liberté,* and the flag is French."

Half a dozen heavily armed marines had landed on the beach, and now the zodiac was returning to the patrol boat. Alan spoke to them in French and then turned back to his group of captives.

"You said we were under arrest," said Nagle.

"And so you are."

"But why? And by what authority?"

"I am an officer of the Direction Générale de la Sécurité Extérieure."

"The DGSE," said Nick. "That's the French Secret Service."

"You are well informed, Nick. That is quite correct. I hold the rank of major in that organization. This is a fully authorized K-Cell operation: authorized from the very top of Division Action and approved by the highest authorities."

"What's this all about?" demanded Dr. Sommerville, her voice quivering with anger.

"You have uncovered a top-secret French military science and technology research base."

"Cavendish Island?" asked Nick.

"Precisely."

"But Cavendish Island belongs to Australia," protested Cathy.

"What claim can Australia possibly have, when the island has been unoccupied and unused since 1823?" was the swift reply.

"That doesn't change its legal status," snapped Nagle, "or the illegality of what you're doing."

Alan replied, "It is unfortunate that you will never have the opportunity to test that opinion in a court of law."

The zodiac returned to the beach carrying crewmembers from the patrol boat. After the men had disembarked with their equipment, it headed back to the vessel anchored in the bay.

Alan spoke to the sailors in French, and they began assembling their equipment on the beach.

"Do we get any fuller explanation?" asked Nick

Alan considered his request, then replied, "I will give you an explanation—a brief explanation."

"Let's hear it then," grumbled Ingrid. "And it had better be good."

Alan faced them, his right hand cradling the pistol resting on his hip.

"It began in 1985 with a series of neutron bomb tests at Moruroa. There was a problem with one of the blasts. It accidentally released a massive electrical charge. In that environment the result was totally unexpected. It surprised and pleased the particle physicists who were supervising the tests."

"What was this unexpected result?" asked Nick.

"A massive discharge of tachyon particles. Wave upon wave of tachyons was released from the center of the charge."

"What are tachyons?" asked Vic.

When Alan was slow to answer, Cathy said, "An elementary subatomic particle that always moves at speeds greater than the speed of light. According to the special theory of relativity, ordinary matter can only move at speeds less than the speed of light. As matter speeds up and approaches the speed of light, time slows down for it. If an ordinary particle of matter ever actually reached the speed of light, time would stop for it. But tachyons appear to exist on the other side of the light barrier—unable to slow down to the speed of light, always moving faster."

"You explained it very well, Miss Samson, very well indeed," said Alan patronizingly. "Would you care to tell us what happens when there is a massive discharge of tachyon particles into the atmosphere?"

"I don't know what happens. In fact, I've never heard of it being done."

"Quite right. This is a French scientific breakthrough."

"So, what does happen?" asked Nagle.

"Time distortions occur."

"What sort of time distortions?"

"Because of the impact of the tachyon blast on the space-time continuum, a 'warping' effect occurs. Time can pass very quickly. Some young palm trees at Moruroa were found to have grown old, withered, and died, in the space of a few seconds, following the first accidental blast. Traveling faster than the speed of light, the tachyon particles can also make time run backwards, as it were. The exact results of each blast are unpredictable. After the tachyon experiments, some prehistoric creatures were found to be living in the lagoon at Moruroa—carried out of their time zone and into ours by the tachyon waves."

"When you say the results were unpredictable, you mean uncontrollable, don't you?" asked Nick shrewdly.

"To be quite frank, yes, that is true, Nick. Once our particle physicists worked out what had caused the tachyon discharge, they repeated it. But they found they could not control the results. The tests were considered too unsafe to continue at Moruroa."

"So you brought them here, to Cavendish Island?"

"Correct. It is within easy reach of Noumea, it was unoccupied, and it was unused. And there was a large network of caves in which our scientists could live and experiment in secret. So, why not?"

"But you also abandoned the tests," continued Nick. "Why?"

"Because the tachyon waves proved to be so unstable. Some of the scientists were killed, within seconds, by sudden and rapid aging. So the field tests were replaced with computer simulations. But the plan was always to return here once control methods had been developed. All the heavy equipment was left in place."

"But that meant you had to make sure no one visited Cavendish Island, or, if they did, that they did not uncover your secret installation in the caves."

"Precisely. For that reason we have been monitoring your expedition since it was first announced. And now, in the interests of state security, I am going to have to kill you."

64

After pronouncing their death sentence, Alan walked off to confer with the next batch of sailors arriving from the patrol boat. He left a marine standing guard over the group.

"Is that man serious?" asked Sam.

"I'm very much afraid he is, Sam," replied Captain Nagle grimly.

"It's outrageous," shouted Ingrid. "There must be something we can do about it."

"I think this explains a whole lot," said Nick, ignoring the doctor's outburst.

"Such as?"

"Well, such as the creatures—the predators, the reptiles—that killed the Roystons and that almost killed us."

"What about them?"

"They must be dinosaurs, prehistoric animals captured by a tachyon wave."

"Oh, yes," said Cathy, her eyes lighting up. "That makes sense. Pieces start to fall into place when I think about it like that. All along I kept telling myself that creature I saw in the church was vaguely familiar. Now I can place it."

"So what sort of things are they?" asked Sam.

"I'm not absolutely positive, but I think they are some sort of theropod. I used to love dinosaurs when I was a kid, and I often visited exhibits at the museum. They had a reconstruction of a theropod there called a deinonychus. It looked exactly like the creatures we have seen: basic theropod body shape, long snout, binocular vision, around two meters tall. They are, or were, small carnivores. Very fast, very intelligent, very nasty. Believed to hunt in packs."

"That's the beasties we saw all right," said Sam.

"Would they ever attack each other?" asked Nick.

"No one really knows anything about dinosaur behavior, but they might—if they were very hungry."

"Okay, answer me this," said Nick. "If there is one type of dinosaur turning up on this island, why are there no others? Why don't we see the occasional triceratops? Or a stegosaurus? Or even a tyrannosaurus rex?"

"Look, don't treat me as the expert," protested Cathy, "but if you want me to guess, I'll guess."

"Let's hear it."

"Most likely the tachyon waves cause distortions in time, but not in space. So, in other words, the only dinosaurs that will turn up will be those that lived on this island in the distant past."

"If it comes to that," interrupted Nagle, "how could there ever have been dinosaurs on such a remote island?"

"Perhaps in ancient times Cavendish Island was linked by a land bridge to more populated regions. Or perhaps a basic breed-ing stock drifted here on a raft of matted vegetation. But it would explain why one type of dinosaur gets pulled out of its time zone and into ours, but not other types."

"What about the swamp creature?" asked Nick. "Could that be part of these time distortions?"

"It could be. Perhaps in the remote past this island, like the Galapagos, had some unique inhabitants. Perhaps one of them was captured by a tachyon wave and pulled out of its time zone to live in the swamp."

"All of this talk is making my head swim," complained Vic.

"That nice Alan Marchant has a cure for that," said Ingrid

angrily. "About an ounce of lead in the back of the brain, and you will feel no more discomfort."

"I'll bet Alan Marchant is not his real name," suggested Sam.

"I'm certain you're right," agreed Nick. "And this notion of uncontrolled, unstable, waves of time distortions explains something else for me. Something that happened on the voyage here." Nick explained the experience he had on the deck of the *Covenant* late at night, when he saw an old-time sailing ship come out of the mist and cruise past.

"Why didn't you tell us this before?" asked Cathy.

"Because I … I guess I was embarrassed. I don't like seeing visions and hearing voices. That's strictly for people who've gone bananas."

"I feel as though I've gone bananas," complained Vic. "All this stuff about tachyon particles and time distortions."

"It explains why the dark chapel appeared to be rebuilding itself," exclaimed Cathy. "A time wave of tachyon particles passed through the building, replacing the present, dilapidated structure with the original building from sometime in the nineteenth century. These tachyon bomb experiments by the French do seem to explain a lot of the strange things we've experienced."

"Fine," growled Ingrid. "Now explain how we're going to get out of here alive. That's the big trick."

When Alan returned to the group, he was carrying a submachine gun instead of his small pistol, which he allowed to hang loosely at his side. "This, ladies and gentlemen, is a Mini-Uzi. Very compact, as you can see. But still capable of firing at a rate of 950 rounds per minute. It is fitted with a 32-round magazine. It would take me about two seconds to kill all of you. I tell you this so that you will be very careful to obey all my commands."

This was said in a quiet voice and with a pleasant smile. No one responded.

"By the way," he added, his smile getting broader, "while you were worrying about being out of contact with the outside world,

I had a compact satellite radio in a waterproof compartment in my backpack the whole time. You will understand, of course, that I couldn't reveal this fact to you."

"Of course," said Nick, but the Frenchman missed the sarcasm.

"Now, you will all move farther down the beach, over against the cliff face. The crew needs this area of the beach. Leave your belongings here."

"Why don't you just kill us at once?" asked Nagle.

"Because you may be useful as laborers. The tachyon device is very heavy and difficult to move."

Sullenly the group stood and moved to the spot indicated by the French secret service agent.

"You will all sit here and not stir until I come back for you. I will leave an armed marine on guard. He speaks no English, so you will not be able to communicate with him. He will simply be instructed to shoot anyone who moves. Do you understand?"

65

For a long time the group sat in gloomy, depressed silence.

"There's something else going on here," said Nick quietly. "It's very puzzling."

"What is?" asked Cathy.

"Why we are still alive."

"But he said ..."

"I know what he said. But he doesn't need us as laborers—he has those French sailors and marines. So why is he keeping us alive?"

"I don't care, just so long as he is," remarked Toby.

"I'm starting to remember some of my science," Ingrid interrupted. "Cathy, I thought that tachyons were just imaginary particles, that they really didn't exist?"

"Look," replied Cathy, "I don't have all the answers, just a bit I can remember from first-year lectures and textbooks. There is nothing in the theory of relativity that forbids tachyons, and at least one experiment claimed to find them. It was done by a couple of Australians in 1973. They were studying cosmic ray showers in the earth's atmosphere and discovered what they called 'anomalous events' that *preceded* the main shower. The only way for that to happen apparently would be if the so-called anomalous events were particles traveling faster than light—in other words, tachyons."

"I don't understand how speed relates to time," said Vicky. "All of this is way over my head."

"What Albert Einstein said is that all creation is connected. Space and time are part of the same continuum. Gravity can bend light, and speed can slow time. If you take a small amount of radioactive matter that is decaying at a regular rate and spin it on a laboratory centrifuge at an extremely high speed, the rate of decay slows down. As speeds begin to approach the speed of light, time really slows down."

"And on the other side of the speed of light?" asked Vic.

"No one knows for sure. But it's possible that quantum wave functions actually link different points in time."

"Like linking spots on this island with the same spot in the remote past?"

"So it appears," said Cathy with a shrug of her shoulders. "I do remember that as tachyon particles lose energy, they speed up. So, if highly energized particles were discharged by the tachyon bomb, they would speed up as they lost energy—"

"Until," interrupted Nick, "at some point in time they would be going fast enough to cause a ripple, or a wave—a distortion in the fabric of time?"

"Apparently so," agreed Cathy.

"What's happening now?" asked Lois, looking down the beach and shading her eyes against the setting sun.

The zodiac had continued running back and forth between the patrol boat and the beach, each time bringing another load of sailors.

"It looks to me as if almost the entire crew must be on the beach by now," remarked Captain Nagle, puzzled.

Then they saw Alan striding back up the beach toward them, a grim expression on his face.

"This may be it," said Cathy quietly.

When he arrived, he said something to the marine in French. The soldier went to join his colleagues, in a large cluster with the sailors from the patrol boat, at the end of the beach. Then he turned toward the group.

"Three of you," he said, "Mr. O'Brien, Miss Myles, and Miss Shaw, you will come with me."

"I protest," said Ingrid. "What are you planning to do with these people?"

"Shut your mouth, old woman," snarled Alan. "And the rest of you will stay here or be shot."

"Something's going on," muttered Nick quietly.

The marines and sailors had laid down their weapons and were breaking open their rations.

"Look," said Nagle. "There's a light flashing on the bridge of the patrol boat."

"What is it?" asked Cathy.

"A signal of some sort. It's flashing in Morse code."

"Can you read it?"

"Dot, dash—that's A; dot, dash, dot, dot—L. Now it's going too fast, and my Morse is too rusty."

The sound of rapid gunfire drew their attention back to the beach. Alan was holding his Uzi cradled in his arm and, unbelievably, was firing into the ranks of his own marines and sailors. They were taken by surprise, and fell, bleeding, on the sand, too startled even to reach for their weapons.

Somehow Toby had also got hold of an Uzi, and, standing by Marchant's side, was firing into the uniformed ranks. The men were dropping like insects, ugly wounds tattooed across their bodies.

"Stop that butchery!" shouted Ingrid, pushing herself to her feet with the aid of her walking stick. "You vile butchers! Stop that!"

"Dr. Sommerville, sit down," yelled Captain Nagle. But she ignored him and started hobbling down the beach.

"You vicious animals," she was shouting. "Stop that. Stop that at once, I say."

As the firing ceased, Alan heard her voice. He turned around to see her limping across the sand toward him, waving her walking stick angrily.

He ejected a spent magazine from his machine gun and

replaced it with a fresh one. Then he raised the weapon and calmly shot down the doctor. There was a row of ugly explosions of blood and flesh across her body, and then she collapsed.

"Ingrid!" screamed Cathy, starting to rise.

Nick grabbed her and held her down.

A cloud of acrid blue smoke drifted down the beach. At the far end, everyone in uniform appeared to be dead. Left standing were Alan, Toby and, beside them, Lois and Vicky.

"I don't understand what's going on," mumbled Vic.

"None of us do, Vic," said Nick quietly. "Just keep very still. Don't make a move. We've been warned, and these murderers mean business."

66

The zodiac had left the patrol boat and was headed back for the beach with one person on board. Still holding his machine gun at the ready, Alan walked slowly toward the terrified group.

"If you're going to kill us, get it over with now," Nick challenged.

"Oh, but I'm not going to kill you. As I said before, I need you as laborers."

"I … don't … understand," stammered Captain Nagle.

"Of course you don't, Captain. It would be impossible for you to understand. All along you have had no idea what was really going on."

"Are you going to tell us?" demanded Cathy defiantly. "Or just stand there and gloat?"

"I will tell you. It is time you knew the truth."

"Why did you kill those men?" demanded Sam, his Tongan geniality gone from his scowling face.

"Following instructions," replied Marchant calmly.

"Whose instructions?" asked Cathy.

"The Grand Master of the Order of the Crimson Circle."

This explanation produced nothing but blank expressions.

"I will explain. As well as being an officer of the DGSE, I am also a sworn servant of the Order of the Crimson Circle. It was always possible that one day my two loyalties would conflict, and when they did, I knew I would choose the path of the Crimson Circle. That has happened today."

"I still don't understand," protested Nick.

"There were only four crewmembers left on board the *Liberté*," Alan continued. "When I saw the signal from my colleague, I knew that she had killed the other three—shot them with a silenced pistol—and dumped their bodies over the side. That was my signal to act—to ensure that the Order of the Crimson Circle obtains the tachyon device by removing all the obstacles in the way."

"They weren't obstacles—they were *men*!" shouted Nagle.

Alan just shrugged.

"And what about Toby, Lois, and Vicky?" asked Cathy.

"Also agents of the Crimson Circle."

"That's right," said Lois as she and the others approached the small group of prisoners. "Vicky and I were infiltrated into this expedition to look after the interests of the Crimson Circle. Although we didn't know until just now that Toby was also an agent."

"My role was rather more undercover, as you might say," remarked the Irishman with a self-satisfied grin. "Just like Alan here, I've been carrying a concealed radio and reporting every day to the headquarters of the Circle."

"And just what was your role supposed to be?" asked Nagle, his voice filled with disgust.

"I was to be the 'heavy,' so to speak—to take drastic action, if and when such became necessary. My IRA training comes in useful on occasions. As, for instance, when it became necessary for me to sink the *Covenant*."

Nagle's face flushed red with anger.

"It was just a small amount of plastic explosive, fitted with a primer charge, a detonator, and a battery-operated timer fuse," Toby announced calmly. "Pretty basic, really."

"But I thought you were part of the Roystons' group," protested Cathy, looking puzzled.

"So did they. It took the Crimson Circle a long time to infiltrate me into the Secret Coven, but it was worth it just to know what they were up to."

The zodiac had landed by now, and a woman with short blonde hair was walking up the beach toward them. She was also armed and was wearing a French commando's uniform.

"Your colleague?" Nick nodded toward the approaching figure.

"Allow me to present to you Dominique Turenge," said Alan. "Dominique has been in the DGSE for as long as I have, and in the Order of the Crimson Circle for even longer."

"What is this Crimson Circle?" asked Nick. "Explain it to us."

"Perhaps later. Right now we are all returning to the *Liberté*, where you will be locked in the crew's quarters overnight. In the morning you will help us remove the tachyon device. You will be taken out to the patrol boat one at a time. Dominique will pilot the zodiac, and Toby will keep you covered."

The crew's quarters turned out to be a long, narrow space behind a lockable bulkhead, fitted with double bunks. When the last of the prisoners was delivered from the beach, Alan stood in the doorway.

"First, my apologies to Miss Samson. It is unfortunate that you must share this space with the four men, but security demands it."

"Thank you for your gallantry," replied Cathy sarcastically.

"Second, you will be taken one at a time to the crew's bathroom where you may shower and change into clean clothes. I have found some overalls in the lockers that you may change into if you have no clean clothes of your own left. Indeed, considering the heavy work you have ahead of you tomorrow, overalls would be a good idea. Miss Myles here, who I assure you is an excellent shot with that automatic pistol in her hand, will guard you to and from the bathroom. And I will bid you *bonsoir*."

Later that night, Alan, Toby, Lois, and Vicky sat in the officers' mess room with Dominique making their plans for the next day.

The French woman was tall and slim, with a round face accented by small features.

"The prisoners have been secured for the night?" asked Alan.

"Locked up tight," replied Lois smugly. "There's no way they could escape."

"Excellent. Tomorrow morning at sunrise you and Vicky will prepare breakfast for everyone, including the prisoners. They will need the energy for the work they have to do. I have no idea what you will find in the galley, but I am certain it is well stocked."

"Yes, sir," said Vicky quietly. She was stunned by the turn that events had taken, but glad she was on the winning side.

"And then?" asked Dominique in her heavily accented English.

"Then we will all remove ourselves to the caves, disassemble the tachyon device, and bring it on board. We four," he explained to the French woman, "have seen it as we have passed through the caves."

"That big black metal tube?" inquired Lois.

"Precisely. It is very large and very heavy. The captain, the journalist, and the engineer are all fit and strong. The big Tongan would be strongest of all, but he is still recovering from the loss of blood. Nevertheless, I am sure he will still be useful. Even Miss Samson is a fit young woman—she can contribute to the lifting."

"What about us?"

"One of us needs to stand armed guard over the prisoners at all times."

"I'll do that," volunteered Toby.

"No, one of the women can manage that. You and I will have to help with the disassembly and the lifting. I stress again that this will be a heavy and difficult task."

"And what do we do with the prisoners once the tachyon device is safely stowed on board?" asked Lois.

"We kill them all."

The five prisoners lay on their bunks, in the dark, in the quarters once occupied by the murdered crew, unable to sleep. All of them had showered and eaten, and all were wearing dark blue overalls.

"Nick?"

"Yes, Cathy."

"What will happen to us once they have their precious tachyon device disassembled and loaded on board?"

"They are planning to kill us. I have no doubt of that. We've seen how ruthlessly they behaved toward the crew of this ship. And why should they keep us alive once we've served their purposes?"

"When I go, I want to take that Toby O'Brien with me," muttered Captain Nagle. "He's a lying, murderous, cold-blooded … Well, he's a lot of things, but with Miss Samson here, I'd better not say them."

"Aye, sir. We all understand," said Vic, "because we all feel the same way."

"Will they get away with it?" asked Sam.

"They might, Sam, they just might," replied Nick reluctantly. "I assume the five of them will be able to operate this patrol boat. If that were not so, they would have kept some of the crew alive. And in this age of high-tech, computerized seafaring, a crew of three or four is probably sufficient. So, they'll sail out of here on the *Liberté* with the tachyon device on board."

"And then what?"

"Well, if this Order of the Crimson Circle is as well resourced as it appears to be, they will probably be met at sea by a private boat owned by the Order, which will transfer the tachyon machine and the five conspirators to the yacht and sink this patrol boat in deep water."

"Have you ever heard of this Order of the Crimson Circle before, Nick?"

"I've been racking my brains ever since Alan Marchant—or whatever his real name is—mentioned it. And I have heard of it, or read about it, but I only know a little."

"What do you know?" asked Cathy.

"It's some sort of New Age organization—part of the modern 'occult explosion' that approaches the supernatural, the paranormal, and the realm of the spirit seeking to dominate and gain control. Some time back I read an article on the Crimson Circle, which claimed it was a very disciplined organization with a rigid hierarchy and a strict chain of command."

"As we saw today," growled Nagle, "when their Grand Master says kill, they kill."

"According to the article," continued Nick, "this group claims to be the inheritors of ancient pagan traditions. On the basis of today's evidence, I'd say this bunch is as dangerous as the Charles Manson family—on a larger scale."

"Are you saying these people are simply nuts?" asked Vic.

"No, I'm saying they're wicked. And those giving them orders are even more wicked."

67

*T*he next morning they entered the tunnel system once more through the sea cave above the rocks around the headland from the beach.

Alan was in the lead carrying a tool kit from the ship. He was followed by the five prisoners. His four colleagues, all heavily armed, brought up the rear. They brought with them five large, high-powered flashlights.

There were puddles of water on the floor of the cave system, and the walls were still damp, from the flooding of the day before.

"How are you feeling, Sam?" asked Captain Nagle as they made their way deeper into the honeycombed rocks of the dead volcano that was Cavendish Island.

Although he spoke quietly, his voice echoed and rolled around the rocky walls.

"I'm fine, Captain."

"Are you sure? You lost a lot of blood two days ago."

"I guess I feel about ninety percent. And that's not bad."

"Stop that conversation," snapped Dominique Turenge. "And keep moving." Her emotionless face was as cold and hard as a machine.

Eventually the group reached the cave that contained the tachyon device. They sat on the rocky floor and rested after their long walk from the beach. Marchant arranged all five flashlights in a semicircle so the device was brightly illuminated.

It was a large metal pipe, some half a meter in diameter and three meters long. Its outer skin was a dull, burned black, and it was connected to heavy cables at both ends. On top was a flat control box with rows of switches, and underneath were large bolts anchoring the device to concrete blocks.

Alan moved back and forth for some time, examining the device in detail.

Then he began to hunt through the toolbox. Finding a heavy-duty wrench, he started to work on the large bolts that held the tube to the concrete blocks. He rapidly became red in the face with the effort. Despite the beads of sweat appearing on his forehead, he clearly could not loosen the bolts.

"Give me a hand with this," he ordered Nick and Vic.

All three men grasped the long handle of the wrench and pulled. This work continued for several minutes, but their efforts remained fruitless.

"This is getting us nowhere," said Alan in disgust, throwing the wrench on the cave floor and sending metallic, clanging echoes rolling back and forth for a full minute.

"Neal," he snapped, "you're a ship's engineer. What can you suggest for loosening those bolts?"

Vic took up one of the flashlights, got down on his hands and knees, and closely examined several of the bolts.

"I don't know why they won't come free," he said as he stood up again, brushing the dust off his hands and knees. "The only suggestion I can make is to cut them free. Is there an oxy torch on the boat?"

"I am not certain how safe it would be to use an oxyacetylene cutter so close to the device," said their captor thoughtfully.

"Why?" asked Nagle. "What's inside that thing? How dangerous is it?"

"The problem is," confessed Alan, "that we don't really know. Much of the material concerning these experiments is so highly classified even Dominique and I have been able to find out very little about it."

At this point, Dominique spoke to him rapidly in French for several minutes, running her fingers through her short, blonde hair.

"Don't you have any idea what's in that tube?" demanded Lois, when the torrent of French had stopped. "Are we in any danger just by standing this close to it?" As she spoke, Vicky was backing up against the far wall.

"There is no need to panic," said Alan, making pacifying gestures with his hands. "As far as we know, there is a small amount of radioactive material in the very center of this tube. A small amount—I stress—a very small amount. And the tube is heavily shielded. The key to the operation of the device, as I understand it, involves bombarding that radioactive material with an enormous high-tension electrical charge. The tube is filled with some sort of gas that facilitates the process."

"What sort of gas?" asked Nick.

"We were not able to find out. So we don't know if it is an inert gas such as you would find in a light bulb, or if the gas is a catalyst, or even an active component in the whole process. But on the whole, I think it would be best if we did not breach the tube and allow any of the gas to escape. That is my concern with using an oxy torch."

"What about a grinder?" suggested Vic. "Are there any portable power tools on the boat?"

There was a short exchange in French between Alan and Dominique. The French woman, stern and thin-lipped, kept shaking her head.

"Dominique says no," explained Alan. "Perhaps we can move the tube with the concrete blocks it rests on still attached?"

"The job is getting heavier and harder all the time," commented Captain Nagle.

The only response was an angry scowl from the Frenchman who had masqueraded as a Canadian.

"Why don't you disconnect the cables," suggested Toby, "and see if we can lift it at all?"

"Yes," said Lois, "try that."

Alan took a large insulated screwdriver from the tool kit and approached the cable connections at one end. The moment he touched the connection there was a massive spark that hissed and sizzled and flashed blue-white light around the cave. He leaped back quickly.

Dominique asked a question in French, Alan replied in English, "No, I'm fine. I was just startled, that's all."

"Perhaps the water has damaged it," suggested Nick. "That flood surge was ocean water—saltwater—and salt is very corrosive."

"Surely there wouldn't have been enough time since the flood for the salt to corrode anything, would it?" asked Cathy.

"It was just a thought," Nick said with a shrug of his shoulders.

"Keep your thoughts to yourself," growled Toby, raising his Uzi and pointing it at Nick.

"But he may be right," Alan remarked as he approached the cable connections again. As he did so, the other occupants of the cave moved back, well away from any possible arcing electrical discharge.

But Alan didn't touch the connectors with his screwdriver this time, he simply looked.

"There's no sign of corrosion or water damage," he said. Then he reached forward with his screwdriver. Another brilliant blue-white spark arced from one end of the black tube to the other.

Alan Marchant swore in French as he leaped back a meter or two. Then he knelt down and began rummaging through the tool kit.

"Unless we remove the cables," he said to no one in particular, "we will never be able to budge the tachyon device."

In the quietness that followed, Nick heard a low humming sound that he recognized. It began very quietly and built very slowly—so slowly that no one else seemed to be paying any attention to it. *Perhaps,* thought Nick, *their ears are still ringing from that last electrical explosion. Alan's should be—he was standing so close to it.*

Then Nick remembered that no one except him and Alan would recognize the significance of the humming, buzzing noise that was very slowly building in intensity and pitch. And Alan seemed to be paying no attention, so preoccupied was he with searching through the tool kit.

Nick listened and concentrated. He waited until what he judged to be the last possible moment, then he turned to his fellow prisoners and shouted, "Get down!" They looked at him, blankly, startled, for a moment, and then copied his example and hit the rock floor. They did so just in time.

Massive fingers of forked lightning arced out of the black tube and crashed around the cave. The light was, for a moment, as brilliant as the sun. The thunderclap was a deafening explosion.

When it was over, and with his ears still ringing, Nick raised his head. The first thing he noticed was that Vicky was dead, her body burned and blackened where the lightning had stuck her. Together with the smell of the ozone generated by the lightning came the awful smell of burning human flesh.

Everyone else was flat on the floor of the cave, slowly and cautiously raising their heads. Toby got up on one knee, holding his Uzi machine gun nervously.

Captain Nagle also started to rise. "Don't move," hissed Nick. "Stay down." He had noticed that the humming hadn't stopped, but was building again in volume and pitch.

This time it built to a louder, whining, buzzing noise before the crash came and the charge was released in a simultaneous explosion of thunder and lightning. Immediately the hum resumed, and began building even more quickly toward its discharge rate.

"Somehow," said Nick to Cathy, "he's set that thing running on overload."

They pressed their faces against the floor, with their ears covered, as once again the cave lit up like the sun, and a deafening crash reverberated against the rocks.

"After the next one," whispered Nick urgently, "start crawling toward the tunnel." His fellow prisoners nodded. Nick noticed that Alan looked terrified and appeared to be frozen by his fear into inaction. Dominique was crawling across the floor toward him.

"She's going to tell him to turn it off," guessed Nick. "And he'll tell her he doesn't know how."

Then it came again. It was like being in the very center of a terrifying electrical storm.

"Now!" shouted Nick as the thunder died away. He and Cathy, with Nagle on one side and Sam on the other, began crawling on their hands and knees as rapidly as they could toward the entrance to the tunnel that would take them back to the beach.

"Stop!" yelled Toby behind them. They didn't. Nick turned around and saw Toby groping for his machine gun. "Come on!" yelled Nick to Vic Neal who was lagging behind. "Catch up!"

They had crawled another two meters when the caves rang with the horrible chatter of the machine gun. Nick looked back. Vic was dead, his body riddled with bullets. Toby raised his machine gun again and pointed it directly at Nick.

Then the tachyon device exploded again. Before Toby could regain his balance, Nick crawled through the tunnel entrance and out of the line of fire.

Nick saw that Cathy, Sam, and the captain had struggled to their feet. They were dazed and stunned by the repeated blinding flashes and ear-splitting explosions.

"We can't stop," urged Nick. "Come on, back to the entrance cave."

But before they could move, the rock beneath their feet began to tremble.

"Those explosions," shouted Nagle over the roar, "are going to bring the whole cave system crashing down."

"Come on then, run!" shouted Nick.

"Look what I grabbed on the way," said Cathy, holding up one of the flashlights.

"You're a genius," laughed Nick. "Lead the way."

They began to run down the long, narrow tunnel. They had to duck their heads as the ceiling lowered in places in uneven rocky bulges. No one seemed to be following them. They had traveled no more than two hundred meters when Cathy came to a sudden halt. Something was happening directly ahead of her—something she recognized.

The air was full of mist and was shimmering strangely. Expressions of fear and panic passed rapidly over Cathy's face. She turned back toward Nick as if asking what to do, but Nick was also staring, hypnotized by what he knew was about to happen.

"What is going ..." began Sam. But Nick gestured to him to be quiet.

The mist swirled and spread in the narrow tunnel. Then it merged into a shimmering distortion of the light, and suddenly the tunnel ahead of them was no longer empty. There was a pack of dinosaurs, jaws open, razor-sharp teeth bared. Nick counted them: nine, ten, eleven, twelve. They completely filled that narrow space. Their snouts were in the air sniffing, their green reptilian eyes were blinking, and already the hissing and snarling had begun.

The rock beneath their feet trembled again, and Cathy screamed. The lizard-like carnivores began to stalk slowly and cautiously up the tunnel toward the group. Two of them bumped each other, snarled and hissed, and one flashed at the other with his long, sharp fore-claw, drawing blood from the other's scaly side. The smell of blood seemed to excite them. The leader's long jaws opened wider as he roared, revealing the rows of curved teeth designed to cut and tear.

Nick looked around desperately.

"In here," he said, pointing to a shallow indentation in the tunnel wall. "Everyone press yourselves back against the rock. Don't move. Don't make a sound. And turn off that light."

Seconds later all four of them were lined up side by side in the small gap, in pitch darkness, hardly daring to breath.

They could hear the dinosaurs getting closer. Their long,

talon-like claws scratched on the floor of the tunnel, they hissed and snarled, and they had the horrible smell of carnivores.

They were closer now—directly opposite them in the tunnel. Cathy felt the hot breath of one as it passed. Nick thanked God the vicious creatures were not good hunters in the dark.

At that moment a bright light shined into the tunnel, and Toby ran around the bend. "Come back, or I'll kill all of you!" he shouted, and then stopped dead in his tracks.

The ex-IRA sniper and explosives expert had seen one of these creatures once before: He had seen it eating Stella. Now he was facing twelve of them. He dropped his flashlight on the floor and raised his Uzi. The flashlight did not break, and Nick saw clearly what happened next.

The hunting pack moved with astonishing speed. Before Toby could fire, the leader had slashed open the Irishman's thigh. With blood streaming down his leg, Toby squeezed the trigger on the Uzi. He fired off one complete magazine in a single burst. The leader's long neck was hacked in two by the wall of bullets. For a moment the others hesitated. Toby fumbled in his pocket for another magazine. It was still in his hand when two of them rushed him. Nick heard the scream and turned away.

A moment later, the whole pack was on top of Toby, each fighting for its share of the fresh meat.

"Now," hissed Nick, "while they're preoccupied. Run!"

They ran. Cathy flicked the flashlight back on and led the way. The rocky walls around them rumbled again, and cracks began appearing. Nick pushed Sam and Nagle to follow Cathy, and then he brought up the rear.

Adrenalin pumping, they ran hard, their lungs hot and bursting and sucking in air; so fast they bumped, grazed, and bruised themselves against outcroppings of rock—but they reached the sea cave.

Ahead of them was daylight, and the sounds of the sea, and the smell of salty air. Once inside the cave they stopped, exhausted, out of breath, desperate to rest their burning muscles.

"Nearly there," puffed Nick. "Must keep going."

There was a snarl behind them, and they all spun around. It was a single dinosaur. Perhaps it had not been able to get its share of the feed in the struggle over Toby's corpse. Perhaps it had been attracted by their light, and by the noise they made, and had turned back. Perhaps it had just appeared as the tachyon device continued to fire.

Wherever it had come from—it was there.

The four of them backed away. The creature advanced with a hiss. Its eyes flicked back and forth, as if picking which one it would attack first. It reared up on his hind feet, flashing its powerful fore-claws. *I know what happens next,* thought Cathy. *It's about to charge.*

Rising higher on its back legs, it snarled ominously, and then shot forward. But before it could cover the five meters that separated it from its victims, the rock shook violently, and a crack opened up in the floor of the cave. Out of the crack belched sulphurous smoke and the ominous red glow of flames. Their savage attacker reared back and stopped in its tracks.

"Now!" yelled Nick. "Out of the cave and down to the beach."

The others needed no more encouragement. They ran to the cave mouth and jumped down onto the rocks, stumbling over the boulders, around the headland, and back to the beach. Nick looked over his shoulder. He saw dense smoke billowing out of the cave.

By the time they reached the beach, Sam was limping. Captain Nagle put an arm around him and said, "Into the zodiac. The only safe place is out on the patrol boat."

68

Nick and Cathy stood on the deck of the patrol boat, looking back at Cavendish Island, while Captain Nagle and Sam made their way down to the engine room.

"It looks as though the grass on the island is on fire," said Cathy, her arm around Nick's waist.

"You're right," he replied, hugging her closer. "There's smoke and flame everywhere. All the grass and bush seems to be burning."

As they watched, the dense gray smoke from the burning vegetation was joined by the yellow sulphurous smoke billowing out of the cave system.

"And it's not just smoke," said Cathy.

The beach and the cliffs were now wreathed in a strange, white mist—a mist that seemed to shimmer and distort the light.

"We've got the engines going," announced Captain Nagle as he joined them. "Sam is about to weigh anchor, and I'm about to try and master the controls on the bridge. Nick, you help Sam. Cathy, you come with me."

"I can remember a little of my high school French," she offered, "perhaps I can help read labels on the dials and controls. Or, at least, guess at them."

"Good girl," said Nagle.

Ten minutes later, both the fore and aft anchors were up, and Nick and Cathy stood beside Captain Nagle as he took the wheel, and the patrol boat began to slowly make way. Sam remained in the engine room, keeping an eye on the powerful marine diesel engine that would take them to safety.

With painful slowness, the bow of the patrol boat swung around until the vessel was facing out to sea. Captain Nagle rang down for more speed and set a course out of the bay.

"Where do we go, Captain?" asked Cathy.

"Noumea is the closest major port," replied Nagle, "but I have no intention of sailing a French patrol boat into a French port, with all the crew missing. We would spend years in a French jail."

"Where to then?"

"I suggest we turn south, toward Lord Howe Island. It's not a big port, but we could get ashore there in the zodiac, and the Australians would be a lot friendlier than the French."

"Yes," agreed Nick, "and there'll be a lot of interest in what the French have secretly been up to on an island that is legally still part of Australia."

"I've been thinking about that, Nick," said Nagle.

"Yes?"

"I've been wondering how we're going to explain all this to the world. Maybe it would be simpler not to try to explain it."

"What do you suggest?"

"When we're in Australian waters we could send out a distress signal. Once we know the Australian navy is on the way, open all the sea cocks on this boat, and put to sea in the zodiac to wait for them."

"And what story would you tell them when they picked us up?"

"We could think of something between us."

Nick looked at Cathy. They smiled at each other, and Nick said, "Captain, Cathy and I would rather take our chances with the truth."

Nagle nodded. "If you insist."

Sam joined them on the bridge, sweat trickling down his cheerful face. "That is a beautiful engine, Captain, and it's purring as sweet as a kitten." Then he flopped down into the navigator's chair and added, "I'm pooped."

"Nick! Captain! Sam!" said Cathy. "Look at the island."

They all walked to the side of the wheelhouse and looked back toward Cavendish Island. It was now wreathed in black smoke and appeared to have changed shape.

"I can't remember there being a hill in the middle of the island," said Sam.

"There wasn't," responded the captain. "So, what's going on?"

"That tachyon device," muttered Nick grimly, "it just kept on firing, didn't it?"

"That's right, it did," Cathy agreed.

"I think we can see the result. That is the ultimate time distortion—Cavendish Island is reverting to the form it held in the remote past."

As he spoke, the island exploded, shooting lava and rocks high into the air. Captain Nagle slowed the engines, and for the next few hours the fascinated spectators watched the island turn back in time.

"The good thing is," said Cathy quietly, "when the island dies, the tachyon device dies with it."

"Amen to that," said the captain, vigorously.

Shortly afterward there was a second mighty explosion, and as ash rained down on the sea around the patrol boat, Cavendish Island settled beneath the waves.

"Is it over?" asked Cathy.

"It's over," said Nick.

References

Chapter 15
Psalm 23:1-4 KJV
Psalm 23:5-6 KJV

Chapter 18
See Revelation 6:1-8
Psalm 91:6

Chapter 20
Psalm 91:1-6 KJV

Chapter 25
See 2 Corinthians 5:8 KJV

Chapter 39
Psalm 2:9
See Psalm 23:4
John 10:11, 17-18

Chapter 52
See 2 Corinthians 5:8 KJV
See Matthew 25:21 KJV

Chapter 60
Ephesians 6:12

READERS' GUIDE

For Personal Reflection
or Group Discussion

Readers' Guide

Many of us live our lives without any awareness of the battle raging all around us. Life is simply what can be seen and touched; the only true realities are those that command our attention on a daily basis—sickness, finances, relationships, war, terrorism, death. We don't like to consider the reality of the supernatural. That is somehow equated with flaky new-agers, fanatic cults, or extremist factions of the Church. But the Bible warns us to be diligent: "For our struggle is not against flesh and blood, but against the rulers, against the authorities, against the powers of this dark world and against the spiritual forces of evil in the heavenly realms" (Ephesians 6:12).

Dark Storm tells a harrowing tale of what can happen when the tangible, physical world collides with the supernatural realm. Nick, Cathy, and the others are faced with an evil they would not have imagined possible, and their lives are forever changed.

The battle *is* real, but God has not left us powerless. Second Corinthians 10:4 says, "The weapons we fight with are not the weapons of the world. On the contrary, they have divine power to demolish strongholds." Consider the following questions with an open heart. The conflict is as old as time itself: good versus evil. The good news is that in the end, God always wins.

1. At first Nick's assignment to cover the expedition to Cavendish Island seems to be little more than an innocuous pleasure cruise. But what early warning signs point toward real danger ahead? What motivating forces lie behind Nick's decisions?

2. The journal entries of Lieutenant Edmund McDermott provide great insight into the history of the island. In what ways do his experiences parallel those of Nick? What other similarities exist between these two men?

3. W. H. Muir tries to convince the team to abandon the expedition and warns of dark spiritual forces that have been unleashed on the island. He writes that these evil spirits "are always deceptive. They present themselves as 'angels of light' while being, in reality, agents of darkness." Why does Satan attempt to disguise himself as goodness and light? What examples come to mind— particularly in our popular culture—of darkness posing as light?

4. Lieutenant McDermott and Nick see each other clearly as their ships pass in the night. What purpose might God have for allowing their lives to intersect—despite the distance of almost two centuries? What does this reveal about God's perception of time?

5. What significance can be found in *Covenant*, the expedition ship's name? Is it merely coincidence that Commander Black's ship also was named the *Covenant?*

6. As a result of the witchcraft practiced by Commander Black and others on the island, Lieutenant McDermott becomes deathly ill and then is offered up as a human sacrifice by the pagan worshipers. Since the lieutenant was a committed Christian, how is it possible that he was so personally affected

by evil? Although he finds some comfort in prayer and Scripture, why didn't God save him from his enemies? Is it wise to believe that Christians are immune to the destructive work of evil spirits?

7. While she works to record details of the ancient church, Cathy quickly becomes terrified of the old building and is desperate to get away from it. Is this God's way of warning her of the peril to come? How important is it to heed the "still small voice"?

8. What light does Ephesians 6:12 shed on the supernatural realm? How does prayer affect the outcome of the ongoing battle between good and evil? In what ways do the faithful prayers of Christians affect the outcome of this story?

9. The Bible is full of references to dreams and the interpretation of dreams. Acts 2:17 says: "In the last days, God says, I will pour out my Spirit on all people. Your sons and daughters will prophesy, your young men will see visions, your old men will dream dreams." What is the meaning of Frank Gordon's dream? What does each of the two houses that he approaches represent? What is his mentor—Sir Alfred Stocker—repeating to himself and what message does it offer Frank?

10. When Frank declares he doesn't believe in evil spirits, Mr. Muir responds, "Which is exactly what they intend, and it pleases them a great deal." Why do so many deny the existence of evil? Does this make Satan, demons, and hell any less real? What are the potential consequences for living in ignorance of the spiritual realm?

11. Cathy has a vivid dream in which death pursues her and she becomes consumed with fear. But as she is lifted up high

above the situation, the darkness that at first seems so over-whelming is minute when compared with the vast Center of Light. What peace does Cathy gain from her dream? What does the vision teach us about God's eternal perspective?

12. Paul Marshall is "bitten" by a stone statue and dies the same evening after being attacked by a giant slug. Later, Max is bitten by the same statue and—convinced the gargoyle is "after him"—dies just hours later after being attacked by a large, ferocious animal. Are specific individuals being targeted for death? Why? Are the creatures of the island being controlled by an outside power?

13. When the Roystons take Cathy captive and force her to take part in their ritual Black Mass, Cathy is saved despite their evil intentions. How does God deliver her? What significance is found in the fact that the Roystons are consumed by the very "demon" they conjure and worship?

14. Perhaps somewhat foolishly, Nick eagerly explores the island's underground cave system. What impact do his discoveries have? What events are set in motion that directly affect the outcome of the island? What evidence can be seen of God's hand at work?

15. Jesus said: "I am the way and the truth and the life. No one comes to the Father except through me" (John 14:6). But many people believe that any belief system is acceptable as long as its followers are devoted. Some even claim that all religions are equally good. Captain Nagle expresses this world view when he says, "Well, I've always said it doesn't matter what people believe, as long as they're sincere." How do the events on the island dis-prove this theory? How do world religions—including the

occult—mislead their followers? In what ways do they counterfeit or contaminate the Truth?

16. Many bizarre and terrifying events are attributed to the experimental tachyon device operating beneath the island's surface. Does this scientific explanation undermine the spiritual component of these experiences? What elements of the story are still left without a logical or tangible explanation? Which force is the controlling factor—science or the supernatural?

17. Soon after the surviving team members escape the island, it reverts to an active volcano. Shooting ash and fire, the inferno destroys everything—even the island itself. How is this similar to the future planned for Satan and his demons? In what ways are Nick, Cathy, and the others privileged to experience such a dramatic illustration? What sign of promise can be found in their survival?

The Word at Work Around the World

A vital part of Cook Communications Ministries is our international outreach, Cook Communications Ministries International (CCMI). Your purchase of this book, and of other books and Christian-growth products from Cook, enables CCMI to provide Bibles and Christian literature to people in more than 150 languages in 65 countries.

Cook Communications Ministries is a not-for-profit, self-supporting organization. Revenues from sales of our books, Bible curricula, and other church and home products not only fund our U.S. ministry, but also fund our CCMI ministry around the world. One hundred percent of donations to CCMI go to our international literature programs.

CCMI reaches out internationally in three ways:

· Our premier International Christian Publishing Institute (ICPI) trains leaders from nationally led publishing houses around the world.

· We provide literature for pastors, evangelists, and Christian workers in their national language.

· We reach people at risk—refugees, AIDS victims, street children, and famine victims—with God's Word.

Word Power, God's Power

Faith Kidz, RiverOak, Honor, Life Journey, Victor, NexGen — every time you purchase a book produced by Cook Communications Ministries, you not only meet a vital personal need in your life or in the life of someone you love, but you're also a part of ministering to José in Colombia, Humberto in Chile, Gousa in India, or Lidiane in Brazil. You help make it possible for a pastor in China, a child in Peru, or a mother in West Africa to enjoy a life-changing book. And because you helped, children and adults around the world are learning God's Word and walking in his ways.

Thank you for your partnership in helping to disciple the world. May God bless you with the power of his Word in your life.

For more information about our international ministries, visit www.ccmi.org.